THE COWBOYS AND BABIES COLLECTION

For the men in this special 2-in-1 collection nothing is more important than the family that surrounds them and the women they love.

From cowboy hats to baby booties, and horseback rides on the range to candlelit dinners for two, these romances are sure to lasso your heart.

We dare you not to fall for these rugged men who know the value of a hard day's work, hold family loyalty in the highest regard and would do anything for the love of a good woman!

CATHY GILLEN THACKER

is married and a mother of three. She and her husband spent eighteen years in Texas, and now reside in North Carolina. Her mysteries, romantic comedies and heartwarming family stories have made numerous appearances on bestseller lists, but her best reward, she says, is knowing one of her books made someone's day a little brighter. A popular Harlequin author for many years, she loves telling passionate stories with happy endings, and thinks nothing beats a good romance and a hot cup of tea! You can visit Cathy's website at www.cathygillenthacker.com for more information on her upcoming and previously published books, recipes and a list of her favorite things.

CATHY GILLEN THACKER

A Family Man

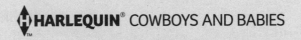

HARLEQUIN® COWBOYS AND BABIES

Recycling programs
for this product may
not exist in your area.

ISBN-13: 978-0-373-60611-5

A FAMILY MAN
Copyright © 2014 by Harlequin Books S.A.

The publisher acknowledges the copyright holders
of the individual works as follows:

MOMMY FOR HIRE
Copyright © 2009 by Cathy Gillen Thacker
A BABY FOR MOMMY
Copyright © 2009 by Cathy Gillen Thacker

HARLEQUIN®
www.Harlequin.com

Printed in U.S.A.

CONTENTS

MOMMY FOR HIRE

Chapter One

"So you're the best ForeverLove.com has to offer." The silky male voice seemed to engulf Alexis Graham the moment she walked through the imposing double mahogany doors into the executive suite of Grady McCabe Enterprises.

"And you must be Mr. McCabe," Alexis replied, striding forward and holding out her hand. Although why the eldest son of the legendary Josie and Wade McCabe would need to hire a matchmaking agency was beyond her.

At thirty-five, the wildly successful Texan was renowned for the skyscrapers he built and leased to businesses throughout the Southwest. He was no slouch in the looks department, either. Six foot four inches tall, with the kick-butt physique of a Hollywood heartthrob, he had a strikingly masculine face that commanded attention. He wore his dark brown hair in a short, sexy cut that looked great even now in rumpled disarray. His tie was loosened, the first two buttons undone, and the sleeves on his pale blue dress shirt were rolled up to his elbows, revealing strong, sinewy forearms. As he moved, Alexis couldn't help but notice his flat stomach and lean hips.

His lips curved upward. "Call me Grady." He clasped her hand in his big, rough palm. "And let's get right to it, shall we?"

Her skin still tingling from his brief, warm touch, Alexis sat down and removed a notepad and pen from her leather briefcase.

Grady circled his desk and sat down in his high-backed leather chair. "I need a mommy for my five-year-old daughter, Savannah, and I'm willing to marry to get one."

Alexis made a note of that, before gazing up into his deep velvet, blue eyes. "I have to tell you—that's not the best opening for a man on a first date."

Grady McCabe obviously couldn't have cared less. "I'm not going to be less than honest," he told her bluntly. "Which is where you come in."

Alexis was beginning not to like this. Or at least not like the commercial real estate developer's attitude. She had gotten in the matchmaking business because she believed wholeheartedly in the possibility of life-long love. She knew how short life was, how cruel fate could be, and she wanted to be instrumental in helping well-meaning couples find each other. But what she did *not* want to do was promote loveless unions. Unfortunately, her employers were not as idealistic. The four business partners who owned ForeverLove.com only cared that the customers left happy, and the bottom line remained healthy.

Grady McCabe was an important client. Not only was the multimillionaire a member of the famed McCabe clan of Laramie, Texas, he was one of the premiere businessmen in Fort Worth. His mixed-use development projects were the pride of the downtown area.

Alexis had been given the task of ensuring that Grady found whatever he wanted in a woman, no matter what it took. A lot was riding on her success.

Grady sent her a level look. He seemed to know that what he was asking was highly unusual. That made him no less serious in his ambition, however.

"I already had the best. I lost my wife shortly after our daughter was born. A few days after we took the baby home from the hospital, Tabitha had an aneurysm and cerebral hemorrhage that resulted in her death."

Alexis recalled reading about it in the paper. Grady had been at work and had come home to find his wife, but by then it was too late. The funeral had brought many prominent people to Fort Worth. Grady's grief, the tragedy of a young mother dying so suddenly and the newborn baby growing up without a mother, had been all folks talked about for weeks. "I'm sorry."

Grady accepted Alexis's sympathy with a grim nod. "Since then I've had nannies. A lot of them, actually. My eighth one just quit."

"Goodness," Alexis murmured before she could stop herself.

Grady kicked back in his chair with a heavy sigh. "I'm not surprised. Savannah doesn't need a nanny. She needs a mother." He paused to give Alexis a pointed look. "Which is where you come in."

Alexis did not deny Grady needed help, when it came to the domestic front. "I'm supposed to find women for you to date and hopefully marry."

He shook his head. "You are supposed to find a woman who will make a great mommy for Savannah."

It was Alexis's turn to disagree. "That's not really what we do at ForeverLove.com."

"I've spoken to your boss, Holly Anne Kirkland, and she assures me that not only will it be done, but you are the right person to do it." Grady's blue eyes narrowed in obvious displeasure. "Was she wrong?"

THAT SHOULD HAVE BEEN an easy question, Grady thought. One that brought forth a flurry of apologies and assurances that yes, his demands would be met, without any further delay.

Instead, Alexis Graham studied him in thoughtful silence.

He couldn't say he minded. The pause in conversation gave him a chance to size her up, too. Decide if she was indeed the right woman for the task.

Outwardly, she certainly looked it.

The thirty-something matchmaker had the city-chic sophistication of the upwardly mobile career woman she was reputed to be. Her figure-hugging suit was made of a pale yellow fabric perfect for the balmy June weather. Understated makeup accented the delicate, feminine features on her oval face, drawing attention to her high cheekbones, soft full lips and long-lashed, teal-blue eyes. Her shoulder length, honey-blond hair only added to the aura of pulled-together perfection. Had he been in the market for a dalliance with an intelligent, engaging female, he would have had to look no further. He wasn't.

All he wanted was a solution to his problem.

And the sooner Alexis Graham understood that, the better.

"Should I ask for another matchmaker from the agency?" Grady drawled.

"No. Of course not." Alexis exhaled sharply. "I've been assigned the job. I'll do it."

"Good, then let me tell you what I want."

She picked up her pen and notebook and began to write, but Grady couldn't help but notice her exasperation.

"First and foremost, my daughter has to like this woman. She has to be the mommy of Savannah's dreams."

"What does Savannah want?" Alexis inquired coolly.

If Grady had a clue about that, he wouldn't be in this position. "You'll have to ask her." His little girl was not cooperating with him on any level right now, for reasons known only to her.

With no discernible change in her expression, Alexis continued taking notes.

Grady added even more seriously, "Second, and equally important, the candidates you present to us will have to understand a marriage to me will be in name only. There will be no romance, no sex, no emotional intimacy—other than the normal family dynamic. There, I can promise everything will be status quo."

The elegant arch of Alexis's blond brows lifted slightly.

"You have a problem with that?" he asked.

"I don't think any woman in her right mind will agree to that. Unless…" faint color tinged Alexis's cheeks "…you're giving your potential mate license to look elsewhere for, um…companionship?"

Grady frowned. "Absolutely not. Any woman who marries me will have to be completely faithful to me and our family. Otherwise, it would be too confusing for Savannah."

Alexis sighed. "So this woman is just supposed to do without sex and romance for the rest of her life?"

Her sarcasm grated on his nerves. "It's not impossible." He had been doing without both since his wife died and had been managing okay. "Particularly when one trades that for the love of a family and a luxurious lifestyle." He paused, discerning that Alexis was still not convinced. "I am sure there are women who get that," he said dryly.

She nodded and scribbled something else. "Oh, I have no doubt that you're right."

"Then…" he prodded.

Looking reluctant to speak her piece, but also determined, Alexis sat back in her chair and eyed him carefully. "If I may?"

Grady had a feeling he was going to regret this, but not knowing what was on the tip of her tongue would be worse. "Go ahead."

She lifted her slender shoulders in a shrug. "I think you're selling yourself short. It's not just the woman who deserves more, Grady. You do, too."

"So how did it go?" Holly Anne asked when Alexis returned to the penthouse offices in downtown Fort Worth.

Alexis looked at the managing partner. The forty-year-old entrepreneur had founded the matchmaking business fifteen years prior. Of the four investing partners, she was the only one involved in the day-to-day operations. The others came and went as the demands of their other business ventures allowed.

Holly Anne was the one who delivered the sales pitch that brought in all the wealthiest clients. She was also a pretty tough taskmaster, expecting nothing less than absolute devotion from the firm's twenty-seven employees. Alexis figured her boss had thought long and hard about whom she was going to send to see Grady McCabe.

Alexis followed her into her office. "You knew what he was going to ask me to do, didn't you?"

Her boss ran a hand through her sleek black bob, paused to adjust one of her diamond earrings, and sank down in her custom leather chair. "He might have mentioned his request was unusual."

Alexis looked past her toward the view of the skyline. Without warning, she could feel a hint of melancholy coming over her. She pushed it away and began to pace. "Unusual or ridiculously heartless?"

Holly Anne gestured for her to sit down. "He has a lot of money."

Reluctantly, Alexis complied, crossing her legs at the knee. "Not to mention the McCabe name."

"The family is legendary," Holly Anne agreed.

And notoriously warm and loving, Alexis had heard, wishing she could be part of such a large, inclusive clan. Unfortunately, she'd been an only child and had lost both her parents in a car accident. She sighed and let loose some of her pent-up emotion. "Which makes me wonder if they know what he's up to."

Holly Anne tilted her head to one side. "I imagine they want to see him married again."

"Not this way."

"Maybe any way. He was completely in love with his late wife."

Alexis knew how that felt. She had been completely in love with her late spouse, too. She swallowed, then forced her mind back to the present, and the ethical problem in front of her. "So he said."

Her boss paused again. "I chose you, Alexis, because I thought you would understand where Grady is coming from, better than anyone else on staff."

She did, Alexis thought, as silence fell. And she didn't....

Holly Anne leaned forward, a compassionate gleam in her eyes. "I know this is an unusually tough assignment, but you're the right matchmaker for the job. Unless...your heart isn't in this anymore?"

Lately, Alexis had been wondering that herself. Had she been doing this way too long? Not always for the most idealistic of reasons? Or was she just feeling blue as she always did when the second weekend of June approached and she was forced to confront all those painful memories? She turned back to her boss. "Is that what you think? That I'm burned out?"

"I think you've been on track for a promotion for many years. Finding that perfect woman for Grady McCabe would not only make his little girl very happy, but it would put you at the top of the list to run the new office in Galveston." Holly Anne paused. "The move to the coast would be a fresh start for you. And the bump up in salary is considerable."

And money, Alexis thought, was essential if she ever wanted to get out of debt, put the past behind her and live in something more than a tiny efficiency apartment in a not-so-great neighborhood. And Holly was right. In the middle of this crazy request was a little girl who'd never really known her mother, and wanted—as every child did—to have a mommy in her life. If Alexis could find someone who was right for Grady and his daughter, it was possible love could blossom. Grady McCabe could get more than he expected. He could do what she was trying to do right now—come all the way back to life again.

Alexis smiled. "Then I'll do it." And in the process, maybe convince Grady McCabe that it's plain crazy to give up on love.

GRADY WASN'T SURE what had happened in the last month or two to make his daughter so uncooperative where her schoolwork was concerned. He did know that at-home assignments were a stringent part of the curriculum at the prestigious Miss Chilton's Academy for Young Women.

Not that it would take the incredibly bright child very long to actually do the work sheet, if she would just get to it.

Savannah slumped on the leather sofa in his study, the picture of five-year-old distress. "But, Daddy, I don't *want* to do my homework."

Grady worked to curtail his exasperation. "It's not up for discussion, Savannah," he reminded her gently.

"I want to go outside and swing!" she whined loudly.

"*After* you've finished your work sheet," he promised.

Savannah's lower lip slid out, and tears welled in her eyes.

The doorbell rang.

Grady sighed and went to answer it.

Alexis Graham stood on the other side of the portal. She looked every bit as beautiful as she had that afternoon in his office. Briefcase in hand, she was clearly ready to get to work. "Come on in." He stood back to let her pass. "I've got someone I want you to meet."

The only problem was, when he entered his study, his daughter wasn't there. "Savannah," Grady called, and was greeted with silence. "Savannah!" His voice turned stern. He looked behind the sofa, the desk, in the storage closet concealed behind paneled doors.

No sign of her anywhere.

Her abandoned homework sat on the child-size wooden table in the corner, next to her pushed-back chair. Figuring he knew where she had gone, Grady grumbled, "You may have to interview her outside."

Alexis's shapely brow lifted in inquiry.

"Savannah's going to have to approve of anyone I marry," Grady explained, leading the way through the sprawling first floor of his multimillion-dollar home, to the French doors that opened onto the patio. "So I figured we'd start by finding out precisely what she wants in a mother."

As suspected, his misbehaving daughter was seated on her swing, knowing full well that she was doing something wrong. "Look how high I can go, Daddy!" she exclaimed, pumping her legs.

Figuring the lecture could wait, Grady said, "Savannah, this is Ms. Graham. She's going to help us find someone to take care of you."

Savannah's eyes narrowed. "I don't want another nanny!"

"I know you don't." He stopped the swing, then hunkered down in front of her, so the two of them were at eye level. "Which is why we're now looking for a *mommy*."

NOT EXACTLY THE WAY Alexis would have put it. But now that the matter-of-fact declaration was out there, she figured they were just going to have to go with it.

"Your daddy," she said, picking up where Grady had left off, "is looking to get married again. His new wife will be your mommy and that's why we want to know what kind of one you want, before I actually start searching."

Savannah McCabe scrunched up her eyes and twisted her mouth thoughtfully. The face she was making did nothing to diminish her prettiness. Grady's five-year-old daughter was incredibly beautiful. A halo of wild honey-blond curls framed her expressive face. She had bright blue eyes and thick, curling lashes. Round cheeks, a pert nose and a pugnacious little chin added to her angelically stubborn aura. She was tall and athletically built—like her daddy—yet feminine, too.

She was dressed in a ridiculously frilly pink organza dress, with mismatched purple-and-yellow-polka-dot tights and lime-green cowgirl boots. A red-and-white striped barrette in the shape of a candy cane had been shoved into her uncombed hair.

She clearly had Grady McCabe wrapped around her little finger.

Although Alexis doubted he saw it that way.

"I don't want a mommy, either," Savannah declared. "I just want my daddy." She hopped down off the swing and pushed herself into his arms.

Grady hugged her close. Over Savannah's head, he met Alexis's eyes.

This, he hadn't expected.

However, Alexis had.

No little girl who'd had her father's undivided attention was going to want an interloper in their lives.

"Sweetie, you know you need a mommy," he was saying.

"My mommy's in heaven."

"That's right. Which is why," Grady continued, "your mommy wants you to have another mommy now. Someone who can be with you and help you do things."

"Like what?"

"Like…go shopping, bake cookies and go to the park—and comb your hair and all that stuff."

"*We* do that." Savannah pushed away from Grady and hopped back on her swing.

He moved back as she began swinging madly, the petulant look again on her face.

Alexis put a hand on Grady's arm before he could say another word. The tensing of his bicep made her fingers tingle. When their glances met, she silently beseeched him to let her handle this.

Dropping her hand, she stepped away from him and turned to Savannah. "Let's pretend that I'm your fairy godmother."

Savannah's eyes widened in interest. "Like in *Cinderella?*"

"Sort of." Alexis smiled. "Only instead of me making you into a princess, I will help you and your daddy look for a real live princess to come and be your new mommy. What do you think about that?"

"A princess could be my mommy?"

For the kind of lavish lifestyle Grady was offering, Alexis figured he could get anything he wanted from a woman interested in that.

She nodded. "Of course, she would look a lot like everybody else's mommy." She set down her briefcase in the grass and sat in the swing next to Savannah's, nodding at Grady to do the same.

Reluctantly, he took the swing on the other side of his daughter.

Alexis began to swing at the same level and speed as Savannah. "And she'd be kind and loving...and lots of fun."

"Would she play games with me?"

Alexis smiled. "Oh, yes."

"And dress-up?" Savannah pressed.

"Absolutely." Or else she wouldn't be a candidate, Alexis thought.

"And she'd help you with your homework," Grady interjected.

"Then I don't want one," the little girl declared. "Because I don't want to do my homework ever again!" That said, she hopped out of the swing and stomped inside the house.

Alexis offered a sympathetic smile. "Do you want to go after her?"

He shook his head. "I'll give her a few minutes to cool off first."

She couldn't help but feel bad for the man. He obviously loved his daughter very much, but was at a loss as to how to handle her. At times like this, another parent would come in handy. "I gather homework is an issue?"

"Recently, yes, for no reason any of us can figure out. Savannah knows how to write all her letters and numbers and color in the lines, and she does those things without a problem at school." He shrugged helplessly. "She just doesn't want to do them at home."

"You've talked to her teacher?"

"She can't understand Savannah's increasingly recalcitrant behavior either, but it's to the point now that if Savannah doesn't perform as required, they're going to have to hold her back a year. I don't want that to happen," he said emphatically. "I think she's more than ready for first grade, intellectually. Emotionally, well, I think not having a mother is beginning to be an issue for her. So I'm hoping that if I solve that problem, I'll solve the homework problem."

Feeling as if they were finally getting somewhere, Alexis guessed, "Which is why you decided to get married ASAP."

Grady nodded with determination. "I'd like to be married by the Fourth of July."

Once again, Alexis was knocked off-kilter by his demands. "Why so fast?"

"Savannah's in a year-round school program. She graduates from kindergarten on June thirtieth and then is off until first grade starts on August first. I think it would be helpful to her to spend the month of vacation getting to know her new mother."

Alexis understood that Grady was used to getting things done quickly, in business. "You don't want to work that fast," she warned. There was no possible way they could find a suitable wife in less than a month!

His jaw set. "I think it can be done in that time frame."

She knew the customer was always right. Still, she felt she had to at least try and talk sense into him. "What Savannah needs," she urged gently, "is for you to take as much time as necessary to do this right."

He looked irritated, but at least willing to listen to what she had to say. "Then what would you suggest? How can we do this right and still do it fast?"

Alexis drew a bracing breath. "First, I need to spend time with Savannah. If I'm to find someone who is going to be compatible with you both, I've got to understand a lot more about what the two of you want. And while you certainly can fill out the detailed questionnaires that the agency provides, Savannah can't."

Grady caught her drift. "Want to start by staying for dinner with us tonight?"

He's just a client. Albeit a very handsome one. "Sure." Alexis forced herself to maintain a business-like attitude. "If that would make it easier."

"A lot, actually."

The French door from the family room flew open and Savannah stomped out. She was wearing a violet feather boa, a red cowgirl hat…and an attitude that begged for some one-on-one attention. "How come you're still out here swinging—when I'm mad?" She planted her hands on her hips and glared at both of them.

Grady seemed to know that what his daughter really needed at that moment was some tender loving care. "We were talking about what to do next," he soothed.

"Your dad asked me to stay for dinner with the two of you," Alexis reported. And in an effort to include Savannah, she added, "Is that all right with you?"

The child lowered her head and dragged the toe of her cowgirl boot across the patio flagstone. "Well…." She drew out the word. Threw up her hands even more dramatically. "Okay. I guess!"

"Great!" Grady winked at Alexis. "I'll throw something on the stove while you girls get to know each other."

Chapter Two

"Close your eyes, Daddy!" Savannah shouted from the hallway just beyond the kitchen. "And don't open them until I tell you to, okay?"

Grady grinned. He didn't know what Alexis and Savannah had been talking about in her bedroom while he'd been preparing dinner, but his little girl sounded a lot happier.

"Okay." After setting the baking tray on top of the stove to cool, he leaned against the counter and closed his eyes. "I'm ready," he shouted back.

"Are you sure your eyes are closed?" Savannah called.

"Yes." To convince her, he put a hand over them. "I can't see anything!"

"Okay!" Savannah exclaimed, "'Cause ready or not, Daddy, here we come!"

This ought to be good, Grady thought.

He heard the familiar clomp of Savannah's cowgirl boots coming down the hardwood hallway. Followed by the tapping of Alexis's high heels.

Seconds later, he felt the movement of bodies, and inhaled the sexy, feminine scent of Alexis Graham's perfume.

Savannah giggled. "Okay, Daddy, you can look now!"

Grady opened his eyes and found his daughter in one of her dress-up costumes. Her cowgirl boots peeked out from beneath the hem, a jeweled crown adorned her head, and the boa encircled her neck.

Beside her, Alexis stood. Her honey-blond hair was swept into an elegant knot, on the back of her head, and she, too, wore a child-size tiara and a great deal of play jewelry. Her regal attire consisted of a makeshift shawl wrapped around her shoulders and a ruffled pink-and-white cotton "skirt" that suspiciously resembled one of Savannah's bedroom curtains.

"We're playing dress-up," Savannah announced. "I'm the princess and Alexis is my fairy godmother!"

"So I see." Grady worked to contain his pleasure before trading glances with Alexis.

She solemnly waved a magic wand at Savannah, and the little girl beamed up at her. To his surprise, Alexis seemed to be enjoying herself every bit as much as his daughter.

"And she said I can call her Alexis if I want!" Savannah declared.

Grady grinned. He wanted his daughter attaching herself emotionally to her new mother, not the woman he had hired to *find* them one.

Alexis met his eyes. Seeming to understand his reservation, she said, "I think it's important if Savannah and I are going to be friends that the two of us be on a first-name basis."

Put that way, Grady decided, it was acceptable to forgo the traditional method of address.

"You can call her Alexis, too, Daddy," Savannah chimed in.

Grady wasn't sure he wanted even that level of intimacy with a woman he found so physically attractive. But if it made his daughter happy… And Savannah did look happier than he had seen her look in a very long time. "Then I will," he agreed with a smile.

"And you know what else?" Savannah babbled as she sat down in her chair at the breakfast room table, her poufy skirt fluffing out around her. "Alexis is going to find me the kind of mommy I always wanted to have, and she's going to do it right away! Isn't that awesome?"

"It is awesome." Surprised that Alexis had been able to change Savannah's mind so easily, Grady put dinner on the table. Breaded fish sticks from the freezer, macaroni and cheese out of a box, creamed corn from a can and applesauce from a jar.

If Alexis was surprised at the pedestrian fare, she didn't show it.

Grady checked to make sure they had everything, and realized he had forgotten the tartar sauce and ketchup.

He got both from the fridge.

"Do you want anything else for your fish sticks?" he asked Alexis.

Looking impossibly at ease in curtains and a tiara, Alexis spread her napkin across her lap. "Tartar sauce will be fine, thanks. This looks delicious."

Savannah leaned toward her eagerly. "My daddy's a very good cook. He knows how to make all my favorites."

Grady filled her plate, put a puddle of ketchup next to

her fish sticks and handed it to her. "So what else have you ladies been doing?" he asked curiously.

"You tell him," Savannah said, her mouth half-full.

Grady gestured to remind Savannah to remember her manners, and Alexis grinned. "We've been trying to figure out what kind of mom a princess would want her fairy godmother to bring her."

"And what kind of mother would that be?" he asked.

Alexis regarded Grady with a deadpan expression. "The kind that likes to read stories and play dress-up and never makes Savannah do her homework."

He worked to suppress a groan. He should have seen that coming. But when it came to his daughter, he was a total pushover.

Alexis responded to Savannah's wordless pantomime and reached over to cut up the fish sticks on the child's plate—something Grady had forgotten to do.

Savannah basked in the extra attention and help, even saying a polite thank-you afterwards.

Alexis added a tiny amount of tartar sauce to her fish. "She should also let Savannah stay up as late as she wishes, and wear whatever she wants to kindergarten. And she should let her eat candy and cake instead of vegetables and fruit. And buy only chocolate milk at the store."

"I can see you've given this a lot of thought," Grady remarked to his daughter.

"And most important of all—" Alexis looked at Grady steadily "—she wants her new mother here in time for her kindergarten graduation. That way she'll have a mommy and a daddy there with her, just like everyone else."

"THANKS FOR STAYING," Grady told Alexis several hours later. The curtain, play jewelry and tiara were gone. One again Alexis was garbed in a sophisticated business suit and heels. Her hair was still in an elegant knot on top of her head, but a few strands had slipped down the nape of her neck. She looked even prettier than she had before.

He pushed the thought away. It was not like him to notice. That wasn't why she was here, a fact they were both very well aware of.

"Where would you like to talk?" Alexis asked, tilting her face up to his.

"The formal dining room," Grady decided, since it was the closest thing he had to a conference room in his home.

They sat opposite each other. Alexis opened up her briefcase and removed a pen and notepad emblazoned with the company logo and her name. "I don't know about you, but I think we may have made a mistake involving Savannah so closely in the selection process."

"You're referring to her list of desired traits in a mother?"

Alexis nodded, observing him as keenly as she had his daughter. "Savannah now has a very clear picture of what she wants."

Grady stretched his legs out in front of him and slumped back in his chair. "She also knows granting all those wishes is impossible. No parent with the best interest of their child in mind behaves that way."

Alexis was silent. "You and I know that. I'm not so sure Savannah does."

"What are you saying?" Grady prompted.

Alexis cupped her chin in her hand and predicted

glumly, "It's going to be tough finding someone by graduation."

Grady shrugged. He refused to lower his expectations just because they had hit a snag. He didn't think Alexis should, either. "I've closed more than one impossible-to-pull-off business deal in less than two weeks."

Her blue eyes darkened. "That's just it," she countered. "This isn't business, Grady. It's personal."

Only to a degree, Grady thought; since he did not plan to get emotionally involved with the woman who would be rearing his child. Had this been anything other than a business arrangement, it *would* have been complicated. "Just go through your files," he advised, not bothering to mask his impatience. "Find some likely candidates. Introduce them to Savannah. And don't make this any more complex for any of us than it has to be."

Alexis tensed. After sending him a look of thinly veiled displeasure, she asked with forced politeness, "Are you certain you don't want to meet them first?"

Grady had vowed when his wife died that he would never love a woman that way again. It was a promise he had kept—and intended to go right on keeping—no matter how much his little girl wanted a mother. "A bit pointless, don't you think, if my daughter doesn't warm to them first?"

Alexis compressed her lips. "I'll be frank. I'm worried she could get hurt."

"She's already been hurt, from the first moment she figured out what a mommy was and learned hers was already in heaven."

The matchmaker's expression turned compassionate. "I need to know what you're looking for, too," she said, writing Grady's name across the top of the page.

Finding it too uncomfortable to look into her eyes, he studied the way her hair gleamed in the light of the chandelier overhead instead, then wished he hadn't noticed. "I already told you my requirements."

She waited in silence until he looked straight at her. "For this to work on even the most rudimentary level, you and Savannah both have to be compatible with the match. So let's start again. What do you want in a woman?"

Grady curbed his temper with effort. "A loving mother for my daughter. An undemanding but understanding wife for me."

"Is she going to need to be able to entertain?"

"Yes." He folded his arms across his chest.

"Cook?"

He pushed away the too-intimate memory of Alexis having dinner with them in their kitchen. He wondered if she had any idea how hard it was for him to let a woman into his life again, even in theory. How hard it was going to be to open himself up to even the possibility of loss.

Savannah had already lost one mother.

How would they survive if it happened again?

Grady snapped out of his reverie when he realized Alexis was still waiting on an answer to her last question. "I don't care if she can cook or not. Any woman you bring into our lives is going to have to be able to eat Savannah's favorite foods with as much gusto as I do, though."

Finally, the faint hint of a smile tugged at the corners of Alexis's lips. She wrote "fish sticks, mac'n cheese and applesauce" on the pad in front of her. "What else does Savannah like to eat?"

This, Grady thought, was a lot easier to talk about. "Chicken fingers, hamburgers, hot dogs, grilled cheese, spaghetti, pizza and tacos."

She kept writing. "That's it?"

"It's enough that we don't have to repeat anything for eight days. And I don't have to expand my culinary repertoire."

Alexis chuckled. "What does she eat for breakfast?"

"Cereal, toast, pancakes and waffles. Lunch is peanut butter or bologna sandwiches." Grady waited for Alexis to finish her list.

Warming to the subject, he said, "It would probably also be nice if she was good at talking Savannah into doing things she doesn't particularly want to do—like homework or brushing her hair."

Alexis wrote down *diplomatic* and *persuasive* in big bold letters.

"And energetic," Grady added as an afterthought. "She needs to be able to keep up with Savannah, especially with the month-long summer break coming, since I don't plan to hire any more nannies."

Despite his decision to keep an emotional wall between them, Grady found himself fascinated by how quickly and delicately Alexis's hand moved as she took notes. "And last but not least, any woman who wants to come into our lives has got to be able to love my little girl as much as I do."

Alexis nodded in agreement. "Well, I can see I've got my work cut out for me."

Grady stood. "How soon can you introduce prospective mommies to Savannah?"

Alexis slipped her notebook in her briefcase. "I can have the first one here tomorrow, when Savannah comes home from school. But you're going to need to do something, too, Grady. You've got to fill out that questionnaire I gave you when we met at your office."

Grady scowled. "It has four hundred questions."

She held up a palm—her left hand, he couldn't help but notice. And the ring finger was bare.

"I know it's long," Alexis said. "I'm sorry about that. Just e-mail me the results when you're done. Our computer program will analyze the data and present us with a list of potential matches. We'll go from there."

GRADY SHOULD HAVE FELT good. The process of finding the replacement mother his little girl wanted had begun. Instead, he felt unsettled. Deeply, peculiarly so. Worse, every time he tried to figure out why that was, he ended up thinking about Alexis Graham instead.

He supposed that was because the straight-talking matchmaker was in charge of finding him a suitable wife, and her success rate of pairing up clients with someone to marry was close to one hundred percent.

Fortunately, a series of phone calls on his latest development project kept him busy the rest of the evening. The next morning was spent getting himself off to work and the unusually cooperative Savannah off to school.

As he arrived home with Savannah that evening, Alexis was pulling into his driveway.

He watched her get out of her white BMW.

Today, she was wearing a trendy teal suit that brought out the blue-green of her eyes. Her honey-colored locks had been drawn into a sophisticated french twist. A heart-shaped locket hung on a golden chain around her neck and nestled in the V of the silky teal blouse she wore beneath her jacket.

Her high heels clicked on the drive as she made her way toward his Cadillac Escalade.

Savannah, who had been pouting over the prospect of doing homework again, cheered up as she approached. "Daddy, it's my fairy godmother! She's here again!"

And she was supposed to have a likely candidate with her, Grady recalled.

He stepped down from the driver's seat and greeted her.

After returning the greeting, Alexis waved at Savannah, who was still strapped in her booster seat.

The little girl waved back vigorously.

"The first candidate should be here any second."

Grady breathed a sigh of relief. He really wanted to get this business over with as soon as possible. "Good," he said.

As if on cue, a station wagon pulled into his wide circular drive in front of the house.

An attractive woman stepped out.

She had a kind face, short dark hair and brown eyes. She was wearing the type of clothes a well-to-do suburban mom might wear—tailored beige slacks, a matching summer-weight sweater set and sensible shoes.

Alexis made introductions. "Grady McCabe, I'd like you to meet Desdemona Bradford. Desdemona, this is Grady McCabe—the client I was telling you about."

"Nice to meet you." Desdemona shook hands with Grady, while Savannah, who had unsnapped her safety belt, looked on curiously before opening the rear passenger door.

Grady smiled and said hello, then turned to help his daughter from the car.

"Savannah, this is Ms. Bradford."

"You can call me Desdemona," she said with a smile.

"She's a librarian and she knows a lot about story-books," Alexis stated.

"I brought some books for us to read." Desdemona walked back to her station wagon to get them.

Savannah studied the librarian skeptically. She was more thrilled at the items accompanying the stack of brand-new books. "Cookies and milk!"

Desdemona shrugged. "I thought an icebreaker might be nice."

"Good move," Alexis murmured.

"You could join us," Desdemona said to Grady.

He nixed the offer with a brief shake of his head. "Actually, I've got some phone calls to return. But thanks."

Alexis, Desdemona and Savannah headed for the kitchen. Grady retired to the study that served as his at-home office.

An hour later, there was a knock at the door.

It was Alexis.

"How's it going?" he asked.

"I really like Desdemona. I think she's a wonderful person."

"But…?" Grady prompted.

"Maybe you should come out back and see for yourself," Alexis suggested.

Curious, Grady rose. He had taken off his suit jacket and tie, unfastened the top buttons on his shirt and rolled up the sleeves when he had sat down to work.

Alexis had also taken off her suit jacket—probably

due to the unusually warm June afternoon. The sleeve-less silk shell she wore moved fluidly about her slender torso, and exposed her arms to view. Grady had always considered himself a leg man—and Alexis's legs were spectacular—but for the first time he found himself equally entranced by the feminine shape of a woman's arms. There was no doubt about it—Alexis's shoulders, the supple curve of muscles in her upper arms, were every bit as alluring as the rest of her.

Not that he should be thinking this way.

Frowning, admonishing himself to stay on task, he followed her down the hall toward the back of the house. They walked through the breakfast room, out into the sunny family room and over to the French doors, which stood ajar.

Alexis put out a hand to stop him from stepping outside.

"Just stand here and observe a moment," she urged quietly.

"I want more cookies!" Savannah was saying.

"Sweetums, you've already had five."

"Daddy always lets me have six."

"No I don't," Grady murmured.

"Hush," Alexis said. She tapped the back of his hand lightly. "Pay attention!"

"All right. But you can't tell anyone I've given you another one!" Desdemona slipped another cookie from the bakery box balanced on top of the play fort platform.

"I want you to do somersaults for me," Savannah demanded.

Desdemona flushed and wrung her hands. "I can't. I'm too old, sweetums."

The girl sized her up shrewdly. "But that's what I want!" she demanded around a mouthful of cookie.

"How about we read books instead?" Desdemona pleaded.

Realizing she had the upper hand, Savannah shook her head. "No! I want you to do what I say…and I want you to do it now or I'm going to scream!"

"That's enough," Grady muttered.

He strode through the French doors and out onto the grass.

Desdemona had already slipped off her sensible shoes and was bending down, awkwardly attempting to figure out how to roll herself into a ball.

Grady stopped her with a hand on her shoulder, then removed the half-eaten cookie from his daughter's hand. "Savannah, you owe Ms. Bradford an apology."

"But, Daddy…!"

"Right now, Savannah."

The child flushed and sighed, then mumbled, "I'm sorry."

Grady picked up the library books and what was left of the box of cookies, then turned to Desdemona. "Let me walk you out," he said amicably.

"DADDY'S MAD AT ME," Savannah reported, when the two adults had disappeared through the wooden gate.

"With good reason, it would seem," Alexis answered. "You took advantage of Desdemona's kindness."

Savannah scuffed her sneaker in the grass and said in a low, hurt tone, "She didn't really want to play with me." She paused, to make sure Alexis was listening. "She just did it because she had to."

And Savannah, understandably, hadn't wanted any part of that. So she had acted out to get rid of her.

Without warning, Grady was back. "Don't you have homework to do, young lady?" he said.

Savannah's beleaguered look indicated she did.

"Is it in your backpack?" he continued.

She lifted one shoulder. "I guess so."

"What is it?"

"A picture. We're s'posed to finish coloring it."

Grady turned his daughter in the direction of the house. "All right. Please sit at the kitchen table and do your homework while I finish talking to Alexis."

Savannah tipped her head way back, so she could see her daddy's face. "*Then* can she stay for supper and play with me like she did last night?"

"I don't think so. Go. Now."

Savannah uttered a dramatic sigh and trudged toward the door. By the time she reached it, however, she was skipping. Whether in joy or relief, it was hard to tell.

Grady made sure she was out of earshot before he turned back to Alexis. "That was a disaster."

Alexis couldn't disagree. "It's not going to be easy to find a woman who will accept your criteria," she warned. "A marriage without sex or emotional intimacy is going to be a tough sell."

Grady ran a hand through his hair. "I'm sure there is someone," he stated in a low, aggravated tone.

Alexis contained her own frustration with effort. "I didn't say I was going to stop trying." She turned to face him. "I want Savannah to have a mommy as much as you and she do—I think she deserves that and so much more. But clearly the next candidate can't be someone who will let Savannah walk all over her."

Grady exhaled, his expression guilty. He massaged the muscles at the nape of his neck. "It's all those nannies I've had."

Alexis paused. "How many were there again?"

"At last count? Eight."

Wow. No wonder Savannah was having problems....

"The first two were great. They were a lot older—in their early sixties. They each stayed two years, before health woes forced them to retire." He sighed. "The next bunch were a lot younger. Physically able to keep up with Savannah, but each one wrong for some other reason."

"Such as...?"

"Where do I begin?" He took a deep breath before forging ahead. "Marabelle let Savannah get away with everything and anything, so she had to go. Liza tried to hit on me. Penny was always on the phone. Grendel had allergies that wouldn't let her spend any time outdoors. Xandra thought twelve hours of daily TV was just fine." He threw up his hands. "And last but not least, there was Maryellen, who, as it turned out, spent the majority of her time practicing her yoga on the living room floor while Savannah sat in a corner with a book."

It sounded like a nightmare. One that could have been avoided? "How'd you find so many bad child care workers?" Alexis asked curiously.

Grady stepped onto the shaded patio. "Don't ask me. They all had references. Experience." He waved her out of the sun, too. Once Alexis was beside him, he looked down at her and continued. "I guess the main problem was that the two older nannies I had were so great with Savannah, she was devastated when they left. Although both Olivia and Graciella keep in touch, it's not the same. To the younger, more energetic nannies, taking care of Savannah was just a job.

"By the time they came, she was old enough to observe the other kids in her preschool and kindergarten classes with their mothers, and realize what they had and she didn't. She wants a mother who loves her, and I don't blame her. I want that for her, too." Grady paused, his eyes clouding over. "I can't pretend I'm ever going to feel for another woman what I felt for my late wife. It's impossible."

Alexis nodded, understanding. "Grief like that can be very hard to overcome." But hopefully, not impossible, for him or for her. Otherwise, she'd never have what she wanted out of life, either.

An increasingly uncomfortable silence fell between them.

Finally, Grady looked deep into Alexis's eyes and stated quietly, "I still have to give my daughter what she needs. Even if it means entering into a marriage of convenience."

Alexis could see there was no changing his mind. A marriage of convenience it would be.

Chapter Three

"Burning the midnight oil?" Holly Anne looked pointedly at the extra-large latte in Alexis's hand, as she entered the conference room and took command.

Alexis smiled politely and made a mental note to work a little harder to cover up her growing disillusionment. As much as she was loath to admit it, the deep-seated frustration she felt this morning was only partly due to the heavy rainfall. It was more about the demanding client in her care.

The dozen other staffers already at the conference table regarded her with thinly disguised envy. Everyone there wanted the plum task of spending time with the delectably handsome, oh-so-eligible Grady McCabe. Of course, Alexis reassured herself practically, that probably would change if they knew how impossible he was going to be to match. It wasn't that she couldn't find a woman who would be willing to trade money for love. There was always someone viable in that category, of either sex. It was trying to find someone who would do so who would still be good for Savannah. That, Alexis wasn't sure was possible. And she did not want to let the adorable little girl down.

"Grady McCabe is particular," she said finally, wincing slightly when lightning lit up the dark morning sky.

Sandi Greevey sighed and said, over the rumble of thunder, "If you ask me, he's fooling himself if he thinks a woman is going to sign on without even the possibility of love or sex."

"I don't know," said another colleague, as rain lashed the windows with gusty force. "Hope burns eternal."

"Tell that to Russ and Carolyn Bass," Doreen Ross quipped.

Holly Anne frowned, clearly disappointed by the recent divorce filing that had flooded the morning airwaves. "I thought those two would last forever," she lamented.

So had Alexis, when she'd matched them.

"Just goes to show money doesn't buy happiness," Sally Romo said.

The receptionist walked in just then and handed Alexis a note.

She let out a breath slowly. Just what she needed to make her day even more difficult.

Six hours later, it was still raining heavily as she drove to Grady McCabe Enterprises's most recent acquisition.

The three-block area just south of downtown Fort Worth was blocked off as a construction zone and surrounded by a twelve foot high fence. Entrance to the muddy, rubble strewn demolition zone was monitored by an electric gate and a uniformed guard in a gray-and-black rain slicker.

"Alexis Graham, here to see Grady McCabe," she said when he stuck his head out the window of the gatehouse.

"He's expecting you, Ms. Graham. Proceed straight ahead to the last trailer. You can park behind it. Mr. Mc-Cabe is waiting inside."

Resentful that she was going to have to take her company-leased BMW through the car wash after this expedition, Alexis drove slowly through the gravel and mud, past a sign proclaiming this as the site of the new GME high-rise, to the quartet of construction trailers parked near the back of the sprawling lot.

There were six vehicles parked next to the last trailer.

She slid her BMW into the last available slot, grabbed her umbrella and briefcase, and got out.

THE MEETING HAD JUST broken up when the knock sounded on the trailer door.

Through the rain beating against the windows, Grady could see Alexis Graham standing on the wooden steps.

He rushed to open the door so she could get in out of the rain.

Water darkened the fabric of her vivid yellow trench coat. Her heels, stockings—even the hem of her raincoat—were coated with mud. Too late, he realized he should have suggested she dress more casually and maybe wear boots.

"Sorry I'm a little early," Alexis said, shaking out her umbrella. "I wasn't sure how long it would take to get here."

"No problem." Grady paused to introduce his four best friends: Dan, the architect of all his developments, and Travis, who owned the construction company that built them. Jack, the wiring genius whose company installed the networks, phones and satellite systems. And last but not least, Nate, the CEO of the Texas-based financial services company that was going to be leasing eighty percent of the available space in this latest project.

"Nice to meet you," Alexis said.

The four men murmured the same, grabbed their jackets and headed out.

Grady and Alexis were alone. Dumbstruck by how lovely she looked, with raindrops glistening on the tip of her nose and her cheeks, he said the first thing that came to mind. "Sorry about the weather...."

Merriment sparkled in her eyes. "You control that?"

Her teasing brought a smile to his face, too. "Sorry about having you meet me here in the middle of a monsoon," he corrected. "I thought the rain would have let up by now."

"We're in the midst of a tropical storm—or what's left of it this far inland. The precipitation isn't going away until tomorrow evening, at the earliest."

Normally, Grady would have known that. But he'd been too preoccupied lately. "Guess I should have paid more attention to the forecast."

"You seem to have your hands full."

Grady thought about Savannah's temper tantrum that very morning, when he'd told her she had to wear her school uniform—not her princess costume—to school, as always. "I do at that," he said dryly.

The phone rang, and Grady held up a hand, wordlessly asking her to wait before he pulled his BlackBerry from his pocket. He listened, but the words made no sense. He blinked in stunned amazement. "Could you repeat that...?"

Slowly but surely the meaning sunk in. Words not polite for fit company filled his head, the inner diatribe directed exclusively toward himself, for his increasingly poor parenting. "No. Thank you for letting me know. I'll be right there."

He ended the call with a push of a button.

Alexis looked at him and lifted a brow.

"It's Savannah," Grady said, already searching for his umbrella. "She's in trouble."

"WE CAN GO OVER your picks for the next introduction on the way over," he promised Alexis as the two of them headed back out into the rain.

She had insisted that this time he consider at least three women, before selecting one. She hoped going through the process would show him what a valuable screening tool it was. Unfortunately, despite the fact she talked nonstop on the fifteen minute drive to Miss Chilton's Academy for Young Women, Alexis was fairly certain Grady didn't absorb a word of what she said.

Before she could quiz him on his thoughts, however, they were turning into the visitor parking lot of the city's oldest and most prestigious all-girl school. "Would you like me to wait in the car?" she said.

Grady shook his head. "It's too warm. I have no idea how long this will take. And I may need female reinforcement."

"Mind telling me what's going on, then?"

He held the umbrella over her head as they hurried toward the door. "The headmistress said something about a contretemps in ballet class, whatever that means. All I know is I am expected to come and get Savannah and take her home early—after stopping in the school office."

Grady held the door, then escorted Alexis through

the lobby to the glass-walled principal's office. There, seated on a bench, was Savannah. Next to her was a little girl with long red hair and the kind of to-the-manor-born-air about her that Alexis had always hated.

Both were wearing hot-pink leotards, tights, tutus and ballet slippers. Their hair was askew. Their faces were flushed and pouty, but otherwise both looked fine.

The school secretary shot Grady a sympathetic look. "I'll let the headmistress, Principal Jordan, know that you are here."

Behind Grady, the door opened and closed.

An elegant red-haired woman in a slim black Prada skirt, electric-blue silk blouse and black Jimmy Choo boots glided in. She'd drawn a silk Hermes scarf over her head, to protect her hair. She whisked it down to lie against the diamond pendant around her neck. "Grady." She turned a regal nod in his direction.

"Hello, Kit," he replied. "Principal Jordan. I'd like you-all to meet Alexis Graham. She's a friend of the family."

Alexis tried not to read too much into the acknowledgment.

Savannah, however, was looking at her with an expression that clearly said, I'm so glad you're here! Now save me!

"Nice to meet all of you," Alexis said politely after the introductions had been made.

"What's going on?" Grady asked the principal.

"I'd like to know that myself," Kit Peterson said, clearly unhappy to be there under those circumstances.

"Savannah and Lisa Marie disrupted ballet class with a brawl. The teacher sent them to my office. Hair pulling, pushing, shoving, name calling—none of that will be tolerated at our school."

Grady looked at his daughter. Clearly in shock, he knelt down in front of her. "Honey, what do you have to say for yourself?"

Nothing, apparently, Alexis noted.

"She started it." Lisa Marie pointed the finger at Savannah, who remained stubbornly silent.

"I expect both girls to apologize to each other right now," Principal Jordan said.

"I'm sorry." Lisa Marie Peterson piped up immediately.

Her mom beamed in approval and relief, as did the headmistress.

Grady's little girl remained silent.

"Savannah?" he prompted.

Her expression grew stonier. She refused to look at her father, or any one else, even Alexis.

"Perhaps you should discuss this matter at home," Principal Jordan suggested, with slightly less patience.

Mrs. Hanford appeared with two backpacks and child-size rain slickers, one set of which bore outrageously expensive designer labels.

The principal looked at Grady, her frustration with his daughter apparent. "Although she does not have to do it right now if it is not sincere, I will caution you both that Savannah will not be allowed back in school until formal verbal restitution is made."

"I understand," Grady said.

So, apparently, did Savannah.

She wasn't budging.

"You okay with dropping by our house for a while, before we go back to the construction site to pick up your car?" Grady asked Alexis, after settling Savannah in the back seat and climbing behind the wheel.

"Sure."

"Good." His jaw set determinedly. "Because I still want to go over those files you brought, as soon as we get a minute."

"I wasn't certain you'd be interested...in, um..." Alexis paused to cast a brief glance at the back seat, where a glum Savannah was silently staring out of the rain-streaked window.

"In what?" Grady prompted, with a sidelong glance of his own—at her.

Alexis's cheeks warmed self-consciously beneath his scrutiny.

"Um..." She dropped her voice another notch. "Continuing your search for a new..." She gestured rather than complete the sentence out loud.

Grady exhaled, his own frustration with the situation apparent. "I think this latest 'contretemps' proves more than ever that I need to do something to provide the missing female guidance."

"There are other ways to do that." Alexis spoke before she could stop herself.

He gave her another, sharper look. "None I am interested in."

They both fell silent. Five minutes later, they turned into the driveway of his 1920s bungalow-style home in the River Crest Country Club area. The two-story gray stucco home with the dark gray roof and sparkling white trim was situated on a tree-lined cul-de-sac. Approximately half the size of many of the other luxurious homes in the area, it had an understated elegance and cozy, charming appeal, unobscured by the rain still pouring from the skies.

While Grady shut off the engine, got out of the Escalade and opened the rear passenger door, Alexis followed suit.

Grady lifted Savannah, who was clad in her yellow rain slicker and ballet slippers, down to the pavement. She didn't seem to care that her slippers were getting soaked for the second time. "Let me grab your backpack, then I'll carry you the rest of the way," he offered.

Finally, Savannah sparked back to life.

"No!" she shouted. Fists balled at her sides, she spun around, and before he could stop her, took off at a rapid pace for the front of the house. Several inches of water had gathered in the drive and water splashed up around her knees.

"Slow down!" Grady called, striding after her.

"No!" Savannah shouted again. Clearly in a temper, she increased her speed, breaking into a run. And that was when it happened. The slippery soles of her flimsy slippers went out from beneath her and she went flying.

Alexis and Grady both gasped as Savannah landed facedown on the concrete drive, the bulk of the impact taken by her outstretched elbows and knees.

There was a moment's awful silence as her tiny body shook with soundless sobs, and then, a second later, loud wails.

Grady didn't hesitate. Tossing Savannah's backpack to Alexis, like a quarterback handing off a ball, he rushed forward and scooped his sobbing daughter into his arms.

He carried her through the rain to the front porch,

punched in the code on the keypad next to the door, then stepped inside.

Alexis followed, her own eyes filling with moisture that had nothing to do with the rain coming down.

It didn't matter how old she was, or who was hurting. Alexis couldn't stand to see someone in pain. Never had been able to. Which was what had made the last years of her ill-fated marriage so very hard.

Grady continued through the foyer, down the hall and into the state-of-the-art kitchen, soothing his daughter with low, comforting words all the while.

Arms locked around his neck, Savannah cried uncontrollably.

He buried his face in her damp curls, gently patting her back, still soothing her verbally.

Finally, when she hiccupped and seemed to be calming down, he said, "Let me have a look at those 'owies'."

Savannah shook her head and clung all the more tightly.

Grady glanced at Alexis over the top of his daughter's head. "Can you…?"

"Sure." She slipped out of her drenched trench coat and moved closer, trying to inspect the damage. "Looks like she scraped both knees," she reported.

And that had to hurt!

"Check her elbows."

"We're going to have to get her slicker off."

"I'll help."

Still sobbing, Savannah refused to cooperate.

Together, the two adults finally managed, without Grady ever having to put his daughter down. "They look a little raw, but they're not…" *Bleeding,* Alexis mouthed. "Her palms, unfortunately, are both scraped raw."

Whoo boy, Grady mouthed back. "Savannah, honey, we need to get your owies cleaned up, and get you out of these wet clothes."

"No," Savannah wailed, even more hysterically. "It's going to hurt!"

"Then how about," Grady suggested, barely missing a beat, "we have your fairy godmother do it?"

ALEXIS HAD TO HAND IT to Grady—that was inspired. The suggestion got his daughter's tears stopped—momentarily at least—as she lifted her head and looked at Alexis. "Can you do it?" she whimpered. "Can you make it stop hurting?"

Alexis had made people in far worse straits comfortable. "Of course I can fix you up," she said calmly, slipping into caretaker mode. She tapped her index finger against her chin. "The question is," she added thoughtfully, "do you want to clean up those scrapes here in the kitchen, or in a nice warm bubble bath?" Which would do a better job and be a lot easier. "If we can get you in the tub to soak the dirt and germs out of your owies, I bet you can have a Popsicle, too."

Savannah sniffed and looked interested. "While I'm in the tub?" she asked incredulously.

Alexis turned to Grady, shifting the ball right back to him. "Daddy? Is it okay?"

Respected glimmered in Grady's eyes. "Sure."

"I'll tell you what. I'll get her in the tub, and you follow with Popsicles, the first aid kit and whatever dry clothes you want her to wear."

His lips curved into a grateful half smile. "No problem, fairy godmother."

Alexis looked back at Savannah, who was still ensconced in her daddy's strong arms. "Do you think you can walk upstairs, or do you want me to carry you?"

The child sniffed again. New tears trembled on her lashes. "I want you to carry me," she whimpered.

"I'll be happy to." Alexis held out her arms.

Savannah slid into them.

Together, they went up the stairs, down the hall, to the private bath in Savannah's suite. It was just as girlie and pink and suited for a princess as her bedroom was. "My goodness, you have a big selection of bubble baths!" Alexis exclaimed. She sat on the rim of the sunken tub, Savannah on her lap, and reached over to turn on the tap. "What kind do you want? Lavender? That's supposed to be very soothing. Or the one that smells like baby powder?"

"Baby powder." The lower lip was out as far as it would go.

Alexis snapped open the lid. "You want to help me pour it in?"

"Uh-huh." Savannah leaned over to let a generous amount stream beneath the tap. Bubbles sprung up immediately. She smiled slightly at the sight.

"I'm going to warn you," Alexis said. "It might sting when you first sit down in the tub, but then it's going to get much much better."

"I know," Savannah acknowledged miserably. "I've had to do this before when I falled down and hurted myself."

Alexis helped her slip out of her worse-for-wear ballerina outfit. "Me, too."

Savannah's eyes widened in amazement. "*You* fell down?"

"All the time when I was a kid," Alexis admitted with a rueful grin. "I had the worst time trying to learn to ride a bike...."

She was still regaling Savannah with stories of her own mishaps when Grady appeared, three pineapple-flavored Popsicles in hand.

Savannah brightened, seeing the frozen treats. Grady's eyes met Alexis's. "One for each of us." He telegraphed his gratitude, then turned back to his daughter. "So how are we doing?" he asked, lounging against the counter. "Are you okay?"

Savannah nodded and averted her eyes.

A sure sign, Alexis noted, that she was not.

"Savannah asleep already?" Alexis asked an hour later, when Grady joined her in the kitchen. She had been sitting at the table, catching up on her end-of-business-day e-mails, while he put his daughter to bed.

Grady nodded, his compassion for his little one evident in his gentle expression. "She didn't even get past the first page of the storybook."

Alexis sent him a commiserating glance and closed the lid of her laptop computer. She could finish that later. It was time to get back to setting up her primary client. "She had a rough day."

"I'll say." Appearing as restless and distracted as Alexis felt Grady plucked the skillet out of the dish drainer and put it away.

"But a good dinner," Alexis said, as he handled the very last of the cleanup. "Those two grilled cheese sandwiches and a glass of chocolate milk really did the trick," she teased.

Grady grinned, as if knowing it wasn't the healthiest array of foods he could have provided. He leaned against the sink, arms folded in front of him. "It was what she wanted," he said with an unapologetic lift of his broad shoulders. "Speaking of which…" He paused to look Alexis in the eye. "Thank you for staying and helping get her all fixed up. And hanging out with her while I made dinner. And eating with us once again."

He acted as if it had been a chore. It hadn't been. The truth was, Alexis hadn't felt so happy and content in a long time. Part of it was being around a child, because she loved kids. Had always wanted them. Fate had kept her from having any so far, but she hoped it wouldn't always be the case.

"It was my pleasure," she murmured, doing her best to keep the situation from getting too intimate.

"I'm serious." Grady strolled closer. "You were really good with her today."

Thinking maybe it was time they called it a night, Alexis pushed back her chair and stood.

The Savannah who'd hung out with them at suppertime was cuddly and cheerful and cooperative. Which made Alexis think all Grady's little girl really needed was a lot more tender loving care from people who genuinely cared about her.

Marriage, Alexis realized, might not be necessary.

Was it possible that a family friend—filling in as an occasional mom slash mother figure—would do?

Alexis wanted to suggest just that, rather than have Grady rush into a marriage that potentially might not work out over the long haul…and hence create a bigger void than Savannah already had in her life.

Unfortunately, Alexis's role as matchmaker, the responsibility for bringing in more business to a firm that had stood by her during the best and worst of times, precluded her doing so.

Aware that Grady was gazing at her quizzically, she turned the conversation back to the reason they were both here. "I enjoy spending time with her."

Grady studied Alexis. "She adores you, you know."

Alexis felt a lump of emotion well up in her throat, and the equally strong need to protest. "She barely knows me."

He stepped close enough to inundate her with his brisk, male scent. Some emotion she couldn't quite define flickered in his eyes. "She knows enough."

Alexis stared at him in confusion. She felt they were on the brink of some kind of epiphany. "Meaning…?"

"You're one of a kind, Alexis," Grady observed slowly. He cupped the side of her face with the palm of his hand.

Her breath hitched, even as she tilted her head up to his. This couldn't be happening. Could it? He couldn't be putting the moves on her. "What are you doing?" she murmured.

He gave her a look of determination that was as unexpected as it was compelling. His eyes shuttered to half-mast. "What I've wanted to do all day. Hell—" his head lowered and his mouth dropped even lower "—why not be honest here? From practically the first second we met…"

Alexis splayed both hands across his chest. His muscles were warm and hard beneath her palms, and she could feel his heart pounding. "That's…this…" Oh, hell, he was going to kiss her! "It's impossible…."

"No," he murmured. "It's not."

And then all was lost in the feel of his body pressed up against hers and the wonder of his lips moving over hers.

Chapter Four

The rational, practical part of Grady knew he shouldn't be kissing Alexis. Shouldn't be trying to ease the loneliness and isolation that had dominated his life for the last five years with the incredibly warm and tender woman in his arms. He should be walking away from the softness of her lips, and the femininity of her body pressed against his. Ignoring the sweet taste of her mouth, and the passionate way she kissed him back.

A physical relationship with her could only get in the way of what they were trying to do—find a mommy for Savannah…and a wife for him who would accept the limitations he set. A woman he could be honest with. A woman who understood. A woman Savannah could love, and who would love her in return.

Grady wanted a kind of wife Alexis didn't seem to think could be found. Unless… He broke off the kiss as the next idea hit.

Hands on her shoulders, he shifted her away. Working to keep himself from surrendering to temptation once again, he noticed the surprising vulnerability in her eyes. Her lip was trembling slightly, and she seemed as taken aback by the flare of desire between them as he was.

"Are you available?" Grady asked bluntly.

Alexis blinked and stepped away. "You mean single?"

For the first time in a long time, he felt fully, physically alive once again. With effort, Grady curtailed his spiraling emotions. "As a potential match."

"For you?" Alexis's brow lifted as the meaning of his words apparently sank in. She stepped back again and lifted both hands, as if to ward him off. "No. I'm not."

Grady hadn't gotten where he was in life by accepting no for an answer, especially when he wanted something as much as he suddenly wanted this. Eyes trained on hers, he asked, "Sure about that?"

Resentment laced her voice as she answered, "Matchmakers at my company are not allowed to date clients, Grady."

Most of the important decisions in his life were based on instinct. And right now it was telling him he'd already found the mother his daughter wanted and needed. A woman his daughter could love—and who would love Savannah back. "We're not talking about a date." Or anything near that insignificant. "We're talking about a match."

"Same thing," Alexis replied. "And it's out of the question, Grady."

Frustration tightened his muscles. "Why?"

She packed up her laptop, picked up her handbag and began searching for her cell phone. "Because you're in too much of a hurry to find someone and get this done." She pushed the words through gritted teeth.

He shrugged, not about to back down, now that he'd put the idea out there. "So I value efficiency."

She lifted her chin. "Efficiency is fine when it comes

to business. But this isn't business, Grady, or at least it shouldn't be. It's your personal life."

He'd heard as much from the few friends and family who knew what he had planned. He shrugged. "So?"

She shook her head in mute exasperation. Finally looked him in the eye. "Ever heard the expression, 'Pick a spouse in haste and repent in leisure?'"

He exhaled. "More or less."

Alexis stepped closer, clearly not afraid to stand up to him. "When clients are in as much of a hurry as you are to get matched up," she explained, as if to someone in need of a great deal of counseling, "it's usually because they don't want to stop and think about what it is they are doing. Because—" she inched even closer "—they know if they do stop and think, they'll realize what a giant mistake they're making, and they won't go through with it."

Grady gazed down at her. "I won't back out," he stated confidently.

"You say that now. But when it comes time to commit to a lifetime without love, you may feel differently."

"I probably would if I thought I could love again," Grady said honestly. The sad thing was... "I don't."

"You really loved your wife that much?" Alexis whispered, backing away once more.

It was almost as if he could see an invisible force field go up around her heart. "Yes," he said.

A mixture of sadness and commiseration shone in Alexis's eyes. "And you still miss Tabitha."

Grady found himself wanting to talk about something he never discussed. "I don't know. Sometimes—" he shook his head, gulping around the sudden knot of emotion in his throat "—I can barely remember her.

Other times, the void in my life…" He paused, searching for words. "Let's just say I really feel it."

More gently now, Alexis asked, "How did you meet?"

Grady lounged against the kitchen counter again. He took a deep breath, let it out. "Tabitha was an interior designer who specialized in commercial buildings. I was right out of college and had just purchased my first run-down commercial space. The location was good. The interior of the building was not. I wanted to redo it and then lease it out." He smiled reminiscently. "She helped me achieve my dream. After that, we were inseparable. Worked on one project after another and got married three years after we met."

Alexis went back to the table and took a notepad and pen out of her briefcase. She sat down in the chair and began to write. "Was she close to your family?"

Grady watched Alexis's movements, for the first time realizing she was left-handed. "Yes."

She looked up, intent. "Is that important to you— that the person you marry be loved by your family?"

He nodded.

"What about prenups?" The questions now were rapid-fire. "Are you going to ask for one?"

"I didn't before," he admitted, remembering he'd been called a fool for that, too, by everyone who knew his own earning potential, plus what he one day stood to inherit from the trust his folks had set up for him.

Aware that she was still waiting for an explanation, Grady said, "When I married it was for life. I just didn't know Tabitha's would be so short."

Empathy radiated in Alexis's eyes.

She took a moment to consider that, then asked, "When you marry again, will it be for life?"

Grady hoped so. But he knew, under these circumstances, which were quite different, he had to take steps to protect himself and Savannah from anyone who might be in it purely for the money. He regarded Alexis steadily. "This time, I will require prenups for both of us, should the union not work out. Although I would hope and expect it would never come to divorce."

Alexis made a face and kept writing. "If you ever get married again," she murmured, in a cynical tone he hadn't heard her use before. She paused, looked up. "I'm not convinced you will. Not without being in love."

Grady stayed rooted in place. Not sure why, only knowing he was enjoying the sparks of mutual aggravation arcing between them as much as he had enjoyed kissing her a few minutes before. She seemed to be reluctantly attuned to their chemistry, too. "If you expect me to back out," he countered, "then you don't know me very well."

Alexis nodded. "Exactly."

A fact, Grady thought, that could easily be remedied. "So back to you and me…"

She drew a deep breath that lifted her breasts. "There is no you and me."

Grady noted she wasn't looking at him—a sure sign there could be a "them," given half a chance. He pushed away from the counter, closed the distance between them, took her wrist and raised her to her feet. "That kiss we shared just now said otherwise."

Twin spots of color touched her cheeks. "That kiss meant nothing," she declared. But her breathing was slightly agitated.

"On the contrary." He made note of the absence of

her customary cool as he tucked a hand beneath her chin. "It was a wake-up call to me."

She jerked back abruptly. "And what did it say?"

Grady lifted both his hands and determinedly held his ground. "That maybe, just maybe, I've been selling myself short with the parameters I set for my next spouse."

ALEXIS HAD THOUGHT, after the kiss—and Grady's equally inane suggestion that they consider marrying for his daughter's sake—that he couldn't surprise her further. She was wrong. Momentarily tabling her decision to call a cab to take her back to her BMW, which was still parked at his construction site, she sat back down for the third time in twenty minutes and picked up her pen, determined to get as much information as possible from him while he was in the mood to talk. "Okay, obviously you've refined your notion of what you want in a potential relationship. What are you looking for now?"

"Someone who could enjoy sex without the romance and a child...and a life together as man and wife."

She tried not to leap to the conclusion that the kiss they had shared had in any way jump-started Grady's latent physical needs. "But no love," she ascertained, a great deal more coolly than she felt.

"I've already had the love of a lifetime. To think lightning would strike twice..." He paused, his guard going up again. "Let's just say the odds are very much against it."

Grady took a seat at the table catty-corner from her, and surveyed her with surprising intimacy. "Oddly enough, you look as if you understand why I can't love anyone else the way I loved my wife."

Maybe this was an area where they could in fact relate. Finding she wanted him to know at least a bit about her, she said quietly, "I do. I was married, too."

He was silent, absorbing that, then dropped his gaze to the unadorned ring finger on her left hand. "And?"

It was her turn to talk about matters she found difficult to discuss. "I got married right after college, too. We were together for seven years. If Scott hadn't died, two years ago, we would still be together now."

The loss she felt was reflected in Grady's eyes. "What happened?"

Alexis swallowed. Her voice took on a raspy note. "Cancer. He'd had it as a kid. Had been in the clear for almost fifteen years. And then the leukemia came back and…" Their lives, their dreams, everything they had hoped for and wanted had been turned upside down. Alexis shook her head. Even now, it seemed like such an impossible, bad dream. She forced herself to go on, "For two years, he had all the latest treatments. Something would start to work, we'd think we were out of the woods, and then…we weren't. He got sicker and sicker, until finally nothing worked and he just couldn't fight it anymore."

Grady reached across the table and took her hand. The feel of his strong fingers around hers was as warm and reassuring as his presence. "I'm so sorry, Alexis."

She hadn't felt the need to lean on a man for a long time. She felt it now. Finding comfort in the empathy in his eyes, even as tears blurred her vision, she said, "So am I. I still love Scott. I always will. But I also know that part of my life is over."

Grady withdrew his hand reluctantly. Sat back. "So you will marry again."

Alexis nodded, knowing what she had just recently begun to realize herself—that the only way to leave sorrow behind was to move on. Not just partially, but all the way. "If I find love again, you bet I will." Because marriage was the best thing that had ever happened to her.

"What if you don't find true love again—at least not on that heart and soul level?" he asked, practical as ever.

She knew where this conversation was going. She cut him off at the pass. "I'm not going to settle, Grady. I'm not going to do what you're contemplating, and enter into a marriage of convenience. I'd rather be alone than be with someone and *feel* alone."

Deciding this session had gotten way too intimate for either of their sakes, she stood, began to pack up her belongings one last time. "In the meantime, I need you to look through the potential matches I've selected for you. If any of those three women appeal to you, or seem—on paper and on videotape—as if they might be a good match, let me know and I'll set something else up as quickly as possible."

"Under the guise of this match being a friend of yours, instead of a potential mommy," Grady cautioned.

Normally, there was no way Alexis would agree to anything so convoluted. But then, a little girl's feelings were not usually involved. She nodded. "Savannah may figure it out, if we have to do this too many times. But I'm willing to go with that plan as long as it works."

THE NEXT MORNING, Alexis's cell phone rang just as she was heading out the door. Caller ID indicated it was

Grady. Wondering if he had found a match who intrigued him, she picked up. "Hello, Grady."

"Good morning, Alexis."

It was ridiculous, really, how happy she was to hear his low, gravelly voice. Ridiculous how warm it suddenly felt in the small studio apartment she had lived in since her late husband had first gotten sick.

Frowning, Alexis walked over to the window unit in charge of cooling the place, and turned the dial to maximum. Enjoying the resulting blast of icy air, she sat down on the windowsill in front of the air conditioner. "What can I do for you this morning?" she asked.

"How much do you know about defiant little girls?"

Not the response she was expecting. Alexis promptly switched into problem solving mode. "Enough, I think. Why?" She tensed in concern. "What's going on?"

Grady exhaled. "It's Savannah. She's refusing to go to school. She won't tell me why."

Alexis unbuttoned her jacket. Was it her imagination or was the air blowing out behind her warming slightly once again? She turned around and fiddled with the dial. "Is it because of what happened with Lisa Marie Peterson yesterday?"

"I don't know. She won't talk to me."

Alexis heard the mixture of hurt and frustration in his voice. "I'm not sure what to do." He sighed. "I think she needs a woman's tender loving care—if that makes any sense."

It made perfect sense to Alexis. Women were better at handling certain things, men others. "Where are you?" Deciding to give her air conditioner—which had been working overtime lately—something of a rest, she switched the dial back to low.

"Home."

Alexis retrieved her briefcase and purse. "I'll be right over and see what I can do."

"Thanks." Grady's relief was palpable. "You're a lifesaver."

Maybe not that, Alexis thought as she let herself out of her studio apartment and walked outside to her car. But she figured she could be of some help.

Grady was waiting for her when she arrived at his home fifteen minutes later. He was dressed for work, in a suit and tie. Savannah was still in the pink princess pajamas she had put on after her bath the night before. She was seated at the kitchen table, her breakfast of cold cereal and glass of juice in front of her, untouched. She had her right arm stretched out on the table, her head on top of that, face hidden from view.

Grady looked at Alexis, clearly concerned. Now that she was here and could see what he was dealing with, Alexis was concerned, too. She set her purse on the kitchen counter and walked over to the table. "Bad morning?" she asked gently.

Savannah looked up at Alexis, her blue eyes swimming with tears. She nodded, let out a heartfelt sob, and thrust herself into Alexis's waiting arms.

IF GRADY HAD HAD ANY doubts before, he had none now as he watched Alexis gather Savannah in her arms and sit down, cradling her in her lap. Alexis had a mother's loving touch.

And Savannah knew it.

"Oh, honey," Alexis soothed, stroking one hand through his little girl's tangled ringlets, another down her back. "It's all right."

Stubbornly, Savannah shook her head. "No, it's not," she insisted.

Now that, Grady thought, sounded like his head-strong daughter.

Savannah sniffed. Ignoring him completely, she drew back to look into Alexis's face.

"Are you still upset about the fight you had yesterday with Lisa Marie?" Alexis pressed.

Grady had asked the same question—to no avail—so he was surprised to hear his daughter answer right away.

"I don't want to say sorry to her!"

Was that what this was about? Grady wondered.

"Because…?" Alexis prodded.

Savannah's whole body tensed. "She's mean!"

"Mean how?" Grady asked. He pulled a chair up next to them and sat down.

Savannah cuddled closer to Alexis, but told him, "She makes fun of me and I don't like it!"

"Be that as it may, that's no reason to get in a hair-pulling fight with her," he stated firmly.

Over Savannah's head, Alexis gave Grady a look that told him very clearly to back off and let her handle this.

"I'm not going to say I'm sorry," Savannah repeated, even more stubbornly.

Exasperated, Grady pointed out, "Then you are not going to be able to go back to school." To his chagrin, his daughter clearly didn't care.

"Hmm. Well…" Alexis grew thoughtful. "I suppose that is one option."

Savannah looked up in surprise.

Grady gazed at her in shock.

"You could stay home alone, away from all your friends, and never get to play on the school playground again. You'd probably be a little lonely, and maybe bored. But I guess it would be okay."

Grady gave Alexis a look Savannah couldn't see. This was not helping! Alexis ignored him.

"But…" Savannah's resolve began to waver, just a bit.

Alexis shrugged. "Or you could apologize and say you were sorry you lost your temper, because I'm sure that is true. I'm sure you were not happy that you let someone push you into behaving that way. Because that's not who you are, Savannah McCabe." She looked meaningfully at Grady's daughter. "You're not the play-ground bully who shoves everyone else around and makes them feel bad. You're the girl who is nice to ev-erybody, the girl who just wants to be friends."

For once, Savannah didn't disagree.

"What did she say to you, anyway, to get you so mad?" Grady asked gently after a moment.

Savannah's lower lip shot back out. "Lisa Marie said I did not have a fairy godmother and that I was never going to have a mommy, 'cause my mommy was dead."

Whoa, Grady thought. That *was* cruel.

Alexis looked as upset as he felt. "That wasn't very nice, was it?" she said quietly.

"No." Savannah looked relieved to have emotional backup.

"And it's not true. Because—" Alexis smiled "—as we've already established, I am going to help your daddy find a new mommy for you. Now, it's not going to be easy, because sometimes these things take awhile. But if you are persistent, you can make your dreams come true. The question is, how do we handle this?" Alexis asked as Savannah's brow furrowed. "Do you want me to talk to Lisa Marie and tell her I am indeed your fairy godmother, so to speak?"

"You'd really do that?" Grady found himself cutting in once again.

Alexis grinned, the picture of maternal confidence. "I'll even go with you and Savannah when she apologizes to Lisa Marie and anyone else who feels the need for an apology."

Savannah sat there on Alexis's lap, clearly considering.

"Of course, we can do this whenever you want, Savannah," Alexis continued amiably, "but I have always found that when you don't particularly *want* to do something, it's better to just do it and get it over with."

"ALEXIS GRAHAM, you are a miracle worker," Grady declared an hour later, as the two of them walked out of Miss Chilton's Academy for Young Women.

She waved away his praise. "Savannah just needed moral support." And as Grady had already intuited, a mother figure's loving presence in her life, to help her with some of her girl problems.

Grady paused next to Alexis's BMW. "Do you think Lisa Marie will leave her alone now?"

Alexis hit the unlock button on the keypad and opened the door to let the searing summer heat out of the vehicle. "Knowing female bullies—probably not." She tossed her purse onto the passenger seat, next to her briefcase, and turned back to Grady. Trying not to notice how his dark hair shone in the morning sunlight, she predicted, "It'll just be more of a stealth operation than ever."

With the mean-girls-in-training in Savannah's kindergarten class doing everything they could under the school administration's radar to taunt the little girls they perceived as undeserving of kindness and respect.

Grady leaned against his Escalade, which was parked next to her sedan. He pushed the edges of his suit coat back and braced his hands on his waist. "So what do we do?"

Alexis gestured vaguely, wishing like heck she could do more to protect his little girl from even the potential of hurt. "You do what all parents do. Keep an eye out for trouble. Help Savannah learn to develop a thicker skin and rise above the petty manipulations, of which, sad to say, there will be plenty in the years ahead."

"You sound so cynical."

Maybe because, Alexis thought, in this one aspect, she was. "Your wife never had problems with female bullies?"

"I don't know. It's not something we talked about. Did you?"

"As a child, yes." These days, she could take care of herself in the mean girl department.

Grady favored her with an appreciative smile. "That's no surprise, I guess. It's usually the good-looking girls who get chased the most on the playground."

If the two of them had been children, Alexis figured Grady would be chasing her right now.

"And that makes the other girls jealous," he continued.

And sometimes ridiculing and vindictive. Finding herself in no more of a hurry to get to the office than Grady appeared to be, Alexis fiddled with the car keys in her hand. "Which is why, I guess, you put Savannah in an all-girls school, to keep her away from little boys?"

Grady shook his head. He took off his suit coat, opened the back door of his car and tossed it in. "She's going there because that's where Tabitha attended school, and I promised her before Savannah was born that any daughters of ours would go there, too."

So, it was a sentimental choice. That made more sense. Alexis nodded thoughtfully. "About those three profiles that I gave you last night…"

"I looked through them," he reported. "Twice, as a matter of fact. I couldn't really see any of them being a good match."

Alexis sighed.

"I might feel differently, meeting them in person, if there was some spark between them and Savannah, but…"

Alexis wasn't sure whether she was relieved he hadn't been drawn to anyone else, or frustrated to the point she wanted to shout aloud in irritation. She had been so sure those three women were all his type. "I'll keep looking," she promised.

"How come we're going shopping before I do my homework, Daddy?" Savannah asked.

Because Alexis had called with a potential match she was very excited about, and wanted them both to meet. Having decided, however, that it probably wasn't a good idea to have Savannah giving any future mothers the runaround before they even saw if there was any chemistry there, Alexis and Grady were taking a new approach. They were doing this one on the down-low.

Did he feel good about it? No. Did he think the end justified the means? Yes.

If Savannah's meltdown yesterday afternoon and again this morning had shown him anything, it was that his little girl needed a woman's presence in her life. And since Alexis had made it clear she wasn't interested in being anything more than a temporary stand-in, he had no choice but to keep looking.

"We're going to the mall because it's raining again, and you can't play outside today," Grady said. Another storm had blown in that afternoon, which wasn't that uncommon for June. "Plus I figured, since you did a very grown-up thing this morning and apologized nicely to everyone, even though you still don't think you did anything wrong—"

"That's 'cause I didn't, Daddy," Savannah interrupted.

Figuring they'd leave the discussion about solving conflict in a peaceful manner for another day, Grady continued "—that we would take advantage of the fact that there is a covered parking deck as well as a very good ice cream shop in this mall, and take some time to smell the roses."

"There are flowers there, too?"

Grady shook his head. "It's an expression."

"Huh?" Savannah blinked.

"I meant we should enjoy ourselves today," he clarified.

Savannah skipped along, holding his hand. He grinned down at her. This had been a good idea. One that might make the inevitable take-home work sheet a little easier to get completed before dinner this evening....

"Hey, Daddy, look!" Savannah got so excited she jumped up and down.

There, on the other side of the mall atrium, were two blondes standing side by side in front of a shoe store.

"It's Alexis! And some lady!" Savannah jumped again and clapped her hands together. "Can we say hi to them, Daddy? Please! Please! Please! Please!"

"Calm down, honey, and yes we can." Before he could say anything else, Savannah raced off across the floor. She skidded to a halt just short of Alexis, and taking a deep breath, looked up at her shyly.

Alexis turned away from the display of shoes she and her companion had been admiring. She dropped the shopping bag she was carrying and knelt down, arms open wide. The way, Grady figured, a mother would greet her child. "Well, hello there, sweetheart," she said. "Fancy meeting you here!"

Savannah barreled into Alexis's embrace. Small arms wreathed around her neck and she held on tight for a long time. One would have thought, by his little girl's reaction, she hadn't seen Alexis in ages, instead of just seven hours ago....

"What are you doing here?" Alexis asked at last, when they had stopped hugging each other and were face-to-face again.

"Daddy and I are having ice cream! Want some?"

Alexis looked up at Grady.

A glimmer of apology shone in her eyes. This wasn't going exactly the way she had hoped, but it was pretty much how Grady would like to see things evolve.

"We'd love to have you join us," he said cordially. He looked over at the pretty blonde next to Alexis. She was thirty something, with a trim, athletic figure, kind eyes and what appeared to be an abundance of energy. He held out his hand. "I'm Grady McCabe. My daughter, Savannah."

"Nice to meet you. I'm Tina Weinart."

"Tina's a nurse at the Children's Hospital," Alexis said, getting slowly and gracefully back to her feet.

"We'd love to have you join us, too, if you can," Grady told Tina.

"I'd love to." She smiled, then looked at Savannah. "I heard you had a fall yesterday."

The little girl slipped her hand in Alexis's and pressed in close as they walked to the ice cream store at the end of the aisle. She demonstrated by holding up first one knee, then the other. Beneath the tartan skirt of her school uniform, two Band-Aids were visible on each knee. Savannah then held up the heels of her hands. No Band-Aids there; the scrapes had been light enough to do without. "It hurt!" she declared. They entered the shop and took a horseshoe-shaped booth in the center. Savannah slid across the banquette seat and onto Alexis's lap. She rested her head on Alexis's chest and continued recounting her sad tale to Tina. "And that's how come I'm not supposed to run in the rain. 'Cause," she added for emphasis, "I might fall down."

Tina nodded, clearly as enthralled with Grady's little girl as he was.

Savannah, however, had affection only for Alexis. Forty-five minutes later, when they'd finished their sundaes, Alexis took her into the ladies' room to wash her hands and face.

Tina looked at Grady. "She's adorable. I'd like to get to know her better—without Alexis around. Otherwise, I'm not sure she'll even give me a chance to connect with her."

Grady knew Tina had a point. Alexis was a hard act to follow. Especially where his daughter was concerned.

"SO? WHAT'D YOU THINK of Tina?" Alexis asked Grady over the phone later that evening, after Savannah was fast asleep.

He tried not to think how lonely it was, with Alexis at her place and he at his, or how much he and Savannah had both missed having her there with them during the evening routine.

"Tina was very nice. Personable," Grady responded. "I'm a little concerned about the lack of chemistry between her and Savannah, though." The affection and interest, while genuine, had seemed all on Tina's side.

"Tina mentioned she wanted to get together with the two of you, without me," Alexis continued, with a cheerfulness that sounded slightly forced. "I think it's a good idea. In this case, four probably is a crowd."

Grady agreed with that. He just wasn't sure they were talking about the same three. Still, he knew Savannah needed a mommy, and Tina was happily volunteering to enlist…on his terms.

Alexis was not.…

"I haven't told Savannah yet, but Tina's going to be stopping by tomorrow evening with a new puzzle she thought Savannah would enjoy. I'll step out to make a phone call—and we'll go from there."

There was a slight pause. "You'll let me know how it goes?" Alexis's voice was brisk.

Grady reminded himself he was done wishing for

the impossible, and adapted Alexis's businesslike attitude. "You'll get a call as soon as the 'next date' concludes," he said.

Chapter Five

Grady's visit from Tina was slated for five o'clock Friday evening. At four forty-five, Alexis received a call from him. "I've got a problem," he said without preamble.

Instinctively, she quipped back, "You seem to have a lot of those lately."

He sighed. "No joke, Sherlock." The ding of a car door opening sounded in the foreground. "I don't have much time to talk. I'm on my way into the school to pick up Savannah from her after-school program."

Alexis hoped he hadn't changed his mind about Tina. On an intellectual level, anyway, she knew the two might be a good match. Certainly, Tina would be a good mother to Savannah.... Emotionally, well, Alexis couldn't help but feel a little wistful that she and Grady were not looking for the same things in their future.

"What can I do for you?" she said more seriously, pushing away the memory of their one fantastic kiss.

"Run interference," Grady stated.

Alexis furrowed her brow in confusion. "How?"

"Get ahold of Tina. Make some excuse. Tell her this evening is not a good time."

Alexis pushed the send button on the e-mail she had

just written to another client, and rocked back in her desk chair. "May I ask why?"

When he answered, his tone was wry. "I just had a call from my parents. Surprise! They're in town for the weekend and they want to stay with us."

Alexis had lost her own parents two years after she got married, so she no longer had to deal with what they would think about what she said and did. But she could still imagine all too well their reactions to things.

"I can see where that would be complicated."

"You have no idea. Anyway, would you please call Tina and tell her we'll have to reschedule for next week? I've been trying to reach her on her cell, and all I get is voice mail. And I can't keep trying, because of course I don't want Savannah to know…."

Alexis reached for Tina's contact numbers. "What if I can't find her?"

Grady groaned. "Let's hope you can, because by the time I get to my place with Savannah, my parents will be there, too."

Alexis tried all the numbers she had for Tina—to no avail. Working quickly, she shut down her office computer, grabbed her briefcase, purse and keys, and headed for Grady's home.

By the time she got there, it was too late.

There were three cars in the drive. Grady's Escalade, a bright yellow pickup truck with WILDCAT on the license plate and a Wyatt Drilling Company logo on the side and a Toyota with a Children's Hospital Staff parking sticker.

Still trying to figure out how she was going to usher a disappointed Tina out of the house, Alexis walked up to the door and rang the bell. Grady opened it. The look on his face said *Rescue Me*.

"It's Alexis!" Savannah broke away from her grandparents and ran toward her. The little girl had on the athletic clothing she had worn for the after-school soccer practice, and her curls were more a mess than ever. She threw her arms around Alexis's waist, then turned to her grandparents and said, "This is my fairy godmother!"

GRADY WASN'T SURE what was worse—the coming together of all these people at exactly the wrong time, or the look on everyone's faces. His parents were clearly amused—and perplexed—while Savannah was deliriously happy. Tina Weinart looked ticked off. He was doing his best to keep a poker face. Only Alexis looked pleasantly composed—but then she was clearly in her element. "Hello, everyone," she said with a smile.

"Are you going to play with me today and have dinner with us again?" Savannah asked.

"Actually, I came over to see if Grady's company was still interested in tickets for the cancer research fund-raiser tomorrow evening," Alexis said. She looked around the room. "I'm on the committee that's hosting it."

Good save, Grady thought. "Absolutely. If a table is still available."

"I'm sure we can fit one in."

"Great. Let me get my checkbook."

"Can I go?" Savannah asked, when he had walked back out into the foyer.

Grady shook his head. "It's just for grown-ups, honey."

Her face fell.

"Children's Hospital has fund-raisers you can attend," Tina Weinart interjected.

Savannah brightened. "Really?"

She nodded. "I think the next one is in July. But in the meantime, I can arrange a private tour of the hospital, if you like."

The little girl looked interested.

Grady opened his checkbook and glanced at Alexis. "If you'll tell me who to make it out to…"

"I'd like to go, too," Tina said, opening her purse.

"We'll babysit," Grady's mother offered. She extended her hand to Alexis. "By the way, I'm Josie Wyatt McCabe, Grady's mother. This handsome guy next to me is my better half and Grady's father, Wade McCabe."

Her husband chuckled.

Alexis smiled. "I'm Alexis Graham."

"Do you know Tina?" his mother continued, obviously curious as to why he had two beautiful single women in his house at one time. Up to now, he had hardly been socializing, never mind actually dating.

Before Grady could formulate a reply, Tina jumped in to explain, "Alexis is the matchmaker who introduced Grady and me to each other."

EVERYONE WAS SO STUNNED, the foyer so quiet, you could have heard a pin drop, Alexis noted. Fortunately, the implications of what Tina had just said had gone completely over Savannah's head. The child frowned. "What's a matchmaker?"

Wade McCabe, a handsome man with silver threading his short dark hair, explained kindly, "That's a person who helps like-minded people get to know each other."

Again, the explanation was too adult—and circumspect—for Savannah to completely understand. Which was, Alexis figured, the intent.

Josie propped her hands on her blue-jeans-clad hips. Tall and slender, with glossy brown hair, the youthful-looking woman fixed her azure eyes on her son, as if indicating they would talk—when the time was right.

Alexis smiled cordially. "Tina, I have something I'd like to discuss with you, so if you'll—"

Her client dug in her heels. "Actually, Alexis, it's not a good time for me. I haven't given Savannah her new puzzle yet."

"It'll just take a moment," Alexis insisted.

Savannah ambled back to Tina's side. She peered in the cloth carryall. "Can I see?"

"Certainly." Tina smiled, digging into it. "If it's all right with your daddy, of course."

Apparently realizing the benefit of having Savannah out of earshot, at least momentarily, Grady nodded and said, "Of course. Honey, why don't you take Tina outside? You can sit on the patio and look at the puzzle, and I'll bring out some lemonade for everyone in a minute. I want to talk to Grandma and Grandpa first."

"Okay, Daddy. Alexis, do you want to come, too?" Savannah asked.

"Alexis needs to stay here," Grady replied. "But we'll all be out in a moment."

Tina and Savannah departed.

When the back door had opened and shut, Grady gestured toward the formal living room. "Why don't we sit down?"

His parents sat on the sofa. Following reluctantly,

Alexis perched on the edge of a wing chair. Grady took the other.

"We know how tough Tabitha's death was for you, and we're happy you're ready to move on, at long last," his mother began. "But—sorry, Alexis—a *dating service?*"

"Since when have McCabe men had any trouble finding a woman to go out with?" his dad asked.

"Not to mention the improbability of finding someone via third party," his mother continued.

"Isn't that what a blind date is?" Grady continued amiably.

His father chuckled. "Got a point there, son." He looked at Alexis. "How do you match people up?"

"We have detailed questionnaires about hobbies, interests and opinions, and we run a computer program that sorts out likely matches. But that's just the first step. After that the program sorts information gathered in one-on-one interviews with clients. When all the appropriate data is collected, we present the client with promising candidates. They review files and look at video interviews of likely matches, and if a rapport seems possible, we set up a meeting. If that doesn't work out, we set up another, and so on until a match is made."

"How long does it usually take?" Wade asked.

She shrugged. "Anywhere from weeks to months or even a year or two. We keep looking as long as the client is interested."

"ForeverLove.com is the agency the Basses' daughter, Carolyn, used," Grady added.

It was all Alexis could do not to wince.

"Russ and Carolyn Bass are getting divorced," Josie said. "I talked to her mother a couple of weeks ago. She said that, in retrospect, Carolyn is sorry she ever went that route."

Alexis imagined she was.

"Did you know them?" Josie asked.

Reluctantly, Alexis admitted, "I matched them."

FOR THE SECOND TIME that afternoon, silence fell. Alexis stood. "I think I'll check on Tina, see if she's ready to go."

Grady stood, too. "I'll walk with you."

He fell into step beside her. As they reached the hall, he took her lightly by the arm. "But first, I do want to give you a check for the benefit tomorrow evening, before it slips my mind. If you'll come in here…" Cupping her elbow, he steered her into his study and shut the door behind them.

Alexis felt the warmth in her cheeks. She told herself it was because she was embarrassed she'd put him on the spot that way, pretending she was there for charity. "You don't have to purchase any tickets. Never mind an entire table—"

Grady took the checkbook and pen out of his shirt pocket. "It's for a good cause. I want to support it. I'm sure I can round up however many people need to be there, as my guests. Perhaps they'll write checks, too."

Alexis couldn't say no to the help it would provide in finding a cure. "Thank you," she said, gratefully.

Grady sat on the edge of his desk and opened the checkbook on his thigh. "How many at each table?"

Alexis looked down at the rock solid muscles beneath his suit pants, and tried not to think how those same muscles had felt pressed up against hers. "Eight. At a cost of two hundred fifty dollars per person."

He wrote a check for two thousand dollars and gave it to her. Their hands touched as they made the exchange. "I'm sorry if my parents embarrassed you."

Aware of how her fingers were still tingling, she slid the check into her purse. "It's no problem," she managed to reply.

"It is for me." He caught her by the shoulders before she could step away. "I believe in what you're doing for me and for Savannah."

Alexis only wished she could say the same.

She thanked him and they walked together toward the back of the house.

A few moments later, they stepped out onto the patio.

Savannah was cuddled up next to Tina, as they put in the last two puzzle pieces. "There you are," Tina said to Grady with a smile.

"Daddy, this puzzle is awesome!" Savannah said, showing him the finished picture of brightly colored fish.

Grady admired her accomplishment with obvious paternal pride. "Did you thank Tina?" he asked.

"She did," the nurse told him with a smile.

"Tina, could I speak to you privately?" Grady glanced at Alexis. "If you could just hang out here for a second…"

Alexis had the feeling Tina would refuse to go, if she thought she was leaving a rival for Savannah's affection behind. "Actually, I need to get going." She bent down to the little girl. "I just wanted to say goodbye before I left."

"Will you come and see me again?" Savannah asked.

Alexis smiled, not sure what to say. Was her presence helping or hurting here? If it interfered with Savannah's ability to bond with a woman who wanted to become her mommy—and Grady's wife—her growing relationship with Savannah could hardly be considered a positive thing.

"Alexis will definitely be back," Grady reassured her.

Knowing Grady still wanted to talk to Tina alone, Alexis held out a hand to his daughter. "Want to come with me while I say goodbye to your grandparents?"

Savannah slipped out of the curve of Tina's arm. "I had fun doing puzzles with you," she told the other woman shyly.

"I had fun spending time with you, too," Tina answered fondly.

Hand in hand, Alexis and Savannah set off.

THREE HOURS LATER, Holly Anne stopped by Alexis's office. "What has you here so late on a Friday evening?"

Not much, Alexis thought. *Jealousy. Guilt. Worry.* She fretted that she wasn't doing the right thing for Savannah, in fixing her dad up with someone he swore he would never be able to love. She sighed heavily. She'd never admit this to her boss, but she was also starting to wonder if her budding feelings for Grady—complex and mixed up as they were—had begun to cloud her judgment.

"Grady McCabe?" Holly Anne guessed, coming all the way into the office.

She nodded. These days it was always Grady Mc-Cabe. "I'm just pulling up some more profiles for him to peruse." Alexis studied the photo on the screen, ignoring her own lingering resistance to this matchmaking assignment, then hit the print command once again.

Her boss moved to the window and looked out at the

dusk falling softly over downtown Fort Worth. "Tina Weinart didn't work out?"

All business, Alexis rose, plucked the pages out of the printer and added them to the folder on her desk. "She did better with Savannah the second time they met, but I just can't see her with Grady McCabe."

Holly Anne studied Alexis with a sharp eye. "Any particular reason why?"

She shrugged, not sure what was bothering her, just knowing something was. "Instinct," she said finally.

"Keep working on it. Make this match. And the Galveston office will be yours to run."

And if she didn't, Alexis thought, she'd probably be fresh out of luck, because there was no way the other three partners would vote to put her in charge of the new branch office.

Holly Anne drummed her fingers on the windowsill. "By the way, I had a call from Carolyn Bass...."

Alexis squirmed. "I heard she wants her money back."

The executive's jaw set. "We don't guarantee happily ever after. We deal in possibilities."

"Right."

"It will blow over," Holly Anne promised.

Alexis nodded. She certainly hoped so.

Otherwise, there would be yet another reason she could kiss that promotion and pay raise goodbye....

A rap sounded on her open office door, and both women turned. Grady McCabe stood in the doorway. His dark hair was rumpled, as always, as if he had been running his hands through it. A hint of evening beard rimmed his jaw, giving him a sexy, ruggedly attractive, all-man look. Since she had seen him last, he had changed into a V-necked T-shirt, knee-length shorts and deck shoes appropriate for the hot June evening.

Holly Anne smiled and slid off the corner of Alexis's desk. "I'll let you two converse. See you in the morning."

Alexis nodded as her boss headed for the exit. "Good night."

Grady came closer. The scent of soap and cologne clinging to his skin told her he had recently showered. After a day spent working and running around in the fierce June heat, Alexis yearned to do the same.

"I figured you would be here," he said.

The office was so quiet at this time of night. In the distance, a door shut. Alexis realized she and Grady were completely alone. Playing it cool, she rocked back in her swivel chair. "I thought you'd be with your family."

"Savannah's asleep. Mom and Dad wanted to hit the sack early, too—they were up at dawn checking out drilling sites of my mom's. Not sure if I told you—she's a wildcatter. Runs the oil exploration company she inherited from my grandfather, Big Jim Wyatt. My dad specializes in making money on business investments of all kinds, including but not limited to oil exploration."

Alexis was touched by the affection in his voice. "From what I've heard, they make a good team," she said softly.

One corner of Grady's mouth crooked up. "They met when my mom was drilling for oil on property my dad owned. To hear them tell it, there were a lot of fireworks at first, but then they fell madly in love, married and had five sons."

Alexis watched Grady stroll back and forth, checking

out the photos and award plaques on her office walls. She shook her head. "To be the only woman in a family of six men...wow."

Grady grinned. "The testosterone in my family has never overwhelmed my mom. She was a tomboy herself. But the lack of steady women in all her offspring's lives does rankle. She wants all her sons married. And me being the oldest, I'm supposed to do that again ASAP."

Alexis recalled the affectionate way Josie and Wade had interacted. "She wants you to be in love, though."

"You bet." Grady seemed to steel himself. "Which is why I didn't tell my folks about my plan to marry without it."

"So they..."

"Still don't know, and I would prefer to keep it that way," he stated flatly.

A less comfortable silence fell between them. Alexis knew Grady thought he wasn't ashamed by his attitude. However, his actions, when it came to his parents, said otherwise. "It is a hard thing to explain," she said eventually.

"It's also the way I feel."

Alexis wished lightning would strike twice. Grady and Savannah deserved to be happy. They deserved to have a complete family, and all the love life had to offer.

"But maybe it can still be good," Grady said, sounding more upbeat than before.

Although her spirits plummeted, she forced herself to smile. "Things went well with Tina?"

Grady's gaze roved over Alexis's pale-blue sheath, his glance lingering on the bare skin of her shoulders, before drifting thoughtfully back to her face. "She left right after you did," he murmured, sounding as if he was suddenly having as much trouble staying on track as she was.

Alexis reminded herself that it was nearly nine o'clock, and had been an exceedingly long day at the end of an exceedingly long week.

"I explained I needed time alone with my family," Grady continued, in a low, matter-of-fact tone.

Without warning, Alexis's heart kicked into a faster beat.

She told herself to calm down. To slip back into matchmaker mode. She looked Grady in the eye, all business once more. "Are you going to see her again?"

His gaze still locked with hers, he shook his head. "I don't think so."

Inexplicably, her heart slowed down once again. Alexis tapped a pen on the surface of her desk. Swallowed. "Any particular reason why?" she asked, surprised how normal her voice could sound, when her emotions were all awhirl.

Grady's lips thinned. "Tina's a very nice person. I think she'd be great with Savannah."

"But?"

"I'm not sure how comfortable I'd be with her."

A feeling akin to relief slid through Alexis. She did not want to match up any other couples who were wrong for each other. She didn't want that on her conscience. Bad enough that Russ and Carolyn Bass were divorcing after just one year...

"I'll let Tina know," Alexis promised.

And when she did so, she'd have another match ready for Tina to consider. A doctor, maybe.

"Thanks."

Alexis reached for the folder on her desk. "Would you like to look at other profiles?"

He paused, and she wasn't sure what he was thinking. Only that he looked conflicted. "How about I take the info with me?" he suggested finally. "And look at it later."

"That would be fine." She gathered up the relevant video interviews and slid them inside the folder, alongside the printed pages, and handed them over.

"Are you done for the day?" Grady asked.

"Yes."

"Walk you out?"

Alexis tried not to think how good that sounded. "Sure."

He waited while she logged off her computer and shut it down. "Want me to carry that?" He indicated the briefcase she had slung over her shoulder.

They were already feeling too much like a couple. And honestly, how ridiculous was that? "That's okay. Thanks."

He strolled beside her, respecting the parameters she'd set. When they reached the elevator, he pushed the down button, then turned to her with a sexy smile. "Have you had dinner?"

"I stopped for a salad on the way back to the office."

His eyes crinkled at the corners. "Bet you didn't have dessert."

"You're right. I did not."

"I know a great French bakery not too far from here that stays open late."

She knew the place he was talking about. The desserts were to die for. But if she went there with him, they would end up talking, and feeling even closer to each other. Which might have been fine, had they been able to keep their relationship strictly platonic. But they had already proved the hard way that they couldn't do that. They had kissed one another, avidly. And she had the feeling if she went anywhere with him tonight they might end up doing so again.

Which again would have been fine, if they wanted the same things. But they didn't. Which meant she had to stay focused. Find Grady a woman who wouldn't mind being in a loveless marriage—and then move on herself. "Thanks, but…" she had to pause to clear her throat "…I've got other plans."

Big ones. A cold shower. A good book. Another long, lonely night.

His expression inscrutable, he studied her, seeming to know instinctively how much she wished they were on the same page. "Another time then," he said eventually.

She nodded, pretending for cordiality sake that that was so.

They got into the elevator without speaking and he walked her to her car, waited until she was safely inside. "I'll see you at the fund-raiser tomorrow evening," he said in lieu of goodbye.

And that, Alexis noted—trembling slightly as she drove away—was that.

Chapter Six

"Are you going to talk about why you aren't going out this evening?" Josie asked Grady on Saturday as soon as his dad had gone off with Savannah to read bedtime stories.

Grady carried the dirty dishes to the sink. "You and Dad are here."

His mother spritzed spray cleaner across the tabletop. "And you bought a tableful of tickets for the cancer research fund-raising dinner this evening."

From a woman who will be there but does not want to spend time with me, Grady thought.

He opened the dishwasher. "I gave them all to friends."

Josie tore off a paper towel. "I bet you could still get another ticket if you wanted. They'd find a way to fit you in."

Grady imagined that was so. When it came to raising funds for cancer research, every dollar was appreciated.

He watched his mom wipe down the table. "Why would I want to do that?"

She shot him a knowing glance. "Probably the same reason you got cleaned up before heading out last night on 'errands' and came back early."

Grady couldn't deny he had been disappointed at the way things had turned out. He'd hoped to get to know Alexis better last night, spend a little time together. To what end he wasn't sure—given the fact she'd made it pretty clear she wasn't interested in being "matched" with him. All he knew for certain was that he longed to be with her, surprising as that was... He sent his mother a censuring glance. "I stopped reporting in when I was eighteen."

She ignored his complaint. "What's going on with you and Alexis Graham?"

Grady finished loading the dishwasher, added detergent and shut the door. "What are you talking about?"

Josie tossed the paper towel in the trash. "I haven't seen you look at a woman that way since you met Tabitha."

Grady tensed. The two situations were not the same. They couldn't be. "Just because you were the first to call that romance..." he muttered.

"Does not mean I've lost my intuition around my sons," Josie declared. "I saw the hope in your eyes when you left here last night, and the quiet disappointment in your expression when you returned less than an hour later." She gently touched his arm. "So what's the problem? Is Ms. Graham not interested?"

She's holding out for the kind of love I can't give, Grady thought. *And doesn't want to consider anything else.* And while he was deeply disappointed about that, he couldn't say—in all honesty—that he blamed her. Alexis was the kind of woman who deserved the best life had to offer. Not a pale imitation of the deeply satisfying unions they had both had in the past.

Aware that his mother was still waiting for an answer, he said, "It's a little more complicated than that, Mom. Alexis was married before, too. She lost her husband to cancer a few years ago."

Her expression compassionate, Josie guessed, "So she's not altogether ready to move on, either."

Was that true? Grady recalled the passionate way Alexis had kissed him back, before coming to her senses and ending the embrace. Much as he wanted to forget the way it had felt to hold her in his arms, he couldn't. And his gut told him Alexis couldn't forget *her* attraction to him, either. He shrugged. "Alexis *says* she's open to the idea of getting involved again."

Disappointment resonated in the room. "Just not with you."

Leave it to his mom to hit the nail on the head. "Your sons do strike out from time to time, you know," he reminded her drolly.

Josie grinned. "I know that," she said, rebounding to her usual sunny outlook. "I just would have sworn that wasn't going to be the case in this situation."

AT EIGHT-THIRTY THAT evening, Alexis checked off the final guest stopping by the ticket desk. At last, all the name cards had been picked up. And although Grady McCabe had purchased an entire table, his name had not been on one of the placards, which meant he was not planning to attend.

Given the attraction simmering between them, Alexis should have been relieved she wouldn't see him tonight.

"Well, we did it," Holly Anne, one of the event's organizers, said. "We sold all four hundred and fifty tickets!"

That was a great deal of money, Alexis calculated with satisfaction. It would go a long way toward funding more cancer research.

And hopefully, more lives would be saved. She was very happy about that.

Holly Anne pushed away from the cloth-covered table and regarded Alexis gently. "Scott would be very proud of you—"

"Got room for one more?"

They both turned, to see Grady striding toward them. He looked incredibly handsome in a black tuxedo, pleated white dress shirt and black tie. Alexis's breath caught in her chest. For a second, as their eyes locked and held, time seemed suspended.

Holly Anne greeted him, then turned to Alexis. "I'll let you handle this." She slipped inside the ballroom, shutting the door behind her.

Pulse racing, Alexis looked at Grady. She really should not be so happy to see him tonight. But she was, even though his presence presented yet another dilemma. "Your table—"

"Is full. I know." His gaze swept her from head to foot, obviously taking in her upswept hair and silk halter dress, her silver stilettos and sapphire jewelry. Then he closed the distance between them. "I was hoping I could sit next to you. Assuming you came, as I did, without a date who might object."

She had.

He withdrew a check from his inside jacket pocket and handed it over.

Doing her best to contain her pleasure, she murmured, "Hang on a minute. I'll see what I can do."

Flushing self-consciously, she went off to make the

necessary accommodations. She returned to find Grady lounging next to the ballroom doors, looking as if he had all the time in the world.

"They're fitting in an extra place for you now. I have to warn you, though. We have one of the worst tables in the room, at the very back, next to the entrance."

"No place I'd rather be."

She tried not to take his declaration literally. Her spirits rose nevertheless, maybe because he was looking at her as if he was thinking about kissing her again.

Aware the first course was already being served, they slipped inside and found their seats. On the dais, the first guest speaker was recounting his own battle with cancer, the way ongoing research and a clinical trial had saved his life. He was followed by half a dozen more throughout the meal. Listening to the speeches brought it all back to Alexis. More than once she found her eyes welling with tears, of both sadness and joy. Grady —indeed everyone at their table—was similarly touched.

Thanks were given to everyone in attendance, and then the orchestra started up again. His expression compassionate, Grady leaned over to whisper in her ear, "I think you could use a spin on the dance floor."

Alexis knew she needed to do something to ward off the memories crowding in.

Grady took her hand, and she reveled in the warmth and strength of his grip, the callused feeling of his palm.

They were halfway to the dance floor when Lisa Marie Peterson's mother appeared before them.

"Hello, Grady!" she said, ignoring Alexis. "I'm glad you're here tonight. I've been wanting to talk to you about the situation with our little girls."

ALEXIS WOULD HAVE BEEN completely content to let the two parents go off to have their conference alone, but Grady clamped his hand around hers as Kit led the way out of the ballroom, into the corridor. Alexis went along reluctantly.

When Kit finally turned and saw her there, she looked as unhappy as Alexis felt.

But she turned to Grady. "Lisa Marie told me what a nice apology Savannah gave her. Her father and I are very appreciative."

Alexis noted there was no mention of Kit's daughter's culpability in the brouhaha.

Grady nodded, waiting for whatever was coming next.

The redhead flashed an ingratiating smile. "I just want to let you know there are no hard feelings on our family's part. Savannah will be invited to the mother-daughter tea at our home—the day before kindergarten graduation—like all the other girls in Lisa Marie's class. It'll give them a chance to sit down like the little ladies they are and practice the etiquette they've been learning all year."

"Thanks for letting me know," Grady said, his expression inscrutable.

"I understand this could present a problem for Savannah, bless her heart, since she's the only one in her class who doesn't have a mother...." Kit continued.

Then why do it this way? Alexis wondered. Why design an important end-of-year social event that she knew in advance was only going to make Savannah acutely aware of the deficiency in her young life? Surely there had to be a way to have a tea party without making a child feel ostracized! But then, Alexis thought, going back to the mean girl experiences in her own life, maybe that was the point. To isolate and demean Grady's little girl…so Lisa Marie and her friends would feel better about themselves.

"So," Mrs. Peterson continued brightly, "if you would like to break with tradition and attend along with Savannah, Grady, that would be fine with us."

"Thank you for letting me know that," he repeated, with more politeness than Alexis would have been able to muster, under the same circumstances.

"Naturally," Kit said as she shot an openly condescending look at Alexis, "we want each child to attend with just one adult, so it won't be possible for you to bring a guest."

Meaning me, or any other female, Alexis thought, not sure why Kit's snub should bother her, only knowing that it did. Maybe, she mused, because her feminine intuition told her that Savannah needed to be protected whenever she was around Lisa Marie and her friends. And the deeply maternal part of her wanted to be there to do it.

Not that this was her job, of course. She knew full well that she wasn't Savannah's mother.

She just felt that way sometimes.

"And now," Kit finished cordially, "I'd like a word with Alexis privately, if I may."

Alexis could tell Grady didn't want her conversing with Kit Peterson. She didn't want to have a tête-à-tête with the stunning redhead, either. Unfortunately, as a member of the event committee, she could hardly say no. Especially since she had no idea what this was about. "How can I help you?" she asked, as the two of them walked a short distance down the corridor, to an alcove around the corner.

Without Grady there for an audience, Kit dispensed with the saccharine smile and got straight to the point. "I heard you're looking for a new mother for Savannah."

Alexis reluctantly confirmed what was now, thanks to the brawl that had landed Savannah in the principal's office, common knowledge around Miss Chilton's Academy for Young Women. "I work for ForeverLove. com." And that was all the information Alexis was going to give.

Excitement gleamed in Kit's eyes. "Well, look no further. A friend of mine—Zoe Borden—is perfect for Grady."

Alexis put up a silencing hand and stated firmly, "I can't discuss clients."

Kit stepped closer. "You need to call me," she said urgently. "Between the two of us, we can set something up."

No, we can't, Alexis thought, as a shadow loomed in her peripheral vision.

They turned to see Grady. Seeming to realize they were close to what Alexis guessed would be a vehement disagreement—at least on Kit's side—he planted his palm on the small of Alexis's back and brought her in close to his side, his manner as resolute as it was protective. "Alexis, your presence is requested inside the ballroom."

She had an idea who wanted her there. And he was standing right beside her.

"Enjoy the rest of your evening," Grady told Kit deliberately.

Clearly taken aback, the redhead nodded curtly and flounced off.

"What was that about?" he asked, when the two of them were alone once again.

Alexis shrugged off the near-unpleasantness. "The usual." *More or less,* she added silently to herself. "She heard I was a matchmaker."

A hint of devilry came into Grady's blue eyes. "Let me guess. She has a friend who is looking to get married."

And not just to anyone, Alexis thought sarcastically. Out loud, she affirmed, "Something like that."

"Are you going to help her?"

Alexis couldn't imagine any friend of Kit Peterson's would be right for Grady. She shook her head. "If her friend signs up with the agency, she'll be given to someone else. I have my hands full right now with the clients I have."

"I've heard one of 'em is nothing but trouble," Grady teased.

No kidding, Alexis thought, her heart fluttering once again. Already, she wanted to kiss him. And if she kissed him, she was going to want to kiss him again, and if she did that... She really couldn't go there, even in her thoughts.

Alexis held her ground with effort. "There's trouble," she said lightly, "and then there's trouble with a capital T." Grady fell into the latter category. Worse, he seemed to know it.

Still grinning, he took her hand once again. "About that dance..."

Alexis knew that if he held her in his arms, the chemistry she felt whenever she was near him would ignite into a dangerous desire. Life had already dealt her enough heartache without her voluntarily signing up for more. She called on every bit of willpower she had, took a deep, bolstering breath and withdrew her tingling hand from his. "You're a client, Grady. I shouldn't be dancing with you."

His smile faded. "You were willing before."

Still was, if the truth be known… Coolly, she responded, "Only because you didn't give me a chance to say no."

He studied her perceptively. "And now that you've had time to think about it…?"

Alexis pushed aside her romantic fantasies and forced herself to come to her senses. One of them had to be practical. It looked as if it was going to be her. Doing her best to erect another wall between them, she said, "Our becoming close can only get in the way of what I'm trying to do for you and Savannah."

Grady's dark brows drew together. "And dancing together would accomplish that?"

Alexis gave him a withering look. "What do you think?"

"STRUCK OUT AGAIN, hmm?" Wade McCabe asked, when Grady walked in shortly after eleven.

He hadn't had this much commentary on his love life or lack thereof when he had been in his teens. Ignoring the frustration and disappointment roiling in his gut, he tossed his father a droll look. "I thought you'd be asleep by now."

His dad grinned, not about to be diverted. "Your mother is."

Knowing a heart-to-heart was in the offing, Grady

grabbed the open container of orange juice from the fridge.

"Your mother is worried about you," his father continued.

Grady uncapped the plastic jug, lifted it to his lips and drank the half cup or so that was left. "She worries about all her kids, all the time."

Wade watched as Grady wiped his mouth with the back of his hand. "You especially. She thinks that, apart from the time you spend with Savannah, you aren't enjoying life the way you should."

Grady tossed the empty container in the recycling bin. As long as they were talking honestly… He looked his father in the eye. "There hasn't been a whole lot to be happy about, beside my kid and job success."

His dad put the lid on the tin of cookies on the counter. "Maybe this matchmaking service will work out. At least help you get back in the game, if you know what I mean."

And maybe it wouldn't, Grady thought.

All he knew was that Alexis had been working on his situation for almost a week now, and he was no closer to finding a mother for his daughter.

He also knew that he was lonelier than ever.

Fortunately, he had a lot of work to do. And since his parents were going to be in town until Monday morning, now was a chance to get caught up.

HE WAS ELBOW DEEP in the latest cost projections the following afternoon when his cell phone rang.

A burst of pleasure warmed his chest when he saw the caller ID flash across the screen. Lifting the phone to his ear, he found his smile broaden as a soft sexy voice rippled through the receiver. "Grady?"

"Hey, Alexis." He rocked back in his chair.

"Is this a good time?" she asked.

"The best," Grady said. "What's up?"

She continued in the gentle, businesslike voice he had come to know and appreciate. "I've compiled another list of potential mates for you. I wanted to drop by and give them to you." She paused.

He could picture her scraping her teeth across her lower lip....

"I thought—hoped—because it was the weekend you might have a chance to look at them and give me your opinion, so I could get dates set up for you every day this week. But if you're busy with family..."

Despite his own resolve to provide a mommy for his little girl, the idea of dating was no more appealing than it had been at the outset. Nevertheless, he knew he had to keep trying. Savannah needed a woman in her life.

Grady turned his chair so he could look out over downtown Fort Worth. As always on a Sunday afternoon, the streets were quiet, with only the occasional car or pickup driving by. "I'm at the office. My parents took Savannah for the day. So if you want to drop them by—"

"I'll be right over. Thanks, Grady." *Click.*

Twenty minutes later, building security called to let him know that Alexis was on her way up to see him. Grady met her at the elevator and walked her through the deserted executive suite to his private office.

He was painfully aware he could have done more in the grooming department today—he had showered, but not shaved. Put on a faded burnt-orange-and-white

Texas alumni T-shirt with an ink stain across the hem, jeans and running shoes.

Not that she seemed to mind.

He shut the door behind them. Gestured for her to take a seat. Took a moment to survey her as she got settled.

Her silky hair was caught in a clip on the back of her head. She was dressed casually—in a pale pink sundress, a thin white silk cardigan and flat-heeled sandals with a rose in the center of the thin straps across her feet.

He had never seen her bare feet, he realized. They were small and delicate, the toenails polished a sexy hot pink. Her legs were bare and smooth, without the usual panty hose....

She leaned forward to open up the carryall that served as both purse and briefcase, extracted a sheath of papers and half a dozen DVDs bearing the company logo.

It was only when she straightened and looked him square in the face that he noticed the faint puffiness around her eyes.

TOO LATE, Alexis realized the makeup she had applied so carefully before leaving her apartment had not done the trick.

"What's wrong?" Grady asked. He came back around the desk.

It had been a mistake coming here today. Thinking work—and possibly, time spent with Grady—would erase her overwhelming sense of loss and grief. "If you're talking about my eyes..."

"It looks like you've been crying."

"It's allergies," Alexis fibbed. Deciding to just hand the information over and flee while the going was good, she stood.

"Bull. It's something else, if your eyes are that swollen."

"I don't want to talk about it." The words were no sooner out than the tears began to well once again. The next thing she knew his arms were around her, hauling her against him. While her tears fell in a river, dampening his shirt, he stroked her hair, saying nothing. But then, nothing needed to be said.

Alexis struggled to get ahold of herself once again. She pulled away from him and rubbed the moisture from her cheeks. "I don't know what's wrong with me today," she murmured, averting her gaze.

He studied her closely. "It's because of last night. Something the speakers said…"

What had been meant to be uplifting had brought up everything she wished never to think about again. Suddenly, she couldn't hold it all in anymore.

In a choked voice, she cried, "I just wish it had never happened!" She looked in Grady's eyes and saw understanding. Like it or not, they were both in a club no one ever wanted to join. "I wish that Scott had never gotten sick or suffered the way he did, or had his life taken away from him."

Knowing Grady had lost a spouse, too, gave her the courage to admit, "I wish we'd had a chance to have the children we wanted. Although…" Alexis's lips curved ruefully "…seeing Savannah deal with the loss of a parent makes me realize how selfish that is."

"It's okay to want kids," he said compassionately. "It's okay to want things to be different. But at the same time…" he shrugged "…you've got to know our lives are what they are…."

And nothing they said or did would change that.

Alexis relaxed slightly. "Usually, I can deal."

"Then what was different about yesterday?" Grady asked, edging closer.

She reveled in the warmth of his nearness. "It was the anniversary of Scott's diagnosis."

Grady nodded, as if knowing firsthand that the date life as you knew it had screeched to a halt was always hard to bear. It didn't matter how much time passed.

Alexis gulped. "I thought by being involved in the fund-raiser this year I would be able to turn the day our lives went all to hell into something good, really start moving on…instead of being stuck in what was…."

Grady stroked a hand through her hair. He looked as if he approved of her decision to move on—and why not, since he was attempting to do the same thing? "You could start by taking a day off every now and then."

Alexis scoffed. "You're one to talk!"

He favored her with a sexy half smile. "I took yesterday off."

"So did I."

"You worked a benefit—I wouldn't call that time off. I'm talking about time to just be."

He had no idea how good that sounded.

Alexis focused on the strong column of Grady's throat. She splayed her hands across his chest and felt the steady beat of his heart beneath her fingertips. "I wish it was that simple." But it wasn't. For starters, the two of them, though wildly attracted to each other, did not want the same things. She had to keep remembering that.

As for the rest...

Alexis sighed.

Grady sifted his hands through her hair, lifted her face up to his. "Why isn't it that easy?"

He wouldn't understand unless she told him. And suddenly she wanted him to know at least this much about her. "I need to work every second I can because I'm up to my neck in debt." It was why she lived in a less-than-ideal apartment instead of a house, and drove a company-leased car. When his brow furrowed, she explained, "Insurance only funded a portion of the cancer treatment, and Scott battled leukemia for two years. Luckily, his co-pays were capped at twenty-one thousand a year, but that's still forty-two thousand dollars, plus another twelve thousand for his funeral, and countless other expenses, like hospital parking fees and lost wages."

She took in a quavering breath. "Suffice it to say, I'll be paying off that debt for a very long time. Unless I get the job running the new Galveston office, and the increase in salary that comes with it. Then it will happen a lot sooner, of course."

Grady was silent, looking down at her with compassion. "I wish I could help."

She knew he was rich. Did he think she was asking him for money...?

Oh, God, no.

Embarrassed she had told him so much about the private details of her life, Alexis stepped back abruptly. "It's not your problem." And it wouldn't be.

Suddenly, she needed to get out of there as soon as possible, and head back to work. She grabbed her carryall, slung it over her shoulder. "Let me know what you think about the candidates so I can set something up as soon as possible."

He studied her closely. "Meet me at the Reata Restaurant at seven o'clock," he said. "We'll go over it, and I'll tell you what I think then."

NOT SURE WHY she'd agreed to have dinner with Grady when she could just as easily gotten the information from him over the phone, Alexis went back to her own office. She spent the rest of the afternoon tending to several other clients, and pulling up another half dozen files, just in case Grady did not like any of the six women she had profiled for him. She went straight to the restaurant from work.

He was there, waiting for her. Dressed in a sage-green dress shirt, khaki pants and boots. He had shaved since she had seen him last, and put on aftershave. Suddenly, this felt like a date.

It shouldn't.

Marshalling her defenses, she slid into the chair he held out for her. "Well?" she said brightly, reminding herself she had handled much tougher situations than seeing a guy she was secretly attracted to pick someone else, at her urging. "What did you decide?"

"The kindergarten teacher, Pauline Emory. On paper, she sounds perfect."

That was depressingly easy. Alexis kept her hurt feelings to herself. "That's what I thought, too," she agreed cordially, rummaging through her notebook so she wouldn't have to look Grady in the eye. "I would have recommended her sooner, but she just signed on Friday, so her information wasn't in the system yet. Anyway, I'll call her and set something up." Unable to help but feel disappointed that their business had been concluded so swiftly—she'd been looking forward to having dinner with Grady, even if it was strictly business—she reached for her carryall and started to rise.

Grady caught her wrist. It was his turn to look flustered. "Where are you going?" he asked in surprise.

"Well…" Alexis tried not to focus on the intimate feel of his skin on hers. "We don't need to have dinner," she said, feeling as if her heart would bolt right out of her chest. "Our business is concluded."

His grasp tightened protectively. "Not quite." Grady caught the eye of a man sitting at the bar.

Alexis's eyes widened. Why was Grady's father here?

Wade McCabe strolled over to join them. "Hello, Alexis."

Completely dumbfounded, she nodded. "Mr. McCabe." Alexis turned back to Grady. "What's going on?" His father couldn't want the services of a matchmaker! He was already married. Why hadn't Grady mentioned that his father would be joining them?

"Grady told me about your situation," he stated affably, as he pulled up a chair.

"You already indicated you didn't want my help," Grady explained.

Wade nodded and flashed her a genial grin. "So we were hoping you'd accept mine."

Chapter Seven

"C'mon, Alexis! Talk to me!" Grady called through the closed apartment door a short time later.

He could hear her stomping around the small space, obviously angry and insulted. "Go away, Grady!" she shouted back.

The door behind him opened, and Alexis's neighbor, a short and burly Latino man, stared ominously at him.

"This guy bothering you?" he shouted.

The door to Alexis's flat swung open. Jaw working, she planted her hands on her slender hips and stared at them both. "No," she told her neighbor. Her face softened in appreciation. "Thanks, Augusto."

The man surveyed her a moment longer. "Then keep it down, will you?" he said gruffly at last. "The baby is asleep."

"Right." Alexis nodded, contritely. "Sorry."

He then glared at Grady, as if expecting him to leave. Grady looked at Alexis.

She appeared to be weighing her options, then exhaled loudly and motioned him in. "You've got two minutes to speak your piece," she snapped.

"You call me if you need me," Augusto stated.

"Thank you." Alexis looked warningly at Grady. "But it won't be necessary."

He followed her inside.

The first thing he noticed was how small her place was. Located in an area known for housing young families, the efficiency rented—according to the sign outside—for six hundred a month, utilities not included. She had a window unit air conditioner, which, although noisy, seemed to be putting out plenty of cool air. A worn tweed sofa bed was unfolded for sleeping, and there was a table with one chair for eating, a small desk with the other chair for working. The door to a tiny bathroom was ajar, and he glimpsed an ancient pedestal sink inside. The kitchen held an under-counter dorm-style refrigerator, microwave and hot plate. No dishwasher or disposal.

One entire wall of the flat was taken up with books, another with racks of neatly maintained and organized clothes and shoes. He wasn't surprised about that. Her line of business demanded she dress nicely, when interacting with clients.

The portable TV in the corner was tuned to a popular home decorating show. She snapped it off. "You've got one minute and a half," she said.

The clock was ticking. "Why did you walk out of the restaurant like that?" he asked.

She crossed her arms in front of her. "Because the meeting was over."

They faced off in silence. "Obviously, I offended you."

"Duh." She glowered at him, letting him know with a searing glance how humiliated and embarrassed she had been. *"You think?"*

It was a good thing he liked a challenge. "I was trying to help."

She propped her fists on her hips, her feet planted slightly apart. "I do not need you or anyone in your family to loan me money to consolidate my debts."

"My dad wasn't going to loan you the money himself," Grady told Alexis calmly. "He was simply going to underwrite it, the same way he does for any business or person he's interested in investing in, so the bank would issue you one at a premium interest rate."

Grady was disappointed to see that the distinction did not win him any points with her.

"I'm sure your father's heart was in the right place, Grady," Alexis stated carefully, "but I don't need his help any more than I need yours."

Grady thought about the crushing debt she had described. "This—" he gestured to the five-hundred-square-foot living area, which seemed in many ways as joyless as his own life had been after his wife's death "—tells me otherwise."

"I'm fine."

Was she? "You deserve better."

Alexis angled her chin. "And I'll get it without anyone's help or interference, when I've paid off my debts."

"Anyone ever tell you that you're stubborn to a fault?"

Anger flashed in her eyes. "Anyone ever tell you that you're clueless to a fault?"

His parents had tried. They'd both felt it was a bad idea to make the offer. Grady had convinced them otherwise. And because they liked Alexis, they'd agreed to go along with it…even as they shook their heads and predicted disaster.

"I was just trying to help you out, one friend to an-other."

"Really." She shoved a hand through her hair. "And how many other 'friends' of one week have you offered to loan upwards of seventy-five thousand dollars to even through a third party?"

Silence fell between them again.

He noticed she had taken off her thin sweater. The sundress she was wearing had a figure-hugging bod-ice and spaghetti straps, one of which had fallen down her shoulder.

Reluctantly, he tore his eyes from the expanse of bare, silky skin.

The relationship that only hours before had seemed so full of possibilities now seemed like a metaphor for the confused state of his life.

"That's not the kind of thing a guy does for a female friend—it's the kind of thing a man does for his mis-tress or *potential* mistress."

That woke Grady up. He stared at her. "Excuse me!"

"You heard me! That's the kind of move that typi-cally comes with strings attached—if not sooner, then later."

The idea that she could even for one red-hot second imagine him that calculating and crass, rankled. "You think I went to all that trouble because I wanted to sleep with you?" he asked incredulously, watching the play of emotions across her face.

Alexis swallowed, looking almost sorry she'd brought it up. But now that she had, she was obviously not about to back away from the rash statement. "Maybe not consciously…but yeah," she blurted. "I think ro-mancing me is in the back of your mind!"

Grady stepped closer, purposely invading her physical space. "Then I guess you missed the part where I told you, when you interviewed me about my revised requirements in a potential wife, that I had no interest in having a romantic relationship!"

Alexis scoffed. "Oh, no! I got that!" She thrust her index finger at him. "And I have to tell you, it hasn't exactly made my job of matching you with a woman any easier! I also got the part where you kissed me like there was no tomorrow. The part where I realized that although you may want a mother for Savannah, what you're really looking for here—for yourself—is a friend with benefits! And I have to tell you, you're not the first to present me with that option!"

The idea of Alexis being treated as anything less than the wonderful woman she was filled Grady with fury. He stared at her in shock. "You've been propositioned before?"

She didn't answer right away, but then she didn't have to, as a mixture of rueful recollection and bitterness filled her eyes. "What is it about guys and heartbroken widows, huh? What makes them think that we're all just begging to be bedded? That being crazy with grief equates to being crazy with lust? Because I have to tell you that hasn't been the case with me."

The same as it was with him. When it came to him and her... It was a very different story. He wasn't going to let her pretend otherwise, and group him with every other selfish jerk who had tried to make a move on her.

Alexis wasn't just a conquest to him. She was a person. Flesh and blood, with the heart and soul of a woman, who was every bit as lonely—and in need of companionship—as he was.

"I don't want to be intimately involved with anyone right now," she declared. "Casually or otherwise."

He wasn't just anyone. He was someone who had suffered the same kind of crushing loss she had. Like it or not, that gave them a unique bond. Drawing on that rapport, he said softly, "I thought you said you wanted to marry again someday."

She flinched, for a moment looking as vulnerable as she had that afternoon in his office. "*Someday* being the operative word," she answered quietly.

Grady would have accepted that declaration had the present not been filled with such incredible chemistry.

"And you know why?" she added. Her eyes glimmered as she glanced at him. "Because I haven't given up on having it all."

Grady figured he had—and with good reason. The odds were stacked against either of them ever finding that kind of love again. But he also realized life was too short to let the passion they were experiencing— even here and now as they argued—slide by. He knew better than most that life could change in an instant. All anyone ever really had was the present. And in this moment of time, there was only one thing…only one person…he wanted.

He gave in to a whim and lifted the strap that had fallen down her arm back onto her shoulder, then let his hand slide beneath her hair to the nape of her neck. Luxuriating in the silky feel of her skin, he tilted her face up to his. The way she looked at him then, all soft and wanting, prodded him to risk even more. "The kiss you gave me the other night said otherwise."

Alexis's lips compressed. She lowered her lashes and

retorted in a low, unsteady voice, "That kiss was ill-advised."

"Sometimes ill-advised is what's called for," Grady said, aware that his heart was suddenly slamming against his ribs. And then he did what he'd been wanting to do ever since the first time they'd embraced. He guided Alexis closer and slanted his lips over hers, taking everything she had to give.

Grady hadn't come here for this, but he couldn't say he was sorry it was happening. Instinct told him she needed this—needed him—as much as he needed her. Something about feeling her pressed against him, reaching for him, made him come alive. Made him want to connect with her in the most intimate of ways.

Basking in the gentle surrender of her body, he kissed her deeply. As he inhaled the sweet scent of her skin and the lingering fragrance of her perfume, he knew he'd been resurrected at long last. No longer moving numbly through his days, he was totally immersed in the here and now. The warmth of her touch. The womanly taste of her tongue. The softness of her breasts brushing up against his chest. Blood thundered through his body.

She was on tiptoe now, wrapping her arms around his neck, threading her hands through his hair. Her hips pressed against his, and still it wasn't enough....

"Alexis..." It was an effort to get the words out. "If I stay..." he warned, retaining control with effort.

"I know what will happen, Grady," she whispered back, looking deep into his eyes. Every emotion was stripped bare, yet her gaze never wavered. "I want this, too."

And tonight, wanting was all it took....

With the intoxicating scent of her filling his senses, he guided her backward to the sofa bed. "Then show me," he demanded gruffly.

And that, as it turned out, was all the encouragement she needed.

Alexis ran her hands across his shoulders, down his spine. Fused her mouth to his, stroking his tongue with hers. Until all he could think about, all he could feel, was the way her firm body fitted against him. Through the thin fabric of her sundress, her nipples beaded against the muscles of his chest.

Impatient, he slipped a hand beneath her and eased the zipper down, past her hips. He drew away the bodice, revealing a pale yellow, strapless bra. Her pink, jutting nipples were visible through the transparent lace. Lust poured through him, along with something else a lot more difficult to quantify. The need to touch…more than just her body. The need to possess…more than just her momentary will.

Reassuring himself this was only physical, he dipped his head, kissing the swell of her breasts through the cloth. With a low moan of pleasure, she arched her back, offering herself up to him, with a purity and innocence that rocked him to his core. Refusing to acknowledge how much this would have meant to both of them under other circumstances, he pushed the dress lower, past her navel, over her thighs.

Her panties, in the same pale yellow, were cut high on the thigh, revealing an expanse of fair, smooth skin. Pulse racing, he dispensed with the dress, slid his hands beneath her hips and lifted her to him. "Incredible," he murmured, loving the way she opened herself up to him.

And then she was shifting, pushing him back, rising

up to kneel beside him. Still clad in panties and bra, she reached for the buttons on his shirt. His belt. His fly. Minutes later, he was naked. Seconds after that, she was, too. "Protection," she murmured.

He stopped as reality crashed upon them once again. "I don't suppose…"

She shook her head.

Aching, but no less determined to have her, he said, "So we won't do that." Eyes locked with hers, he drew Alexis back down beside him. Wrapping an arm around her trembling body, he draped her thigh over his and guided her against him for a long, leisurely kiss. "There are other ways…." he promised.

The last thing Alexis had expected to be doing was lying naked with Grady on her bed, making out like two teenagers, but as they continued to kiss and caress each other, the frustration at their lack of foresight was replaced by a steadily building pleasure.

Grady was right. There were other ways to be close.

Ways that felt just as good. Just as satisfying. He hadn't just led her into a firestorm of heat. Grady knew how to touch her, how to caress her just so, how to make her feel as if she was the only woman on earth for him. And her own instinct was just as strong. Before she knew it, the pleasure was soaring out of control. She was coming apart, and so was he. He caught her to him. Their hearts thundered in unison. Together, they climaxed, and just as slowly and inevitably, drifted back to earth.

ALEXIS'S EYES WERE CLOSED. Grady was not entirely sure that was a good sign. He wished to hell he'd had a condom with him. A box of them. But the truth was, it had been so long since he'd been with someone he hadn't even thought about it. He kissed her shoulder, making a mental note to stop by the drugstore at the first available opportunity so they wouldn't be limited to a hot and heavy make-out session. "Next time...I'll have more foresight," he murmured.

Alexis stiffened.

Obviously, Grady thought, the wrong thing to say.

She pushed him away and sat up. "There isn't going to be a next time, Grady."

O-kay. Maybe, under the circumstances, he should have expected this. Still, being iced out only moments after lovemaking was a kick in the groin.... He watched her grab the blanket and wrap it around her, toga-style. "Mind telling me why?" He forced himself to sound casual as she disappeared into the tiny bathroom.

She came out seconds later, wrapped in a pink, jersey knit robe that clung to her slender curves with just enough accuracy to get him hard again. "Because we don't love each other."

What could he say to that? Grady wondered, tearing his eyes from the hint of breast exposed in the V neckline. Except what he had already repeated to Alexis and every other woman who had crossed his path since his wife died? He steeled himself against unnecessary complications. "That's not in the equation for me." He didn't want to be hurt like that again. Didn't want to hope that this time it would be different—this love would last. It felt too much like tempting fate.

She sat down next to him on the bed, looking impossibly composed for a woman who had just given herself to him with no reservation. "I know that. You were perfectly clear on the topic from the very beginning."

"So?" His frustration mounted.

She turned away. "So this was cathartic, in that neither of us has been with anyone in a very long time."

Too long, Grady was beginning to conclude. Otherwise, he would have done the smart thing and kept their relationship platonic, so the two of them could remain friends.

"Don't get me wrong. I enjoyed it," she admitted. "But it can't happen again."

ALEXIS WASN'T SURE how she did it—behaved as if her whole world was not crashing down around her. But somehow she got Grady dressed and out of there in record time.

When the door closed behind him, she went back to her rumpled bed. She had turned the window unit on high when she came home, and cool air was still blasting out of it. Shivering, she climbed beneath the covers and closed her eyes. The overwhelming guilt she expected, at having made the first real attempt to move on after her husband's death, was nowhere to be found.

For the first time in a very long time, there was no sorrow. There wasn't really even any loneliness. There was just the warmth of their bodies, still in the covers. The smell of Grady—that unique mixture of soap, man and aftershave lotion—mingled with the muskier scent of their love.

Thinking about the unabashed way they had pleasured each other filled her entire body with heat. She couldn't believe they had gone at it like teenagers. That she had very nearly risked pregnancy and more, for a moment's pleasure with a man she knew in her mind—if not her heart—was all wrong for her.

Instead, all she had been able to think was about the way he made her feel. So completely, wonderfully alive. So impatient for more. For the first time since she could remember, she was ready to get on with her life.

She wanted, she realized belatedly, to put an end to the long, lonely nights. She wanted someone to talk to. She wanted children. She wanted a real home, with a yard, and a backyard swing, instead of the cheapest apartment she could find.

She wanted Grady.

It was just too bad he wasn't available. Not the way she needed him to be.

ALEXIS DIDN'T HEAR FROM Grady McCabe again that night. She told herself it was for the best. She had asked him to leave. His parents were still in town. Tomorrow was a school day....

Still, when Monday morning dawned, and she received a short e-mail indicating that he still intended to meet with kindergarten teacher Pauline Emory for breakfast, as scheduled, Alexis breathed a sigh of relief.

Or at least she told herself it was relief, not despair. What had she expected? That one hot and heavy tryst would lead him to some great epiphany about wanting romance and commitment, after all?

Telling herself to grow up, she dressed and went to the office. No sooner had Alexis booted up her computer than her boss strode in. "How's it going with Grady McCabe?" she asked.

Alexis pushed the image of Grady making love to her from her mind. She forced a smile. "He's seeing a potential candidate this morning."

Holly Anne frowned. "You're usually so quick to

find the perfect someone for a client. I was hoping you'd have Grady matched by now."

Same here. The less time I spend with the sexy heart-breaker, the better...

Alexis struggled to keep her emotions under wraps. "It's not a typical case. Usually romance is involved."

"He's rich. Successful. Handsome. He has an adorable daughter in desperate need of a mommy. How hard can it be to get women lined up to marry him?"

"Not difficult at all." *Sad to say.* Alexis was disappointed at how many women were perfectly willing to throw love out the window, if they could have everything else.

She took a sip of iced coffee. "The problem is Grady. He's proving very difficult to please."

Holly Anne checked her messages on her Black-Berry. "How many clients has he met thus far?"

"Pauline Emory is the third," Alexis replied.

Her boss sent a text and looked up. "That's not so bad, is it?"

"It wouldn't be if he weren't in such a hurry." *If I hadn't lost all sense of propriety and succumbed to him.* Alexis gulped and pretended to look at her computer screen. "He wants this wrapped up in the next two weeks."

"Or sooner," a familiar male voice said, "given the fact that Savannah's summer break starts July first, and I'm going to need someone by then."

Well, if it wasn't the man of the hour.

Doing the best to ignore the jump in her pulse, Alexis glanced at her watch as Grady strode in the door. "I thought you were supposed to be with Pauline Emory."

If he was thinking about the passion that had flared

between them the last time they'd seen each other, Alexis thought, he was definitely not showing it. "I met with her after I dropped Savannah off at school," he said.

"And?" Alexis prodded.

Grady flashed an inscrutable smile that did not reach his eyes. "Pauline's great," he said, his tone devoid of emotion. "I think Savannah will like her. Her experience as a kindergarten teacher should help her connect with my daughter."

"Good. I'm glad." Lamenting her sudden hoarseness, Alexis reached for her iced coffee and took another long sip. What was wrong with her? She was supposed to feel happy about his interest in Pauline, not sad and rejected.

Grady continued matter-of-factly, "Pauline's off for the summer—she teaches at a school on the regular calendar—so I asked her to tutor Savannah after school every day for the next week and a half. See if she can't get Savannah enthused about doing her homework, so it's not such a hassle."

Tutoring wasn't exactly the same as dating with a view toward marriage, Alexis thought. She could tell that Holly Anne was having the same troubled reaction. "And Pauline agreed?"

Grady's contained expression told Alexis that Pauline Emory hadn't exactly been thrilled about it. He shrugged his broad shoulders. "She understands I'm doing this for Savannah, not for me."

So nothing had changed, Alexis realized pensively. Grady was still keeping every woman who was interested in him at arm's length. He was only looking for a suitable mother for his daughter. And while that might work in the short run, she knew it would not work in the long run. Unfortunately, it wasn't her decision to make. Her job was to cater to Grady's whims.

"In the meantime, do you want me to keep presenting you with other candidates?"

Grady shook his head. "Not until I see whether this works out."

It sounded as if he was getting serious, Alexis noted with alarm.

"I can only juggle one potential wife at a time," Grady said flatly.

Which means I'm out of the picture entirely, Alexis thought with a sinking heart. *Not that I was ever* in *the picture...except as a means to an end.*

She forced herself to meet his gaze. "That's good to know."

Holly Anne beamed, obviously seeing this as progress. "Sounds like you'll be in Galveston before you know it," she whispered to Alexis.

Seeing her secretary appear in the doorway, Holly Anne asked, "Problem?" At the answering nod, she hurried out.

Once again Grady and Alexis were alone. A brief, uncomfortable silence fell between them. Finally, he raised his brow. "Are congratulations in order?"

Was it her imagination or was there the faintest hint of concern—and maybe even disappointment—in his eyes?

She shrugged self-consciously to let him know any such talk was way premature. "I haven't been offered the job. The four partners still have to vote on it at the end of the month." And there was no way of telling how that would go, particularly if Grady remained as hard to please. ForeverLove.com was an agency that prided itself on *results*. Unsatisfied customers hurt—not helped—profits. Holly Anne and her partners were all about the bottom line.

As was Grady, apparently, Alexis noted.

"Will you take it if offered the position?" he asked her casually.

Pack up and move several hundred miles away? A week ago, thinking the change of pace, not to mention the extra money, would be helpful to her, Alexis would have said yes unequivocally. Now?

Honestly, she didn't know.

But if she told Grady so he'd think she was only staying in Fort Worth because of him.

And if he thought that, he'd think she was ripe for a continuation of their never-to-be-repeated encounter.

She wasn't.

So, for both their sakes, she told him what she knew he least wanted to hear, even though she was no longer sure the statement was accurate. "From a financial standpoint, I'd be a fool not to."

Chapter Eight

"Grady?" Pauline Emory paused in the door of his study. "We've got a bit of a problem." She glided on in, looking every bit the suburban mom. Smart, energetic, friendly, the slender brunette was everything most Texas men would want in a potential wife.

Except him.

Despite her many laudable qualities, when he looked at her, all he could see was what she wasn't. Namely, Alexis.

If only Alexis were willing to settle for what he could give her…instead of what he *couldn't.*

But she didn't want to settle.

And he couldn't pretend he would ever believe in happily-ever-after again.

Grady sighed, forcing himself to listen to what Pauline was saying as she paused next to his desk, the bangle bracelet sliding down her wrist, drawing his attention to her expertly manicured hands.

Which was another thing he didn't like, Grady thought.

Acrylic nails.

"We've been at this for over an hour now…." Pau-

line heaved a distressed sigh. "Savannah absolutely re-
fuses to finish her homework. She said she can't do it."

Not couldn't, Grady thought. Wouldn't. He looked
at Pauline, recalling from the file he'd read on her that
she had twice been named Teacher of the Year at the
elementary school where she worked. He lifted a brow.
"Surely—"

Pauline cut him off. "I've tried every pre-k method
I know. She's not budging."

No one had to tell him how stubborn his daughter
could be, especially when she had it in her mind not
to cooperate. Grady pushed away from his computer
keyboard, lamenting the fact that his plan had already
hit the skids. He headed for the door. "Where is she?"

"On the swing set." Pauline touched his arm before
he could get past the portal. "Listen, I think I should
go," she said gently.

This was a surprise.

"Savannah's in no mood to spend time with anyone
new today. I don't think we should push it. Maybe just
try again tomorrow. With the three of us."

That wasn't what Grady had had in mind. He could
see Pauline had reached her limit, however. He walked
her to the front door. "I'll call you later," he said.

She smiled. "I'm sure Savannah will do better if it's
the three of us," she repeated.

Or not, Grady thought.

He said goodbye and headed to the backyard.

Savannah was sitting on the swing. She was still in
her school uniform. Surprised that she hadn't changed
into one of her princess costumes, as was usually the
case, Grady leaned against the tall wooden post just to

the right of her. He shoved his hands in the pockets of his trousers. "What's going on?" he inquired.

Savannah looked up at him. "I want Alexis," she said.

"WHAT'S GOING ON?" Alexis asked Grady, the moment she arrived. She had been on her way home from the office when she got the message that he had some sort of emergency at his home and needed to see her ASAP. "Where's Pauline?"

"She left." Briefly, Grady explained.

"You don't look thrilled," Alexis noted.

"To be truthful, I'm not sure it's going to work out with her. She and Savannah didn't really seem to hit it off. Not the way the two of you did. And that kind of rapport is what I'm looking for."

Alexis couldn't blame him. Anything less would not hold up over time. "How'd the tutoring go?"

"Terrible. Savannah wouldn't cooperate. Pauline gave up and went home."

Alexis made a face. That wasn't good. "How much did they get done?"

"Not one problem. Which is why I sent out the SOS to you. Savannah said only *you* could help her with her math."

Alexis shook her head in silent remonstration. She propped her hands on her hips as the mood between them lightened considerably. "And you fell for that?"

A guilty-as-charged-but-so-glad-to-see-you grin tugged at the corners of Grady's lips. "You're always so good with her," he answered wryly.

Not exactly a reason to set her heart to pounding. Although, Alexis admitted reluctantly to herself, it felt kind of good to know that Savannah missed her as much as she missed the little girl. And, truth be told, it warmed her heart that when in trouble, Grady didn't hesitate to call. She hadn't been needed—or wanted— like that in someone's life since her husband died.

"Alexis!" Savannah came running into the room. She was still in her school uniform and a pair of purple cowgirl boots, a tiara perched precariously on her head. "Daddy, you didn't tell me Alexis was here! Where've you been? How come you didn't come and see me? Do you want to go upstairs and play Fairy Princess?"

Alexis grinned—she couldn't help it. Knowing full well she shouldn't be encouraging this "little diva" behavior, she wrapped her arms around Grady's daughter and returned her exuberant embrace. "I've been very busy working, sweetheart."

Still holding on tight, Savannah looked up at her. "Did you miss me as much as I missed you?"

"Yes," Alexis told her sincerely. "Very much."

Savannah beamed.

"I hear you have homework to do," she continued gently.

The child collapsed to the floor dramatically, then brought her arms and legs in close to her torso, resting her chin on her upraised knees. "I can't do it today," she said, suddenly looking distressed and completely overwhelmed. "I'm too upset."

Alexis knelt down beside her. "About what, honey?"

"I don't have a dress for graduation."

Grady looked stunned. "I thought you were wearing your school uniforms to graduation."

Savannah shook her head, more distraught than ever.

"No, Daddy," she explained with exaggerated patience. "My teacher said we all have to wear party dresses."

Grady shrugged, clearly not getting the importance. "Well, that's no problem. You have a half a dozen nice dresses upstairs in your closet."

Savannah scrambled back to her feet, full of animation once again. "It has to be brand-new, Daddy." She spread her hands wide for emphasis, frustrated that he didn't intuit this on his own. "Everybody is getting *brand-new* dresses to wear. Everybody went shopping for their very special dress with their mommy except me." Tears filled her eyes. "And I didn't get to because I don't have a mommy!"

Talk about a dagger to the heart, Alexis thought.

Grady looked as crushed as Savannah and she felt. "Why didn't you tell me this sooner?" he asked hoarsely.

Mutely Savannah lifted her shoulders in a shrug.

"Grandma and Grandpa were here over the weekend," Grady continued mildly. "We could have done it then."

She shrugged again. "I guess I forgot—till I heard everybody talking about it at school today and then I got real, real sad. So you see, I can't do my homework if I don't have a pretty dress to wear."

"Sure you can." Alexis stepped in kindly. "And I'll sit with you in the kitchen while you do it."

Savannah was not happy about the idea. "But what about shopping?" she asked anxiously.

"We'll go this weekend," Grady promised.

"ONCE AGAIN YOU CAME to my rescue," Grady said an hour and a half later, after Savannah had been tucked in bed—at the child's insistence, by both of them. "I can't believe how easily you got her to complete her homework?"

Alexis shrugged off his comment. She didn't want to feel too comfortable here, or be this needed. It made her realize just how lonely she had been the past few years, while she was grieving the loss of her husband. She smiled at Grady, eager to get back to business. "We need to talk about where you go from here."

Grady walked into the kitchen. He plucked Savannah's insulated Princess lunch bag from the drying rack on the counter. "It's clear Savannah needs a mother more than ever, but the timing could be wrong."

Alexis's heart sank. "You want to wait?"

He got leftovers out of the fridge. "Yes."

Alexis could only hope this meant he was starting to come to his senses. Even though it meant they would have little or no reason to communicate with each other in the meantime. "For how long?"

He put chicken strips and dipping sauce in the lunch bag for school the next day. "Until after she graduates in ten days."

Alexis lounged against the counter and accessed the calendar on her BlackBerry. "So you want to pick it up again on July first?"

Grady added yogurt and a bag of precut apple slices. Tossed in a plastic spoon, a kid-size bottle of water and a napkin. "We're going to Laramie to spend the holiday with family. Maybe after Independence Day."

Alexis tensed. "You realize finding a mother for Savannah is going to take time," she warned. "Delaying the search won't help matters."

Arms folded in front of him, he lounged against the opposite counter. "Actually, I disagree." He shot her a significant look. "I think it will actually help in the long run."

"How so?"

He quirked a brow. "You see…I have a plan. But I need your help to pull it off."

"Grady McCabe wants to *what?*" Holly Anne said first thing the next morning, when Alexis went in to talk with her.

"Suspend his search for a wife and have me spend more time with him and his daughter instead. On the clock."

Her boss never minded more billable hours on a project, as long as the client didn't. As far as Holly Anne was concerned, that was simply money in the bank. This request, however, was unusual. "He's paying you to spend time with them?" she repeated, stunned.

Alexis nodded. Her initial reaction had been much the same. "Grady thinks if I can spend more time with Savannah and him, I'll get to know them better and will have a more accurate idea of what kind of woman they need in their lives. And he'll be better able to assess how much of a hurry he needs to be in, when it comes to finding a mate."

Holly Anne continued opening up her mail. "You sure he's not just looking for another matchmaking service on the sly? Maybe thinking of going with one of our competitors?"

At the moment, Alexis honestly didn't know what to think. "I offered to set him up with another matchmaker here."

"And?" her boss pressed, putting one letter into the In basket, another in the trash.

"For whatever reason...Grady's little girl has gotten rather attached to me," Alexis stated carefully. "She's been having a hard time. That translates into a lot of chaos in his life. Which is why he wanted a wife as soon as possible. Now that he's met with three women, none of whom were right, he's not so eager to continue screening candidates and introducing them to his daughter." She exhaled. "And I can hardly blame him for that. He's busy enough as it is, with this new project he has going downtown. To put all this additional pressure on himself—and by association, Savannah—well, it seems to be making the situation worse."

Holly Anne picked up the last letter in the stack. "Will you being there, billing him by the hour, help the overall situation?"

Truth time. "It could."

"Will it lead to him looking again?"

Alexis hesitated. "Maybe." She hated to think how much she loathed the idea of seeing him with yet another marriage-hungry woman. "But I'll be honest. I still can't promise anything."

Holly Anne sat down at her desk, switched on her computer. "Why not?"

"Because even though it's been five years, I just don't think he's completely over losing his wife." Instead, he seemed to be waiting for something awful to happen again the moment he got happy, and Alexis knew how that felt. Once life had taken a truly devastating turn, you were never without that niggling bit of fear in the back of your mind.

It was hard, moving on.

Her boss knew that, too.

When she finally spoke, her tone was grave. "The

other partners are excited about having someone with Grady's stature as a client. If you don't match him with anyone, or at least get him looking again, this will impact your chances of getting the Galveston job and the substantial pay raise that goes with it—no matter how many hours you bill."

Alexis nodded. "I assumed that would be the case." How many times had she been told that, in their company, *results* were what mattered?

"Don't disappoint me, Alexis," Holly Anne warned quietly. "We're counting on you to make the match of the century for Grady McCabe."

SAVANNAH'S MATH HOMEWORK looked easy enough to Alexis, when she sat down at the kitchen table with Grady's little girl early that evening. "Hmm…" She pretended to be perplexed as she studied the mimeographed sheet of eight problems. "I'm not really sure what we're supposed to do here…."

Savannah's eyes widened, as if amazed Alexis could be so dense. Glancing back at the paper, she picked up a crayon. "It's easy. We just count the pieces of fruit in each box."

Alexis pointed to a box in the middle of the page, just to shake things up. "Want to do the apples first?"

"Okay!"

"Do you know how to count them?"

"Of course!" Savannah sighed in exasperation. "One, two, three!"

"Now what do we do?" Alexis probed.

"We find the number three in the box. See? Here it is. And then…" Savannah stuck her tongue between her teeth as she wielded her crayon. "We circle it, just like this!"

"Wow. That was really good," Alexis praised. "You want to show me how to do another one?"

"Sure!"

Five minutes later, they were all done. Savannah had counted objects, located the appropriate number beneath and marked it, without a single mistake. There was no doubt she was not in the least bit academically challenged by the work assigned to her. If anything, it was all too easy…and hence, boring.

"Good job, sweetheart!" Alexis said.

"Can I have a look?" Grady strolled in. Even in a rumpled shirt and jeans, with the shadow of beard on his face, the guy looked good. What could she say? No wonder the women who came over to meet him were instantly smitten. He would be quite a catch, if he ever deigned to let himself fall in love again, that was.

"Okay, but then I have to put it in my backpack to take to school tomorrow," Savannah told her father importantly.

Gravely, Grady perused the work sheet with Savannah's name written awkwardly across the top. "That's excellent!" he told her. "I'm very proud of you!"

Savannah beamed. Familial warmth permeated the room. Amazed that her work there could have been completed so quickly, Alexis looked at Grady, wondering what was next.

"Want to help Savannah and me make dinner?" he said.

"What are we having?" Savannah asked excitedly.

"Your favorite. Pizza. Run upstairs and change into

some shorts and a T-shirt and I'll let you pat out the dough."

"Okay, Daddy!" Savannah raced off, anxious to get out of her school uniform.

Grady and Alexis exchanged glances, the air vibrating with tension.

Once again, Alexis noted, she and Grady were alone. And having all that raw male power focused on her was unsettling, to say the least.

ALEXIS WASN'T SURE what she had expected for the rest of the week. What she got was more of the same. She worked all day at the office, matching other couples with her usual exceptional success. Then arrived at Grady's shortly after Savannah got home from her after-school program, at five-fifteen. Homework was done at the kitchen table, followed by dinner, which more often than not was now a group cooking project. Then there was bath, story and bedtime, and finally a casual adieu.

Savannah was always overjoyed to see her and sad to say goodbye. Grady treated Alexis with kindness and reverence. Occasionally she found him looking at her a tad too long. But out of respect for her previously stated wishes, he always turned away.

There were no accidental touches or near kisses. No physical contact between the two of them of any kind.

His chivalry was driving her crazy. She wanted, she realized belatedly, to connect with him again. Even if it wasn't what *he* wanted.

And yet she knew he was right, keeping the relationship between them strictly platonic.

When Savannah completed the school year, Alexis

still had to match him with someone else. A woman who wouldn't require love.

Which was why, Friday evening, Alexis was thinking about making an excuse to leave early, as soon as Savannah's homework was done. Before she was overcome with wistfulness for what could never be.

And that was, of course, exactly when Savannah turned her hope-filled gaze upon her. "Are you coming shopping with me and Daddy tomorrow morning?" she asked. "For my graduation dress?"

"Actually…" Grady stepped away from the fridge, where he was busy studying the contents. "I was meaning to talk to you about that."

"Daddy said you can come with us and help me try on the dresses!" Savannah said.

His eyes on hers, Grady moved closer. "She wanted a woman's point of view, and since my mom's off on an oil rig in West Texas, and can't be here until the day of graduation…"

"Say yes!" Savannah grabbed on to Alexis and held on tight.

There went her plan to have a respite from the family that was beginning to feel far too much like her own.

"Please, please, please!" Savannah looked up, waiting.

There was no way Alexis could deny the need shimmering in those sweet blue eyes. She caved. "Of course I'll come," she promised. It was little more than an errand, after all. Something she'd do for any friend with a daughter Savannah's age. And if Grady happened to be along for the trip, so be it.

He grinned, his smile so wide and all-encompassing it crinkled the corners of his eyes. "That's great," he said, looking more cheerful than he had all week. Despite her decision to keep a wall between them, Alexis found herself smiling back at him.

"Now for the bad news." Grady twisted his handsome face into a comical parody of apology. "I thought we still had some stuff in here to make tacos, but we don't, so what do you ladies say about going out for dinner tonight? It is Friday, after all."

Savannah jumped up and down in enthusiasm. "I want to go to a restaurant!" she declared.

"And then maybe stop by the grocery store on the way home?" Grady looked at Alexis. "That is, unless you've got other plans…?"

Was he fishing to find out if she had a date? The thought that he might be sent a thrill of excitement through her. Alexis forced herself to calm down. Since their one ill-advised tryst, Grady had given her no reason to think that he wanted anything more from her than help with his daughter.

Before she could stop herself, she smiled again, more casually this time, and said, "Nothing I'd rather do."

Grady grabbed his keys and BlackBerry while Savannah ran upstairs to change into a ruffled T-shirt, matching lavender shorts and sandals. The three of them walked outside. They were nearly to Grady's SUV when a sleek Jaguar sedan pulled into the driveway.

Kit Peterson was behind the wheel. She waved, turned off the engine and got out. The statuesque redhead strode toward them, her high heels clattering on the driveway.

"Hello, Grady! Savannah. And—?" She slid her sunglasses partway down her nose and peered over the rim.

"Alexis Graham," Alexis reminded her, trying not to grimace.

"Oh, right…" Kit greeted her with a dismissive nod, then turned back to Grady, an exaggerated expression of sympathy on her perfectly made up face. "I just came over to see how you all were doing!"

Wild giggling emanated from the back of the Jaguar.

Lisa Marie and two other little girls from Savannah's class were clearly visible. They were pointing and ducking down in the back seat, obviously making fun.

Alexis felt Savannah tense beside her.

She put an arm around the child, who leaned against her with a slow exhalation. Alexis sensed her unhappiness. She knew it wasn't her place, but oh, how she wanted to reprimand the trio responsible for Savannah's obvious discomfort.

"What's going on?" Grady asked Kit.

"Just a minute." The woman tottered back to the sedan. "Girls!" she scolded. To no avail—the giggling died down momentarily, before starting up again. Kit leaned into the open window, treating her audience to a view of the tight white skirt encasing her slender backside, as she retrieved a ribbon-wrapped bakery box. Nose in the air, she did her beauty queen walk back, knelt and gave it to Savannah. "Here you go, darlin'. This should make you feel all better."

Savannah held the box, from a popular cupcake emporium, as if it were radioactive.

"I have no idea what you're talking about," Grady said.

Kit looked flummoxed. "Well, I assumed," she said dramatically, "you would have chatted with Principal Jordan…."

"About?" he demanded, still in the dark.

"Oh, dear!" Kit draped a hand across her chest. "It seems I spoke too soon."

The lenses of the woman's sunglasses were opaque, so Alexis couldn't see her eyes, but was pretty sure she knew how they'd look. Mean girl, all the way…

Grady must have known it, too. And he was beginning to get really ticked off.

"You know what?" Having done the damage she clearly intended to do, Kit gave an airy little wave. "I think I'm just going to go ahead and leave. I'm taking the girls to a movie tonight and I don't want to be late. So we'll talk later. You call me if you need to, Grady dear." She smiled condescendingly at his daughter. "Savannah, good to see you, darlin'. And, Alexis, do call me. I think I can help you out with some ideas for…" She smiled at Grady mysteriously. "Well, you know…."

As if, Alexis thought grimly, she would ever match Grady with one of Kit's friends!

"Thanks for the cupcakes," Grady stated politely, sounding anything but grateful.

Kit Peterson drove off, the three little girls in the back of her car still giggling unkindly.

Savannah appeared ready to cry.

Grady glanced at his watch. "You know what, ladies? I forgot I have to make a call first. So if you want to take those cupcakes inside and put them on the counter, I'll slip into my study and do that before we get on our way."

Savannah didn't say anything. Head down, still carrying the pastry box, she headed for the front door.

Grady traded glances with Alexis over his daughter's head. On this, Alexis knew without saying a word, she and Grady were in perfect agreement. They both wanted to throttle their recent visitors for hurting his little girl's feelings.

Chapter Nine

"Did you get hold of Principal Jordan?" Alexis asked.

"Finally." Grady set the tray of food on the table next to the play area in the popular fast-food restaurant. From where they were sitting, they could see Savannah, and four other children racing around the elevated tunnels, mesh-sided walkways and dual circular slides. All were well out of earshot, and clearly having a fabulous time.

Grady handed Alexis her flame-grilled burger and onion rings, and confided, "She said she didn't want to get into it over the phone. That we'd talk in her office Monday morning at nine o'clock."

Alexis tensed. "That sounds ominous."

"I asked Principal Jordan if Savannah was in some sort of trouble and she assured me that was not the case," he continued, obviously sharing Alexis's concern.

She studied Grady's worried-looking face. He didn't let his guard down very often. She knew the fact he was doing so now—with her—was significant. "You're not buying it?" she guessed in the same low tone.

Grady tore the paper wrapper off his own burger and stuck a straw in his soft drink. They had promised Savannah she wouldn't have to eat until after she had played awhile, so her meal remained on the tray.

There was a moment of warm familiarity when his gaze met Alexis's. This was what it would be like to be married to Grady and raising his daughter. This feeling that whatever problems came up, they would handle them together....

"If it wasn't bad news, why all the mystery?" Grady mused, searching her eyes.

"Why Kit Peterson's sanctimonious attitude?" Alexis countered.

"Exactly." He spread his napkin across his lap and picked up his double cheeseburger. "I hate this, having her in an all-girls school. I feel so out of my league."

Alexis imagined everyone who wasn't in the school's estrogen-driven in crowd felt that way.

"Which is why," he continued, some of the brooding intensity leaving his face as he looked at her yet again, "I was hoping you'd go with me Monday morning."

"For moral support," Alexis suggested, trying hard not to read more into it than that. "For you and Savannah."

He acknowledged it with a shrug, adding, "And you're a woman. You've worked with Savannah on her homework. You know how bright she is. And last but not least, I think you have more objectivity than I do right now."

Alexis wasn't sure about that. She was feeling pretty emotional about the way Savannah was being treated by Kit Peterson, her daughter and classmates, as well as the school administrator. None of it seemed on the up and up, but then what did she know about the rarefied world of private girls schools? "If you think I can help," she allowed, pushing away those turbulent thoughts.

Grady reached over and briefly touched her hand.

And in that moment, all the casualness of their conversation transferred into something deeper. "I do," he confirmed.

The touch of skin on skin created a ripple of sensation within her. Her pulse skittering, Alexis stared into Grady's eyes. It would be so easy to fall in love with him, she realized. And so very dangerous.

"Hi, Daddy! Hi, Alexis! We're having fun up here!" Savannah shouted from up above, her grinning face pressed against the mesh-sides of the walkway.

Just like that, Alexis noted in disappointment, the spell was broken.

Grady withdrew his hand and waved back. "Be careful!" he called.

"Okay, Daddy!" Savannah raced off, the other little girl and the three boys right behind her.

Grady looked at Alexis, happier now. Knowing she needed to get the conversation back on a safe, platonic topic, she took a long sip of her diet soda and asked casually, "Where did you go to school, when you were a kid?"

Grady relaxed even more. "Public school in Laramie, Texas. College at University of Texas in Austin. What about you?"

"I attended public school in Arlington, then the University of North Texas in Denton."

He dipped an onion ring in ketchup. "I guess we have that in common."

Alexis ate hers plain. "I guess we do."

They exchanged smiles again.

Okay, she thought, they really had to stop this. It was beginning to feel like a date. She concentrated on cutting her burger in half, reminding herself for the millionth time that all she was ever going to be was a family friend. "Where did you want to look for a graduation dress?"

Grady's dark brows drew together. "No clue. I thought you might have some ideas."

"Depends on how fancy you want to go, I guess."

"Knowing her classmates?" Grady said grimly. "We're aiming for the Little Princess level." He looked back at Savannah, who was still racing around, happy and carefree, then turned to Alexis once more. "Any ideas?"

Her mind jumped ahead to the possibilities. "We'll find her something every bit as special as the day. I promise."

ALEXIS MET THEM Saturday morning. Together, they hit all the high-end department stores. Savannah tried on dozens of dresses and modeled them for her daddy, but did not like a single one enough to purchase it. The more dresses she tried on, the more pouty she became.

The look Grady sent Alexis, over Savannah's head, said he was just as perplexed by his daughter's temperamental behavior as she was. Usually, he'd told Alexis before they started out, Savannah loved trying on pretty clothing.

"Maybe we should try a boutique," Alexis said.

"What's a boutique?" Savannah asked.

"A store where they only sell little girl's clothes." She consulted the list she had drawn up from her computer research, and they headed for the first shop on it. Located in a strip mall, the small store was bright and cheerful and had a rack of summer party dresses, perfect for the hot weather.

Alexis showed Savannah the ones in her size. They picked out half a dozen and went into the dressing room, while Grady sat outside to wait.

"Which one do you want to try on first?" Alexis asked.

The corners of Savannah's mouth turned down. She rubbed her toe along the carpeted floor.

Alexis sat down on the bench along the mirrored wall, so they would be at eye level. "What's wrong, sweetheart? Can you tell me?"

She shrugged, but didn't look up.

Was she overwhelmed? "Is it too hard for you to try to pick out a dress?"

A few tears trembled on Savannah's lashes and trickled down her cheek. "They're going to make fun of me," she said.

"Who is?" Alexis asked, even more gently, fearing she already knew.

The child sniffed. "Lisa Marie and all her friends."

Alexis reached out and drew her onto her lap. "Why would they do that?"

Savannah cuddled close and rested her head against Alexis's shoulder. "They're going to say I look stupid, 'cause I don't have a mother to help me buy a dress, and then they're all going to laugh at me."

Savannah wrapped her arms around Alexis's neck, and the damn broke. She cried silently, her whole body shaking. As she witnessed the little girl's misery, it was all Alexis could do not to break down, too. Her own eyes blurred with tears as she murmured soft reassurances.

Finally, Savannah got it all out and settled down.

Alexis stroked a hand through her curls. Still holding her tight, she pressed a kiss to the top of her head. "I am so sorry those girls hurt your feelings. That is not nice. Not nice at all."

Savannah sniffed some more. Still holding on, she leaned back enough so she could see Alexis's face. "I'm not mean to them."

Unfortunately, Alexis thought sadly, that did not always matter. "I'm glad to hear that, Savannah. Because all being mean to someone else does is make you feel bad inside."

Savannah clearly didn't quite believe that. Which was why they needed to bring Grady into the situation, to offer counsel and advice, Alexis decided. "Tell you what. I think we've had enough shopping for one morning. Why don't we forget about trying all these dresses on and go get your daddy and have lunch instead?"

Savannah's body sagged with relief. "Okay," she said with a tremulous smile. She took Alexis's hand. Together, they went to find Grady.

GRADY DIDN'T ARGUE WITH the abrupt break in the shopping excursion. In fact, he looked every bit as relieved as his daughter to be able to go to a nearby barbecue place. Exhausted, Savannah fell asleep in the car on the way home afterward. He carried her inside and upstairs to her bed. When he came back down, Alexis was waiting in the living room.

"Is she still napping?"

He nodded. "Out like a light."

Alexis was glad. "We need to talk."

"I figured." Grady sat down next to her on the sofa. Once again it felt more like they were co-parents than just friends. "What happened in the dressing room at the last place?" he asked. "When Savannah came out she looked like she had been crying."

"Yes. I wanted to speak with you about that privately before you talked to her." Briefly, Alexis filled him in.

Grady's jaw hardened at the news of what the other little girls were saying to his daughter at school, when the teacher wasn't within earshot.

"Normally, knowing there are two sides to every story, and sometimes things can be said one way and taken another, I'd suggest you investigate more," Alexis stated. "Give the kids the benefit of the doubt. But having seen Lisa Marie and her little pals in action last night, the way they seemed to be taunting Savannah from the back seat of Kit's Jaguar, I imagined Savannah's account is all too true."

Grady looked deeply concerned, and once again way out of his league. "What do we do in a situation like this?"

Alexis tried not to focus on the "we" in his sentence. It was figurative, just an expression. She shrugged. "I was going to ask you."

"That's the hell of it." He shoved his fingers through his hair, stood and began to pace. "I don't know."

Alexis stayed seated. Savannah was Grady's child— it should be his decision. "What's your first instinct?"

"To talk to the kids' parents. In this case, though, I don't think it would do any good, since children model their parents' behavior."

And Kit Peterson was snotty to the core.

Grady stared off into the distance. "If she were a boy—"

"What would you advise?"

"That he fight back. Stand up for himself."

Alexis thought about her own counsel to turn the other cheek. "What would your late wife have said?"

"She probably would have gotten into it with Kit Peterson. Called her out and had a row. Tabitha was not one to shy away from quarrels with other women. In fact, I think there was a part of her that enjoyed those cat fights."

Interesting. It was the first time Alexis had heard Grady speak about his wife with anything other than total reverence. "Of course, the real problem is that these girls are in her class at school and she can't just avoid them."

Alexis thought about the mother-daughter tea party coming up. "Maybe you could bring this up at the meeting on Monday with the principal."

"I don't think we should involve her." He paused. "At some point, Savannah does have to learn to stand up for herself."

"Grady. She just turned five."

"So you think the fact I want to give those little girls a talking-to myself without involving Principal Jordan is not out of line?"

Alexis exhaled slowly. "Not at all." She looked up at him. "Your mom seems very capable. What would she say?"

Grady's eyes glimmered. "She always wanted us to fight our own battles, but I can remember a time or two when she stormed into a school to give someone her opinion."

Alexis rose and moved closer. "Did it help?"

"Sometimes." Grady shoved his hands in the pockets of his shorts. "Sometimes not. I always felt better knowing she was on my side, though. There's something to be said for having a parent as your staunchest defender. It makes you feel safe."

"Yes," Alexis said, remembering a time or two when her own parents had gone to bat for her. "It does."

They looked at each other, in sync once again. Grady flashed her a bemused smile and she smiled back.

"Fortunately," he said with a sigh, "kindergarten graduation is just six days away. After Thursday, she won't see those girls until the new term school starts on August first."

Not much of a break, Alexis thought. And nothing much would change to help the situation. Plus, there was the tea party at the Peterson home coming up in five days, although she figured they should hold off discussing that and just concentrate on one problem at a time.

Grady turned back to her. "What do you think we should do about the dress?"

Alexis shrugged helplessly. "I'm not sure. Savannah isn't confident she can pick anything out that's going to be bully-proof."

He leaned against the fireplace mantel with a rueful grimace. "Nice way to put it."

"I call it like I see it in instances like this," she said quietly.

Grady's eyes narrowed. "You think I should take her out of Miss Chilton's Academy, don't you?"

Yes. The sooner the better. But Alexis knew she was on dangerous terrain here—he was still a client, after all. "That's up to you, Grady. As her parent, it's your decision," she stated carefully. "I would, however, suggest that you talk to Savannah and counsel her on how you think she should deal with female bullies. Because mean girls are tough to handle, even at that age."

Grady took Alexis's hand, then, as if realizing what he was doing, released it. "You sound like you've had some experience with this."

Alexis's skin tingled from the fleeting contact. Somehow, she forced a smile, before she edged away again. She was flirting with danger, getting so personally involved with him like this.

"I was picked on a time or two, growing up."

His gaze drifted over her lazily. He, too, seemed to be struggling to hold on to the threads of the conversation. "What did you do?"

Alexis backed up even more, pretended to inspect a photo of Grady and Savannah on the bookshelf next to the fireplace. "I usually went off to hang out with the guys." She tossed him a wry look over her shoulder. "They were much easier to get along with, even when they didn't particularly like someone."

"That's true," he admitted without a grin. "When boys get in an argument with each other, they lay it all out in the open and deal with it, and it's over."

Alexis could imagine him tussling with one—or even all four—of his brothers when he was growing up. She imagined Josie and Wade had had their hands full back then.

She swallowed around the parched feeling in her throat. "So back to the dress…?" she prodded, knowing it was time to get on task once again.

He studied her as Savannah came downstairs to join them, sleepily rubbing her eyes from her nap. "I'm guessing you have an idea?" he said as he swept his daughter up into his arms.

Alexis watched Savannah lay her head on her daddy's broad shoulder. "I do."

"YOU DON'T GET TO COME in with us, Daddy," Savannah told Grady a short time later, as the three of them stood in front of a popular bridal salon in downtown Fort Worth. Looking well-rested and in a much better frame of mind after her nap, she cupped both hands around her mouth and hissed, as if it were a secret, "This place is only for *girls*."

Grady nodded as if it was news to him. "Oh," he said gravely. He turned to Alexis with mock seriousness. "How long am I supposed to get lost?"

"I think an hour should do it," she answered. "There are some bookstores and coffee shops down the block...."

Grady patted his cell phone, in the pocket of his sport shirt. "You know how to reach me. Otherwise, I'll see you ladies in an hour." He headed off.

Alexis held out her hand. Together, they went inside.

Savannah gasped in delight as she walked across the velvety red carpet. Eyes wide, she looked at the wedding gowns displayed on the mannequins, the rows of gorgeous white dresses on hangers. "These are so fancy!"

Alexis's friend Lynn Delgado appeared. Alexis had already made prior arrangements with the bridal shop proprietress, explaining the need for TLC during this sensitive dress shopping expedition. Lynn knelt before Savannah and introduced herself. "I understand you're looking for a dress for a special occasion."

Savannah nodded vehemently. "Savannah is graduating from kindergarten on Thursday," Alexis explained.

"And I don't want to be made fun of," the child said.

Lynn, who made a living soothing nervous brides and members of the wedding party, had no problem reassuring her. "Well, I promise we will find something that is absolutely perfect for you!"

"Like a fairy princess?" Savannah suggested hopefully.

"Like the little princess you are," Lynn agreed. She led Savannah and Alexis to an area full of multicolored flower girl and bridesmaid gowns. She had already pulled out three beautifully made frocks in a classic tea-length style. "What do you think?"

Savannah shyly touched the silk chiffon with breathless reverence. "It's soft," she said.

"And very comfortable," Lynn promised. "But you should find that out for yourself. Try it on. And then come back and stand on the pedestal so you can see yourself in the three-way mirror."

Savannah glanced over at a bride-to-be doing that exact thing. Still a little awestruck, the child turned to Alexis. "But you've got to try one on, too, Alexis."

Given all it had taken to get this far, Alexis wasn't about to rock the boat. She reached for one of the bridesmaid gowns. "Not that one!" Savannah protested. "A white one!"

Alexis flushed and knelt in front of her. "Sweetheart, those are wedding dresses."

"That's okay," she said enthusiastically, "you'll look real pretty."

"Sounds fun to me!" Lynn said.

And that, Alexis found, was that.

Grady paced and browsed, and got a cup of coffee he didn't particularly want. Finally, forty-five minutes had passed, and he couldn't wait another moment longer.

He had to know if things were going better for Savannah than they had this morning.

He pitched the paper cup in the recycling bin and headed back toward the bridal salon, figuring there'd be no harm in walking by and sneaking a look in the window.

As he reached the plate glass, a happy bride-to-be and her mother swept out of the shop, laughing and smiling, two gowns in tow.

Grady stopped to hold the door for them and then turned to shut it, noticing as he did so that his gallant action gave him a clear view all the way to the rear of the store, where three pedestals were located.

Standing on one was Savannah, in a pale yellow dress with a ribbon sash, perfect for her age. She was playing with a wreath of flowers on her head, looking happier than he had seen her in a long time.

On the pedestal next to her was an ethereal vision in white satin. The world slowed down. Nothing existed but this moment in time. He stood rooted in place as he gazed at the stunning beauty who had become such an evocative presence in their lives.

Chapter Ten

"I want you to put a wreath in your hair, too!" Savannah said, giggling.

"I already have a veil," Alexis protested, feeling a little silly—and a little magical—in the gorgeous off-the-shoulder, embroidered wedding gown.

"Pretty pretty *pretty* please!" Savannah jumped up and down on the pedestal next to hers. "I want us to match!"

"Then that's what you shall have, my little princess." Alexis stepped down off her pedestal. Savannah did the same. Closing the distance between them, Alexis gathered her train in both hands and bent down, in a deep curtsy. Grinning, Savannah stood on tiptoe, and with all the reverence of a flower girl assisting a bride, gently laid the wreath of flowers on top of Alexis's hastily upswept hair.

Finished, Savannah stepped back to admire her handiwork, then clapped her hands together. "Now you look really pretty!"

Silly was more like it, with a tiara and veil perched on the back half of her head, a wreath of flowers slanting down over her forehead. Still, Alexis couldn't help but laugh aloud. She had forgotten what it was like to let go of life's problems and difficulties and just do whatever made her happy.

She bent down and gathered Savannah into a heart-felt hug. "You look incredibly pretty, too, sweetheart."

"This is the dress I want to wear to my graduation," Savannah declared, "because it's the color I like the mostest."

Alexis stepped back to admire her once again. "I think that's a very good choice, Savannah. You look very pretty in yellow."

"You both look very pretty," a male voice interjected.

In unison, Savannah and Alexis turned toward the sound. Grady stood there, smiling as widely as his daughter.

Alexis blushed as she hadn't since she was a gawky teenager.

"This time we tried on dresses together!" Savannah said. "And it was way more fun, Daddy."

"I can see that," he murmured, an appreciative glimmer in his eyes.

Lynn, who'd been busy with another customer, came bustling back. "How are we doing?" she asked.

Alexis confirmed the purchase with both father and daughter, then said, "We're going to take the yellow dress for Savannah."

"Are you going to get yours, too?" the child asked.

"Not this time," she answered.

Savannah's face fell. Then she perked up. "Does this mean we get to come back and try on dresses again?"

Aware of Grady's eyes upon her, Alexis blushed all the more. "Maybe the next time you need a special dress," she allowed.

To CELEBRATE THE successful purchase of a graduation dress, they stopped by the park to let Savannah romp in the shady playground. While Alexis lounged on a bench, watching her race over climbing equipment with a group of other kids, Grady ambled off to purchase cold drinks for all of them.

He returned with three tropical slushies. Savannah ran over to take a long drink of hers, then left the icy beverage with her daddy while she returned to her new friends.

Grady dropped down beside Alexis and stretched out his legs. The look in his eyes made her flush from the inside out. "You can stop blushing now," he teased.

Alexis focused her gaze straight ahead. "You can stop looking at me as if you're still seeing me in that gown."

"Can't help it." He shrugged and glanced away. "You were gorgeous."

Alexis took a pull on the straw, enjoying the tropical fruit flavor, the crushed ice melting on her tongue. "I know I shouldn't have tried it on. I just wanted to distract Savannah, wipe out the memory of our disastrous shopping trip this morning. And I know how much she likes playing dress-up, so when she insisted I try on a gown alongside her, I said yes."

His gaze returned to hers. "You don't have to explain."

She knew that. So why was she? Why did it matter so much how Grady McCabe saw her?

His dark brows lifted slightly and one corner of his mouth turned up in that lopsided smile she found way too sexy for her own good. "I enjoyed seeing you in a wedding dress. It gave me an idea of what you must have looked like the first time around."

Not quite. "Scott and I didn't have a big wedding."

Clearly, that surprised him. And she knew why. Most self-avowed romantics like herself insisted on them. "We eloped."

"Is that what you wanted?"

Yes and no. "I really wanted to be with him," Alexis said softly.

"Why do I think there's more to this story?" he mused.

Because there was. Aware she had never talked about this with anyone, Alexis shrugged, as if it hadn't really mattered, when she knew, deep down, that it had. "He was pushing us to move in together." And at the time, she had lacked the confidence to stand up to him. "Economically, it made sense. We were both just out of college, and neither of us could afford much on our own. Together, with both of us working, we could afford a nice two bedroom apartment and two decent cars, and to start saving for a down payment on a house. And he thought eloping was the most romantic way of all to marry."

Grady's face softened. "And you went along with it to please him. Circumventing what you really wanted— a fairy-tale wedding."

Alexis sipped her drink and looked into his eyes. "It seems Savannah and I have that in common. We both love really fancy dresses."

They fell into a thoughtful silence once more.

"Any regrets?" Grady asked, gauging her reaction.

Alexis shook her head. "I've always believed that things work out the way they should. Forgoing the big wedding gave us another year of marriage. I thought about that a lot as Scott battled leukemia."

"Next time," Grady said quietly, with understanding reflected in his deep blue eyes, "maybe you'll get what you want."

"I will," Alexis said. Or she wouldn't marry. She turned toward him, her knee nudging his thigh slightly in the process. "What about you?" she asked, shifting slightly on the bench, so they were no longer touching. "Did you and Tabitha have a formal wedding?"

Grady nodded, and waved at Savannah, who was still happily monkeying around on the climbing gym. "We married here in Fort Worth."

Alexis regarded him curiously. "Was it everything you wanted?"

"Except for the location." He shrugged. "I would have preferred having it in my hometown, but I deferred to her wishes."

Alexis appreciated his gallantry. "Seems you and I have that in common." A habit of putting others before themselves....

"As well as something else," Grady said.

She shot him a baffled look.

"When I saw you in that dress today, laughing and hugging Savannah, I realized it's not just my little girl who wants me to be married again," Grady explained. "I want that, too."

ALEXIS SWALLOWED, not sure she'd heard right. "You're serious?" she said, when at last she could speak again.

Grady nodded. He waved at Savannah, who was now sitting atop the fort-style play gym, talking to two other little girls and a boy. Although they had never met before, they seemed to be having a good time.

His expression sober, Grady continued, "It made me think how much Savannah and I have both enjoyed having you with us this last week, helping with homework and dinner and bedtime and dress shopping. I realized how much we would be shortchanging ourselves if I married someone under the guidelines I originally set up with your matchmaking service."

At last he had come to his senses! Alexis thought jubilantly, aware how much easier that would make her job, professionally speaking. Emotionally was another matter. It was going to be tough for her to watch him fall in love with someone else. Harder still to watch another woman step into the intimate day-to-day activity of Grady and Savannah's lives. And yet she knew he would be so much better off if he let himself be loved again, so she had to be happy about that.

Determined to do the right thing and help make that happen, she forced herself to be the premiere matchmaker he had hired. "So you want to change your requirements in a potential spouse? Redo your profile and questionnaires and video interview?"

"Not necessarily," he said, with that Difficult Man note in his tone again.

Her emotions awhirl, Alexis tightened her grip on the drink clutched in her hands. "Well, I guess I can just interview you about what you want in a wife, and make the adjustments myself." It wasn't the usual procedure, but then what about her relationship with Grady had been ordinary thus far?

He turned toward her and draped his arm along the back of the park bench behind her. "To tell you the truth, I'd like to bypass the process altogether and just go with what I know, what has been proven to work."

She studied him, more confused than ever.

"I'd like," Grady said, "to go with you."

OKAY, GRADY THOUGHT, that hadn't come out right. But maybe there was no correct way to say it.

As the meaning of his words sank in, Alexis's mouth dropped open. Then slammed shut.

He held up a hand before she could jump to the wrong conclusion. "Obviously, that's not going to work," he admitted. "You want someone who still has all the hearts and flowers stuff in him." The kind of guy who would give her that big wedding and enjoy every second of it.

She squirmed uncomfortably.

Afraid she would bolt, given half a chance, he reached over and laid his hand on her arm. "And I want a woman who's not going to ask me to pretend to have stars in my eyes anymore," he said practically. "Unfortunately, there's no way to fix that." He dropped his voice a notch, regretting that he didn't have half her optimism where his personal life was concerned.

"And that's a shame, because we get along really well in every other way." So well that he wanted nothing more than to make love to her again—without restraint this time.

"Savannah adores you," he added, "and I can see you adore her, too."

As if unable to argue with any of that, Alexis looked away. Guilt flooded Grady when he saw the sentimental glimmer in her eyes. This was exactly why he needed to stay away from her.

He forced himself to continue. "But one good thing has come out of this."

She turned back to him, and Grady lifted his hand from her arm. "The three of us have the start of a beautiful friendship. The kind that can last a lifetime. And I want it to last a lifetime, Alexis." He wanted her to know he could always be there for her, even though as yet she'd let him do precious little for her.

For a second, she looked as if they had been dating and he had just tried to break up with her. Which was kind of funny, because it was starting to feel that way to him, too. Again, not what he intended...

Then she shook her head, moved slightly away from him and visibly pulled herself together. Which was good, because he needed things to be friendly and platonic between them. In an attempt to lighten the mood, which had gotten way too serious, he teased, "If we could just clone you..."

She flashed him a feisty smile. "Or make a few slight adjustments and clone you."

He couldn't help it—he laughed.

"But," he drawled, while Alexis made a great show of sighing, "since that is out of the question, at least for now, back to finding me a wife who will accept my limitations."

Alexis plucked her BlackBerry out of her purse. "You want to start looking right away?"

Grady thought about it. Although he had realized today he wanted to be married again, the thought of spending time with another woman besides Alexis just did not appeal. "No," he said firmly. "That's going to have to wait until after the Fourth of July Day holiday."

Alexis squared her shoulders, as if preparing to do

battle. "So we're talking two weeks from now?" she inquired crisply.

Grady nodded, apprehensive that in trying to be as honest as possible with her, he had nonetheless taken a grave misstep. "At the very least."

ALEXIS WAS IN THE OFFICE Sunday afternoon, filling out her time card for the previous week, when her boss walked in. "You've been logging a lot of hours lately," she noted. "How's it going with Grady McCabe?"

Alexis rocked back in her chair. "He decided yesterday he's no longer just looking for a mommy for his little girl. He wants to be married."

"Hmm. That's good." Holly Anne pulled up a chair. "Isn't it?" she asked, studying Alexis.

Doing her best to put aside her own tumultuous emotions, she picked up a pen and rapped it on the top of her desk. "I haven't a clue."

Holly Anne ran a hand through her dark hair. "What's the problem?"

"I just…" Alexis sighed and plucked at the crease on her cotton capris. "I don't know that I can please this guy."

Her boss shrugged. "You've had difficult clients before. What's different this time?"

I think I might be falling in love with him. Once again, Alexis pushed the unwanted emotion away. She had bills to pay, a promotion to earn. She had to get a grip. "Nothing, I suppose, except… He's been so determined not to get hurt again that he hasn't dated anyone since his wife died, five years ago. If he's on the rebound, it might be impossible to find a match for him that will last."

"So if we do match Grady McCabe and it doesn't work out…" Holly Anne theorized, quickly seeing the business implications of that. Alexis had already had one socially prominent couple that she'd matched— Russ and Carolyn Bass—file for divorce this month.

"I don't want to fail," Alexis said. *For more reasons than I can count.* "I don't want to put his daughter through that. Raise her hopes that she'd finally get the mommy she wants, only to have it all fall apart in the end. I think that might be devastating for Savannah." Almost as hurtful as it had been for Alexis herself, the previous day, when Grady told her he had decided he wanted a full relationship with a woman again—just, for obvious reasons, not with her.

Alexis's boss shrugged again. "I see your point regarding his daughter, but I still think you can do it."

Nothing like a little pressure.

"When is his next match supposed to take place?"

Alexis stood and went over to her bookshelves, pretending to look for something. "He doesn't want to set anything up for two weeks."

"And in the meantime?"

She picked up a stack of client videos and returned to her desk, facing her boss again. "He still wants me spending time with him and his daughter. He thinks the better I know them, the better a match I'll eventually make for them."

"I'm not certain that's necessary," Holly Anne said. Assured everything was under control, she was already on her way out. She tossed her parting words over her shoulder. "But as long as you're billing him for your time, and he's paying, who are we to quarrel?"

Who indeed? Alexis wondered.

In the meantime, she would concentrate on her other clients, while she did her best to be pals with Grady and Savannah, but nothing more.

"THANKS FOR GOING to this meeting with me," Grady told Alexis, as they walked into the lobby of Miss Chilton's Academy Monday morning.

"Happy to do it," Alexis murmured. She didn't want to see Savannah treated unfairly any more than Grady did. And it quickly became clear, as the closed-door session began, that was exactly what the headmistress had in mind.

"Before we start—I'm curious." Principal Jordan eyed Alexis with obvious disdain. "Why did you bring your matchmaker to this meeting, Mr. McCabe?"

"Ms. Graham is also a family friend. She's been working with Savannah on her homework issues and, I'm happy to report, it's no longer the problem it was for a while. Savannah sits right down every day and does her work in five or ten minutes, and puts it in her backpack."

"I'm glad to hear she is behaving responsibly." Principal Jordan paused. "However, as you know, that is not the only difficulty we have had with your daughter this spring. She's still having quite a bit of trouble socially."

Grady's jaw set. "Are we referring to the way the other little girls are picking on her?"

Briefly taken aback by his blunt assessment of the situation, the administrator responded, "We're referring to her apparent inability to hold her own in a convivial setting. Which is why we still think it would be wise for Savannah not to graduate with her classmates on Thursday afternoon, and instead repeat her kinder-garten year."

Silence fell.

"You've got to be kidding," Grady said finally.

Principal Jordan shook her head. "Quite the con-trary."

"There's no way I'm going to agree to this," Grady stated, his expression grim. "She has done all the work, and earned the right to move on to first grade, along with all her friends."

Alexis admired the way he stood up for his daughter. It was exactly what she would have done.

"That's the problem," the principal admitted with ob-vious discomfort. "Savannah doesn't have many friends in her class. We were hoping—the other teachers and I—that it would be different next year."

"How? Can you guarantee there will be kinder, more empathetic girls in her class? Or just more of the same, tormenting her over her lack of a mother?"

The administrator leaned across her desk. "I would thank you," she said tightly, "not to refer to our stu-dents that way."

Grady stood, a muscle working in his jaw. "I paid twenty thousand dollars in tuition for Savannah to at-tend kindergarten at her mother's alma mater. She has attended school regularly and done the work. She will graduate with her peers and be promoted to first grade, along with everyone else in her class."

Principal Jordan stared at Grady. "Very well. Sa-vannah will be promoted—with reservation—and can attend her graduation on Thursday, along with all her peers. But I must warn you, Mr. McCabe. Should her problems with Lisa Marie Peterson and some of the other little girls *continue* next autumn, we will revisit this issue. And if necessary, move Savannah back to kindergarten then."

So *that's* what was going on here, Alexis thought angrily. Kit Peterson was behind this! She'd had a feeling ever since Kit showed up at the house on Friday that she had something up her sleeve.

Grady took a moment to absorb the thinly veiled threat, then stated in a low, implacable tone, "It won't be an issue when the new school term starts."

Alexis believed him. She just didn't know what his next move was going to be.

She followed Grady out the door, and together they left the school and headed across the parking lot toward his SUV. Grady opened the passenger door for her. "I shouldn't have lost my temper in there," he said, starting the engine a moment later.

Alexis fastened her safety belt. "You had every right to be disgusted. I certainly was."

Grady looked at her. "Well, now we know why they brought cupcakes for Savannah Friday evening."

"And were giggling and making fun of her that way."

Stopping at a traffic light, Grady turned to Alexis. "Why would they want Savannah out so badly?"

Noting he was hurting for his daughter, as much as Alexis was, she tried to explain. "She's very pretty and smart. Maybe too nice to be in a cutthroat environment like that. Unless…"

"What?"

She had to say it. "You want her turning into a mean girl, too."

"Hell, no." Grady's jaw set as he drove on.

"Well, then, it looks like you're going to have to do

something about it. Either take on Kit and her daughter's entourage and make them all behave, or move Savannah out of there and put her in another school."

They reached his driveway, where Alexis had left her car. "Do you have time to come inside for a moment?" he asked, his expression pensive.

Alexis glanced at her watch. Her first appointment with a new client was not for another hour and twenty minutes. "Sure."

"I'm going to have to find another private school for Savannah," he said, leading the way into his study and switching on his computer. "I was hoping you'd help me look for a good match. On the clock, of course."

His mention of money sent her spirits into a nose-dive. Alexis had to work to keep from showing her hurt. "Of course. And here I thought I was just put on this earth to help people find love."

The sarcasm in her voice caught his attention. "Very funny." He motioned for her to have a seat at his desk. "Seriously, it's going to be difficult, at this late date, to find a spot for her this fall."

Alexis slipped into his swivel chair. It felt oddly in-timate, sitting where he usually did. She lifted her face to his. "If you don't mind my asking…what's wrong with public school?" She didn't let the hesitant look on Grady's face keep her from speaking her mind. "I went there," she continued. "You went there. We both had good experiences. Why does it have to be private?"

Grady sat down on the edge of his desk, facing her. "Why indeed?" he murmured. "You're right that I should consider it. Whenever I take Savannah to the playground—or anywhere there are kids from varied backgrounds—she does great. It's only when I stick her with a bunch of little blue bloods that the atmosphere becomes intense."

Alexis rebuked him with a look. "Well, I don't think we should discount all rich kids, as a rule. I mean, you come from wealth, Grady, and you turned out pretty great."

He flashed her a sexy grin. "You think so?"

She caught the look in his eyes. Hitched in a breath at the warm intimacy beckoning her near. Aware that she was way too close to falling head over heels in love with him as it was, she reminded herself that Grady was not interested in letting anyone into his heart again, even if he did want to marry. As for her, she needed much more than a simple legal commitment from a man to say "I Do" to him.

But from the determined look in his eyes, he clearly had his mind made up.

Grady wrapped one hand around her wrist, pulled her up out of his chair, and reeled her in to his side. Caught off balance, she crashed into him, her body rubbing against his. He clamped an arm around her waist, holding her close, then reached up to tuck a strand of hair behind her ear. She trembled as he stared soulfully into her eyes. "Have I told you," he asked softly, "just how fantastic you've been the last couple of weeks?"

A ripple of need swept through her, followed swiftly by a wave of feelings she could not deny. "Grady…"

"Just one kiss, Alexis," he murmured tenderly, his lips shifting toward hers. "Just one…simple…kiss. What can that hurt?"

Chapter Eleven

What one kiss could hurt, Alexis knew, was her ability to go on being this close to Grady without losing her head and her heart. Spellbound, she closed her eyes as his mouth captured hers, and then all was lost in the taste and touch and feel of him.

He was so big and blatantly male. His kiss so incredibly tender and sweet. A sigh rippled through her. She lifted her arms to encircle his neck, burying her fingers in the thick strands of his hair. Giving back even as she took, she pressed forward, meeting him kiss for kiss.

Heat swept through her. Her knees wobbled with the effort it took to remain upright. The next thing she knew, he'd swung her up into his arms and was heading for the stairs.

She didn't have to ask where he was going.

She knew.

She didn't have to ask if this time they had what they needed.

She was certain that would be the case, even before he stopped to grab the box from his top bureau drawer.

Alexis had never been in his bedroom before. The furniture was heavy and masculine, the king-size bed large enough to accommodate both of them, no matter how they wanted to lie.

Legs quivering, she sat down on the taupe paisley sheets. Watched as Grady took off his coat, tie and shirt.

She'd seen him naked before. She already knew what a tremendous body he had. His shoulders were broad, his chest muscles defined, his pectorals covered with crisp, dark hair that arrowed down to the waistband of his trousers. He dispensed with those, too. Clad only in a pair of gray jersey boxer briefs that left very little to the imagination, he knelt in front of her, like a knight paying homage to a queen.

"Tell me this is what you want," he said.

Heaven help her.

"This is what I want," she agreed breathlessly.

He smiled and used his hands to part her knees. Her skirt slid up past her thighs. It was too hot to wear panty hose, so all that stood between her and what he wanted was a thin scrap of lace.

Smiling, he kissed his way from knee to inner thigh, then stood and guided her to her feet.

Their gazes locked.

He unbuttoned her suit jacket, drew it off her arms, laid it gently aside. Her lace-edged camisole came next. Then her skirt. He tugged her to him once again, one hand flattened across her spine, the other threaded in her hair. He tilted her head back, and their lips met in an explosion of pent-up heat and need.

Alexis heard the groan in the back of her throat as if from a distance. Felt the hardness of his muscles and crisp chest hair teasing the taut tips of her breasts. Lower still, there was a burgeoning pressure and heat. Dampness flowed between her thighs. She held on to his shoulders, on to him, unable to stop the sway of her body, the flood of need.

He kissed her with a sure sweet deliberation that reminded her of everything that had been missing from her life, for so very long. Feeling as if she had come home at long last, she returned his kiss with everything she had. The brisk masculine fragrance of his cologne and the soapy clean scent of his skin filled her senses. She recalled how it had felt before, when they'd brought each other to climax, and couldn't help but want to experience the pleasure of it again—this time, with Grady buried deep inside her.

She whimpered as his fingertips played over her nipples, turning them to tight aching buds. And again, when he followed the path with his mouth, lips and tongue.

Still holding her against him, he dropped once again to his knees, this time taking off the single scrap of cloth that covered her. Grasping her hips, he buried his face in the softness of her body. He caressed the slope of her abdomen gently, ran a hand between her thighs. She cried out, feeling heat spreading through her in undulating waves, as he loved her. "Oh, Grady." She trembled helplessly as the obsession to be one with him grew ever stronger. "Not...yet..." Needing to give as well as receive, she pushed away and reached for the protection he'd provided. "Not without you."

He grinned.

Together, they removed his shorts and lay on his bed. Blushing, Alexis struggled with the wrapper, and oh so tenderly and carefully slid the condom on. Caressing him with her hands, she straddled his hips, then slowly lowered herself until they became one.

Grady groaned and grasped her waist, drawing her into an even deeper union. Then his fingers were trailing over her body, finding every responsive area, until need overwhelmed her and pleasure skyrocketed. She cried out, self-control evaporating, and the next thing she knew she was beneath him once again, euphoria flowing through her. His hard, hot body was draped over hers, and they were moving together in unison.

His hands slid beneath her. With a low moan, he lifted her higher still, possessing her fiercely. Surrendering willingly, she arched into him. Raw need gripped them both as they crested together, washed by wave after wave of sensation. Afterward, hearts pounding in unison, they slid slowly back down, into the most wonderful peace she had ever experienced in her life. And in that moment, Alexis knew there was no question about it. She was in love with Grady McCabe and always would be.

GRADY GENTLY disengaged their bodies and rolled to his side, bringing Alexis with him. Part of him couldn't believe that had just happened. The rest of him knew it had been inevitable from the start.

He hadn't been looking to fall in love. Still wasn't. Hadn't been looking to make love without any sort of commitment, either. He wasn't impulsive. He thought things through. Weighed consequences first, acted only once he knew what the stakes were, what the outcome would be. But this was different. When he was with Alexis, nothing mattered but the present moment. He felt connected to her in a very fundamental way.

She shifted, shuddered. He saw her studying him thoughtfully. Maybe even regretfully. Grady took a deep breath. Yes, the days ahead would be tricky, but together they could navigate them, if they worked together. "We don't have to figure out everything today," he murmured.

"You say that as if there is more to this than just… this," she replied.

He caught her arm before she could leave the bed, and forced himself to be ruthlessly honest. "There is," he said quietly. She was always in his thoughts. When he wasn't with her, he would find himself wondering just how long it would be before he saw her again. And since the first time they had ended up in bed, he had known they would find a way to be together again.

Apprehension laced her low tone. "I don't see how."

He paused, still struggling with his emotions. "Exactly why we shouldn't talk about it just yet," he said.

"Because we want such radically different things?"

Because he didn't want to misstep. He touched a hand to her hair, burying his fingers in the silky softness. "Because where there's a will there's a way, Alexis." He drew a long breath and looked deep into her eyes. "And what I want more than anything is you. Right here, right now, with me."

Confusion warred with the quiet deliberation on her face. "Grady…"

"We'll work it out eventually," he promised. They had to. She was the one—the only woman for him. The only mother for Savannah. Somehow, he would figure out a way to give Alexis everything she needed, to bring her all the way into their lives.

His mouth crooked up in an affectionate smile. But for now, there were more pressing needs. The desire heating their skin. The gentle give of her body that said

she had been just as long without intimacy and fulfillment as him. Between the two of them, they had a lot
of pent-up sexual energy. It was past time they put it to
good use, because there was no way they were letting
anything this good go.

Determined to make her see how great things could
be if she would only put her reservations aside, he
shifted so she was beneath him once more. Their eyes
met. Her hands came up to clasp his shoulders and her
breathing grew uneven. Slowly, deliberately, he lowered
his mouth and fused his lips to hers. She ran her fingers
through his hair, across his shoulders, down the center of his back. He felt her body soften as he began to
explore her breasts. And knew that, no question, they
were meant to be together.

This time, when the last shuddering spasm had
passed, they clung together. Silent and content, they
made no effort to sever the physical and emotional intimacy that had been missing for so long from both
their lives.

ALEXIS WOKE TO THE late morning silence of Grady's
house and the faraway sound of a cell phone ringing.
A glance at her watch told her the time. She had slept
through her eleven-thirty appointment with a new client!

She leaped from the bed, wrapped a sheet around
herself and raced down the stairs. After checking the
message and her cell phone, she swiftly dialed the office. Martha, the office receptionist, whispered, "Where
are you? Holly Anne is furious! Zoe Borden asked for
you personally and has waited almost a week for you

to work her in—and not very patiently, I might add—and then you're a no-show?"

"I was unavoidably detained," Alexis said with as much coolness as she could muster, which wasn't a whole lot under the circumstances. She had never been this irresponsible in her life! Getting emotionally involved with a client, sleeping with him, and then missing an appointment! What was next in her long litany of mistakes? Aware that Grady had come up behind her, clad only in his boxer briefs, Alexis turned away so she could continue to concentrate on her conversation, instead of how great he looked. "Were you able to reschedule?"

"Are you kidding?" Martha yelped. "I thought she was going to blow a gasket!"

Alexis could imagine it hadn't been pleasant. Zoe Borden was Kit Peterson's friend—the one who had wanted to be fixed up with Grady. Alexis had tried to avoid taking her on as a client, to no avail. Zoe was very wealthy and accustomed to getting what she wanted, when she wanted it. Because the customer was always right at ForeverLove.com, her wishes had prevailed.

"Holly Anne is meeting with her now. You better get here as soon as possible."

"I will. Thanks, Martha."

Alexis ended the call. Clasping the sheet around her with one arm, lifting the hem with both hands, she headed back for the stairs.

Grady followed, looking disappointed that their interlude was coming swiftly to an end. "Problem?"

"You could say that." Briefly, Alexis explained, as she rushed into the bedroom and began gathering up her clothes. What a mess. A glance in the mirror confirmed her worst suspicions: she looked like she'd spent the morning making love. Her hair was tousled, her lipstick all kissed off. Her skin radiating a postcoital glow. Holly Anne would take one look at her and know this delay had not been strictly business.

"How can I help?" he asked.

Alexis grimaced. "You can't."

They exchanged another tension-filled glance, then he went downstairs to check his own messages. Alexis finished dressing, and slipped out while he was still on the phone.

She had no choice but to stop by her apartment for a quick shower on the way to the office. When she arrived, Zoe Borden was still in with Holly Anne.

Alexis gathered her resolve, knocked, and strode on in.

Holly Anne made the introductions, adding compassionately, "Zoe has just weathered her second divorce."

And had responded, Alexis observed, by having a little "freshening" done, with mixed results. The woman's face still had the telltale puffiness and immovable quality commensurate with recent Botox. Her perfectly taut body appeared to have been enhanced by a tummy tuck and breast lift. Who knew what it looked like beneath her clothes?

Showing no evidence of the irritation Alexis knew her boss must feel, Holly Anne continued, "She'd heard that Grady McCabe was looking for a wife."

Zoe radiated cougarlike determination. "I'd like to be matched with him," she stated firmly.

"I've explained that's not how it works," Holly Anne interjected.

"But I already know Grady McCabe is exactly what I want in a man!" Zoe said petulantly.

Me, too, Alexis thought ruefully. With the exception of one tiny roadblock. As far as she could tell, Grady was still not ready to fall in love.

"There's no point in matching me with anyone else!" Zoe continued, sounding ever more agitated.

"First of all," Alexis soothed, with the most comforting smile she could conjure up, "you haven't seen any of the other candidates we might be able to match you with. We have dozens of eligible, successful, wealthy men in our database who are also looking for love, companionship and someone to build a future with. You would be limiting yourself terribly if you don't allow us to show you who all is out there, before you make up your mind."

As Alexis suspected, the ka-ching of the cash register resonated with this particular client. "Well…" Zoe hesitated. "I suppose…"

Alexis slipped into the mode that had made her one of the best matchmakers of the company. For every money-minded client like Zoe, there was a money-minded man. "Let me take you to my office and we'll get you set up with the personality questionnaires and wish lists, so we can figure out together who your dream man might be…."

An hour later, Zoe left the building with high hopes and a much more open mind. Directly after that, Holly Anne walked into Alexis's office and shut the door behind her.

Time for the mud to hit the fan.

"I think I deserve an explanation," she announced grimly.

Alexis flushed guiltily. "I'm sorry." She hesitated, not sure where to begin.

Holly Anne's eyes narrowed. "I assume your absence this morning had to do with Grady McCabe?"

"He's proved to be a very demanding client," she said finally. "So demanding, in fact, that you and I need to talk."

"WHAT'S THE MATTER, pumpkin?" Grady asked Savannah when he picked her up from her after-school program that afternoon. He knew it couldn't be homework. The last take-home assignment had been given the previous Friday.

His daughter slumped dispiritedly in her seat. "Everybody else has *two* dresses. One for the graduation, and the other for the tea party at Lisa Marie's house. I only have *one*."

Uh-oh, Grady thought. *Crisis.* "So what should we do?" he asked calmly. "Go shopping again?"

A glance in the rearview mirror showed his suggestion had gone over well.

Savannah sat up straight, smiling now. "Can we go with Alexis?"

Good question. He had left messages on Alexis's cell, home and office voice mail, but she had yet to return his calls. He hadn't spoken to her since she had slipped out of his house this morning. Not about to make a promise he couldn't keep, he said, "I think she's working late tonight. I could take you, though."

His offer was followed by silence.

Grady hazarded another glance in the mirror. Savannah's eyes met his and she gave him a soulful look, the one that always came up when the topic of her not having a mommy came up. She sighed.

"Been there, done that, hmm?" Grady mused, when they stopped at a traffic light. Another glance showed tears trembling on his daughter's lashes.

As soon as he could, Grady pulled the car over into a parking lot and put the engine in Park. He unfastened his seat belt and turned around to face his daughter. "Is anything else wrong?" he asked gently. Had Savannah heard about his private meeting with Principal Jordan that morning? Had someone told her there was pressure to hold her back a grade? If so, he thought grimly, there would be hell to pay.

Savannah turned an accusing glance his way. "Everybody else has been drinking tea and eating little sandwiches, too. And *practicing,* Daddy."

It took a moment to decipher that. "You mean they've been going to tea?"

Savannah nodded vigorously. "At a hotel."

Talk about keeping up with the Joneses! This was getting ridiculous, he thought, a little disgruntled. On the other hand, he did not want to withhold anything he could easily provide his little girl when her self-esteem and self-confidence were already shaky.

Fortunately, Grady thought, he'd have her out of this quagmire of snobbery and bad behavior soon, but until then he had a job to do. "Let me make a call. I'll see if I can figure out a good place to go."

Grady punched in a number on his speed dial. Once again, he got the voice mail for Alexis's cell. He dialed her office. Martha, the receptionist, picked up. "Grady McCabe, calling for Alexis Graham."

"Oh, hello, Mr. McCabe! Alexis said you might call.

She's in a meeting. She wanted to let you know she won't be stopping by this evening. She left a message to that effect on your home phone."

She'd known he'd been at the office.

Not sure how to decipher that, Grady figured he'd find out later. He thanked Martha and cut the connection. "Looks like we're on our own tonight, pumpkin."

Grady wasn't surprised to discover Savannah wasn't any happier about that than he was.

AS THE HOURS WORE ON, Alexis's Monday went from bad to worse. She was assigned three new clients, all of them difficult personalities. The temperature in Fort Worth topped one hundred ten degrees, and the window unit in her apartment, which had been acting a little off lately, took that moment to decide to blow out nothing but hot air.

She was standing in front of it in a cotton skirt and lace-edged camisole, trying to decide if it was broken or just unable to handle the extreme heat, when a knock sounded on her door.

Already exhausted and stressed out, she walked over, peered through the viewer and saw Grady standing in the hall. He looked really ticked off. She opened the door. "Grady?"

"Just when?" he growled, shouldering past her, "were you going to tell me?"

Chapter Twelve

"Tell you what?" Alexis asked, ushering him inside.

Grady looked around, as if noticing the stifling heat inside her apartment, but didn't comment on it. He turned his intent blue eyes to hers and clarified, "That you asked your boss to assign another matchmaker to me!"

Doing her best to quell her racing pulse, she moved around him to shut the door. "You spoke to Holly Anne?"

"She telephoned me this evening." Grady's voice was calm. His emotions clearly were not. "She wanted to be sure I was okay with it."

Alexis wished she could do something about the moisture gathering between her breasts. It was beginning to seep through her camisole. And worse, Grady had noticed.

She edged toward the stream of air blowing out of her air conditioner and stood with her back to it, figuring a hot breeze was better than no breeze. Discreetly, she plucked at the fabric of her camisole, pulling it away from her moist tummy. "And were you?"

"Actually, no." Looking uncomfortably warm in his stone-colored dress slacks and starched, pale blue shirt, even though the top button was undone and the sleeves rolled up to his elbows, Grady moved toward the unit, too. "I told her I didn't want to work with anyone but you."

Alexis shifted so Grady could stand in front of what circulating air there was.

"And Holly Anne told you it was out of the question," she guessed, wishing her boss had given her a heads-up, so she would have been prepared for this confrontation tonight. She had hoped to put it off until she figured out what to say—and when to say it—knowing all the while there would never be a good time to tell Grady she was ditching him as a client.

"She said you felt someone else would do a better job." Displeasure filled his voice. "Why didn't you tell me you were going to do that?"

Alexis shrugged, and tried not to think about kissing him. "Because I thought you might try to talk me out of it."

Perspiration beaded on his face. "You would have been right."

Alexis felt her own skin dampening, too. She stepped closer, trying to adopt a practical tone as she said, "Grady, surely you can see, after what happened this morning, that I'm the wrong person to be trying to set you up with someone else."

He regarded her with the steady resolve she'd come to expect. "I don't want to be with anyone else."

A thrill shot through her at his matter-of-fact determination. "Only because you got involved with me," she countered, with the same resolve he was showing. "It still doesn't solve your problem—the lack of a mother in Savannah's life." *Or a woman you can love with all your heart and soul—in yours.*

Grady took her in his arms. "I've come to the conclusion, as has my daughter, that she doesn't need just any woman. She needs you. And so," he murmured fervently, "do I."

Before Alexis could answer, his lips captured hers. Everything she had been trying so hard to forget was suddenly at the center of her world. No one had ever kissed her as tenderly as he did, as if he cherished everything about her and wanted to experience even more. No one had ever brought forth such a wellspring of need, passion, and yes, love. When Grady pressed her against him, and made her feel as if the two of them were a perfect fit, it was all she could do to control the raging lust and soul deep yearning that blazed inside her. She wanted to be part of his life. His future. His present. She wanted to take what they had and use it as a foundation to build a love that would endure forever. She wanted to be singed by the hard muscles of his body, and filled with the most intimate part of him.

But making love with him meant being vulnerable. And she wasn't sure it was wise to feel that way tonight....

Shakily, they drew apart.

Alexis splayed her hands across his chest, forcing some distance between them. "This is what always gets us into trouble."

Grady lovingly stroked a hand through her hair. If he had any misgivings, he was not showing them, she noted.

He rubbed his thumb across her damp lower lip. "I like this kind of trouble."

So did she, on some level.

On another, more practical one, she knew she had to retain some perspective. Otherwise heartache lay ahead, and it wouldn't be just her heart that would be broken. Savannah could end up devastated, too, and what hurt Grady's child hurt him.

Still struggling to regain her composure, Alexis went to the refrigerator and got out a pitcher of water flavored with fresh mint leaves.

Grady studied her as she put ice into two glasses and then filled them to the rim. He seemed to know intuitively there was another reason why she hadn't contacted him. "What aren't you telling me?" he asked after a moment, accepting the beverage she handed him. "What else was said between you and Holly Anne?"

Alexis sat down at the café table, relieved to be able to talk about work. "A lot, actually. She's right to be very disappointed in me. You're a big client, with a lot of money and the McCabe name, not to mention being one of the movers and shakers in this city. She expected me to make a match for you that would dazzle everyone and make you very happy."

Taking a seat opposite her, Grady favored her with a lopsided grin. "Who says you haven't?"

She refused to let him distract her; he had done that far too often as it was. "I should have been focused on my job." *Instead of how attracted I am to you.* Pressing the cold glass against her forehead, to bring down the heat, she continued her litany of regrets. "I forgot what my goal as your matchmaker was, and got personally involved with you and your daughter. I ended up billing for time spent helping Savannah with her homework!"

"At my request," Grady argued, shifting his big

frame in the small chair. "To help you get to know Savannah, so you would know what kind of woman she needed in her life."

It didn't matter that she had gotten her boss's approval prior to caving to Grady's request. Alexis had known on a gut level it was the wrong thing to do, professionally, but she had acquiesced because she'd wanted to spend time with Grady and Savannah. Because being with them made her feel like part of a family again. And she had needed that more than she wanted to admit—to the point she knew her judgment was hopelessly skewed, in his favor. For both their sakes, she needed to reassert her boundaries. She took a long sip of her mint-flavored ice water. Was it roasting in here or what? "Grady, I'm not a tutor."

"I agree." He drained his glass and went back to the fridge to retrieve the water. Returning, he poured them each another glass, put the pitcher on the table and sat down again. "You're more in the class of miracle worker, where Savannah is concerned. Do you know how happy you've made her and me, just being with us and resolving problems?"

As happy as it made me, taking on the mommy role? Alexis thought pensively. She sat back and rubbed at the tense spot in her neck. "But I'm not her mother, Grady. I never volunteered to be."

He studied her quietly, looking every bit as hot and uncomfortable as she felt.

"I'm not your girlfriend. I'm barely a family friend."

Grady continued to gaze at her in silence. She had the impression he wanted to argue with her about all of that. Instead, he inquired, "What does all this have to do with your job?"

Alexis let her hand drop back to her lap. "In failing you and Savannah I severely damaged my chances to run the Galveston office."

There went the promotion, the pay raise that would have quickly paid off her medical debts, the move that would have helped her start a new life. A new beginning without the reminders of the husband she had lost, and the temptation of Grady and Savannah nearby. Because as much as she loved them—and she did, Alexis realized—Grady did not love her the way he should love a woman he intended to make his wife. And she could not pretend that didn't matter to her. It did. She just wasn't sure it was enough of a deterrent to keep her from seeing Grady and Savannah again.

Had she been wrong all this time? Was getting everything she wanted from her personal life—*except* romantic love—better than being alone?

Alexis's mind told her no. Her heart felt otherwise whenever she spent time with Grady.

He reached across the table and took her hand. "You shouldn't be held accountable for my actions."

Alexis tried not to notice how good her palm felt wrapped in his. She swallowed and forced herself to look him in the eye. "My boss has every right to be unhappy with me at present. I should have been focused on business when I was working with you. I should have looked at the big picture for the Fort Worth office and thought about what my success with you could mean in jump-starting the Galveston operation. Instead..." Alexis sighed. "I lost sight of all of that, Grady, to the point Holly Anne now questions how much I want to relocate."

"How much *do* you want to relocate?" Grady asked.

That, Alexis thought, was the million dollar question. For both their sakes she forced herself to tell him what was in her heart. "I don't know." Briefly, she looked down at their hands, luxuriating in the warmth and strength of his grip. "I thought it would be a fresh start for me. A way to move ahead and put the past behind me. Now, it almost seems like I'd be running away."

From something I never should have allowed myself to get so tangled up in.

She shrugged, withdrew her hand and sat back in her chair. "I'm not sure I want to do that." Restless, she stood and walked back over to the air-conditioning unit, which was now blowing out a lot less hot air than before, although the control was still set on high.

Grady ambled after her. "I know what you mean. I've been having a few doubts myself lately."

At the mention of the word *doubts,* Alexis felt herself tense. She swung back around. "In what way?"

"This process of finding someone through a third party isn't right for me." His expression sobered. "I think part of me knew that going in—I just didn't want to admit it."

Alexis didn't know whether to feel elated or worried. "Then why did you sign up with ForeverLove.com?" she asked, before she could stop herself.

"Because Savannah needed a mommy. Still does," Grady told her seriously. "And I didn't want to go through the ups and downs of dating and all that to find her one, when I had no expectation of falling in love."

His words felt like a jab to her heart. Alexis struggled to be as professional as she should have been all along. "If I had found the right woman for you to date,

I could have changed all that," she said as her AC unit made a weird crunching noise.

Grady's lips twisted ruefully. He looked past her to the poorly functioning cooling agent. "I'm not so sure. In any case," he added pragmatically, "it wasn't your fault we struck out on that score—I was an uncooperative client."

Wasn't that the understatement of the decade! Alexis began to pace, afraid if she stood next to him for much longer they would end up kissing again. "Plenty of clients are uncooperative, Grady." She went over to her hanging clothes rack, in search of cooler clothing. "In fact, when it comes to finding love via a matchmaker, I'd say that's pretty much the norm."

He watched her sort through the racks of casual clothing. "It doesn't matter. Like I said, you shouldn't be penalized for my indecision. If you want that job and the promotion that goes with it, I'll move heaven and earth to get it for you."

Alexis whirled around, not sure whether to be horrified by the possibility or amused by his offer of assistance. "You would, wouldn't you?" she observed wryly.

"All that and more," he promised. "I owe you, Alexis. For bringing me back to life."

Another ripple of longing swept through her. Alexis took another step back, banging into a row of shirts on hangers. "I don't want you to owe me."

He closed the distance between them in three long, lazy strides.

"I don't want us to be on the clock." She gulped as he ran his hands up and down her bare arms. She trembled, asserting, "If we ever make love again—"

"We will," he said emphatically, as sure about that as she secretly was.

"I want it to be…" Alexis searched for the right words "…without complications. I don't want to worry about the ethics of it, or the long- or short-term implications, Grady. I just want to live in the moment, appreciate what we have while we have it."

At least for now, until she figured out whether or not she was going to be content with the limitations he'd set over the long haul. "Can we do that?"

"We can do anything you want." Grady pulled her into his arms and delivered another searing kiss. "But there's one thing I want *you* to know, Alexis. I told your boss I'm out, no longer a client of your company. I already know what I want…and it's not that."

GRADY EXPECTED ALEXIS to be happy about that. Instead, she looked upset. "How did Holly Anne take it?" she demanded.

He shrugged. "About how you'd expect. She tried to talk me out of it. When that didn't work, she wanted to know if you were to blame. I assured her that was not the case. You had gone far above and beyond your responsibilities as my matchmaker to try and pair me up with someone, under the very trying parameters I had set." He sighed. "To no avail. Savannah wasn't happy. I wasn't, either. I was trying to hire a mommy slash wife the same way I'd hired a nanny—and it just wasn't a workable situation."

"I'm glad you realize that." Alexis's eyes softened. "Because I think you and Savannah deserve a whole lot better than that, too."

Grady nodded in agreement. "In any case, I promised Holly Anne if I decided to go that route again, I would use ForeverLove.com. And to make up for the way I've monopolized your time, and distracted you to the point you missed a client meeting this morning, that I would give a testimonial the company could use in their advertising."

"That must have pleased her!"

To put it mildly. "I did my best to turn a negative into a positive for you."

"Thank you."

Grady walked over to see what he could do with the AC—it was hotter than blazes in here! "So when will you find out if you get the Galveston job or not?" he asked, over his shoulder.

"Thursday." She followed.

"The day of Savannah's graduation." He studied the controls. Nothing seemed amiss.

"Speaking of the little darling, where is Savannah?"

Grady smiled fondly. "With a sitter. I tucked her in before I left. She was so tired, she was asleep before the lights were out."

"Poor kid."

He noted the perspiration dampening Alexis's clothes—and his. "What's wrong with your air conditioner?"

"It doesn't seem to be working. I called building maintenance, but I doubt I'll hear back from them until morning."

"Well, you can't stay here. People die in this kind of heat. It must be a hundred degrees in here."

Alexis lifted the hair off the back of her neck. "I was just thinking about going to a hotel."

Grady had already cost Alexis enough. This was one

expense he could easily alleviate. And since he already knew she wouldn't let him pay...

He took her by the hand, anxious to get her someplace cool and comfortable. "You're coming home with me."

ALEXIS WOKE TO THE JOYFUL sound of Savannah's voice. "Daddy! Daddy! Alexis is here! She sleeped in one of our beds!"

Footsteps sounded outside the guest room door. "Slept," Grady corrected. "And shhh! We don't want to wake her."

"I'm up." Alexis opened her eyes.

Savannah dragged Grady all the way into the room. "Hi, Alexis!" She dropped his hand and climbed up on the bed. "What are you doing here?"

Alexis stifled a yawn and struggled to sit up. Unlike her own place, Grady's house was blissfully cool and comfortable. "The air conditioner in my apartment is broken, so your daddy invited me to sleep here last night."

Savannah cocked her head. "Your hair is pretty when it's all messy like that."

Grady seemed to think so, too. "I'll get you some coffee," he said with a grin.

Savannah sat cross-legged on the bed. "Grandma Josie is sending me a new dress for the tea party at Lisa Marie's house tomorrow."

Grady came back in with a mug, the coffee fixed just the way she liked it, with milk and a little sugar. "We talked to Mom on the phone last night." He sat on the edge of the mattress and briefly outlined the crisis that had ensued. "My mother was a Dallas debutante years ago. She has a few friends who are still in that social scene. And one of them knows an up-and-coming children's clothing designer who's going to messenger something Laura Ashley-ish over, whatever that means."

"It's going to be pretty and pink!" Savannah clapped her hands. "So now I get to wear a *pink* dress tomorrow when I go to the tea party and the *yellow* dress on Thursday when I graduate!" She held up a pair of fingers. "That's two days and two dresses!"

Alexis patted Savannah's messy curls. "Yes, it is."

The child's eyes lit up. "Can you sleep here every night?"

Alexis ignored Grady's assessing gaze as she took a sip, then set her coffee mug on the bedside table. "Um... no. Thank you for asking, though. But I'm going to have to go home when they get my air conditioner fixed."

"Is it going to be fixed today?"

"I'm not sure."

"She can stay with us until it is," Grady interjected.

"Can she go to the tea party with us tonight?" Savannah asked, slipping beneath the covers and snuggling close to Alexis. "At the hotel?"

Alexis looked at Grady. "Apparently, everyone is practicing tea party etiquette," he explained. "So we're having tea at the Adolphus Hotel this afternoon at five-thirty. Savannah and I would like it very much if you would join us."

That sounded like fun. "I would love to come," she said.

Savannah leaped up, gave Alexis a big hug and then raced off.

"Is it like this every morning?" Alexis asked.

Grady nodded. "Afraid so." He winked. "Better get used to it."

She wanted nothing more than to do just that.

Tea in the Lobby Living Room at the Adolphus Hotel in Fort Worth was lovely. Grady had on a jacket and tie, Alexis wore a summer business suit and Savannah looked adorable in a smocked mint-green cotton dress with short sleeves and a round, embroidered collar.

The waiters were very attentive, bringing back plate after plate of delicate sandwiches and cakes, and even serving Savannah cups of milk flavored with a bit of mild, decaffeinated tea and cubes of sugar. It was all so grown-up and "fancy" that the little girl was beside herself.

Watching her partake of the repast, Grady couldn't stop smiling. Nor could Alexis.

Finally, they'd eaten their fill, and were waiting for the check. Relaxing in his chair, Grady told his daughter, "Now you know what to expect tomorrow when I take you to the tea party at the Petersons."

Savannah had been lounging in the curve of her daddy's arm. She sat bolt upright, utterly horrified. "Daddy, you can't go! Only mommies and little girls can go to that!"

Grady patted her on the arm. "Pumpkin, it's going to be okay. I've already RSVP'd Lisa Marie's mommy that I would be taking you, and she was perfectly fine with it."

Savannah wasn't. "But I don't want you to go, Daddy! I want Alexis!"

"Sorry to put you on the spot like that," Grady told Alexis several hours later, when Savannah was in bed.

Alexis couldn't say she wanted to spend time at the Peterson home, but when it came to protecting Savannah from further hurt and humiliation it was a no-brainer. "I'm happy to fill in for you. Especially if it will make the event less awkward for her."

Grady took a load of clothes out of the dryer. "I'm tempted to have her skip the party entirely, but with everyone else in her class going…"

They both knew how long Savannah had been anticipating this end-of-year event. "I'll keep an eye out for her," Alexis promised, lending a hand by folding towels.

She wasn't sure whether to be grateful for or to lament the ongoing problem with her apartment air conditioning. Because the unit needed to be replaced with a new one, her place wouldn't be livable again until Friday. It seemed, with the current heat wave broiling the Fort Worth area, a lot of people were having trouble with their systems. Grady's, however, was working just fine. The heat she felt welling up inside her had everything to do with his nearness, and nothing to do with the room's temperature. "So…" she swallowed, trying not to think how much she would like to throw caution to the wind and make love with him again. "How is the search for a new school going?"

Grady went back to transfer clothes from the washer to the dryer. "I'm putting her in our neighborhood public elementary school. I spoke to the principal earlier today. It's not going to be year-round, but there's an after-school program run by the local YWCA. It includes tutoring if they need it, as well as a time for the kids to do their homework, so that's all good."

He won't need someone like me in his life.

Alexis followed Grady out into the kitchen. He opened the refrigerator and pulled out a box of pizza leftover from the evening before. The restaurant tea that had filled her and Savannah up hadn't put a dent in his hunger. Alexis shook her head, declining his offer for a wedge of pizza. "When does school start?"

Grady put two slices on a baking sheet and slid them into the oven to warm. "Last week of August." He paused to set the temperature, then went back to the fridge and got a bottle of water. "Which means she's going to have seven weeks off. And that could be a problem, as my investigation of summer day camps shows a lot of them started when the public schools let out in May, and are already full."

"Do you want me to help you with that?" The words were out before Alexis could prevent them. He was no longer her client. She was no longer billing him by the hour. But she couldn't seem to extricate herself emotionally from their problems.

Grady shook his head. "I've got it covered," he said.

A phone call from work, and some sort of emergency on the development project he was helming, occupied Grady for the rest of the evening, and was still commandeering his time and attention the next morning. So Alexis took Savannah to school, with a promise to meet her at the house in time to help her get dressed and take her to the tea party.

"Okay!" the little girl said happily, as Alexis came around to help her with her car door. "Bye, Alexis!" She awkwardly unbuckled her seat belt. Backpack banging against her leg, she tumbled out of the rear passenger seat and gave her a big hug. "See you later!" She skipped off.

Thinking maybe she had been overreacting where Savannah's previous anxiety was concerned, Alexis waved goodbye, then got back in the car and drove on to work. Maybe this tea party wouldn't be so bad, after all.

Wishful thinking, as it turned out. Savannah was tense and upset again when Alexis arrived to help her get ready. She looked adorable in the stylish new pink dress her grandmother had sent her. But shoes were turning out to be a problem. Savannah didn't like her white patent leather Mary Janes.

Grady vetoed flip-flops. "I may not know much, but I know those aren't appropriate."

Savannah scowled.

"Try again," he said.

She flounced off.

"I haven't seen her that temperamental in a couple weeks," Alexis commented.

"I know," Grady murmured, turning to her with concern. "I think it's the stress of the party. She's usually a lot better when you're around, though."

Savannah tromped back along the hall and down the stairs. She had on one red Velcro-fastened sneaker and a hot-pink rain boot. Both were for the left foot. "How's this?" she asked, in full diva mode.

Grady returned her look, his expression droll. "How do you think?"

Savannah tried to keep up the attitude, but the mixture of humor and indulgence in her daddy's eyes soon had her collapsing in giggles. Grady caught her up in his arms and hoisted her until the two were at eye level.

"You know," he told his daughter, suddenly serious, "you don't have to go to this party if you don't want to."

She wriggled out of his arms.

"No." She threw herself at Alexis and held on tight. "I want to go. And I want *Alexis* to take me."

And that, Alexis thought, as she helped Grady find appropriate footwear for his daughter, was that.

FORTUNATELY, the mother-daughter tea party was in full swing by the time Alexis and Savannah arrived at the Peterson home. The unseasonably hot weather had forced the party to be held inside, instead of in the garden. White folding chairs and pastel linen covered tables for seventy dominated the formal living and dining rooms and foyer of the elegant home. Seats were indicated by place cards. A white-jacketed catering staff moved among the tables, setting up tea service and treating the little girls and their mommies to delicate pastries and sandwiches.

Savannah was right to bring her instead of Grady, Alexis thought, as the two of them found their way to their seats—at what was clearly the least desirable table, in a far corner. Already there were two other little girls from Savannah's class. Both were happy to see her. Alexis had a nice time chatting with their mothers.

Lisa Marie and the two girls who had gone out of their way to humiliate Savannah the previous week were seated at the table of honor. To Alexis's relief, they were too busy lording over their party to give Savannah any trouble.

Near the end of the event, some of the children dashed upstairs to hang out in Lisa Marie's room. Savannah stayed where she was with her friends.

And that was when one of the other mothers appeared at their table, introduced herself as Nancy Waterman, and asked to speak to Alexis privately for a moment.

Because it was convenient, they stepped out onto the screened back porch. "I'm in charge of the fittings for the school uniforms. The deadline for getting the measurements for the new first graders was yesterday at five o'clock. I've been trying to get ahold of Grady since last week. I've left messages for him everywhere, and he hasn't returned any of my calls. I thought, since you brought Savannah today, that you might know what's going on."

Before Alexis could respond, Kit Peterson popped out to join them. "Nancy…Alexis, something I should know about?" she asked brightly.

Nancy looked at Alexis, still waiting.

"Grady didn't mention anything about next year's uniforms to me," she said, quite truthfully. "But I can certainly mention it to him when I take Savannah home."

"Would you?" Nancy sighed. "This order has got to go in by Friday, and with graduation tomorrow—and the Fourth of July holiday after that—I am worried it won't get done."

"I'll talk to him. I promise," Alexis said.

"Thank you." Nancy started to go back inside.

Alexis moved to follow.

Kit stepped slightly to the left, barring her path. "We'll be there in a minute," she told Nancy with a smile. "I need to speak to Alexis, too."

The woman nodded and shut the door behind her.

"Just what is your interest in Grady McCabe?" Kit demanded.

Alexis blinked, stunned by the venom in her tone. "Excuse me?"

"You were supposed to be Grady's matchmaker, but would you ever call me back and let me help you with that? No. So I sent my very good friend—Zoe Borden—who is perfect for him, by the way—to Forever-Love.com so you could set them up." Kit's eyes flashed. "Instead, you talk her out of pursuing him! I talk her right back into it, only to find out Grady is no longer looking! And you're now cozily ensconced with him and his daughter!"

"Look." Alexis held on to her temper with effort. "I don't know what you've heard—"

"Savannah told everyone at school today you're sleeping over."

"In the guest room!" Alexis corrected, embarrassed.

Kit crossed her arms. "Mmm-hmm."

Alexis ignored the judgment in her tone. "My air-conditioning unit is broken. There's a heat wave going on, in case you didn't notice."

Kit leaned closer. "Yes, well, it's about to get a whole lot hotter if you think you're going to lay claim to that man, when there are any number of fine, socially suitable women who have been waiting for him to become available again."

When had this become a competition? Never mind one for Grady's heart? "I assure you," Alexis stated, "it was never my intention to jump line." *Never my intention to get emotionally involved with a client. Never my intention to fall in love....*

But she had fallen in love with Grady. Head over heels in love.

"That's good to know." Kit shot daggers at her. "Because all you are to him—all you will ever be—is Grady McCabe's rebound woman." Her voice dropped to a vicious hiss. "And once he's really ready to move on, you mark my words, honey. He'll come to his senses. And he'll pick someone in his own league."

Chapter Thirteen

Grady was waiting for them when they returned from the Petersons' tea. He hoisted his daughter in his arms the moment they walked through the door. "So how did it go?" he asked them, turning his McCabe blue eyes on Alexis. His probing gaze was full of something Alexis couldn't quite put a name to, but mesmerized her nevertheless.

Oblivious to the subtle sparks arcing between the two adults, Savannah snuggled closer, rested her cheek on his broad shoulder and yawned. "It was kind of boring, Daddy. We just sat at tables and ate stuff, and they didn't even have tea for the kids, like at the hotel, only lemonade with some stuff in it."

"Peach slices and maraschino cherries," Alexis interjected, in response to his baffled look.

Savannah yawned again. "I liked the tea party you and me and Alexis went to better."

"Well, I'm glad you were able to go to both," Grady said, with a perfectly solemn face, planting a kiss on his daughter's head. He cuddled her even closer. "Did you thank Mrs. Peterson and Lisa Marie for having you at their party?"

Savannah's expression indicated that was a silly question. "Of course, Daddy." She rubbed her eyes.

"What do you say we take you upstairs and get you in your pajamas and tucked in bed?" Grady smiled down at her tenderly. "You've got a big day tomorrow. You're graduating from kindergarten."

"I want Alexis to come up, too. So she can read me a story and kiss me goodnight." Savannah reached out to tug her closer.

Happy to be included, Alexis winked. "No problem."

Savannah made it through only four pages of the Dr. Seuss book she'd picked out before falling fast asleep. Her heart swelling with love, Alexis tucked the covers around her and kissed her gently, as did Grady. They both tiptoed out of the room and went back downstairs.

"So how was the party—really?" he asked as the two of them settled on the living room sofa.

Good and bad. "The catering company did a very nice job."

He admonished her with a look. "That's not what I'm asking."

She knew that. She had just been hoping to avoid discussing anything that would spoil the peaceful, relaxed mood. Alexis focused on the concern in Grady's gaze. "All the girls were on their best behavior. And it helped that Savannah and I were seated a great distance away from Lisa Marie and her friends." Alexis did her very best to be objective. "I think Savannah really did have a nice time. I believe she felt very grown-up. And she was right about one thing—it would have been a mistake to have you at that party. You would have been totally out of place."

Grady relaxed. "I'm sure she was glad you were there with her."

Maybe too glad, Alexis thought, realizing the two of them were getting as close as mother and daughter. That would be a problem if Grady ever decided to ease her out of Savannah's life.... The last thing she wanted was to break this precious little girl's heart.

Grady saw through her defenses to her distress. "Anything else happen?" he asked gently.

Alexis went to get her purse from the table on the foyer, where she'd left it. Returning, she gave Grady the computer-generated reminder. "I ran into the mother in charge of the uniforms for next year. Apparently, she has been e-mailing and telephoning you to try and get Savannah's measurements?"

Grady put the name and phone number on his desk. "I'm going to contact the uniform coordinator on Friday, at the same time I notify the school that Savannah won't be attending Miss Chilton's Academy for Young Women next year. I didn't want to say anything before graduation. Figured it would create too much of a stir."

Alexis couldn't blame him for that. Savannah had been through enough where Principal Jordan and the mean girls in her class were concerned. She put her purse aside and went back to the sofa, perching on the arm to face Grady. "When are you going to tell Savannah she's switching schools?"

Grady's glance traced the curve of Alexis's stocking-clad knee before returning to her face. "While we're in Laramie, visiting family during the upcoming holiday. I'm going to take her over and show her where I went to elementary school and explain to her that her new school will be just like that."

Alexis could tell he'd given this a lot of thought. "I think she'll be a lot happier in a coed school."

"I do, too." Grady clamped a hand on Alexis's wrist and tugged her down onto the cushion next to him. "Anything else happen?"

Should she tell him? Alexis wondered, straightening her skirt. Heaven knew she didn't want Grady finding out about the mini-contretemps any other way.... "Kit Peterson pulled me aside to let me know that she is not happy with me."

Grady's brow furrowed. "How come?"

Another long story she would rather not have to relate. "Kit sent a friend—Zoe Borden—to my office and had Zoe request me as matchmaker, thinking that she could just ask for a date with you and I would arrange it."

Grady shook his head in irritation. "Kit already tried to set us up last year, right after Zoe separated from her third husband. I told Kit I wasn't interested."

"Well, they're both hoping that will change, now that Zoe is divorced."

"The only woman," Grady said, drawing Alexis close enough for a passionate, lingering kiss, "I'm interested in is you."

"Yes, well..." Forcing herself to remain as composed as she needed to be, Alexis extricated herself from the comfort of Grady's arms, stood and began to pace the length of the living room. "The news is also out that I've been staying here the past couple of nights."

Grady stood, too. "How would they know that?" he demanded.

"Savannah told everyone I was sleeping here."

"In the guest room," Grady corrected, not impressed by the gossip of that particular tale.

Aware what thin ice she was already on, as far as her request for promotion at her company was concerned, Alexis pressed her lips together. "Savannah may have left that detail out."

Grady closed the distance between them, lifted his arms and cupped her shoulders in his palms. "I'm sorry."

Alexis did her best to ignore the warmth of his touch, transmitting through to her skin. "It's all right." She swallowed, wishing she wasn't so emotionally involved. She feigned nonchalance. "I appreciate the hospitality you've shown me the past few days, and I set Kit straight on the matter, so…"

For the first time, Grady looked upset. "Kit's the one who…"

"Let that little detail slip?" Alexis flushed, despite herself. "Yes. She accused me of setting my sights on you from the beginning."

He used the leverage of his grip to bring her ever closer. "We both know that isn't true. What's happened between us…"

Just once, Alexis wished Grady would say or do something to indicate he was beginning to love her as much as she loved him. "Just happened, I know."

When he spoke, his voice was matter-of-fact but kind. "Are you okay with this?"

On the surface…? Sure. Words couldn't hurt her. Privately, Alexis wasn't certain. Like it or not, Kit's spiteful assertion that she was nothing more than a rebound fling to Grady had hit home. Alexis wanted to think it wasn't true. She wanted to believe she and Grady were on the road to something real and lasting and true. But what if they weren't? What if Kit's prediction was correct, that her fling with Grady was all she would ever have?

He was still waiting for an answer.

"I'm fine," Alexis fibbed, working hard to make her expression just as inscrutable as his. "I'm just really tired." She put up a hand, staving off further conversation, freeing herself from his grip. "I think I'll hit the sack early."

Clearly disappointed, he stepped back, too, then inquired softly, "You're sure you don't want to hang out for a while, watch some television?"

Alexis declined his offer with a shake of her head and moved toward the hall. "Thanks, but no."

LONG AFTER ALEXIS HAD departed, Grady couldn't shake the feeling that something more was wrong, something Alexis had yet to reveal. He wondered if her pensive mood had anything to do with the promotion she was still waiting to hear about. Had she received the Galveston job, and had yet to tell him she would soon be moving? Or had she lost the opportunity—because he had dominated her time—and then quit the matchmaking service entirely?

Unfortunately, she was already in bed for the night. By the time she emerged from her room the next morning, showered and dressed, Savannah was up and his parents had arrived.

The five of them drove to the girls' academy together. Then they all watched with pride as Savannah walked up to receive her diploma, a child-size white satin graduation cap with tassel on her head. As she shook Principal Jordan's hand, she turned and smiled for the camera. With a lump in his throat the size of a walnut, Grady snapped the photo, along with the event photographer, then smiled and waved. His daughter waved back, her attention turning to the other guests in their party. Grady couldn't say he was surprised to see his parents were all choked up, too. They burst with pride at every milestone their five offspring took, and now that pride extended to their only grandchild.

What cemented the lump in his throat was the sight of Alexis in the audience, looking as proud—and emotional—as every mother there.

Grady had half expected that. He knew Alexis loved Savannah, and that his daughter loved her back.

What Grady hadn't counted on was the surprising depth of his own feelings, the fact he was experiencing emotions he had never expected or wanted to be subjected to again.

Was it possible? he wondered. Could it be…?

There was no time to contemplate further. Another child was taking the stage and he was in the way. Surreptitiously blinking back the moisture in his eyes, he waved at Savannah one more time, then sneaked back down the aisle and resumed his seat next to his family.

"You know," Wade told Savannah later, over their celebratory graduation lunch downtown, "you are our first grandchild to graduate from kindergarten."

Savannah giggled. "Granddad. I'm your only grandchild."

"For right now," Josie pointed out with a smile. "But we have hopes that some more little darlin's will be joining our family very soon." She looked pointedly at her son.

Grady swore silently to himself. His mother had a matchmaking gleam in her eye. And while he couldn't say his thoughts weren't ambling along the same trail, he did not want his mother saying or doing anything that would alarm an already skittish Alexis, to the point she exited from his life.

Thankfully, his dad stepped in to take his wife's hand. "Hold on there, sweetheart. For that to happen somebody's got to fall in love and get married first," Wade said. Then his father turned and looked at Grady expectantly, the very same gleam in his eyes.

Alexis flushed bright pink and dropped her gaze to her plate.

"Just to be clear…they're not talking about us," Grady rushed to reassure her, in an effort to alleviate some of the familial pressure. He glared at his folks, letting them know it was past time to back off. Sure, they might have figured out what Alexis had yet to discern—that he was more emotionally available than he had realized. But that didn't mean they had to spill the beans.

Telling Alexis that he was a helluva lot more ready for commitment than he had figured was his business. Not theirs.

Grady continued the face-saving explanation of his parents' matchmaking behavior. "They're talking about my four younger brothers."

His folks, getting the hint at long last, just smiled and nodded amiably.

"Speaking of fun," his mother said finally, turning to Savannah, "your granddad and I are headed back to our ranch near Laramie this very afternoon. We're going to get ready for our big Fourth of July picnic and barbecue. And guess what? We could use an assistant. Do you know any big girls of, say, five or so, who might be able to help us?"

"IT WAS NICE OF your parents to take Savannah for a few days," Alexis said a few hours later, after the trio had left.

Grady walked into his study. He turned off his cell phone and set it on his desk, then turned back to her. "They try to give me a break from parenting every month or two. Usually it's pretty lonely around here with Savannah gone. But I have to say…" He stepped toward Alexis and wrapped his hands around her waist "…I'm looking forward to the time alone with you."

She pulled away from him, or attempted to, anyway. He had a pretty good hold on her. "Grady, I—I think we need to talk."

He flattened his hands over her spine, brought her even closer and lowered his head. "First things first," he murmured.

As always, the resistance in her began to fade within the first couple seconds of their kiss. Her body softening, she opened her mouth to the insistent pressure of his, and pulled him seductively closer. A thrill shot through him at the heady sensation of her breasts crushed against his chest. Blood rushed to his groin. Need and want combined.

He lifted her onto the edge of his desk. She caught her breath as he pushed her skirt up and stepped between her spread thighs. Still kissing her, he divested her of the jacket and began working on the single button of her silk blouse at the nape of her neck.

She gave a soft murmur of ascent and lifted her arms

as he eased the fabric over her head. It fell in a puddle on his desk, followed swiftly by her bra. Cupping her breasts with his hands, he took her mouth once again. Moaning, she tightened her grip on him, her body arching. And Grady felt everything he had ever wanted, everything he had ever needed, flooding back into his life.

She was something, this woman.

Alexis made him want to risk again, want to love and live, and count his blessings—not just at times like now, but all the time. She made him want to create a family with the three of them. And she dared him to dream of more than he'd ever thought possible.

For the first time, he could imagine himself having more kids.

Having a wife…

And a relationship that lasted not just until fate cruelly intervened, but for the rest of his life…

For the first time, he could envision a future.

And that future centered around Alexis.

ALEXIS DIDN'T KNOW HOW IT happened, how it always happened. One minute she'd made up her mind to do the cautious thing and take a step back. The next, Grady would be gazing at her, and that have-to-have-you-right-now look of his would translate into a touch, and then a kiss, and the next thing she knew she'd be half-naked and wanting him naked, too.

She moaned low in her throat as the kiss deepened intimately. He kissed her cheek, her chin, her throat, and when his lips dropped even lower, she knew it was all over.

There would be no resisting him—no resisting this. No wait-and-see-if-it-all-worked-out before she got herself in any deeper. She was already in as far as she was going to go. Already in love with him. Already wanting a future that included Grady and Savannah and all the things she'd feared were out of her reach forever...

Her skirt came off. So did his shirt and pants....

Naked, they made it as far as the leather wing reading chair.

He sank into it. She dropped onto him, her head beginning to buzz, as their lips met in a kiss that was hot and hard and sweet. Aroused to distraction, she made a cradle of her hips, easing him into it, every inch of her body beginning to fuse to his. She hung on to that feeling, hung on to him, hands and lips exploring each other's bodies. And then there was no more thinking, no more waiting, nothing but the sheer pleasure of their joining. They clung together afterward, trembling and breathless. Knowing, as good as it had been, that it wasn't over yet.

Aware of how she never wanted to be away from him again, she let him lead her upstairs to his bed. Let him coax her between the sheets and back in his arms again, until she felt the now familiar hardness pressing against her. She knew if she did not extricate herself promptly, she would only fall deeper in love, in lust. But when he slid down, parted her knees and buried his face between her thighs, all thoughts of caution fled.

She could get hurt, handing her heart and soul to him like this. This could only be a rebound for him. But even if it was, had anything ever felt this glorious?

Alexis had never imagined lovemaking could be so tender and hot, uninhibited and fulfilling. Was it any wonder that she caught his head in her hands and brought him closer, thrilled at each expert caress of his tongue? Or found endless ways to pleasure him to oblivion, too? Or that in the end they would end up together again, hips locked, rocking in rhythm. His body felt so warm and strong and good; his weight made her feel so safe, his lips and hands so loved. Every time he moved to possess her, he thrust more deeply home.

Before long, she was teetering on the brink, falling, rising, spiraling into bliss… And then the room grew silent once more, their bodies entwined, her whole being at peace.

ALEXIS WOKE TO THE faraway ringing of her cell phone, discerning by the type of buzzing that it was the office. A glance at the bedside clock told her it was almost five in the afternoon. She groaned, burying her head in the pillow. "This is beginning to be a ritual," she lamented in a muffled voice. "Make love with you…" recklessly and passionately "…and get called by work."

Grady drew her back against him. He wrapped both arms around her and nuzzled the side of her neck. "Don't get it."

Temptation swirled through her, as potent as having him next to her. "I have to." Sighing, she disentangled herself and threw on Grady's robe. "Holly Anne wanted to tell me about the Galveston job."

"Well?" he said when she had finished her conversation and rejoined him in the master bedroom.

Trying hard not to notice how sexy Grady looked, lying back among the rumpled sheets, Alexis dropped the stack of their discarded clothing she had brought upstairs with her on the bench at the end of the bed. Her emotions awhirl, she perched on the mattress, facing him. "I didn't get it."

His expression immediately contrite, Grady sat up. "I'm sorry."

"I am, too, about the money. It would have been nice to be able to pay off my debt a lot faster, get a bit bigger place." She sighed, determined to be as honest with him as she was with herself. "But on the other hand, I really don't want to move to Galveston right now. Not anymore."

He studied her, his expression inscrutable. "What's changed?" he asked gently.

Why pretend she wasn't completely in love with him? Surely he had to have some idea…. Surveying him just as carefully, she said lightly, "You even have to ask?"

Grady pulled her back into his arms. He kissed her warmly, then lounged against the headboard, holding her close. "I feel bad," he told her bluntly. "You lost that job because of me."

"And me." Alexis took credit where credit was due. "I didn't have to get so besotted by you."

He stroked a hand over her hair. "But you did," he murmured in her ear, "which is why I'm thinking we should do something about it."

Alexis's heart began to pound. Suddenly, she couldn't get her breath. "Like what, exactly?"

He ran a hand up and down her back. "Like make it easier for you to pay off your debts faster—and have a nice place to live. And since you won't accept my financial help—"

Alexis's spine stiffened at the idea of being anyone's charity case. "You're right," she said stubbornly. "I will not!"

Grady seemed to be prepared for that. And she supposed, knowing her as he did, he probably was.

His lips turned up in a casual smile. "How about something more neighborly, then?"

She tensed again. Sensing a trap, she asked cautiously, "Like what?"

Without warning, his eyes turned serious. "Like you give up your apartment and move in with me and Savannah permanently."

Chapter Fourteen

Grady looked at Alexis. The stunned expression on her face was not the reaction he had been hoping for. It didn't mean all was lost, just that he had to have a better pitch.

After all, he had the McCabe and the Corbett-Wyatt genes. He knew how to finesse a situation that would leave everyone not only richer, but much happier to boot.

"You're here all the time, anyway. We have a guest room that stands empty. Savannah adores you and she's been longing for a mommy in her life. You've met that need." Feeling her sink even farther away from him, Grady flashed a winning smile. "I love having you around, too."

She started to turn away, but he caught her hands and drew her back. "I love making love with you, being with you," he told her sincerely.

She didn't respond.

He tried again. "I want to help. I want to be part of your life."

Still nothing.

"I want you to be part of ours." *Just the way you have been.* "I want us to be—"

"Like family?" Alexis interrupted, not looking all that pleased.

Well, no, Grady thought, that wasn't what he wanted. He wanted them to *be* family. But, figuring that wasn't what she wanted to hear—at least not this soon in their relationship—Grady said the word he expected she wanted. "Sure."

She let go of his hands as swiftly as if he had burned her. And this time she did turn away, looking thoroughly ticked off. "I don't think so." She pushed the words through gritted teeth, snatched up the scattered pieces of clothing she had worn to Savannah's graduation, and headed into the master bathroom.

Grady followed and planted himself in the doorway, feeling as if he were squaring off with a bear that had caught its paw in a trap. "You're mad?"

She whirled, sending a wave of her perfume drifting his way. "Gee…you think?"

Not giving him a chance to answer, she tossed her clothing on the marble counter and slammed the bathroom door in his face. Grady heard the swish of cloth on the other side. He leaned against the doorframe, trying not to envision the splendid beauty of her nakedness. "Okay. So maybe it's a little soon to be asking you to move in with us."

The silence was broken only by the rasp of a zipper.

"But it's what I want," Grady continued, over more rustling cloth. "I'm not going to lie about that."

The door swung open. Alexis marched out, still buttoning the jacket of her suit. "I'm not going to lie, either. It's not what I want."

He watched her hunt around for her sling-back heels. "I thought—"

"I know." She sat down on the bed to put on her shoes, her skirt hiking up well past her knees. "You had every reason to come to that conclusion." Finished, she stood. "I've behaved like a fool. But no more."

"Alexis—"

She spun around to face him, tears glimmering in her eyes. "I told you when we first met, Grady. I'm tired of only living half a life." She held up her hand before he could interrupt. "I don't want to do that anymore. I don't *want* to settle for friendship when I might have the kind of love I had with my husband."

Grady stared at her, aghast. How could he have been so wrong? So sure she mirrored the way he felt, deep inside? He swallowed, realizing his whole world was crashing down around him, without warning, once again. Fighting to keep a tight rein on his emotions, he swallowed. "You're saying that what I am offering isn't enough?"

It was her turn to look unbearably disappointed. Alexis sighed, swept her hands through her tousled hair and sadly met his eyes. "I'm saying what I've said all along, Grady. I'm tired of living a diminished life. No one knows how much time they have here on earth, but while I'm here, I want it all. And until I get it, I'd rather be alone."

"DADDY, IS ALEXIS STILL looking for a new mommy for me?" Savannah asked three days later, as they walked onto the front porch at his parents' ranch.

Setting down the huge basket of corn his mother had asked him to shuck, Grady took a seat on the cushioned wicker settee. "Um, no, honey, she's not," he drawled as the scents of mesquite and slow-roasting barbecue filled the manicured yard. "I told her it probably wasn't the right time for me to start dating again."

In the distance, his dad and some of his brothers worked on setting up the portable dance floor, while two more minded the wood-fueled smokers.

"That's good." Savannah settled next to him and accepted an ear of corn. She peeled off one green leaf, then another, revealing the layer of cornsilk underneath.

"How come?" Grady asked, husking an ear with two swift pulls.

"Because I don't want a new mommy," Savannah said, serious as could be. "I just want Alexis."

So did Grady. "I know you do, honey."

"How come we haven't seen her?"

"She's been really busy," he fibbed, not about to tell his daughter the woman she wanted in her life was no longer going to be there.

It was hard enough for him to accept. How could he ask Savannah to do the same?

"Is Alexis coming here to eat barbecue and see the fireworks with us?" Savannah struggled to pick the silk off the kernels.

"No." Grady picked up another ear and methodically shucked it, too.

His daughter looked as sad and disappointed as Grady felt. Her lower lip trembled and tears shone in her eyes. "Doesn't she like Laramie?"

Irritated with himself for bringing a woman into their lives, only to have the relationship end as unfairly as his marriage had, Grady worked to spare his daughter's feelings once again. "I'm sure she would like Laramie just fine, if she'd ever been here."

Savannah dropped her shucked ear into the bowl of

cleaned cobs and grabbed another. "Then why won't she come to our Fourth of July party?"

Maybe it was time to be a little more open. "I think she might be mad at me," he admitted finally.

His daughter looked as if she found that hard to believe. "Why?"

Discovering it was more difficult to curtail his emotions with every second that passed, Grady exhaled. "I'm not sure."

Savannah narrowed her eyes. She wasn't buying that for one red-hot second.

"Okay, maybe I have an idea," Grady allowed. "I think I might have rushed her." Either that or Alexis didn't see herself ever falling in love with him, and that wasn't an idea he wanted to wrap his mind around. He didn't want to think he'd been nothing more than a fling to her....

Savannah blinked. "What does that mean?"

It means, Grady thought, *I shouldn't have asked Alexis to move in, when love isn't in the cards for us— at least as far as she's concerned.* The only thing she apparently had wanted from him was temporary passion. The kind that took someone off the bench and put him or her back in the game.

Which was why, he realized way too late, he should have followed his instincts and never gotten off the bench in the first place. He'd been right to think that lightning only strikes once in a lifetime. Correct to feel that the odds of him falling for a woman who would in turn, fall for him were astronomically against it. He hadn't wanted to be hurt again or feel mind-numbing loss. Yet here he was, feeling worse than if he had just remained alone and celibate for the rest of his life. What kind of fool did that make him? What kind of father?

"Daddy?" Savannah said, sounding a little less hurt and a lot more reasonable.

Unable to quell his sadness, Grady looked down at her. "What, pumpkin?"

His five-year-old daughter gave him the stern but loving look he always gave her when he reprimanded her. "I think you should just say you're sorry. Then Alexis won't be mad at you anymore."

Had the situation not been so completely disillusioning, her dictum would have been funny. "Honey, I wish it was that easy. I really do."

Savannah stamped her foot. "But, Daddy, you always tell me—"

"Not in this case."

She slumped in her seat, looking as if her heart would break. As if she'd almost had everything she ever wanted, only to have it cruelly snatched away.

Unfortunately, Grady knew exactly how his little girl felt.

ALEXIS WAS IN THE OFFICE, catching up on work, when her phone rang. Wondering who it could be, since she hadn't told anyone she was spending the holiday alone, she picked up.

"You're a hard woman to track down," Josie McCabe said.

"Sorry." Alexis had turned off her cell. She hadn't wanted to think about the calls she wouldn't be getting from Josie's son. "I've been catching up on a lot of work." Or trying to. She hadn't actually been getting a lot done.

"Honey," the woman chided. "On a holiday?"

Alexis felt a pensive smile coaxed from her lips. If she were in the market for a mom to replace the one she'd lost, she wouldn't mind it being Josie McCabe. But Josie couldn't be her mom unless she was connected to Grady.

"I think I have an idea why you're calling," Alexis said.

"Because you broke my son's heart?" Josie interrupted, with her customary gentleness.

Alexis was a little taken aback. "For me to break Grady's heart, he would have to love me first," she corrected.

Josie paused, then asked incredulously, "Who says he doesn't?"

Who else? "Grady!"

"He said that?" Josie gasped.

Alexis lifted her shoulders in a listless shrug and rocked back in her chair. "It was more what he *didn't* say."

His mother harrumphed. "That sounds like a McCabe male. Thinking it's all obvious and therefore there's no reason to state the obvious."

That made sense. Sort of. Alexis sat forward slightly and rubbed her temples. "What is the obvious?"

Josie paused again. "Don't you think you should be asking Grady that?"

Alexis ignored the gentle teasing in the woman's voice. She traced a random pattern on her desk with her fingertip. "I don't think we're speaking right now."

"And whose decision was that?" Josie demanded.

Good question.

"Look," she continued, her exasperation clear. "I

don't know exactly what happened between the two of you. My son is not telling me anything, as usual. I do know what I saw when you were together. And I know what I see today when you're not with each other. He needs you, Alexis, and unless I'm mistaken, you need him, too."

The truth of the assessment hit home. Tears blurred Alexis's vision. Although the selfish part of her felt she loved Grady enough for both of them, she knew from her work as a matchmaker that one-sided love rarely worked out long term. In those situations, someone always got hurt. And in this situation, it wouldn't be just her and Grady—Savannah would get hurt, too. Alexis couldn't bear that, any more than she could bear the thought of a life without Grady and the little girl she had come to love as her very own.

She didn't want to shortchange either of them. Need wasn't love. Grady deserved to love and be loved as much as she did. "Believe me, I wish you were right, but it's not that simple," she protested in a choked voice, feeling as if her heart was breaking all over again.

She wanted Grady—and Savannah—to have everything they deserved.

"Honey, it's as simple as you want it to be. Follow your feelings. Get in the car and drive to Laramie. Spend the holiday with us."

"Grady—"

"Will be happy to see you."

FINDING THE McCABES' RANCH outside Laramie was the easy part. Getting up the nerve to get out of her car and go find Wade and Josie's eldest son was a lot harder. What if Grady didn't want her there? He hadn't invited her to the party. On the other hand, if she didn't take some risk, she'd never be happy again. And she so much wanted to be happy.

Alexis drew a deep, bolstering breath, opened the car door and got out.

Over the roof of the car, she saw a familiar figure striding toward her. It was Grady. Not in the city clothes she usually saw him in, but in jeans, boots and a white Western shirt. He had a straw hat slanted low over his brow. Although she couldn't see his eyes, she *could* see the serious slant of his mouth. His lips were thinned, his jaw set in the same grim don't-mess-with-a-McCabe tilt she had witnessed the other night, when she'd walked out on him.

Her spirits rose and then sank, then rose again.

And suddenly he was bypassing the three-dozen vehicles already parked on the lawn, on either side of the long elegant drive. Quickly rounding the back of her car, he came to stand beside her. In the distance, Alexis could hear the sounds of a party. Lively music, laughter, shrieking children, the raucous splashes of people jumping into a swimming pool. But here in the quickly diminishing light, there were only the two of them. Only this moment in time. Maybe even only this chance.

Alexis looked up at him, heart in her throat, her emotions on the line. She felt her eyes brim with tears. It was time to take a risk. Way past time. "About moving in with you?" she said simply, her gaze on his face. "My answer is yes."

Grady stared at her, undecipherable emotion flickering in his eyes.

Silence strung out between them.

Finally, he grimaced and said, with what sounded

very much like a mixture of gratitude and regret, "I don't think it's a good idea."

Something crashed inside her once again.

He took her hand. Their fingers twined and he stared down at the place where their palms interlocked. Finally, he looked back up again. "You deserve better."

Suddenly, the happy future she'd once thought would never be hers seemed almost within reach. "I don't want better," she blurted. "I want…you, Grady. Only you."

He grinned and he tugged her closer, the affection she had been craving visible in his eyes. "Maybe you don't want better, but you should have it," he told her, pausing to take her chin in hand and deliver a soft, searing kiss that turned her life upside down once again. Drawing back slightly, he gently caressed her face with the flat of his palm. "You should have everything that's been missing from your life the last few years. Romance, passion, fun, excitement, tenderness. And most of all," he told her solemnly, "you should have a once-in-a-lifetime love. You deserve that, Alexis, and so much more. And so do I. Which is why," he continued hoarsely, "I think we should take a step back."

"A step back." Alexis didn't know why she was repeating his statement. She had understood very well what he'd just said. She just hadn't wanted to hear it. "Okay then…" She started to turn away.

He held fast, refusing to release the grip he had on her hand.

"I know I screwed up," he confessed, his eyes on her face. "I know I pushed you too hard, too fast. I was selfish, but I couldn't help it. I love you, Alexis. I love you with all my heart."

A hiccup caught in her throat. The tears she'd been holding back flowed, full force. "Oh, Grady, I love you, too." Alexis wreathed her arms about his neck. They kissed, long and slow…soft and sweet. "I just said no because I thought you didn't love me!"

He paused, taking that in, then grasped her upper arms. "I thought you walked away because you didn't think you could ever love me."

Joy began to spiral through her. "Well, I guess we were wrong about that," Alexis said, releasing a tremulous sigh.

"Seems so." Happiness radiating from him, he bent his head and delivered another tender kiss.

"So about your offer…" Alexis said between kisses.

"We're not moving in together," Grady announced firmly. "Not just as friends and lovers, anyway." His voice dropped. "What we have is far too special for that."

This, she thought, sounded serious. But she had come to some important conclusions, too. "Life is short, Grady. Sometimes too short. I've waited a lifetime to feel this way again. I don't want to miss a single second of it, due to some arbitrary time frame everyone else thinks we should adhere to."

"I was hoping you'd feel that way…." Grinning, he reached into his pocket and withdrew a velvet box, which he pressed into her palm. She opened it with shaking hands. Inside was a beautiful platinum solitaire engagement ring, with tiny diamonds all around the band. It was the most beautiful ring she had ever seen, just perfect for her in so many ways.

As firecrackers shot off in the distance, illuminating

the sky, Grady dropped to one knee and looked up at her, love shining in his eyes. "Which is why I'm asking if you'll do me the honor of saying you'll be wife."

Epilogue

Three months later...

Savannah bounced up and down with excitement. "I knew we'd get to wear flowers in our hair!"

Alexis secured the last pin, holding the wreath in place, then stepped back to survey her handiwork. Savannah looked precious in a pale blue silk-flower girl dress, white tights and white patent leather Mary Janes.

"How's it going in here?" Grady slipped in the guest bedroom door.

"Daddy!" Savannah shrieked. "You're not supposed to see us yet!"

He grinned, unrepentant. "I won't tell if you won't."

His daughter surveyed him, deciding.

"It's okay," Alexis said, soothing the little girl who would soon officially be her daughter. "I asked Daddy to come in so the three of us could have a moment alone before we go downstairs to get married."

They had decided to wait to get married until Savannah was nicely settled in her new school, which she now was. In the meantime, the three of them had spent every evening together, savoring each other's company and making plans. And Alexis had approached her job as a matchmaker at ForeverLove.com with new energy and commitment, counseling her clients not to settle for anything less than real, lasting love, because, as she and Grady could attest, a love like theirs was worth waiting for.

Now, finally, after counting down the days until she and Grady were to be wed in his home, with only a few close friends and family present, that day had finally arrived. The downstairs was filled with flowers. A harp and flute duo were at the ready. Caterers were setting up a reception beneath a tent in the backyard. The minister had arrived. And Savannah was still considering whether her dad should be allowed to see them.

"I wanted to get a good look at my girls before we went to join everyone else." Grady picked up the explanation where Alexis had left off. He held out his arms and waited.

Savannah did a princess pirouette.

"Beautiful!" Grady said, giving his little girl a hug. He gestured to Alexis. "Your turn."

She did a pirouette, too.

Savannah sighed, completely enthralled. "You look really pretty," she declared.

Grady's eyes glowed. "Absolutely gorgeous," he agreed.

Alexis *felt* stunning, in the strapless, ivory silk gown. She gave Grady a slow once-over. He looked very handsome in a charcoal-gray tuxedo. "You're pretty handsome, too."

"Very handsome," Savannah agreed. Already bored with the conversation, she sprinted toward the door. "I'm going to find my flower basket!"

Once again Alexis and Grady were alone. Contentment flowed, and their future beckoned, as bright and dazzling as the diamond sparkling on Alexis's left hand.

"Have I told you lately," he murmured, taking her in his arms and holding her close, "how happy you've made me?"

"All the time." Alexis drank in the clean, familiar scent of him. "And for the record, you've made me incredibly happy, too." They kissed slowly and sweetly.

Downstairs, the music started. Savannah clattered back up the stairs. Reluctantly, bride and groom moved apart.

"Then there's only one thing to do," Grady drawled as his daughter burst through the door, petals from the flower basket already spraying every which way. "Let's get married."

"Yes!" Savannah shouted. "And live happily ever after!"

"Sounds good to me." Alexis paused to kiss both of them.

So they did.

* * * * *

A BABY FOR MOMMY

Chapter One

Dan Kingsland's mind *should* have been on business. The catered outdoor buffet at the construction site of One Trinity River Place was to celebrate a huge accomplishment, not just for his own architectural firm, but four of his closest friends. Grady McCabe was the enterprising developer who'd put it all together. Travis Carson was the contractor building the three-block office-shopping-and-residential complex in downtown Fort Worth. Jack Gaines owned the electronic and wiring company that would install all the networks, phones and satellite systems. Nate Hutchinson helmed the financial-services company leasing seventy-five percent of the office space.

Instead...all Dan could think about was the incredible lunch being served, picnic-style, to the 150 high-profile guests milling around outside the sleek stone-and-glass skyscrapers culled from Dan's imagination. The food commemorating the end of Phase 1 was literally the best he had ever tasted. And it was all being prepared by one woman, using three portable outdoor stoves and what looked to be an equally portable Sub-Zero fridge.

Dan savored another bite of perfectly seasoned potato salad. Maybe if they could eat like this at home…

Grady McCabe gave Dan a wry look. "We all know what you're thinking. Emily Stayton is *not* the answer to your problems."

Dan turned his gaze back to the dark-haired beauty in jeans, boots and traditional white chef's coat. The young culinary artist certainly *looked* like the solution to his dilemma. He'd lived in Texas all his life and had never had barbecue this good. The fact that Emily Stayton was literally glowing with happiness while she worked made it all the more amazing.

Dan shrugged. "The woman can cook." More important, she handled the multiple demands on her time and attention with aplomb, bringing good cheer and relative calm to the hungry crowd at the portable buffet tables.

"Of course she can cook—she's a chef," Travis said, lifting a brisket sandwich to his lips. The father of two preschoolers, he was always stating the obvious.

"She worked in the best restaurants in the area before deciding she wanted more flexibility in her schedule, and then she struck out on her own as a personal chef," Jack Gaines added with the factual precision of a guy who had founded an electronic-systems company and was single-handedly bringing up his seven-year-old daughter with seemingly none of the problems Dan was having with his own irascible brood.

"Great," Dan said, already imagining what it would be like to have this woman in his kitchen, whipping up one incredible meal after another. "That ought to make it all the easier to convince her to come and work for me." At this point, money was no object. He just wanted a solution to the problem that seemed to be growing larger every day. And if he had to think outside the box to get it, well...wasn't that what he always did? Solve problems in whatever creative way necessary?

"Not so great." Nate Hutchinson held up a cautioning hand. The only one of them with no pressing familial obligations, he made it his business to know all the beautiful, unattached women on the local social scene. And their caterer fit the bill, if the lack of wedding ring on her left hand was any indication. "Emily's leaving Fort Worth."

Frowning, Dan glanced back at the white catering van with the bright blue Chef for Hire logo on the side. "When?"

"By the end of the month. She's closing her business here this week," Grady McCabe replied. "She wants to move back to the Texas hill country, where she grew up. This is her last gig in the Metroplex."

Dan wasn't deterred by the stumbling block. He merely resolved to move around it. "Fortunately," he said, scraping up the last of the ranch-style beans, "she hasn't relocated *yet*."

Having learned early in life that timing was everything, Dan finished his meal and waited patiently until the crowd dispersed and cleanup was under way. He walked over to the banquet tables where Ms. Stayton was busy packing up. She was not only beautiful, but her eyes were a gorgeous blue. Not that this had anything to do with his interest in her. He wanted a chef, not a wife. He was definitely not looking to get married—or even involved—again.

"I hear you're leaving Fort Worth," Dan said casually.

The knowing glance she gave him said she'd noticed

him studying her—and completely misinterpreted why. She stacked empty serving dishes into a large plastic container, then went to the next banquet table to collect some more. "Yep, I'm headed to Fredericksburg."

Admiring the delicate shape of her very capable hands, Dan edged closer. "What's there?"

A mixture of anticipation and delight sparkled in her smile. "An orchard I'm in the process of buying."

As she bent over the table to reach an item at the other end, the hem of her white chef's tunic edged up, revealing the taut underside of her buttock and shapely upper thigh.

Dan tore his gaze from the delectable sight and forced himself to concentrate on the important matter at hand—her skill as a chef. "So you haven't closed on the property yet."

With a determined expression, Emily secured the top of the plastic box with a snap. She straightened and hefted the heavy container. "I will, as soon as I get paid for this gig and secure financing on the property next week. Then I'll be out of here."

Dan took the box from her and carried it to the back of the catering van. He set it where she indicated and turned back to her, noting she was about six inches shorter than his own six-two. "What about Chef for Hire?"

Emily shrugged one slender shoulder and pivoted back toward the banquet tables. To the left of them, two guys from the company that had supplied the outdoor cooking appliances loaded the equipment onto their truck. "It was fun while it lasted," she said.

Dan followed lazily, not for the first time noticing how nicely she filled out the starched white tunic. As he neared her, he inhaled the orange-blossom scent clinging to her hair and skin. The November sunshine glimmered in her mahogany hair, highlighting the hint of amber in the silky strands.

"You're going to quit, just like that, to do something else?"

"Run an orchard," she said as she gathered and folded the linens covering the tables. "And yes, I am, Mr.…?"

Embarrassed he'd forgotten to introduce himself, he extended his hand. "Dan Kingsland."

She accepted his grip with the same ease she did everything else. "Nice to meet you, Dan. I'm Emily Stayton."

Surprised by how soft her hand felt, given the kind of work she did, Dan released his hold on her reluctantly. He stepped back before he could think of her as anything but a potential employee. "Lunch was great, by the way."

Her soft lips curved in an appreciative smile. "That was the plan, but…thanks."

Dan carried a stack of linens back to the van for her. "Since you haven't left yet, how does one go about hiring you?"

Her elegant brow furrowed. "For a party?"

More like…every evening. But figuring they would get to that, Dan looked her in the eye and cut straight to the chase. "I can't remember the last time my family sat down to a good dinner. Not that it was ever that great, given the lack of culinary skill in the family, even before their mom and I divorced a couple of years ago. But now, with the older two in high school and my youngest in elementary, it seems like the dinner hour has become downright impossible." He sighed heavily.

"The kids are always fighting about what we're going to eat. Whereas their great-uncle Walt, who lives with us, just wants hot, home-cooked food and plenty of it."

She gave him a compassionate look. "Sounds stressful. But I'm not sure how—"

He held up a hand, urging her to let him continue. "You see, I watched you today, juggling everything that had to be juggled to feed such a large group under less than ideal circumstances. And I thought, if she could do that for us—help us figure out how to get back on the right track at meal times—maybe we'd have a chance to be a happy family again." Dan paused. He hadn't meant to reveal so much, hadn't expected anywhere near the sympathy and concern he saw in her pretty eyes.

Not sure what it was about this woman that had him putting it all on the line like this, he forced himself to go on. "So what do you say? Will you help us out?"

Emily'd thought Dan Kingsland was attractive when she met him earlier, but that kick of awareness was nothing compared to the sizzle she felt when she arrived on his doorstep at six that very evening for the agreed-upon "consultation."

The single dad of three answered before she could even ring the bell.

He was dressed in boots, faded jeans and a pine-colored pullover sweater that brought out the green of his eyes. His sandy-blond hair was cut in a rumpled, laid-back style that required little maintenance. His five-o'clock shadow only added to his ruggedly handsome appeal.

He looked a bit harried, but as their eyes met and he

said, "I'm really glad you came," he gave her an easy, welcoming grin.

Emily wished she felt the same ease. She sensed that if you gave this man an inch, he'd take a mile, anything to get what he wanted. Which was, apparently, a path to family peace.

Attempting a laid-back cool she didn't feel, Emily thrust her hands in the pockets of her tailored wool slacks. These days, she avoided situations that felt too... intimate from the get-go. Plus, she was a chef—not a consultant—and it was clear from the sounds of rambunctious activity in the foreground that his family was in the midst of end-of-workweek chaos. But in this case, money talked. She needed the extra cash the gig offered to facilitate her move back to Fredericksburg. So she'd taken it, even though she wasn't sure what Dan expected her to be able to do here tonight.

Oblivious to the conflicted nature of her thoughts, Dan led her through the foyer to the rear of the two-story brick home. A messy, hopelessly outdated kitchen was on one side, an equally cluttered breakfast room took up the middle and on the other side of the thousand-square-foot space was a gathering room, complete with an L-shaped sofa and large stone fireplace, with bookshelves on either side. There was stuff everywhere. Briefcase. Schoolbags. Jackets and shoes and caps.

In the midst of it were his three offspring. All had his long, rangy build, sandy-blond hair and green eyes. There the similarity ended, she realized after Dan's brief introduction. Ava, seventeen, had her nose in a book and was busy highlighting passages with a yellow marker. Fifteen-year-old Tommy was standing in front of the fridge with the door open wide, studying the contents.

Eight-year-old Kayla was dividing her time between an easel and paintbrush, and a mess of rainbow-colored modeling clay. She seemed to be working on both art projects simultaneously. Everyone seemed to be in everyone else's way and not particularly inclined to do anything about it.

The little girl got up and rushed over to Emily, skidding to a stop just short of her. Washable paint dotting her arms and face, she demanded, "Are you here to cook for us?"

"Emily is here to consult with us and help us solve our problem," Dan explained. "She's going to give us some ideas on what we can eat for dinner that will make everyone happy."

"Good luck with that," Tommy grumbled. He grabbed a bottle of some sports drink from the fridge, guzzled half and started toward the door. "I'm going for a run."

Dan held up a hand. "You just got home from wrestling practice."

Tommy shrugged and plucked his sweat-dampened T-shirt away from his body. "I didn't get enough of a workout."

Emily gauged the flushed state of his skin and thought maybe he had.

"Not now," Dan repeated with paternal firmness.

Ava stood. "I don't have time for this, either. I've got to study." She picked up her heavy AP Biology textbook and highlighter.

On a Friday night? Emily wondered. Shouldn't the girl be going out with friends or just relaxing after a long week? As Emily had planned to do herself before getting waylaid by Ava's father?

Not to be outdone by her older siblings, Kayla tugged on Emily's blouse. "I've got to paint. Want to watch me?" She grabbed a brush so quickly she knocked over a jar of paint, splattering the table and floor.

Irritated, Tommy said, "Dad, make her get that stuff out of here!"

Kayla clamped her hands on her hips and tossed her long, disheveled blond hair. "I'm supposed to do my artwork in the kitchen, so I don't make a mess on the carpet!"

Ava looked up from her book long enough to put in her two cents. "Yeah, well, your stuff is in our way, as always!"

"Kids, that's enough," Dan reprimanded them just as a stiff-legged older man with a white buzz cut walked in. Dan introduced him to Emily as Uncle Walt.

Walt looked at Dan, perplexed. "I thought you were cooking tonight, Dan."

Dan shrugged. "Change of plans."

Emily looked at Dan. Had she been lured here under false pretenses?

He flattened a hand over his heart. "I wasn't going to try and rope you into it." Dan grabbed a roll of paper towels and knelt to mop up the spilled paint.

"Why not?" Uncle Walt argued, lending a hand, too. "If she can cook and she's here and it's dinnertime… Anything she makes would have to beat your cooking."

Dan took the ribbing with the affection it was given. "Thanks," he said wryly. Standing, he tossed the towel into the trash and went to wash his hands.

"It doesn't matter who cooks—meals around here suck," Tommy grumbled.

Which made Emily wonder if the kids liked the food

anywhere. "What about with your mom?" she asked, curious as to whether Dan's ex had it any better when she had the kids. "What do you do for meals when you're with her?"

The room suddenly grew very silent. No one volunteered anything. Feeling like she'd plunged headlong into quicksand, Emily forged on, searching for information. "I gather meals are a problem there, too, then."

Another heartbeat passed. Then another.

Walt cleared his throat. "Didn't Dan tell you? My great-niece hasn't lived in the United States since she and Dan split up."

Chapter Two

Emily only wished Dan had thoroughly filled her in before she'd accepted this gig. If he had, she would have known this was the kind of situation that tugged on her heartstrings. And hence, one she should avoid. Now, more than ever...

"Mom's in Africa," Tommy blurted out.

"Keep up, will you?" Ava scolded, shoving her glasses up on the bridge of her nose. "That was last week. She's in China this week."

"Whatever." Tommy shrugged, edging toward the back door again. "The point is, she's not here. She's never here."

Kayla picked at the rainbow-colored volcano she had built with her modeling clay. "Yeah, we wish she would come back to see us 'cause we miss having a mommy."

Walt grimaced. "My niece is a physician for the International Children's Medical Service, or ICMS."

Which meant, Emily concluded, that Dan had full custody of their brood, with all the attendant joys and problems. As well as his ex-wife's great-uncle. This was an interesting situation.

Dan paused, his expression filled with remorse. "I'm sorry if I wasn't clear about that."

Emily slowly exhaled, belatedly wishing she hadn't asked a question that had upset the whole clan. On the other hand...what did the former Mrs. Kingsland's on-going neglect of her kids have to do with her? Nothing, she reassured herself firmly, since she didn't expect to be here very long at all. This was Dan's dilemma—not hers!

Kayla tugged on Dan's sweater. "Dad, I need dinner now!"

Appearing frustrated he hadn't made any strides toward solving his problem, Dan silenced the complaining with a motion of his palm. "Fine. We'll order pizza."

"Not again!" the two older kids said in unison.

Dan sent Emily a look as if to say, *See what I'm dealing with here?*

Kayla stomped her foot. "But I'm really, really hungry!" she wailed as tears pooled in her eyes.

"It'll take at least an hour to get here at this time on a Friday night," Ava predicted with a beleaguered sigh.

Once a problem solver, always a problem solver, Emily thought. "How about I just whip something up?" She figured she and Dan could talk and consult while she cooked. Then she'd be able to take her paycheck and exit, before she got hopelessly enmeshed in the ongoing family drama.

"Uh...that could be a problem," Dan said.

Walt nodded. "We haven't had a chance to go to the grocery store yet."

"We only go on the weekends," Kayla said.

Emily knew people generally had more in the pantry than they thought. "Just let me have a look." She opened the fridge and realized she had her work cut out for her.

They were right—pickings were meager. "I can handle it," she said confidently.

"How long is it going to take?" Kayla asked, pouting.

Emily was already assembling ingredients on the counter. "Twenty minutes."

"That's faster than we could get a pizza," Dan enthused with a grateful glance her way.

Happy a meltdown had been avoided, at least for the moment, Emily took charge. "In the meantime I need everyone to sit down with a pen and paper, and make a list of your favorite foods, along with everything you dislike, as well."

Kayla began stuffing her modeling clay back into the airtight storage containers. "Daddy, can you write mine down?"

"Will do," Dan promised.

Walt scrounged in the drawer next to the phone for pens. The older two kids sat down at the kitchen table. Emily filled a big pot with water and set it on to boil. Meanwhile, she chopped up half a pound of bacon into bite-size pieces and put all in a skillet to brown.

"What are we having?" Tommy looked suspicious.

Emily knew that to tell would only invite criticism and argument. "It's a surprise," she said with a firm smile. "Work on your lists."

Ava frowned and looked at her dad. "Can she do that?"

Dan shrugged. "Looks like she already is. Come on, everybody. This is your one chance to have a say in what we're going to have for future dinners around here."

His logic worked. Everyone got down to business, thinking, writing, thinking some more. By the time

Emily put a heaping platter of spaghetti carbonara, green beans with almonds and fruit salad on the center of the table, the pages were filled.

"Hey, that looks kind of good." Tommy surveyed the fragrant pasta, sprinkled liberally with Parmesan cheese.

Kayla smiled. "Fruit salad is my favorite."

"It smells incredible," Walt said.

Dan held out a chair. "Sit down with us, please, Emily."

She hesitated. Wasn't this how she'd gotten into trouble before? By blurring the line between hired chef and family friend? "It's not—"

"Typical, I know." Dan's smile was as kind as it was chivalrous. "But these aren't usual circumstances."

Emily still would have refused had it not been for the growling in her tummy and the fact that she knew she must no longer skip meals or eat at odd hours. For the next year and a half, she had to be as conscientious about her diet as she'd been the past six months. The future of her own family was riding on that. "All right," she said gratefully. "But as soon as we're done eating, it's right back to business."

The serving platters were passed around, and then all was silent as the kids dug in. Ten minutes later there wasn't a speck of food left on the table, and Emily had made plenty.

"Wow!" Dan sat contentedly back in his chair.

Walt agreed. "Incredible."

"I didn't think I'd like that, but it was really good," Tommy said.

Ava smiled. "I liked it, too." She bolted from her chair. "Anyone want coffee?"

Dan and Walt nodded.

They didn't know how good that sounded, Emily thought wistfully. But seeing the label of the can, Emily had to decline. Caffeine was among the things she had to avoid these days, too. "Thanks. No."

"So are you going to come and cook for us all the time?" Kayla propped her chin on her upraised hand and searched Emily's face. "'Cause I would be really, really, really happy if you did."

For a second, Dan noted, Emily looked almost tempted. Then she seemed to catch herself. A hint of sadness and regret flashed in her eyes. "Oh, honey..." she began.

Dan knew she was about to decline.

Across the room, a burst of salsa music radiated from inside her shoulder bag.

Emily rose in relief, all business once again. "I apologize, but I'm really going to have to get that. I've been waiting for a call from my Realtor all day." Phone to her ear, Emily ducked out of the kitchen gracefully and walked toward the front foyer.

"You kids are on for dishes," Dan said. "Kayla, you clear, Ava, load the dishwasher, Tommy, wipe down the table and counters and take out the trash."

For once, there was no grumbling as the kids rose from the table. Maybe, Dan surmised, it was because they were all full, and hence, content—at least as far as their tummies went. Emotionally, well, it was hard to fix the absence of a mom in their lives without getting involved again, and that was something he did not want to do. His life was too complicated and busy as it was.

From the hall, Emily's voice rose in agitation.

"They can't do that, can they? I just got the okay on

my mortgage application!" She sounded distraught. "Of course I can't match that! At least tell me who did this. Tex Ostrander!"

Who was Tex? Dan wondered.

Obviously the guy had some emotional connection to Emily.

Abruptly her voice cut off. Became calm and professional. "Yes. I understand. I'll talk to you in a few days."

"Wonder what's happening there?" Tommy asked beneath his breath.

Dan wondered, too, as did everyone else in his family.

Emily strode back into the kitchen. Tears of frustration glimmered in her eyes. "Sorry about that," she said in a choked voice. "I just got some really bad news." She rubbed her hand across her forehead. "Would you mind if I took your lists home tonight, studied them... and then came back again to talk to you about my suggestions?"

"Of course it's fine." Dan moved toward her. "I'll walk you out."

He waited until they reached her car, then said, "Is there anything I can do?"

Her lower lip trembling, Emily leaned against her van and turned her glance away. "Not unless you can magically buy back the Fredericksburg orchard my family owned when I was growing up." Sighing, she pushed her hand through her mahogany hair and turned her gaze to his, clearly needing to vent. "It went up for sale a few months ago. As soon as I heard, I talked to the owners. Told them I wanted it, put some earnest money down and started saving for the full down payment."

Emily swallowed and gestured ineffectually. "I

mean, I knew technically that, until I secured a mortgage and made the full down payment, the owners could still receive a higher bid, though I had the right to match it—it's written into their contract with me. But I didn't really think someone would come along and offer to pay in cash—never mind my ex-fiancé!" she finished, enraged.

Dan blinked. "Your ex-fiancé just bought the orchard out from under you?"

Emily clamped her arms in front of her, the action delineating the fullness of her breasts. "He outbid me by ten percent."

Dan studied her defensive posture. "You can't match his bid?"

"Unfortunately, no." Emily moved away from the van and began to pace, her hips moving provocatively beneath the loose-fitting black trousers. "I was stretching it as it was."

Silence fell between them.

Clearly still struggling to get her emotions under control, Emily rubbed at the bridge of her nose. "The good news is since my contract with the owner is now null and void, I'll get my earnest money back, but I'm out an orchard and a mortgage application fee."

Dan held her gaze. "Why would he do that?"

Emily threw up her hands. "I don't know. I haven't seen Tex Ostrander since we broke up, and that was ten years ago."

"He knew you were buying the place?" Dan prodded, remembering how soft and silky her hands felt, despite the fact she worked with them all day.

Emily scowled and gave Dan a measuring glance. "Apparently his parents are retiring and he's decided to buy them out and move back to the area, too. If he owns both properties—the two orchards are located side by side—he'll have the biggest peach crop in the area."

And that was saying something, Dan knew, since Fredericksburg, Texas, was famous for its stellar peach crop.

Dan closed the distance between them. "So what does this mean about your move back to the area where you grew up?"

"I don't know." Emily exhaled in frustration. "My Realtor said I'm still approved for a mortgage and the bank has agreed to transfer that approval to another property."

Dan hated to see anyone lose out on a dream—particularly a deeply held one. "Maybe you could purchase another orchard," he suggested kindly.

Her lips parted as she looked up at him. "There aren't any other orchards for sale in the area, and besides, I didn't want any of those—I wanted the one my parents owned when I grew up." She kicked at the concrete drive with the toe of her boot, and Dan tried not to notice how nice she looked in profile. "I had plans to bring it back to its former glory. To… Well, never mind. It's not going to happen now." Her voice rang with disappointment. She fell silent, a morose expression on her face.

Wishing he had a way to comfort her, Dan asked, "So what now?"

Emily sighed. "It puts my plans to leave Fort Worth on hold for now. Which really sucks. Because it's the holidays, and thinking I'd be in the hill country, I turned down all these gigs I could have had."

Dan knew that catering businesses thrived during

the holiday season. "There's still one you could have," he said. He resisted the urge to take her hand in both of his. "And I promise you, it will pay better than you ever dreamed."

"YOU OFFERED HER A JOB, just like that?" Walt said later that same evening when Dan filled him in on what had transpired. "Without doing a background check and getting references?"

Dan loved his ex-wife's uncle. He'd been a lifesaver the past couple years—but sometimes his negativity rankled. "Stop thinking like a private investigator."

Walt looked up from the game of Internet chess he was playing. "I'm the first to admit that the meal she made was wonderful. But we're talking about your kids here. Your home."

Dan frowned at the thought of any delay in getting things back on track at mealtime. "She was great with the kids."

As by the book as ever, Walt countered, "At least have her fill out an application—and let me talk to some of the people she's worked for in the past."

"First of all, Grady's wife has already vouched for her character. Apparently Emily has regularly catered events for the company where Alexis works. Her terrific performance is what led Grady to hire Emily for the lunch yesterday. Second, I don't think Emily has done a job like this before."

"The point is—" Walt's brow furrowed as he took in his Internet opponent's next move "—you don't know."

Dan recalled Emily's enviable ability to bring serenity even to the chaos that had ensued upon her arrival. "I don't want to blow it. Dinner tonight was the first conflict-free meal we've had in years around here."

Walt made his move with a thoughtful scowl. "Still not enough reason to hire Ms. Stayton without due diligence."

"Walt, I appreciate your sentiments. As a private investigator, you've seen things I could never even imagine. But I trust Emily Stayton." On a gut level, Dan amended silently. "And the decision is made. I want her to be our cook. Not a housekeeper, just our personal chef, for however long we can manage to get her." Hopefully in the interim he'd be able to figure out how to get Emily to come to work for them full-time. "And I don't want you doing anything to interfere with that."

Walt turned his attention back to the computer screen. "You ask me," he grumbled, "you're making a mistake."

"I didn't ask," Dan stated flatly.

Still, he couldn't help thinking about it as the night wore on.

He couldn't explain it. He just knew, on some deep fundamental level, that Emily Stayton was The One to help solve his family's problems. And Dan never discounted his instincts when they were that strong.

EMILY HAD PROMISED TO CONTINUE the consultation at nine Saturday morning. She arrived right on time. Dan went to answer the door and found her standing on the porch, much as she had the evening before—with one difference. Instead of looking pink-cheeked and healthy, she looked a little green around the gills.

"Are you okay?" Dan asked.

Emily swallowed hard, waved a vague hand, even as she moved past him. "It'll pass."

What will pass? "Are you sick?"

"Oh. No. I...I... Bathroom?" Her words were more a command for direction than a request.

Able to see what was about to happen, Dan hastened down the hall and opened the door. "In here."

Simultaneously hitting the light and the fan, she barreled past him and slammed the door. The unmistakable sounds of retching followed.

The kids came tromping down the stairs at the commotion. "What's going on?"

"Is someone...?"

"Ohhh." Tommy, Ava and Kayla looked at one another in recognition.

"Go upstairs," Dan ordered. "I'll call you."

They bolted, as was usually the case, when illness that might involve icky cleanup was involved.

"See?" Walt said, passing with his stiff-hipped gait. "You *don't* know everything about her. For all you know, she's got a problem that will leave her unable to do mornings—"

"Actually..." The door opened and Emily stepped out, still looking pale and shaky. She leaned weakly against the door frame. "Walt could be right."

Walt looked at Dan. "I'll leave you to handle this." He went into the study and shut the door behind him.

Dan guided her into the kitchen and onto a stool at the counter. "Can I get you something?" he solicited kindly. "Water? Stomach med?"

Emily regarded him gratefully. "Maybe a glass of ginger ale or a soda cracker if you have it," she said.

Dan paused.

Their eyes met.

As he worked to fulfill her request, he began to put two and two together.

"I'm pregnant," Emily said, flashing a guilty-as-charged smile.

Hence the loose-fitting shirts she wore, the fullness of her breasts in comparison to her slender figure.

"Congratulations!" Dan handed her a ginger ale and pack of crackers.

"Thanks." She ripped open the wax paper and extracted a cracker.

"How far along are you?"

She munched and sipped. "Almost four months."

"Who's the lucky guy?"

Her blue eyes glinted with unexpected humor. "76549823-CBGT."

Dan blinked. "You hooked up with a robot?"

Emily's melodious laugh filled the kitchen. Her soft lips parted as she prepared to take another sip of her ginger ale.

"A sperm bank. All I know about my baby's daddy is that he has an IQ over 140 and is Caucasian, blond, green-eyed and tall. And of course has no major inherited health problems I'd have to worry about."

Dan had lots of questions. None of which would have been polite to ask.

"I'm thirty-five, my eggs aren't getting any younger, and I wanted a family. The luck of the draw wasn't working—I just never met anyone I wanted to settle down with."

"Except Tex Ostrander." Dan recalled the name of the guy who had caused her so much grief the night before.

Emily's lips thinned. "Don't remind me. I'm still mad at him."

She didn't appear to still have romantic feelings for her ex. Although why that should matter to him, Dan didn't know. "Did you talk to him?" he asked casually, forcing himself to move on.

"No." Looking to be bouncing back from her bout of morning sickness, Emily leaned her spine against the back of the stool. "Although, not surprisingly, he called me several times. But back to the job you offered me last night—I've been thinking about it and I can't commit to a permanent family gig. It just wouldn't work out for a lot of reasons," she stated firmly. "But I could help you out on a temporary basis—until I have a chance to get some other chef gigs lined up."

This, Dan hadn't expected. He studied the new color in her cheeks and the professional competence in her eyes. "How temporary?"

"I was thinking through Thanksgiving. That would give me time to figure out what the problems are with mealtime around here—from a cooking perspective."

Maybe there weren't any, Dan thought. Maybe all they needed was a woman in the house again. "There wasn't a problem last night," he said.

Emily disregarded her success. "That was an anomaly. They were caught off guard. They were hungry. Someone set a table of hot food in front of them."

"Hot *delicious* food," Dan corrected.

Finding his mouth dry, he poured himself a glass of ginger ale, too.

"Whatever." Emily waved off the distinction. She rested both her forearms on the breakfast bar and leaned in deliberately. "The point is, these complex family issues are not going to be resolved just because I've showed up."

Trying not to be distracted by the fragrance of orange blossoms and the silk of her hair that fell seductively over her shoulder, he lounged against the opposite counter. "I think you're selling yourself short."

She mocked him with a waggle of her brows. "And I think you're minimizing the problem," she teased. "But we digress—"

Dan frowned in confusion. "Do we?"

Her gaze was completely serious now. "You haven't said if you would be okay with the fact that I'm pregnant," she pointed out softly.

Dan's glance moved involuntarily to the slight swell of her tummy beneath the blue-and-lavender paisley tunic before returning to her face. "Why wouldn't I be?"

"I'm unmarried."

And incredibly sexy, and likely to be even sexier in a deeply maternal way as your pregnancy progresses....

"You have impressionable children," she added.

And I've had thoughts about kissing you...

He shrugged. "You're a responsible adult."

Emily raked her teeth across her soft lower lip. "Not everyone approves of what I'm doing."

Dan enjoyed the experience of being there with her, the pair of them talking with the familiar intimacy of two people who've known each other for years, instead of mere hours. He reassured her with a look. "Not everyone approves of divorce, either. Stuff happens." Old dreams fade. New ones take their place. "As far as I'm concerned, congratulations are still in order."

"Thank you." Emily smiled. "Do you think my pregnancy will bother Walt?"

Dan sidestepped the question as best he could. "He's crotchety."

Her eyes glimmered. She knew there was more. "Meaning?" she prompted.

Candor was something he could not provide. Not yet, anyway. "You don't work for him. You work for me," Dan said, and left it at that.

Emily surveyed Dan warily. "Is there something else I should know?"

Besides the fact that Walt doesn't trust anyone until a thorough background check proves that person is trustworthy? Dan mused. "Not a thing."

ONCE EMILY HAD fully recovered from her bout of morning sickness, they decided to get right down to business. "There's a couple ways we could approach this problem," she told the family gathered around the kitchen table.

"We're not going to be able to solve it," Tommy interrupted, evidencing the same lack of teamwork he had the night before.

Dan gave his son a stern look.

"No offense," Tommy continued, hands raised, "but none of us like the same stuff."

Emily knew sugarcoating the problems would not solve anything. They needed to examine their differences together before a remedy could be found.

"That's true, although you all seemed to like last night's dinner," Emily said. "Anyway, according to your lists, Kayla prefers mainly breakfast foods like pancakes, French toast, eggs, cereal and so on. Ava's into coffee, chocolate and salads. Tommy wants high protein and electrolytes. Dan wants anything everyone will eat. And Walt, given his choice, is a meat-and-potatoes man."

"It doesn't sound like we have anything in common." Ava sighed.

"Sure we do," Dan interrupted sternly. "We're all Kingslands."

"Uncle Walt isn't—his last name is Smith," Ava pointed out studiously.

Eager to join in, Kayla put her crayon down and piped up with, "Emily isn't one, either!"

"That's right." Emily struggled to contain control of the family meeting. "I'm not. My last name is Stayton. It was good of you to notice that, Kayla."

Kayla beamed.

"Back to the problem," Emily said. "I can come up with menus that will please each of you. And I could make enough to feed you for several days if you wanted to eat the same thing every night, reheated."

"Leftovers?"

"I don't really like leftovers."

"Me, neither."

"Or we could draw straws to go first and take turns by night," she suggested. "That way everyone would have at least one night a week where their favorite meal was served."

The kids appeared to be thinking about this option.

"Or I could try to put one thing that everyone likes in each menu. This might make for some odd combinations. Spaghetti and scones, for instance."

All the kids made faces.

"Or we could do something a little less mundane," Emily said, more or less making it up as she went. "We could try eating a lot of new dishes from around the world. Maybe make some of the foods that your mom might be eating in her travels. We could even ask her what her favorite dishes are from some of her favorite places and try that."

The kids looked receptive to that idea. Dan did not.

"I think we should stick to the tried-and-true at first," Dan said.

The kids' enthusiasm faded and they went silent.

"If that means meat and potatoes, sounds good to me," Walt said with a shrug.

"Sorry about that," Emily said a short time later as Dan walked her to her van. "I didn't know you had a problem with international cuisine."

Normally Dan did not discuss his relationship with his ex-wife. Whatever went on between him and Brenda was between him and Brenda. But since Emily was going to be working so closely with his family, he figured she had a right to know. "I don't encourage the kids to try and keep up with their globe-trotting mother."

Emily looked shocked. "Why not? Surely she has e-mail and phone service."

"She does. She's just not good about using it for personal reasons. Sometimes weeks or months go by without a word from her."

"Ava knew where she was."

"Because Brenda put the two older kids on the list-serve that alerts her colleagues to her whereabouts. Getting a mass e-mail every time your mother boards a plane is not the same as having personal contact with her."

Emily appeared to mull that over. "And the lack of personal contact upsets the kids."

"It's always hard when a parent lets you down."

She nodded, for the moment really seeming to understand. Which in turn made Dan wonder what disappointments she had weathered in her life.

"I'm sorry. I didn't know," she said finally.

"Anyway," he said, "Brenda is scheduled to come home between Christmas and New Year's. Hopefully nothing will get in the way of that. Meanwhile, if we could just work on getting us on track to civilized family meals, I would appreciate it."

For the first time Emily looked uncertain. "I'm no miracle worker."

"You wouldn't have known that last night."

"Well, just so you know, I'm not here to step in and cater to their every gastronomic whim."

Dan knew that what he'd asked of her was unusual. In his estimation, that unusualness was what had made that dinner so great. "The thing is, we're not the kind of family who has servants waiting on us. I don't *want* that kind of atmosphere for my kids."

Emily tucked a strand of hair behind her ear. "Then what *do* you want?"

"Have you ever taught a cooking class?"

"Yes."

"Well, you know how, at the end of a cooking class, the chef usually sits down with the class to enjoy the food with the people she's teaching? I'm interested in creating that same convivial mood for my family during the dinner hour. Unfortunately it's something they've never really had. Even before the divorce, the meals at our house were always catch as catch can. So it's going to be like working with a group of beginners."

Sensing she was a woman who liked thinking outside

the box as much as he did, Dan continued, "The point is, I'm not asking you to make a meal and serve it to us in the formal dining room. I'm asking you to create a warm, relaxed atmosphere during the meal preparation, so the kids are free to come in and out and ask questions or just hang out if they want. And if they so choose, they can learn how to cook from you. During the meal, I want you to sit down and eat with us—the way you would if you were a family friend who'd come over to help out in a pinch."

Emily made a face. "But I'd still be an *employee*."

"Only technically. As far as the kids are concerned, you are a friend of my friends Grady and Alexis McCabe, and you've agreed to help us with dinner, using your skills as a personal chef and cooking instructor." Just to be sure she knew he was serious, he named a salary that caused her eyes to widen. And still, he noted in disappointment, no sale…

"While I appreciate your offer," she said, "cooking at the same home day in and day out is not something I choose to do anymore."

"So you've worked for a single client before."

"For a few years, right after I left restaurant work. But I switched to catering small events in different venues because it was more my style."

Dan suddenly had the feeling she was holding back. Was Walt right? Was there more he should know about Emily before bringing her into his home? He decided it didn't matter. He wanted peace in his family—now—and she was the only person who could deliver it.

"Look, just give us a couple of weeks and get us through the Thanksgiving holiday," he persuaded. They both knew she had no other work lined up. And this would give her an income while she regrouped.

"Fine," Emily said reluctantly. "But the first order of business is groceries. You need a lot of staples, Dan."

So he gathered. "You want to give me a list?"

"Actually I'd like to do the shopping myself—unless you're an ace at picking out produce and know the difference between baking soda and baking powder."

"They're not the same?"

Emily winced. "No. They are not."

Dan grinned at her comical expression. "When can you start?"

"I can purchase groceries and fix dinner for you this evening."

Dan couldn't think of a better way to spend his Saturday.

"I don't work Sundays," Emily cautioned.

"What about Monday? Do you hire out for breakfast, as well?"

"How about we just do dinners to begin with?" Emily returned.

Dan knew he'd been pushing it, even getting this far. "Okay," he agreed. "What can I do to help?"

Emily rummaged through her purse for her keys. "Just be here this afternoon around four to let me in, so I can get dinner started."

That, Dan thought, sounded better than she knew.

Chapter Three

Dan was in the study, updating the plans for one of the luxury office condos of One Trinity River Place, when he heard a vehicle turn into the drive. Glancing out the window, he saw Emily emerging from her van. He walked outside, surprised by the drop in temperature. That morning it had been in the low sixties. Now he figured it had to be in the forties. And given the dark clouds on the horizon, looked to get colder still.

"See we've got a blue norther rolling in," Dan said when he met Emily at the back of the van.

She looked as if the change in weather had caught her unawares, too. Her red chef's coat and jeans were little defense against the chill wind.

Shivering, she nodded. "Guess I should have listened to the weather report."

Dan gaped at the sheer volume of food in the back of the van.

"Doesn't look like that when you shop, I gather?" Emily joked.

But maybe it should, Dan thought, noting the abundance of fresh fruits and vegetables. "When I go, it's mostly milk, cereal, bread, frozen pizzas and microwave dinners." Dan took the heavy bags from her arms. "I'll take those if you'll hold the door."

"Sure." She grabbed a bag that looked a lot lighter and moved toward the door.

Being careful not to crash into her, he led the way to the kitchen.

Once there, he was dismayed. The kids had left it in a mess, which wasn't unusual. It wasn't good, either. "Sorry," he said.

Emily sighed, looking less than pleased. She pivoted to go back to the van for more groceries. Dan stopped her with a hand to her shoulder. "Why don't you let me carry everything in? You really shouldn't be lifting anything, anyway, in your condition."

She stepped closer and stood with her hands on her hips. "That's an old wives' tale."

"Humor me?" Dan said. He let his glance rove over her windswept hair, her face, before returning to her mesmerizing blue eyes.

Looking at him from beneath a fringe of dark lashes, she released a beleaguered sigh. "If you insist."

"I do. And don't touch any of those dirty dishes, either! I'll do them when I'm done carrying everything in."

That seemed harder for her to agree to, but finally she nodded her assent. He resumed his task. By the time Dan had finished, every available space in the kitchen was taken up with an overflowing bag or carton. "I've got extra freezer and refrigerator space in the garage," Dan said.

Emily was organizing the condiments, moving most to a cupboard by the sink. "We may need it." She looked around, grabbed a roll of paper towels and a bottle of spray cleaner, and mopped up some spilled milk on the counter.

Dan gathered up plates and glasses and began putting them in the dishwasher. The silence of the house was broken only by the sounds of their activity. "Where are the kids?" Emily asked finally.

Watching the play of worn denim over her slender thighs and delectably sweet butt, it was all he could do not to reach out and caress her. "Ava's with her study group, Tommy went running with a couple teammates and Walt took Kayla to a birthday party at the skating rink. But not to worry—they'll all be back in time for dinner at six."

Emily sent him a quelling glance. "What were you doing when I got here?"

Dan wiped down the tables. "Working."

Oddly, color flared in her cheeks. "Why don't you go back to it? I'm fine here on my own."

Abruptly Dan sensed Emily was as attracted to him as he was to her—and fighting it just as hard. Obviously this situation—and the intimacy it brought—was going to be a lot more difficult to navigate than he'd thought.

"Ordering me out of the kitchen?" he teased.

Emily studied him for a moment, then turned back to her work with maddening nonchalance. "I need to focus."

So did he. Because if he stayed...

"Sure," Dan said. He left, trying not to feel disappointed.

IT TOOK EVERY OUNCE OF WILLPOWER Dan had to stay out of the kitchen and out of Emily's way for the next two hours. For one thing, he was curious about where she was going to stow all the groceries she'd purchased. For another, the smells emanating from the kitchen were damned enticing. And it was his kitchen. He ought to be able to go in there whenever he wanted.

But the main thing he had to fight was his attraction to her. Being around her only increased the subtle sexual tension between them. And giving in to that attraction would not be a good thing. Especially while she was working for him.

Once things were settled in his home life, then perhaps he could see about pursuing this attraction. But for now? Emily was right to put up a wall between them and keep it there, Dan decided. It was the only logical, ethical way to proceed.

So he worked at his drafting table, and as every member of his family straggled home, he warned them not to go into the kitchen where Emily was toiling away. At six o'clock, he gathered everyone up and they headed en masse for the kitchen.

And stared, stunned, at what they saw.

EMILY WONDERED if it was all too much. The linen tablecloth and cloth napkins were nothing special—she'd borrowed them from her store of them at home. The mix of daisies and mums in the vase had come from the farmers' market.

As for the meal itself, she'd decided to go with buttermilk-brined fried chicken, mashed potatoes, corn on the cob and peach cobbler. Comfort foods in the extreme.

She figured, since the kids had welcomed the spaghetti carbonara she'd been able to throw together the night before, they were bound to like this.

She was wrong.

Maybe not wrong, exactly, she decided as the meal wore on with none of the enthusiastic eating of the trial run. But definitely misguided.

Dan, of course, consumed his meal with gusto. So did Walt. Emily was hungry, so she ate, too.

Kayla merely picked at her food, and Emily was pretty sure that Ava didn't actually taste anything. Tommy stripped the breading from the chicken, ate the meat, drank his water, and that was it.

Dan began to get irritated.

He regarded his children with the stern exasperation Emily was beginning to know so well. "What's the problem?" he asked, his tone as impatient as his manner.

Kayla shrugged. "I think I ate too much hot dogs and birthday cake at the skating rink," she said.

That excuse Dan appeared to buy.

He looked at Ava. "I had two mocha lattes while I was studying. So I'm just not hungry!"

Caffeine did cut the appetite, Emily knew.

Tommy shrugged. "I haven't completely cooled down from running. If I eat too much now, I'm likely to do what, um, Emily did this morning."

All eyes turned back to Emily. "Are you sick?" Kayla asked.

Walt, too, lifted a brow, waiting.

Dan hadn't told them, Emily realized. He seemed to not want to reveal it, either. Too bad. If the proverbial mud were to hit the fan, Emily wanted to know it now, before she invested any more in this temporary job.

"I'm pregnant—that was morning sickness," she blurted out.

His uncle gave Dan a look that spoke volumes. Walt could clearly tell from Dan's bland reaction that he was the only one in the room who wasn't surprised by Emily's announcement.

Kayla spoke first. "Pregnant means having a baby, right?"

Dan nodded. "Right. Emily is going to have a baby approximately five months from now. And sometimes, when women are pregnant, they have tummy trouble. She had tummy trouble this morning, but that's okay— it's all part of expecting a baby." *And,* Dan's glance to his children conveyed firmly, *I have no problem with it.*

Nor did they.

In fact, the news didn't seem to faze them, either way.

"Can I be excused?" Ava said. "I really want to study some more."

"I don't feel so good." Kayla held her tummy. "Maybe I should go lie down on my bed."

"The team's going to a movie tonight," Tommy said. "I need to get ready."

Looking relieved her announcement had caused so little upset, Emily stood. "I'll clean up."

"Actually," Dan said, "I'll do it."

Emily's expression turned obstinate again. "It's my job."

He leaned forward and persisted, just as stubbornly. "Not tonight it's not. You look tired. Why don't you go on home? We'll see you Monday evening."

Emily squared her shoulders. "Are you sure?"

Dan nodded. "But you're going to need a jacket. It's really cold out there now." The wind was whipping through the trees, rustling the branches.

"I'll be fine." She moved past him in a drift of orange-blossom fragrance. "The van has a good heater."

It didn't matter, Dan thought. "You're pregnant," he reminded her protectively. He paused at the hall closet and pulled out his wind-resistant, fleece-lined hoodie. It would keep her and her baby cozy-warm. "Take this."

For once, she didn't argue. "Thank you. I'll bring it back on Monday."

He held the sleeves while she slipped it on and zipped up.

Trying not to think how feminine she looked in his jacket, despite it being way too big for her, Dan walked her to the front door.

Emily seemed flustered by the attention. "You don't have to keep doing this," she said. "I'm an employee. Not a friend. Or a—"

"Date?" Dan finished her sentence before he could stop himself.

Emily flushed as they stepped outside. In the soft glow of the porch light, she looked even prettier. "That wasn't what I meant."

On the contrary, Dan disagreed silently. It was exactly what she meant, because that was exactly how it felt—like a date. In his attempt to put her at ease, he was handling this all wrong. He swallowed, felt his throat close. "You'd rather I just stay here?"

Emily dipped her head self-consciously. "Yes."

So, with effort, Dan shoved his hands in his pockets, turned and moved to the door.

Emily got halfway down the sidewalk before she realized, "My keys! I forgot my purse." She hurried back to the door.

"I'll get it," Dan offered.

He stepped inside, Emily right behind him. Walt came out of the kitchen, a cup of coffee in one hand,

Emily's leather carryall in the other. Dan recognized the look on the semiretired private investigator's face and swore inwardly.

"This what you're missing?" Walt asked Emily politely.

"Yes. Thank you. Good night, everyone! See you Monday!" Emily rushed out the door like the hounds of hell were on her heels.

In the driveway, an engine started.

Dan waited until the van drove away, then turned furiously back to Walt. "Tell me you didn't go through that," he muttered.

The older man shrugged. "Well, I had to figure out who it belonged to before I could return it to its rightful owner!"

Bull. "And?"

"She's licensed to drive in Texas. Carries two credit cards and a bottle of prenatal vitamins. Nothing incriminating in there."

The tension between Dan's shoulder blades eased. "Satisfied now?"

Walt ran a hand over his snowy-white buzz cut. "Not without references we can run down."

Dan scowled and immediately took the opposite tact. "Not going to happen," he said.

Walt looked annoyed. "Did you even ask?" he demanded in a low, disgruntled voice.

"No. And I told you, I'm not going to," Dan said, his temper rising. "I trust my gut on this."

Walt paused and shot Dan a telling look. "Make sure it's your gut and not another part of your anatomy you're following."

Dan thought about that as the evening wore on. Why

hadn't he asked for references? He never hired anyone for his architectural firm without a thorough vetting. Walt's P.I. business was the one that did the work. But in this case, he hadn't even thought about it and then when prompted, had resisted the idea. Why? Why did he want to just go on emotion where this woman was concerned? He hadn't done that since Brenda. And they all knew how his refusal to deal with reality had turned out.

Back then, he'd fallen in love with a fantasy of who Brenda was, rather than who she truly was. And three kids and a divorce later, he was still paying the price. Did he really want to go back down that road?

Walt was right.

He had to delve a little deeper, even if it felt uncomfortable. Even though Emily had only agreed to be there through Thanksgiving, he still needed to be sure she was who and what she seemed.

"YOU REALLY DIDN'T NEED to do this," Emily said when she met Dan at the Starbucks just down the street from her loft on Sunday evening. He looked incredibly handsome in a charcoal-gray suede jacket and slacks, his face ruddy with cold. "We could have settled up tomorrow night after I cook dinner. Besides, it's my fault for leaving the house last night before giving you the receipt for the groceries."

Dan gestured amiably as the door to the coffee shop opened and another burst of wintry air swept in. His expression unexpectedly serious, he sat down opposite her, opened a leather portfolio and removed a checkbook. "It's not the kind of thing I want left undone."

Emily sensed there was more than that. She had gotten the impression he wanted to talk to her without his family present. She handed over the receipts from the three stores where she had made her purchases, along with the invoice from Chef for Hire, then watched as he wrote out a check. He sat back, his tall form dwarfing the café-style chair, while she slid the check into her purse.

He continued in a brisk, all-business tone. "I don't know how you normally work, since we got together on the spur of the moment. At my firm, I have employees sign an employment contract. I assume you do the same for your catering gigs."

"Usually, yes, I do," Emily said. But this time she hadn't felt the need to put anything in writing that would have specified her pay and hours. Belatedly, she realized she should ask herself why.

Dan put the checkbook back in the portfolio and pulled out several forms. "I also generally require an updated résumé, completed application, background check and personal references."

That, Emily knew, could be tricky. "Is it really necessary?" she cut in as smoothly as she could. "Sounds expensive and laborious. And really, considering that I'll only be working for you a few weeks, quite unnecessary. Unless, of course, you've had second thoughts about having me in your home."

Dan was silent.

Emily knew that what he was asking was routine business procedure. Yet for some reason she felt insulted on a personal level. After all, he had spent enough time with her to be able to tell she was an honorable person.

He seemed to realize he had offended her. He flashed her a crooked smile meant to conciliate. "You'd almost think you had something to hide," he teased.

Actually, she did. "Ask me whatever you want," Emily said, hoping to give him enough information that a detailed check into her work history would not be necessary.

His eyes still holding hers, Dan leaned back in his chair. "What's your background?"

"I grew up in Fredericksburg, Texas. Only child. My parents ran a peach orchard. It was sold a few years after my dad died." *For many reasons,* Emily added silently to herself, *that still upset me.* "College was out of the question at that point, so I started working in restaurants, liked it and went to culinary school, graduated and worked at three different top-tier restaurants in the Dallas-Fort Worth area until I was thirty. I got tired of the grind and long hours and branched out on my own, freelancing as a personal chef. I've done that for the last four years. And while being a solo operator has been very lucrative, it's also very demanding."

She took a deep breath before continuing. "Now that I'm starting a family, I want a less hectic life, which is why I was trying to buy the orchard. I want to be able to stay home and take care of my child as much as possible, at least for the first four or five years. I thought I had found a way to do that." She sighed. "Obviously, I haven't—since my purchase of the orchard fell through—but I'll come up with a new plan before December first."

"What happens then?" Their glances locked and they shared another moment of tingling awareness.

Emily told herself her unprecedented reaction to Dan was really just another surge of pregnancy hormones. She forced herself to get a grip. "I have to vacate my loft. It's already been rented to someone else."

"So one way or another..."

"I'll be going *some*where," Emily finished, aware her voice sounded a little rusty, and her emotions felt all out of whack, too.

Fortunately Dan had no more questions. Standing up, Emily handed him the jacket she had borrowed from him the evening before, slipped on her coat and gathered her things to leave.

Dan stood, too. "You're going to walk back to your building?"

Emily told herself not to read anything into the concern in his eyes. "It's just down the block." She slipped out the door, Starbucks cup in one hand, keys in the other.

Dan fell into step beside her. "I'd still feel better if I walked you as far as your lobby."

Ignoring the reassurance his strong male presence provided, she shrugged and turned her eyes to the awning that marked her destination. This could not lead anywhere, not if she was working for him. "Suit yourself."

They arrived at the front door of her building. Emily waved at the security man behind the desk in the lobby, visible through the double glass doors. He waved back.

"So how do you want to manage the paperwork?" Dan drawled.

Emily rocked back on her heels. "By fax. I can send you my standard agreement tonight."

Dan rocked back on his heels, too. He braced his hands on his hips, pushing the edges of his jacket back. "So you're still on for tomorrow evening?" he presumed.

Emily tore her gaze from his rock-solid chest and

abs. "Absolutely. Unless we hit a snag in the paperwork, which I'm not anticipating." It was only the thorough vetting of her résumé that would reveal something Emily would rather forget. But she had an idea how to keep that from becoming a problem she would really rather not deal with. Because what happened with the Washburns was not going to happen with Dan's family. She was wiser now. Better able to keep that protective force field around her heart...

"I'll read and sign the contract right away," he promised.

Glad they had come to an agreement that was mutually beneficial, and as thoroughly professional as it should have been from the beginning, Emily nodded. "Thank you."

Another peaceful moment passed between them. Emily smiled and began to relax. Maybe this would work out, after all, she thought. And, of course, that was the moment the next unwelcome complication arose.

Chapter Four

Emily went pale as a dark-haired man, roughly their age, climbed out of a pickup truck parked in front of her building and strode toward them. In a white western shirt, jeans and black leather jacket, he appeared to be both sophisticated and affable.

He touched the brim of his black Resistol hat and stopped just short of them. "Emily," he said, smiling and looking her up and down. "It's been a while."

Emily stood her ground and made no move to greet the interloper with anything even faintly akin to the same familiarity and warmth. Instinctively Dan slid a protective arm behind her.

"Ten years," Emily acknowledged, her voice taut. Turning slightly, her elbow brushing Dan's ribs, she looked up at Dan and said, "Dan, I'd like you to meet Tex Ostrander."

Her ex-fiancé. The man who'd bought the orchard out from under her and thrown her life into chaos.

"Tex, this is my, um, friend—" she stumbled slightly over the misnomer "—Dan Kingsland."

Aware Emily was using him to keep her ex at bay, Dan played along and extended a palm. "Nice to meet you."

"Same here," Tex said.

As the two men shook hands, Dan noted Tex had a firm, no-nonsense grip.

"What are you doing here?" Emily demanded.

"We need to talk about my purchase of the orchard," Tex said. "And since you wouldn't return my calls…"

Emily frowned in warning. "I can't imagine we have anything to say to each other."

Tex clearly differed. "Do you really want to discuss business out on the sidewalk?" Tex asked.

A group of teens walked by, talking and laughing.

Emily's frown deepened. She looked at Dan, a question in her eyes. Getting the hint—she wanted and needed a neutral third party to possibly run interference for her—Dan wordlessly agreed to help her out. He stipulated mildly, "As long as it doesn't take too long. Emily and I have plans for this evening." *Just not together.*

Incorrectly assuming Dan was Emily's date and he was interrupting something, Tex shrugged. "I'm fine with that. I just want a chance to explain and make my pitch."

The three of them walked inside and took the elevator to Emily's loft. The high-ceilinged, brick-walled abode had a bank of windows overlooking the Trinity River. The thousand-square-foot apartment was divided into four areas—work space, living room, kitchen and bedroom. The only space walled off was the bathroom at one end.

She led them to the stylish sofa and a pair of chairs at one end of the room. She sat down on the sofa. Dan sat next to her.

Tex took one of the sling-back chairs opposite them. "I'm here to offer you a job," Tex said.

Emily looked as if she could hardly believe Tex's temerity. Nor could Dan, under the circumstances.

Emily stared at Tex. "You really think I'd accept a job from you after what you just pulled?"

Tex nodded. His expression earnest, he continued in a flat, practical tone, "We both know the only reason you wanted the orchard was to bring it back to its former glory. You don't have the money or the agricultural background to make the sort of improvements required. But I do. And since my parents are retiring to Arizona and have recently sold their orchard to me, and the properties are side-by-side, it makes good business sense to merge the two and have one operation with twice the capacity, rather than two competing businesses."

As much as Dan was loath to admit it, Tex's pitch made sense, from a business perspective, anyway. Personally, it was another matter indeed.

Emily frowned, looking tempted despite her earlier refusal. "What are you offering me exactly?"

"A full partnership if you'll agree to defer most of your salary in exchange for equity, just as I am, until we get the new business up and running. Bottom line—I'm only going to be around part of the time. I need someone I trust to live on the property and run the orchards when I'm not there, and start an on-property restaurant-slash-retail-business that will feature fresh fruit, preserves, pastries, salsas and whatever else you can dream up to produce with our crops."

"Why me, Tex? Why not someone else?"

"Because you're the only one who knows how much blood, sweat and tears went into starting these orchards.

Together, you and I can make them better than either of our folks ever dreamed. So what do you say, Emily?" Tex leaned forward urgently, hat in hand. "Can I count on you? Are you in?"

"THANKS FOR STAYING," Emily told Dan several minutes later, after Tex had left.

Dan looked around her loft. The sleek, minimalist space didn't seem to jibe with her any more than Tex Ostrander did. She seemed much more at home in his traditionally cozy kitchen.

"No problem," Dan said. He had wanted to make certain she was all right. He watched as she walked to the stainless-steel island that served as both work surface and dinner table. She plucked an orange from the fruit bowl and began to peel it with single-minded concentration.

"Are you going to accept Tex's offer?" Dan asked.

"I don't know." She offered Dan half the orange. "On the one hand, I'm really ticked off about the way he subverted my dream."

"But not surprised," Dan guessed as he popped a section of orange in his mouth.

Emily made a face. "He's always been ambitious to a fault. It was never going to be enough for him to help run his parents' orchard until they decided to retire."

Curious, Dan asked, "Is that why you two never married?"

Emily downed one orange section, then another. "We got together when my mom died and I needed someone to be there for me. He stepped in and provided the stability and direction I needed at a time when just trying to decide whether or not to continue subscribing to the daily newspaper was a quandary." She met his gaze. "When my grief ebbed and I no longer needed someone to solve all of life's problems for me, I realized something else that had eluded me. He was always going to put his own needs first and think that his dreams were more important than mine. And that hurt." Her eyes narrowed. "And he's obviously still behaving in that manner—for example, thinking he's doing me a favor by buying the orchard out from under me, because he can run it better than I can."

"I sense a 'but' in there somewhere."

She looked in the fridge. It was crammed with all manner of fresh fruit and vegetables. She moved the milk and cheese and withdrew a jar of dill pickles. Dan shook his head at her offer.

She withdrew a pickle for herself and recapped the jar. "Bottom line—I still want a hand in restoring the property where I grew up." She took a bite of the pickle, catching the dripping juice with one hand cupped beneath the other. Appearing as if the sour taste were heaven—and who knew, maybe it was to a pregnant woman—she continued, "And the thought of having the money to start a restaurant and a line of peach, strawberry, blackberry and plum products with my family's name on it is tempting."

Dan studied the glitter of excitement in her eyes. "Even if it means working closely with your ex?"

Emily turned on the spigot and washed her hands with lavender soap. Some of her pleasure faded. "I think I can handle Tex."

Dan ignored the stab of unaccustomed jealousy and pointed out, "You didn't seem that sure earlier." He watched as she dried her hands with a towel, determined to let her have her say. "When you were pretending I was someone of significance in your life."

Emily flushed, as if guilty as charged. She helped herself to a wrapped candy on the counter, then pivoted toward him. The tantalizing drift of orange-blossom perfume teased his senses. "First of all," she corrected archly, "I never actually said that."

She hadn't needed to. Tex had gotten the message and jumped to the necessary conclusion.

Dan waved off her offer of a candy. "It was implied, in the way you introduced me as your 'um, friend.'"

She removed the foil wrapper from the treat and popped it in her mouth. Dan watched her savor it. Her eyes locked with his, she lifted her shoulders in an aimless shrug. "You could have refused to go along with it."

"And desert a damsel in distress?" he retorted. "I don't think so."

The color in her cheeks went from pink to rose. "Whatever." She waved off Dan's concern. "It's no longer necessary now that I know why Tex did what he did."

"Sure about that?" Dan took comfort in the fact that Emily hadn't given Tex an answer, had merely said she wanted to think about it before deciding.

"What are you insinuating?" she demanded, apparently annoyed.

Aware he did not want to be shown the door as readily as Tex had just been, Dan shrugged and voiced his theory about what was really going on here. "Maybe this is all a ruse to get you back. Maybe Tex is still interested in you—romantically." Certainly Dan couldn't imagine letting Emily go without a fight if she was his woman.

"Don't be ridiculous!" Emily scoffed. "Tex and I haven't been in contact with each other for ten years!"

"Plenty of time for him to realize he made a mistake and want to make amends." And what better way than by being an integral part of Emily's dream of restoring her family's farm to its former glory?

Emily sighed resentfully. "That's *not* going to happen."

"Why not?" Whatever the answer, Dan needed to hear her say it.

She folded her arms in front of her, the action accentuating the fullness of her breasts and the slight roundness of her tummy. "Because I'm not interested in Tex."

The look on her face made him a believer. His heartbeat kicked up. "Not that it should matter to you either way," Emily added bluntly.

Yeah. Well... "It does," Dan shot back just as bluntly.

"Why?" she asked.

Aware she was close enough for him to see the turbulent emotion in her eyes and note the slight unsteadiness of her breathing, Dan retorted gruffly, "Because I don't want to see you—or your baby—hurt." And whether Emily realized it or not, this situation with Tex had the potential to do just that.

"So you're what now?" Emily tossed back. "My unofficial protector?"

Aware that put him in the class Tex had been in—and look where that had gotten the man—Dan exhaled slowly. "And then some," he murmured back.

She stared at him in confusion.

And then he did what he had been wanting to do from the first moment they'd met. He forgot all the reasons they shouldn't tear down boundaries, took Emily in his arms and pulled her against him. She tipped her head back with a soft, anticipatory "Oh!", which propelled him to continue. Caution fled as he cupped the back of her neck with one hand and slanted his mouth over hers. She moved against him provocatively as their mouths met. After that all was lost in the scent and touch and feel of her. Her lips were warm and mobile, and she tasted like chocolate, peppermint and woman. The fullness of her breasts, the slight roundness of her tummy pressing into him, increased his desire. Dan stroked his hands up and down her spine, and let himself fall even further into the kiss, aware all the while of the steady rhythm of her heart against his.

Emily hadn't intended to give in to the simmering attraction any more than she had meant to lean on Dan's solid, reassuring presence when Tex showed up. But from the moment he touched her, her spirits rose. There was just something about Dan that she could not resist. That left her wanting to know and experience more.

Like this kiss. Maybe it was because she was pregnant and had been alone for what seemed like forever, but Emily had never felt such pure, unadulterated passion, never wanted a man more than she did at this moment. He used no pressure, yet she felt overwhelmed. Persuaded. Seduced. And the fierce ardor welling up inside her was reason enough, she knew, to break off the sweet, steamy embrace.

Reminding herself that, like it or not, Dan was still her employer and, hence, she needed to exhibit at least a little common sense, Emily put her hands on his chest and pushed.

Dan lifted his head, his eyes dark with desire.

Breathing hard, flushing with a heat that started deep inside and radiated outward, Emily stepped back.

She noted with chagrin there wasn't an ounce of regret in his demeanor. *Or in her heart.* Her mind, however, was a different matter.

"That," she said flatly, calling on every ounce of inner fortitude she had, "was a mistake that can't happen again. I work for you."

HER TREMBLING WORDS were a shock to his system. As much as Dan was loath to admit it, Emily was right. She was his employee. There would be time to pursue this attraction when that was no longer the case. Right now, there were larger problems to address.

He still needed to bring order to his family's mealtimes—and like it or not, she was the key to that.

Emily needed to figure out what she was going to do after December first. And with Thanksgiving coming up… Concentrating on the two weeks between now and the holiday seemed best.

"I crossed a line I shouldn't have," he admitted reluctantly.

Emily sighed and pushed her hands through her hair. "We both did."

"So what do you say?" he prodded.

"Want to just forget it? Pretend—" she paused and briefly averted her eyes "—it never happened?"

Dan nodded, knowing even as he bid her good-night and left that it wasn't that simple. That kiss had been seared into his memory, and, he suspected, hers, too.

Fortunately the house was quiet when he got home. Kayla was already asleep, the older two kids ensconced in their rooms. Walt was in the study, printing out photos for a client.

Dan noticed the digital pictures coming out of the printer. One glance told him why Walt had waited to print until the kids weren't around. "Another cheater?"

"Unfortunately. Client's not going to be too happy. On the other hand, she'll be relieved to find her husband's infidelity was not a figment of her imagination, as he claimed." Walt indicated the machine connected to the phone. "You had a fax come in a few minutes ago."

Dan plucked the pages out of the feed. It was from Emily. She hadn't wasted any time completing the paperwork and sending him a copy of her agreement. Dan wished her timing had been better. He turned back to Walt. "I imagine you looked at this?"

Walt nodded. "With the exception of your friend Grady McCabe all her references are from the restaurant work she did four to ten years ago."

Before she became a personal chef for hire. Dan scanned the pages Emily had sent, relieved to note that nothing else looked out of the norm. "We discussed that."

Walt ran a hand over his hair. "And?"

She hedged in a way that made him want to back off, for both their sakes. Once again going with his gut, Dan shrugged off his uncle's concern. "I trust her," he said flatly. He held up a hand before Walt could interject. "But to make you feel better, I'm giving you the okay to do a routine background check."

Finally Walt was happy. "Want me to follow up with the references, too?"

Dan nodded. "But don't go overboard," he cautioned. He knew his uncle. The years as a private investigator had left Walt seeing trouble around every corner. And trouble was something Dan did not want to find. Not now, and certainly not before the Thanksgiving holiday.

TO EMILY'S RELIEF, DAN filled out the paperwork as quickly as she did. She reported for work on Monday afternoon at four. Determined to meet the needs of the Kingsland family without becoming emotionally involved with Dan and his kids, Emily set about preparing nutritious after-school snacks to hold the kids until their six-o'clock dinner. And immediately hit a snag.

"I can't do my homework," Kayla told Emily when she got home from school.

Although child care was not part of her job description, Emily reminded herself, creating a warm and welcoming environment for them was. She set a snack of apple slices and yogurt dip in front of Kayla.

"Why not?" Emily cut shortening and salt into flour and added just enough water to make dough.

As if she had no appetite whatsoever, Kayla glumly pushed the dish away. "Because we have to ask our parents what their Thanksgiving traditions were when they were our age, and my mommy isn't here."

"She has e-mail, doesn't she?" Emily asked as she put golf-ball-size rounds in the cast-iron tortilla press.

"Of course Mom has e-mail," Ava said, walking in the door, heavy backpack of books in one hand, a tall iced latte in the other.

"Do you know the address?" Emily asked, determined to solve the problem before it became a full-blown catastrophe that would interfere with the dinner hour.

Ava sat down at the desk in the kitchen and switched

on the personal computer. A series of key clicks later, she had logged on to the Kingsland-family e-mail and started a new message for Dr. Brenda Kingsland. "There you go." Ava grabbed her backpack and coffee and exited.

"Dinner's not for another two hours," Emily called after Ava's retreating figure. "Do you want a snack?"

"Nope. Not hungry!" Ava responded without turning around.

Kayla wrapped her arms around Emily's waist. "Will you type the message for me?"

Knowing the task was beyond the eight-year-old's capability, Emily smiled. "Sure," she said.

A few minutes later, it was done.

The question had been sent, and Kayla began happily munching the apple slices Emily had prepared.

DAN WALKED IN AT SIX to find a make-your-own-taco bar had been set up on the kitchen counter. Emily was standing at the stove flipping fresh flour tortillas on a griddle while the rest of his family, drawn by the delicious scents filling the house, made their way into the kitchen. The scene was cozy and welcoming, despite the continuing lack of total cooperation from his children.

"I thought we'd fill our plates buffet-style," Emily told everyone. Her cheerful smile buoyed Dan's spirits even more than when Walt had let him know—first thing that morning—that the routine background check had turned up nothing at all. There wasn't even a parking ticket on Emily's record.

"I'm not all that hungry," Ava announced, tossing her empty latte cup in the trash.

"Maybe some salad topped with a little meat and cheese?" Emily suggested gently.

"I guess I could do that." Ava reluctantly headed up the buffet line.

Dan relaxed as some of his eldest daughter's recalcitrance faded away. The air of serenity falling over the kitchen was exactly what he had envisioned.

"Will you make mine?" Kayla asked Emily from her perch at the computer keyboard in the kitchen. Behind her, the e-mail screen glowed.

"Sure," Emily said, beckoning Kayla to her side so the little girl could show her what she wanted.

Tommy—who had showered after wrestling practice for once—added spicy beef, greens, pico de gallo and black beans to his plate, passing on the rice and tortillas.

Walt showed no such restraint—he loaded up his plate with a bit of everything, including the freshly made guacamole and sour cream. Stomach rumbling, Dan followed suit.

"Is your baby going to be a girl or a boy?" Kayla asked when Emily had fixed a plate for herself and sat down.

Although technically it was none of his business, Dan had wondered as much himself.

Emily's face lit up, the way it always did when she spoke about her baby. "I don't know yet," she said.

Ava leaned forward eagerly. "Are you going to find out?"

Emily nodded. "In a couple of weeks, when I have my ultrasound."

"What's an ultrasound?" Kayla asked.

Emily briefly explained the procedure. "I'll bring

a picture so you can see. That is—" she flushed and looked at Dan "—if it's okay."

A lot of things were okay, Dan thought. Including Emily's presence there with them. "Sure," he said.

At the kitchen desk, the mail icon sounded with a little ding. Kayla got up so quickly she knocked her chair over. "Look!" she shouted in excitement. "It's a message from Mommy!"

"I WISH YOU HADN'T done that," Dan said as he walked Emily out to her van after dinner.

Emily could see that in the implacable set of his mouth and the disapproval in his eyes. She also thought Dan was wrong. "Kayla got the information she needed, as well as a promise that her mom would try to call the kids tomorrow, talk with them."

His handsome jaw took on the consistency of granite. "A promise that Brenda might not keep."

Emily shrugged. "And that she very well might."

Dan eyed her like a grizzly on a bad day. "Look, I gather you meant well…but my kids have been hurt enough by their mother's abandonment."

Emily turned up the collar on her coat to ward off the chill of the November evening. "And you think you're helping them by encouraging their low expectations of their mom."

Dan looked at the half-moon in the dark night sky. "I'm encouraging them to be realistic."

Emily leaned against the side of her van and folded her arms in front of her. She knew she risked overstepping her bounds by getting involved in this, but she had to speak her mind. "Even if it devastates them in the end? Brenda works in dangerous parts of the world.

She could easily succumb to illness, earthquake, flood or heaven knows what else. You don't want their last thoughts of her to be angry, or for their last contact with her to be hurtful. You don't want your kids to have to carry that kind of burden for the rest of their lives."

Dan paused. "Are we talking about them now, or you?"

"Both, I guess."

He waited.

Emily sighed. She supposed it wouldn't hurt to explain. "My dad was a fantastic businessman and farmer. He grew the Stayton Orchard from nothing. Whereas my mom was dependent on him for literally everything. When my dad died, she fell apart and let the business go all to hell in just a couple years. She destroyed the legacy he'd built, my college funds, everything. I was furious with her when she sold the farm. I hitched a ride to Fort Worth with a friend who went to college here, got a job in a restaurant and didn't look back." Emily shoved a hand through her hair and continued miserably. "Two years later Mom died of complications from pneumonia. Although at the very end we were able to see each other and express our love for each other, I still can't forgive myself for all the time we squandered. I can't forgive myself for not taking the time to understand things better from her point of view."

Dan moved close enough to search her face. "Which is what you think my kids should do."

"Yes—for everyone's sake. It's not as if they're not suffering as it is. Ava's studying nonstop and living on coffee, probably in an attempt to emulate her mom and so feel worthy of her attention. Tommy is channeling all his excess emotion into his physical training, which in itself isn't bad. But he's overexercising and eating just enough to get by to maintain his weight for wrestling, which leads me to think maybe he's in the wrong weight class. And Kayla can't eat whenever she misses her mommy or wants extra attention from you to make up for it, which is a lot, frankly."

He rubbed his jaw contemplatively. "You picked up on all that?"

Emily exhaled in frustration. "It's easier for me. I'm not a member of the family, so I'm able to be more objective about what's making your mealtimes so generally miserable. And it's not really that they can't agree on a menu," she said more quietly after a moment. "It's that they miss having a mom here with them." To the point that Emily's own heart ached for them.

"What do you think I should do?" Dan asked eventually, bracing his shoulder against the side of the van.

"For starters?" Emily retorted wryly. "Tell them what you and I have been talking about all this time."

Dan's brows knit together in confusion.

"Don't look up," she said softly. "But there are three very inquisitive children watching us out their bedroom windows."

Chapter Five

Emily was not surprised to receive an e-mail from Dan first thing the following morning. By 9:00 a.m., he was at her door, looking incredible in a dark green suit, pale olive shirt and contrasting tie.

"Thanks for making time to see me this morning," Dan said, his deep voice sending a thrill coursing through her.

"No problem." Reminding herself this meeting was strictly business, Emily ushered him into her loft and shut the door behind them. She led him to the breakfast bar in the kitchen area, where she'd set up decaffeinated coffee service for two. She stepped behind the counter and went back to whipping up a batch of apricot scones. "I've been curious about what you said to your kids last night."

Dan watched as she cut butter into a mix of flour, sugar, baking powder and salt. "For starters, I told them it's not polite to spy on two people having a conversation, and then I talked to them one on one about what's been going on. Ava admits she's overdoing it on the caffeine, but says it's the only way she can keep up the energy she needs to study." He exhaled slowly. "Tommy acknowledges he is being careful about his weight, but says there's no spot for him in a heavier weight class, and so at least for the rest of the season he's just going to have to continue to maintain his current weight. And Kayla still thinks Brenda is going to call her."

"And you don't." Emily combined cream with beaten egg and then folded it into the mixing bowl with the other ingredients.

Dan compressed his lips. "Let's put it this way. There have been many more promises broken than kept."

Emily stirred in the fruit. "Maybe Brenda will come through this time."

"And maybe she won't. Maybe she'll do what she always does," he said bitterly, "and make a grand entrance and present them with ridiculously lavish gifts meant to make up for all the times she's not been there for them."

Emily turned the dough out onto a floured surface. "Does that work?"

Dan watched her roll the dough out into a circle and cut it into eight triangles. "Initially, no—the kids were so angry they refused to accept anything she gave them. After a couple of years had passed, their need to punish her faded and they slowly began to warm up to her again—albeit in a sort of emotionally distant way."

That sounded sad, Emily thought. She slid the baking pan into the oven and set the timer for fifteen minutes. "How old were the kids when Brenda left?"

"Ava was thirteen, Tommy eleven and Kayla barely four. As you can imagine, Kayla had the hardest time. She just couldn't understand why her mommy was going away like that—that she wouldn't see her for months on end."

Dan drained his coffee cup and Emily reached across the counter to refill it. "It would have been one thing had

Brenda been in the military and had no choice," Dan went on, then shook his head. "But Brenda signing on full-time with ICMS was strictly voluntary."

"And hence hurt everyone, especially Kayla."

Dan nodded. "So in the future, please refer Kayla to me if she needs to contact her mother."

"All right."

Dan rested his elbows on the counter. "As for Ava… I'm not sure what to do."

Emily carried the dirty dishes to the sink. "You can forbid her to use caffeine."

Dan's smile softened. "I'd rather she come to the right conclusion on her own."

"Which is where I come in," Emily guessed dryly.

His eyes followed the swift movements of her hands. "With her knack for science and your ability to cook… I was hoping you could convince Ava to collaborate on some research into the best way to fuel her body for studying. The same with Tommy, only his focus is optimum athletic performance." He sighed. "I know it's a lot to ask, but if we could come up with lists of food that would work for both of them and add those to our menus…"

"You'd have the happy dinner hour you crave?"

"Exactly." Silence fell, more comfortable this time.

"What about Kayla?" Emily asked at last.

Dan kicked back on the stool, his expression pensive. "She takes a lot of her cues from her older siblings. If they're happy, she's in a much better frame of mind, too."

Needing to rest for a moment, Emily came around the breakfast bar and took a stool two down from Dan.

She sipped her decaf. "I'll give it my best shot, at least for the next couple weeks."

Dan glanced at the papers and photos spread out at the end of the breakfast bar. "What's all that?"

"Specs for the Stayton-Ostrander Orchard. Tex e-mailed them to me late last night. He asked me to spend some time looking at them before I make up my mind."

Dan frowned. "What'd you think after looking at it?"

"He makes a good case, that together we'll do a lot better than either of us would alone."

"But…?" His expression was as maddeningly inscrutable as his posture.

"I'm still angry about the way Tex went about this, purchasing the property out from under me with a bid he had to know I couldn't match."

"It does seem if had he wanted a true partner, he would have talked to you first."

Emily traced the rim of her coffee cup with her fingertips. "Exactly."

Dan studied her. "And yet you remain torn."

The compassion in his eyes made it easy to confide. "My father put everything he had into that orchard. It broke my heart when my mother had to let it go. I've felt guilty for years about what happened."

"Why?"

"Because I didn't try to intervene when I knew she was making bad business decisions."

Dan shook his head. "You were just a kid."

"I still could have helped more. Done the research, gathered information, presented it to Mom. It might have made a difference. Instead, I sat back and judged her for everything she did wrong. I should have worked by her side every chance I had to rescue the family business. Finally I have a chance to do something about it, bring it back to its former glory."

"But that means working closely with Tex."

Emily inhaled, taking in the brisk wintry scent of Dan's aftershave. "And I'm not sure I want be in business with someone who constantly thinks he knows what's best for me."

Dan inclined his head. "Signing on as Tex's partner could mean a perpetual power struggle," he agreed.

"But—" Emily bit into her lower lip "—it's also a way to honor my father and make up for my mother's mistakes and my inaction."

"So you're tempted," Dan concluded.

Emily's throat was thick with emotion. "You don't know how much."

THREE HOURS LATER, DURING a pickup game of basketball at the club, Dan was still thinking about the situation. It didn't take long for his friends to notice his distraction. Predictably, after three missed shots in a row, they called him on it.

Reluctantly Dan explained.

Grady dribbled past him. "I can see why you're bummed, thinking Emily might go into a partnership with her ex-fiancé," he said.

"But whether or not such a move is going to be a mistake for Emily is not your problem," Travis reminded him.

Then why did it feel like his problem? Dan wondered. It wasn't as if he and Emily were dating or anything. She was a temporary employee, and a remarkably independent one at that. Just because they'd once had the bad judgment to give in to the physical attraction between them, did not make him her Sir Galahad.

Jack sped past, ambidextrously dribbling the ball. "You have to stay focused, pal. Think about the fact that you need a cook for your family."

"One," Nate added, springing up and catching the rebound with his usual skill, "who gets along with your kids."

"So if it's not going to be Emily, because she feels she has to pick up the banner on behalf of her family..." Grady winced with displeasure as his shot hit the backboard before falling in with a swoosh.

"Then find someone else," Travis concluded.

Easier said than done, Dan thought as the day progressed.

He'd employed enough people in his architectural firm to know that hiring a person with the right skills was one thing. Hiring someone with the right skills who was also capable of seamlessly blending right in was a rare thing indeed.

The simple truth of the matter was that Emily meshed with his family. And although his kids weren't wildly enthusiastic about her presence—yet—at least they hadn't gone all out to drive her away. Which meant he had to do everything in his power to convince her to stay on as long as possible.

His mind made up, Dan showered quickly and headed back to the office. Once there, he quickly settled into a meeting with his staff, discussing the proposed changes to the interior design of a just-sold penthouse condominium at One Trinity River Place. They were deep into a discussion of how the sun would affect the new design when Dan's secretary stuck her head in the door. "Sorry to interrupt, boss," Penny said, "but Dr. Kingsland is on the phone. She said she's about to board a bus into the Changbai mountains and the connection is really bad."

"Keep going," Dan instructed his staff.

He slipped out of the conference room. Penny strode briskly beside him. "The front desk just phoned to let me know that Walt and Emily Stayton are on their way up."

Dan did a double take. What was *that* about?

Penny motioned toward the phone on his desk, and, figuring first things first, Dan strode to the receiver. "Brenda?" he said.

"I don't know who this Emily person is, but honestly, Dan, don't you think you could have consulted me before…" Crackling cut off whatever else Brenda said.

"…I'm coming home as soon as I get done with my work in the mountains…." More static. "I know I said Christmas…but it's going to be Thanksgiving. I've already told the kids…" More snapping sounds. "…an old-fashioned holiday…no restaurants this year…going to cook…"

The line went dead just as Walt and Emily walked in.

Emily looked as perplexed as Dan felt, but Walt's expression was choirboy innocent.

Another bad sign.

"What's the emergency?" Emily asked, still appearing slightly out of breath, like she'd hurried to get there.

Dan speared Walt with a look that let him know this better be good. "I'd like to know that myself," he drawled.

Emily blinked. "You didn't call this meeting?" she asked, suddenly ill at ease.

"Actually, I called it," Walt said.

And Dan had a sinking feeling he knew why.

EMILY WHIRLED TO FACE the older man beside her. In sport coat and tie, his cheeks ruddy with the cold winds currently blowing through the city, he looked like a TV-show cop about to escort a suspect to the interrogation room.

"I looked into your background," Walt told Emily. "Found out your first personal-chef job was with the Washburn family, and that you were there for over a year. I was curious why you would have left that off the résumé you gave to Dan, and so I called Stu and Sylvie Washburn to see what kind of recommendation they would give you." He quirked a brow. "Surprisingly, they refused to talk to me at all. Said they wanted to put the whole sorry episode behind them and move on, and they hoped you had done the same. Naturally I wanted to give you a chance to explain."

Her face burning with embarrassment, Emily glanced at Dan. He appeared as stunned as she was by what was transpiring.

Dan blew out an exasperated breath. "You should have talked to me first," he told Walt in a way that made Emily feel all the worse.

Walt refused to back down. He folded his burly arms in front of him and continued just as stubbornly, "I knew when you stopped letting a pretty face cloud your judgment and came to your senses, you'd realize these questions need to be answered before Emily sets foot in your home again."

The last thing Emily ever wanted to do was cause trouble within another family again. She stepped between the two men as they faced off. "It's all right. I don't mind explaining. It's just I had hoped not to revisit the situation. It's the only time in the eighteen years I've been working that I've ever been fired. And I guess it still smarts."

Dan looked at Emily. "What happened?" he asked gently.

Still feeling a little like she was caught in the middle of a good cop–bad cop game, Emily set her shoulder bag on the floor beside her. Feeling way too warm, she slipped off her coat and scarf and draped them over the back of the chair. Her spine straight, she lifted her chin and continued speaking to both men.

"I was really tired of restaurant work at that point. The stress and long hours and the bickering between all the high-strung personalities had really worn me down. The job with Stu and Sylvie seemed tailor-made for me. They were both high-powered executives. They had sophisticated palates, as did both their twin girls, who were ten. They traveled frequently, so the job was live-in. My duties were only to cook, shop and clean up after meals. They had staff for everything else.

"And at first it was ideal. I worked seven days a week, but I had plenty of time off each and every day to do whatever I wanted. But then—I guess it was about three months into the job—their nanny quit, and I temporarily took on the job of helping the twins with their homework after school. Stu and Sylvie went through the motions of trying to find someone else, but the girls liked me—and I liked them—and so eventually it was decided that I would take an increase in pay in exchange for supervising the girls when their parents weren't around, which ended up being all the time."

She looked away. "The three of us began to get close. I really loved them, and the girls came to love me. Turns out, Stu and Sylvie weren't happy about that. They sat me down and reminded me to remember my place." Emily winced, recalling that uncomfortable meeting.

"That doesn't sound particularly nice of them," Dan said.

"You'd think, since you were caring for their children, that they would want you to be loved and respected by their kids," Walt agreed.

Emily shrugged, facing the two men again. "They had a point. I might have felt like family to the girls, but I wasn't, so I tried to step back emotionally. But that upset the girls because they didn't understand the change in my attitude—so I was perpetually on this tightrope trying to behave in a compassionate and supportive manner and yet not love them as my own, which was tough as hell because they were great kids and I was tremendously fond of them." Emotion filled her voice. "Anyway, I knew it was a bad situation for all of us, and I kept thinking I should leave, but then I also kept thinking what would happen to the girls if I did."

Dan's eyes filled with compassion. "What an awful position to be in. So what happened next?"

"It all blew up in our faces because Stu and Sylvie overheard the twins talking about how they wished I was their real mommy, not Sylvie. I was fired that same afternoon and told never to come back or have any contact with the girls—because if I did, I'd face legal action."

She cleared her throat. "And that was that. My bags were packed for me and I was escorted out without ever having a chance to say goodbye. I've never spoken to the twins or either parent since, and of course never used the Washburns as a reference, either. But some good did come of the situation." She paused, looking both Dan and Walt in the eye. "It made me realize how much I wanted and needed a family of my own, so I decided to go it alone, I selected a sperm bank and, well, you know the rest...."

"I'M SORRY," DAN TOLD Emily after Walt had left. "I never would have permitted Walt to waylay you like that had I an inkling what he had up his sleeve."

More relieved now than upset, Emily shrugged. It felt good not to have this secret between them anymore. Truth be told, she didn't want to have *any* secrets between them. And not just because it made life so much easier, but because she wanted Dan to understand why she was going to have to quit. Sooner, rather than later. Emily forced a smile and slipped into a chair. Although the pregnancy fatigue was beginning to let up a bit in her second trimester, at times like this she still felt physically drained.

"If it's anyone's fault, it's mine. I just should've leveled with you from the start," Emily admitted, smoothing the hem of her black wool maternity skirt and crossing her legs at the knee. Taking a deep breath, she continued, "But I didn't because I figured what happened with the Washburn family really didn't apply to the situation since I was only going to be with you a very short time."

Dan looked at her, and once again Emily felt the electricity crackle between them. He looked a little taken aback, too. Maybe because this seemed to happen every time they were alone together. "I wish you'd given me more credit," he told her quietly.

Emily did, too. And yet she knew, given that the two of them were on such different life paths, it was best they not get too intimately involved with each other. Dan had his hands full running his architectural firm and parenting the three kids he already had. He didn't need to take on any of her concerns, nor did she need to take on his.

"Not that it matters, in any case," she blurted before she could stop herself.

Dan arched a brow.

Emily met Dan's calmly assessing gaze. "I'm pretty sure I'm going to go into partnership with Tex Ostrander."

Dan sat on the edge of his desk and faced her. Concern glimmered in his eyes. "What happened to your reservations?"

"They're still there," she confessed with a shrug. "I know Tex'll try to run roughshod over me."

Dan's gaze narrowed. "And yet you're still willing to go into business with him."

Emily's hand dropped to her tummy. Her palm curved tenderly over the baby growing inside her. "I've got to do what is best for my baby," she said softly. And what was best, Emily knew, was carving out a legacy for her child's future.

DAN KNEW IT WAS A MISTAKE for Emily to ignore her instincts, which initially had been to say no to everything her ex-fiancé proposed. He also knew it wasn't his place to advise her on her career objectives.

Not at this stage of the game, anyway. So instead, he said, "If there is anything I can do…"

"Actually there is," Emily said with a smile, standing once again. She remained directly in front of him, her body braced in challenge. His heartbeat kicked up a notch. "Tex wants to gut the inside of the house I grew up in and turn it into a tearoom, and convert the barn on the property into a retail store. He thinks it will be cheaper than tearing down and starting anew. Before I agree to anything I'd like to get a second opinion. And since you're an architect…" She paused. "I figured maybe you'd know someone reputable in the Fredericksburg area I could contact to take a look at the property."

Finally seeing a way he could help, Dan offered, "*I* could do that for you."

Her high-sculpted cheeks glowed pink against the fairness of her complexion. Her dark silky hair fell in a straight blanket, brushing her shoulders. She rocked forward in her suede shoes. "But you're so busy…"

Dan tried not to recall how much he had enjoyed kissing those soft lips. Or how sweet and feminine her body had felt pressed against his. Even now, he fought the urge to hold her in his arms again…. "So are you," he countered implacably as he pushed his mind back to business, "and you found time to help me out when I needed it."

Again, that slight hesitation. She pressed her lips together, then said, "I'm not sure I could afford your rates."

Dan wasn't sure he could bear to walk away from her and the tantalizing image of what they might one day have, once all the barriers were dispensed with. "How about we barter, then?" he asked casually.

Her blue eyes glittered. "I'm listening."

He shifted forward enough to inhale the soft, womanly fragrance of her hair and skin. "You stay on as personal chef through Thanksgiving weekend—at the salary we've already agreed on. And this is *especially* important—I want you to make our holiday meal and dine with us." His lips quirked. "If you agree to my terms, I'll go with you to Fredericksburg. See the property, give you my honest opinion and draw up any plans you want."

She stepped back slightly. "When would we go?"

Dan mentally reviewed his schedule. "Saturday at noon okay with you?"

"You've got a deal. In the meantime, I'd better get going if you all are going to have dinner ready at six tonight." Emily started for her coat, scarf and shoulder bag.

"Emily—"

She turned.

"Thanks for everything," Dan said softly. "Being so honest in your assessment of my kids and helping us out."

Emily picked up her coat and put it over her arm. "It's my pleasure— Oh!" The garment slipped out of her fingers and fell to the floor.

But, Dan noted, she didn't look as if she was in pain. Just some sort of…shock. He looked at her closely in an effort to diagnose the problem. "Emily?"

She still didn't move. Didn't blink. Barely seemed to breathe.

Dan tensed in alarm. "Is everything okay?"

Chapter Six

Emily stood motionless, hardly able to believe… And then she felt it again. The tiniest movement, a fluttering deep inside. Her breath caught and moisture filled her eyes.

Dan's hand was on her arm, lightly touching, prompting. "Emily?" he said again. "What's wrong?"

The tears she'd been holding back spilled from her lashes and rolled down her cheeks. And still Emily couldn't move, couldn't bring herself to speak. And then…there it was again—the slight fluttering of life. Wanting to hang on to the sensation, this tiny baby she already loved so very much, she shut her eyes and savored the sheer exhilaration of the experience.

"Emily?" Dan tried again. "What is it?"

The tenderness in his voice made her meet his gaze. The warmth in his eyes held her rooted in place. She sucked in a breath, her throat too thick with tears for her to speak. She took his free hand and placed it on her lower abdomen, holding it firmly against her. And there it was again, the push against her skin from deep inside. An unbearable tenderness soared through her. More tears welled and coursed down her cheeks.

Dan finally understood and a smile as radiant as any

she had ever seen spread across his face. "The baby," he murmured, shared joy sparkling in his eyes.

Emily nodded, feeling the love only a parent knew. Together, they stood absolutely still. Waiting. Waiting. And…nothing! It seemed, Emily realized with regret, that the tiny "Hello there!" was over.

Dan wrapped a reassuring arm about her shoulders. "Was that the first time you felt the baby move?"

Emily nodded, embarrassed to find she was still ridiculously choked up from the overwhelming proof that there really was life growing inside her. All she knew was that the sob of sheer joy that had been lodged in her throat made its way to her mouth. She was crying so hard she was shaking. Dan enfolded her in his arms. As he held her, she leaned into him, accepting his warmth and strength. And still, it seemed, she could not stop the flow of tears. Could not resist the soothing feel of his hand moving up and down her spine, or the soft words of comfort he murmured in her ear.

"I'm s-s-sorry," she said finally, trying hard to get it together. And failing.

Dan slid his hand beneath her chin and lifted her face to his. An abundance of emotion flowed between them. Her heart thumped and skittered and filled. "It's okay," he told her. "You've got every right. And look at *me*." He laughed. "I'm a little misty, too."

It was true. He was.

Her voice trembling as much as the rest of her, she forced out, "It's just…"

Dan looked deep into her eyes and finished for her, "A miracle."

"As much as I tried," Emily said, "I couldn't imagine…"

He nodded, touched. "I know."

"The first time I heard the baby's heartbeat in the doctor's office was something, too."

"Really gets you—" Dan's voice was rusty as he thumped his fist over his heart "—right here."

"Yes," Emily said. And then the blissful tears started again, flowing even faster this time.

Dan smiled and wiped the pad of his thumb across her cheek, stopping the flow of salty liquid making its way to her mouth. Emily gazed up at him with her lips parted. His head lowered, and then they were kissing again.

Yearning swept through her, as vital and real as the life growing within her. Dan flattened a hand over her spine, bringing her flush against him. They were touching from shoulder to knee. Giving in to the passion coursing through both of them, she wreathed her arms about his broad shoulders and went up on tiptoe. And still the need swept them along, the happiness brought about by her baby mixing with the reality of discovering this—

Had there not been a sudden, insistent buzzing of the phone on Dan's desk, who knew what might have happened? Emily thought as they reluctantly moved apart. With a look of acute disappointment, Dan let her go and went back to reach across his desk for the receiver. "Yes?" He listened. "No. Tell them not to disband. I'll be right there."

He replaced the receiver. "I've got to get back to my meeting."

Embarrassed, Emily looked around for her bag and slipped it back onto her shoulder. She ducked her head. "And I've got to get to work."

Dan caught her hand before she could reach the door. "We will talk about this," he promised softly.

Which was exactly what Emily most feared. An examination of feelings almost too complex to be borne. "Or not," she said with an equally determined smile. Still tingling from the kiss, she rushed off.

EMILY WALKED INTO THE Kingsland family kitchen from the back door, at the same time Ava dragged herself in from the other direction. The pretty teen tossed her backpack of books onto the kitchen table, where it landed with a hard thump, struggled out of her trendy suede jacket and threw it down, too. "I'm going to die!" she moaned, pressing her hand to the center of her forehead.

Emily had no experience with teenagers. But she knew how to take care of someone who was sick. She edged closer, taking in Ava's pallor and the beads of sweat on her forehead. "Do you think you have a fever?"

Ava shrugged listlessly. Tears gathered in her eyes. "All I know is my head is killing me. I have the worst headache ever!"

Emily risked the teen's wrath. She pressed the back of her knuckles lightly against Ava's cheek. Her temperature appeared normal. "Did you have coffee today?" she asked gently.

"No. I mean, I could have. Dad didn't forbid me to have any more caffeine, but he made me feel like it was so unhealthy—" she grimaced "—I had a caffeine-free soda instead, and have been so drowsy all day I don't think I heard a thing any of my teachers said. And then, to top it off, I got this headache!"

"Where do you keep the acetaminophen or aspirin?" Emily asked.

"In the cupboard above the fridge." Ava dragged herself into a chair and laid her head on the table. "Top shelf."

Emily got out the step stool. Found what she needed and shook out two pills. She took that and a glass of water over to Ava. "Take these. It'll help."

"I doubt it," Ava mumbled, but she complied.

"I think you have a caffeine-withdrawal headache," Emily said gently.

"That's what my friend said," Ava grumbled. "She told me to stop and get an espresso after school, but at that point just the idea made me so nauseous…"

"How about a big glass of lemon water and a snack instead?"

Ava looked desperate enough to try anything. "Sure. If you think it will help."

"I do. You know, I had a caffeine addiction myself when I was just a little older than you."

Ava's mouth quirked up. "I'm guessing you kicked it."

"Had to. I was a prep chef in a restaurant at the time and I was getting the jitters." Emily made a face as she worked, remembering. "Not a good thing to have when you're working with very sharp knives."

"I guess not." Ava lifted her head off the tabletop and sat up.

Emily set a plate of grapes, strawberries and apple slices in front of her. Slices of sharp white cheddar and a fan of soda crackers decorated the edge.

"So what'd you do?" Ava asked, munching on a cracker.

Finding she was a little hungry, too, Emily fixed herself a small plate and sat opposite the teen. "I quit cold turkey, and I'll be honest, I was pretty miserable for a couple of days with the same symptoms you're having, but once I got past that, life got a lot easier. I was able to wake up quicker in the morning, stopped having trouble staying awake in the afternoon and falling asleep at night. And then, of course, I learned all the ways to keep my blood sugar even and my energy level high."

The color coming back into her cheeks, Ava asked, "Will you teach me?"

Emily smiled. "I'd love to," she said.

FOR A MOMENT, DAN THOUGHT he'd come home to the wrong house. It wasn't just the autumn wreath on the front door and the vase of flowers on the console in the front hall. Or even the delicious smells coming from the kitchen. It was the sound of music and the ripple of female laughter.

Walt came in right behind Dan.

Brow furrowed, he muttered, "What the...?"

Dan shrugged. "Beats me." But he was determined to find out.

He set his briefcase down and shrugged out of his jacket, looping it over the banister, then headed for the rear of the house with Walt right behind him.

He stopped at what he saw.

Emily, Ava and Kayla were dancing up a storm in the middle of the kitchen. The lively rock music was turned up so loud and they were having so much fun, they had no idea they had an audience.

Until the back door opened and Tommy strode in, athletic bag slung over his shoulder. He, too, looked

312   *A Baby for Mommy*

incredibly upbeat. Cell phone in hand, he was grinning from ear to ear. "Hey! Did you all get Mom's text message? She's coming home week after next, and she said we're all going to be together for an old-fashioned Thanksgiving!"

The girls stopped what they were doing.

Emily stepped forward and switched off the music.

The sudden absence of sound left them all staring at one another in shock.

"I thought she wasn't coming home until Christmas!" Ava said.

"Does this mean she won't be here for Christmas?" Kayla wailed.

Dan had no clue, so he answered as positively as possible. "I'm sure she wants to be," he said.

Ava tilted her head to one side. "Did Mom say anything to you about this?" she asked her father.

"We talked briefly earlier today," Dan admitted, realizing too late he probably should have mentioned that conversation to Emily when he insisted she be a part of their holiday celebration, as both handsomely compensated head chef and guest.

As it was, she was no doubt as blindsided by the news of Brenda's expedited homecoming as his kids were.

"And so what else did she say?" Tommy prodded impatiently as everyone waited.

Dan forced himself to be as cheerful as the situation required. "Your mom said what the text indicated. That she wants us to be together for the Thanksgiving holiday." For the first time in three years.

"I'm going to draw her a picture right now!" Kayla raced off, beside herself with excitement.

"I'm going to try and text her back!" Ava said.

"She's probably not going to be able to get it," Tommy cautioned her. "Mom said she's headed off into the wilds again, but I'm with you—let's try anyway!"

Ava nodded, for once completely in tune with her younger brother. "She'll get it eventually."

"If dinner is almost ready, I'd better wash up." Walt strode off, too.

Then, abruptly, only Emily and Dan remained.

"I have just one question," Emily said quietly, the depth of her disappointment vibrating between them. "When were you planning to tell me that I was going to be having dinner with you and your ex?"

DAN NEVER HAD A CHANCE to answer that question because Kayla was back, paper and crayons in tow. The actual dinner was equally fraught with excited chatter as plans were made for their mom's unexpectedly early visit.

Then Ava needed help with her physics homework.

Before Dan knew it, Emily had finished cleaning up and left for the evening. So he did what needed to be done to make sure his kids were all set for the evening, told Walt he needed to run an errand and drove to Emily's place. She opened the door, looking none too happy to see him there and not at all inclined to invite him in.

This was going to be harder than he expected. He took in the pushed-up sleeves of her V-neck sweater, fuzzy-slipper-clad feet and her carelessly upswept hair. "First of all—" he looked her squarely in the eye "—I want to thank you for the wreath on the front door."

"I picked it up at the farmers' market on impulse." Her tone was cool.

Dan worked to make peace. "It looks nice. Homey."

To no avail. She simply stood there, one hand planted against the frame, her outstretched arm blocking his way.

"I bought the autumn flowers, too. So…" Emily lifted her shoulders in an indifferent shrug "—if that's all…"

Dan had the feeling he wasn't being pushed away momentarily, but for good. The notion was disturbing, especially after the closeness they'd shared this afternoon. "About Thanksgiving…I'd like to explain."

Noting a man coming down the hall, artist's portfolio in one hand, a bundle of mail in the other, Emily frowned and gestured Dan in. Thankful for the timely entrance of what was obviously one of her neighbors, Dan followed and shut the door behind him.

"What's to explain?" Emily asked, striding to an open packing box sitting next to the bookshelf crammed with all manner of cookbooks. "I'm a temporary family employee. All I need to know is the number of guests and what type of menu you'd like for any given occasion. Along with any special dietary needs…"

Dan moved closer. "Cut the act. I know you're upset and you have every right to be. Uh…you probably should not be packing up these books in your condition."

Emily crossed her arms. In the soft light of her loft, she looked even more beautiful. "Notice I'm not actually lifting any of the book boxes."

Dan studied the determined tilt of her chin. "Yet."

She flushed.

Guilty as charged, Dan thought.

A roll of tape in her hand, she knelt, a feat that wasn't

all that easy, given the figure-hugging cut of her black wool skirt. "Just say what you have to say, Dan."

He held the edges of the box together for her. He sensed he didn't have much time before she booted him out, so he went straight for the bottom line. "There's no reason for you to be jealous."

She dispensed the tape with a ripping sound, patted it none too gently in place, then slowly stood up. He did the same.

"What did you say?" she demanded indignantly.

Exasperated, Dan replied, "That there's no rea—"

The soft press of her index finger against his lips made him stop.

"I'm. Not. Jealous." She enunciated the words.

But she certainly looked it at this moment, Dan noted with a satisfaction that was distinctly male.

"Confused, perhaps," Emily said, dropping her hand.

His lips still tingling from her touch, Dan caught her fingers in his. Confused? "About what?"

She looked down at their intertwined hands, swallowed and said softly, "Why you felt the need to keep it from me."

Dan knew how it looked, but there had been nothing disingenuous about his actions. The truth was, whenever he was around Emily, it was hard to think of anything but her.

"I wasn't doing that," he argued.

To his frustration, her defenses remained firmly in place. Her gaze mocked him. "Really."

"Yes. I was focused on other things at the time," he told her, his eyes still locked with hers.

Emily released a slow, deliberate breath. "Like kissing me?"

A wistful feeling swept through Dan. Suddenly he wanted everything to be different. Starting with the boundaries they had tried to erect between them. "Like…everything about you," he said quietly. He watched as her irises darkened. "The way your hair gleams in certain lights. The softness of your lips. The vulnerability in your eyes and the maternal happiness you radiate. You are so beautiful, Emily." He didn't think she had any idea. "So incredibly, remarkably beautiful that when I'm with you, I can only think of one thing, and that's doing everything I can to make you happy."

He gathered her close. Feeling her melt against him, he kissed her cheek, her temple, the shell of her ear. Intoxicated with the sweet, silky feel of her once again, he inhaled the delicate blend of perfume and woman. Their lips touched in a tender kiss.

"This isn't sensible," Emily said, splaying her hands across his chest.

"Forget sensible," he told her gruffly, as astonished as she appeared to be by the way he was putting himself out there, allowing himself to hope that second chances might actually be possible. "And just be grateful instead," he persuaded her softly. "Grateful that we found each other. Grateful that it might not be too late for either of us to get what we want in this life. Grateful for all the days and weeks and months ahead."

Emily had told herself she wouldn't fall into the trap of being with a man just because she was at a point in her life where she did not want to be alone. She'd told herself that wanting each other desperately wasn't enough of a reason for two people to be together. In her heart of hearts, she knew there should be more than just desire and affection. There should be love and shared ideals and the kind of commitment that would last a lifetime. She and Dan did not have that, might never have all that, and yet…it was so easy to believe that after sharing a few hot kisses and the experience of having her baby move inside her, they just might have a shot at something special.

Dan was certainly everything she could ever have hoped the man in her life would be. Tall and handsome. Smart. Kind. The type of man who would do anything for his kids—and for her.

"Emily…Emily…" He buried his face in her hair and a ragged sigh escaped his lips. "You're going to have to tell me to leave."

Now, she ordered herself sternly, before it's too late. But even as the thought occurred, she knew she couldn't. She had been alone too long. Without comfort and closeness and the exhilarating completion of physical intimacy. She wanted him. She wanted this.

So instead, she pressed a kiss to his collarbone, took him by the hand and led him toward her bed. "Not," Emily said softly, looking deep into Dan's eyes, "before we do this."

DAN KNEW AS WELL AS Emily did all the reasons the two of them shouldn't be together. But damned if he could think of a single one as she sat on the edge of the bed, looked at him expectantly and kicked off her slippers.

His pulse racing as out of control as his heart, Dan knelt before her and pressed a kiss to her knee. She shuddered with reaction. Hands encircling her waist, he brought her hips to the very edge of the bed. Her skirt rode high on her thighs. Wanting to please her, he parted her knees and slipped his hands between them.

The air was thick with lust and the harsh sounds of their breathing.

Emily wrapped her arms around his neck and leaned forward so they could kiss again, and kiss they did. Slowly, patiently, softly, hotly. Dan's body throbbed as he eased a hand beneath her sweater. He caressed her through the fabric of her bra, the fullness of her breasts filling his hands, the tautness of her nipples pushing against his palm. Need spiraled through him. Trembling with passion, Emily reached for the hem of her sweater, lifted it high above her head.

Her bra was black satin and lace that, thanks to a swiftly unhooked back clasp, soon went the way of the sweater. He hadn't been this turned-on…well, ever. "Lovely," he murmured.

"The veins…" Emily ducked her head self-consciously and touched the bluish lines running across her pregnancy-full breasts.

"They're perfect, too," Dan said, never meaning anything more, and to prove it, kissed everywhere he'd touched. Caressed and stroked. When her back arched and she moaned, he moved down the curve of her belly to the elastic insert at the top of her maternity skirt.

"I suppose," Emily said breathlessly, lifting slightly to allow him free rein, "this has to come off, too."

"Most definitely." Aware he'd never wanted to possess a woman more, Dan eased it off, then followed with tights and panties.

"This feels…awkward," Emily whispered as he kissed his way from her navel to her knee. Her cheeks blushed a pretty pink as she looked at him with the same overwhelming need he felt. "I've never…"

"Made love as a pregnant woman," Dan guessed, liking the excited glitter in her eyes.

Emily nodded, her breath coming erratically.

"Then," Dan said, kissing her thoroughly before moving lower still, "you're in for a treat."

DAN HADN'T BEEN KIDDING, Emily thought dizzy moments later as he slowly disrobed and joined her on the bed, pulling her back into his arms. Pregnancy hormones amplified everything and his sensual expertise brought forth even more. "You are so right," she whispered.

Common sense told her they wouldn't be doing this again.

But for now…

What was one night, one moment in time, except something to be grateful for? And she was grateful for the feel of his strong arms around her as he guided her onto her back and stretched out beside her. One arm sliding beneath her shoulders, he lifted her head to his. The kiss drew them closer still. She explored his body as wantonly as he had explored hers. And then they were shifting again, he was bracing his weight on his arms and draping his body over hers. Inundated with the masculine warmth of him, she put her arms about his neck and opened herself to him. To the sensation of being taken, and the knowledge she was taking in return. To the feel of being one with him. To the idea that family was not completely out of reach. And then all was lost in the heat and intensity of the moment, of the rushing adrenaline and the thrill of the pleasure that spiraled out of control and morphed into sweet, hot satisfaction.

For long moments after, they lay like that, bodies shuddering and intimately entwined, his weight still braced on his arms.

With her eyes shut, Emily savored the closeness. It had been so long since she had been held. So long since she had felt so much a woman, so wanted. So long since she had dared hope—

And of course that was when Dan's cell phone went off, the chime breaking the silence of the room. That was all it took to dispel the sensual, carefree mood.

Dan tensed. A second later, he carefully disengaged their bodies. Reached down beside the bed and removed the cell phone from his belt. He glanced at the screen and relaxed slightly. "That was a text message from Walt. He said Ava is upstairs studying, and Tommy's working out one last time before bed. Kayla is asleep… and he's going to bed himself."

Dan texted back, then put the phone aside. Looking completely relaxed, albeit slightly distracted, he rolled onto his side and propped his head on his upraised hand. Feeling a bit guilty for keeping him from his kids, Emily said, "If you want to leave…"

Dan shook his head. "No. That's the last thing I want." He wrapped a strand of her hair around his fingertip. "This is the first time in years I've lost track of the fact I've got kids at home and the responsibility that goes with them. To be honest, I'd forgotten what it felt like to be with someone this way."

Emily had *never* known what it was like to be with someone this way. To feel that nothing mattered but being in Dan's arms, receiving and returning his kiss.

He'd opened up a whole new world of wanting to her tonight.

"You must be looking forward to the empty nest everyone talks about," she suggested.

Dan's lips quirked into a wistful smile. "I have to admit there are times when the thought of being able to do what I want, when I want, sounds pretty appealing."

His longing hit home. Emily wanted to look out for his best interests the way he had unselfishly looked out for hers. "Which is maybe why," Emily supposed softly, trying to be cautious, for both their sakes, "we shouldn't let this go any further."

Dan's brows drew together.

Emily rose, wrapping the sheet around her. She disappeared into the bathroom and came back in a white, terry-cloth spa robe. She sat on the edge of the bed beside him, her natural practicality taking over. "You've carried the never-ending responsibility of fatherhood for eighteen years now." *And you're already looking forward to regaining your freedom.* "I'm just getting started with the whole parenthood thing."

His eyes darkened and he captured her hand with his. "That doesn't mean…"

She stopped him with a smile meant to let him off the hook. "I know you're a stand-up guy—"

"Who isn't into one-night stands any more than you are," Dan interjected gruffly.

Emily nodded and forged on. "And because of that… because you're so decent and honorable, because we've both been alone for so long, we're both going to be tempted to make this more than it is." She placed her finger on his lips before he could interrupt again. "I'm telling you, you don't have to do that." She paused, letting her words sink in. Nervously she traced the seam on the belt of her robe. "I'm letting you off the hook."

He studied her inscrutably, silent now. "You want to pretend this never happened," he said finally.

Realistically? Now that the hormonal need to be with someone had ebbed? Emily didn't see it any other way. "You and I both know that what happened between us was mostly due to the fact I'm pregnant…and alone." *And on the brink of falling hard for you.* Emily swallowed. "Hormones aren't a basis for a relationship." Nor was what had happened earlier that day.

"Today…in my office…" Dan started.

Emily lifted her hand. "There's no denying that was a truly magical moment. It would be for any two people who happened to find themselves together in that particular circumstance."

Dan remained unconvinced.

"I'm really happy you were there to share the moment with me when I first felt my baby move." Okay, now she was babbling.

Dan studied her, his emotions now as tightly wrapped and hidden from view as her own. "So am I," he said warily.

"And that lent an intimacy to our relationship that would not otherwise have been there. Had it not happened, I would've walked out at the end of our conversation. And that would've been that. There would've been no embrace, no second kiss. And certainly no lovemaking tonight."

Once again Dan was silent. He rubbed the flat of his hand across his jaw, looking suddenly so much older than his years. "What do you want to do?" he asked eventually.

Be with you again, Emily thought, without complication or consequence or thought to the future. But she knew she couldn't do that. She would soon be a parent. Just like Dan. She had to be responsible. To her baby, to Dan. And what he needed was not what she had to give.

Her throat tight, she forced herself to do the right thing and say, "I think we should go back to being employer and employee."

And if they were lucky, she mused dispiritedly, perhaps even friends.

Chapter Seven

Dan wasn't sure what he expected when he came in from work Wednesday evening. Certainly not family togetherness.

Ava had her homework and AP textbooks spread out over the kitchen table. A tall glass of ice water and fruit plate next to her, she had her headphones and iPod on and seemed to be studying intently. Through the big kitchen windows, Dan saw that Tommy was outside on the back deck, still in his wrestling-practice clothes, talking on the cordless phone. Walt was outside, too, arranging the wood that had just been delivered into manageable stacks. Emily, in a burgundy chef's smock and trim black pants, had her head bent next to Kayla's as the two pored over a cookbook. The tableau before him made his heart skip a beat.

How long had it been, he wondered, since the members of his family had come together without being forced to do so?

How long since he'd felt the jolt of sweet and tender awareness he experienced every time he laid eyes on Emily?

How long had he been able to go today without remembering how great it had been to make love with her?

And yet, he reminded himself soberly, Emily had made it clear that their lovemaking the night before had been a one-time-only thing. A fling that needed to be appreciated for what it was and then promptly forgotten…if he wanted her to continue working in his home.

"Daddy, we're going to make our own pizzas tonight, and then after dinner we're going to make corn bread," Kayla explained.

Dan looked at the big bowl of salad sitting on the counter and the bowls of toppings, ready to go on six individual-size pizza doughs.

Tommy came in through the back door and set the receiver on the hook. "Some lady from the elementary school called," he announced cheerfully. "You're confirmed for tomorrow, Dad."

Dan blinked. "Confirmed for what?"

"Making corn bread stuffing with me!" Kayla announced.

Frowning at Dan's blank look, Ava took off her headphones. "It's the Thanksgiving feast, Dad," she said, exasperated. "The third-graders get together and make turkey and stuff, and then sit down with their parents and eat together. They do it every year."

"Usually the week before Thanksgiving," Tommy chimed in.

Embarrassed to feel so clueless when it came to his kids, Dan shook his head. "I don't remember that."

"That's 'cause you weren't there when I was in third grade," Ava said matter-of-factly. "Mom was—or she was supposed to be until she had some emergency come up at the hospital."

Tommy studied the pizza fixings, then chowed down on a thin slice of green pepper. "No one was there for me, either," he said. "But all the other kids had their parents there."

Guilt stung Dan. Life had been completely chaotic during those years of his marriage to Brenda. Two careers going full force, no one really minding the store at home. The kids had survived, but they'd been hurt.

With a glance that was equal parts sympathy and censure, Emily plucked a piece of paper off the counter. She handed it to Dan, looked him straight in the eye and brought him up to speed. "Kayla's teacher sent this reminder home with her. You're supposed to show up at school tomorrow morning at nine, with two thirteen-by-nine pans of corn bread and the rest of the ingredients for the stuffing."

"And then you teach the kids in your group how to make it and let them help," Ava said. "Pretty simple stuff."

For an ace in the kitchen, Dan thought. He had his hands full trying to follow the directions on a store-bought frozen dinner.

"What's the matter, Daddy?" Kayla wrinkled her nose.

"I'm not sure I can be there on such short notice," Dan admitted reluctantly.

Kayla's face fell. Her lower lip trembled and she looked ready to burst into tears.

"I can go in your place, if you like," Emily offered.

Their eyes met, held. Dan wasn't sure how he felt about the bailout. Relieved or unfairly spared. He only knew he was glad Emily was there.

Emily put an arm around Kayla's shoulders. "I'm very good at teaching people how to cook," she said.

Kayla glared at her father, then turned to Emily, wrapped her arms around Emily's middle and buried her head against Emily's chest. "I'd like that very much," she said.

EMILY WALKED INTO THE Fort Worth elementary school cafeteria, where bedlam reigned even without the third-grade students in attendance. In the midst of all the women running to and fro setting up the early-morning cooking activity stood a lone man. In a forest-green dress shirt and black slacks, Dan stood uncertainly off to one side. He held a folded-up white apron and wore a mildly confused expression.

Emily hurried toward him as quickly as the box in her arms would allow.

Seeing her, Dan dropped the apron on the table marked Kingsland/Corn bread. "Let me help you with that." He rushed forward.

Their forearms brushed as the transfer was made. "I didn't think you were going to make it this morning," Emily said, tingling at the contact and catching a whiff of his crisp aftershave.

Emily tore her eyes away from the just-shampooed softness of his sandy-blond hair. He'd shaved, too—in the bright morning sunlight flooding through the windows, she could see just how close.

Dan set the box down on the table. "I talked to my clients. Fortunately they were understanding—that isn't always the case—and agreed to reschedule their session with me for this evening."

Emily set the ingredients on the table. "Kayla's going to be really happy."

"I don't know. She was still pretty mad at me this morning."

Finished, Emily rocked back on her heels. Her glance was compassionate. "You didn't know."

Dan exhaled. "I should have."

Nothing she could say to that. It was true. They stared at each other in silence.

The mom in charge came by. She looked at Dan and Emily. "Which of you is making the corn-bread stuffing with the kids?"

"We both are," Dan said, extending a hand. "I'm Dan Kingsland. This is Emily Stayton. I've never made stuffing. She has. So she'll be doing the teaching."

"Great. Glad to have you both." The mom looked at Emily's trim black skirt and green sweater. "Cute, the way you dressed alike, too."

Emily blushed. She'd been so busy looking at Dan and enjoying his company she hadn't noticed. "Completely accidental, I assure you," she murmured.

The mom laughed. "Great minds think alike, hmm?" she said. She hurried off, tossing her departing words over her shoulder. "I'll see what I can do about finding another apron!"

Dan winked at Emily. "If our matching attire embarrasses you, I could go home and change."

Emily's cheeks warmed all the more. "And miss a single second of this gala?" she teased back, determined to hold her own with him. "Not a chance."

Their eyes held again. As the moment drew out and awareness grew, she thought about the night they'd made love, the pleasure they'd both felt, the warmth and tenderness he'd shown her. If only their lives weren't on such different paths, she thought wistfully. But they were, so there was no use pretending they were anything more than boss/employee.

She pulled her gaze away and began rearranging the ingredients on the table.

Obviously perplexed by the abrupt dampening of her mood, Dan plucked his apron off the table and handed it to her. "In case they don't have extra, you can have this one."

Glad to have something else besides the ingredients and his sexy presence to focus on, Emily unfolded the white cotton. "I have a feeling you're going to need it more than me."

His eyes lit up at the teasing jab. "Ha-ha."

She motioned for him to bend down so she could slip the loop over his head. Because he still seemed a little clueless, she straightened the fabric, then grabbed the ties and stepped behind him. "At least you look professional," she joked.

He chuckled and sensual electricity arced through her.

"Careful," he warned with a playful lift of his brows. "I just might show you up."

"That'll be the day," Emily joked back. Although, given the skill he'd shown just about everywhere else, especially in the bedroom…

"Daddy!" Kayla's exuberant voice had them turning in unison.

The eight-year-old barreled into Dan's arms. "I didn't think you were going to come!"

He hugged his daughter tight.

"And Emily, too!" Kayla reached over and grabbed

Emily, bringing the three of them into a group hug. Emily's eyes met Dan's over Kayla's head. *This is what it must feel like to be part of a complete family,* she thought.

When she'd decided to become pregnant, she hadn't felt she needed a conventional family to find the happiness she'd been yearning for. She'd thought a baby alone would do it. Now she couldn't help but wonder. Had she been wrong?

After a few moments, Kayla ended the embrace. She jumped up and down, exclaiming, "Emily, I told my teacher we made the corn bread together last night!"

Kayla's teacher waved all the students to the center of the cafeteria. "Whoops! I gotta go!" The little girl raced off.

Dan turned to Emily and observed dryly, "I think she might be excited."

Still feeling the warmth of the family hug, Emily smiled. "Just a little bit." *Kayla isn't the only one,* she thought.

LUCKILY FOR EMILY, she had plenty to keep her occupied the rest of the day. As did Dan. Hence it was with relief, or so she told herself, that they parted company immediately after the third-grade Thanksgiving feast.

For a change, Tommy was the first one home.

"Where's Dad?" Tommy asked, coming into the kitchen at five-fifteen and carrying his athletic bag.

Noting the teen looked like he needed his dad now, Emily delivered the bad news. "He's having dinner with a client."

Tommy grabbed the next available lifeline. "Uncle Walt?"

"Also meeting with a client. He won't be here for dinner tonight, either."

Tommy's shoulders slumped. She watched as he walked into the laundry room. Moments later she heard the washer rumble on. Then, as she was putting romaine lettuce into the salad spinner, he came back into the kitchen, sat down at the counter and buried his head in his hands.

Her heart going out to the dispirited boy, she asked, "Anything I can help you with?"

Tommy exhaled loudly. "Doubt it."

Emily handed Tommy a big glass of ice water. "Try me."

For a moment Emily didn't think Tommy would confide in her. Then he lifted his head and began to speak. "Friday night is our first official wrestling meet. We had a practice run. I lost my match and I shouldn't have. I'm better than that guy. But I just…I don't know… I ran out of steam at the end."

Emily had been waiting for a chance to talk to Tommy about his eating habits. "It must be hard, trying to stay a certain weight," she sympathized.

"Harder than I thought," Tommy lamented. He rubbed the back of his neck. "It's okay if you're underweight—you can always wrestle in a heavier class. But you can't *exceed* the weight you're supposed to wrestle at."

Emily leaned against the counter, listening. "How are you doing?"

"Actually I was two and a half pounds under today at the weigh-in," Tommy reported proudly.

"That's good."

"Yeah, I was relieved. Some of the guys were over their stated limit."

Which meant, Emily knew, they couldn't wrestle at all. Figuring it was now or never, Emily retrieved her shoulder bag and withdrew a stack of stapled papers she'd printed out. "You know your dad hired me to consult, as well as cook?"

Tommy nodded.

"Well, I was thinking about what I needed to do for you.... So since I don't know a lot about wrestling, I went to the website for the Olympic Training Center and got some information on what their athletes eat." She handed him the papers. "Take a look and see what you think, and then we'll figure out how to best handle your nutritional needs while you're competing."

EMILY WAS JUST GETTING ready for bed when Dan called that evening. "Hey," he said softly, "it's Dan."

She knew. Her consciousness had been imprinted with his voice long before they had ever foolishly made love. Feeling the baby kick, as if to say hello to Dan, too—she climbed into bed. Relaxing against the pillows, she put one hand on her tummy. "Everything okay?"

"Everything's great. Tommy's really happy about all the information you pulled together for him."

Emily warmed at Dan's praise. Trying hard not to think about the night Dan had lain here next to her, she turned her thoughts back to the business of helping his son. "Tommy will have a much easier time making weight if he sticks to the high-carbohydrate diet. Which brings me to the next point. I know you wanted everyone to be eating the same thing—and I can do that to a point—but with Tommy in training, he's going to need some adjustments to his evening meal that the others won't."

"That's fine. I primarily wanted everyone to come together, as a family, and that seems to be happening more and more each day."

"I've noticed the change, too." Emily paused, wishing they could continue to talk personal matters like this. But with the lines between them already hopelessly blurring, she knew it would be wiser to avoid temptation. She forced a brisk professional note into her voice. "Was there anything else?"

Dan cleared his throat. "Unfortunately, yes. I'm not going to be there for dinner tomorrow night, either, although Walt will be."

Emily quelled her disappointment. Wise or not, she had gotten used to seeing him most every evening. "Thanks for letting me know in advance." She forced herself to sound ultracasual. "Do you want me to leave a plate for you in the fridge?"

"If you wouldn't mind," he said just as casually, "that would be great."

Now it was her turn to deliver some not-so-terrific news. Emily took a deep breath. "I hate to do this, but I'm going to need both Friday and Saturday evenings off this week. I'm going down to Fredericksburg on Friday morning to meet with the attorney Tex hired to draft our partnership agreement."

Silence fell.

Emily wished she and Dan were face-to-face. She wanted to be able to look at his expression, see what he was thinking.

Finally Dan asked, in a voice that remained cautiously matter-of-fact, "Does this mean you've decided to go into business with him?"

Emily rubbed her hand over her tummy. "I'm still thinking about it. Considering all my options. But yes, I'm definitely leaning in that direction."

Dan cleared his throat. "Did you and Tex still want me to meet you there Saturday at noon?"

Emily envisioned seeing Dan on her old stomping grounds. Would that be more romantic—or less? Especially given that her ex-fiancé would be there with him. Aware she still hadn't answered Dan's question, she said, "Yes. I'll e-mail the directions to you."

Another pause, and this time Emily could have sworn she heard the reservation in Dan's voice. "I'll see you then."

SATURDAY DAWNED HUMID and cool, with heavy afternoon storms predicted for most of the state. Dan encountered no rain on the four-hour drive south, but the horizon was darkening ominously by the time he turned his luxury SUV into the lane that led to Emily's childhood home. She was already there waiting for him, sitting on the steps of the wide front porch of the small, white-stone ranch house.

Acutely aware he hadn't laid eyes on her in almost seventy-two hours, Dan cut the engine and got out. She was smiling from ear to ear, looking as at ease in the country as she did the city. She stood up and dusted off the back of her pants. "Glad you could make it," she said as she ambled down the steps.

She wore close-fitting jeans tucked into knee-high suede boots, a red, long-sleeved T-shirt that showed off the soft slope of her baby bump and a short denim jacket that no longer met in the middle. Her hair was loose and wavy, her cheeks pink.

Telling himself not to get too excited—this was a business trip after all—Dan slung his camera around his neck and grabbed his notepad. "Tex here yet?" he asked.

Emily stood beside Dan. "He had to go to his orchard in the Rio Grande Valley. They're expecting a big freeze from that cold front moving our way. He's got to make sure his citrus crop is protected."

Dan tried not to look too happy about the man's absence.

Emily stuck her hands in the pockets of her jacket. "I thought we'd tour the house last. See the barn and orchard first."

"Sounds good."

Together they walked across a gravel drive and an unmanicured lawn to a large, white two-story barn. Weathered wood showed beneath the peeling paint. Inside, the cement floor was stained with motor oil, mud and what appeared to be the remains of spoiled fruit.

"I know." Emily sighed. "The previous owners did a lousy job of taking care of the place."

Dan got his camera out. Noting the barn had no electricity, he checked out the integrity of the structure—the place seemed solid—and took flash photos.

"We were thinking the house would eventually be a small restaurant or tearoom, which could be expanded if business proves good enough."

"Gotcha."

Emily gestured expansively at their surroundings. "And this barn would be a retail space."

"Two floors or one?" Dan asked.

"Two—if we can swing it financially," she said.

Dan nodded.

From there, they walked to the orchard. There were rows upon rows of trees. "My dad planted all twelve varieties of Texas peaches," Emily said. "The first crop was ready in early May, the last in early August."

"So you had fruit…"

"For nearly four months. If we were to eventually farm tomatoes and apples, as Tex has suggested, we'd have crop to sell through October."

"That's great."

Emily led the way through the weed-choked aisles. "A lot of these trees are in really bad shape, though. They haven't been pruned in I don't know how long." Emily pivoted on her heel and stood facing Dan, her hands shoved in the back pockets of her jeans. Her posture only accentuated her baby bump—to Dan, she had never looked sexier.

Emily was frowning. "New trees should have been planted in the places where others were lost, but haven't been. Fortunately—" her serious blue gaze meshed with Dan's green one again "—it's nothing a lot of hard work won't fix."

He nodded and took some pictures of the rows of fruit trees, too. "Are peaches all that's grown here?"

"On this farm. Tex's folks expanded to include blackberries, strawberries, nectarines and plums, and he'd like to do the same over here, as well as add the aforementioned tomatoes and apples on the forty acres that aren't being farmed."

"So the orchards would go right up to the house and barn," Dan said.

Emily nodded, not looking happy about that. "Pretty

much, yes. There'd be very little yard when all was said and done."

Or privacy, Dan thought. Especially if they turned the barn into a retail store.

Together, they headed back to the house. All around them, the wind was whipping up, pushing the hair into their eyes and plastering their clothes to their bodies. By the time they reached the front porch of the house, big fat drops of rain were falling.

Emily opened the door. Dan wasn't sure what he was expecting when she led the way inside.

Certainly not what he saw.

EMILY HIT THE LIGHTS, then turned to see the amazed look on Dan's face. Obviously he'd expected an empty home.

"Tex bought the place furnished."

Dan continued to look around. "I see why you wanted to buy it," he said, as impressed as she had been when she'd first laid eyes on the house again.

"It's perfect for a small family."

Emily showed him through the living room with its wide-plank oak floors, steeply angled ceiling and whitewashed paneling. Built-in bookshelves flanked the white-stone fireplace. An overstuffed chintz sofa and chairs formed a conversation area in front of the fire, and floor-length draperies matched the upholstery. Behind the living room was a country kitchen, with wood floor, white cabinets, large farmhouse-style sink, stainless-steel appliances and marble countertops. An oak table accommodated four ladder-back chairs.

On the opposite side of the hall that ran front to back was a master bedroom with a four-poster bed and updated bath, complete with claw-foot tub and shower stall. A small nursery, decorated with a unisex pastel alphabet theme, was at the rear.

The place, which even had plantation shutters covering every window, was absolutely gorgeous and move-in ready. All she had needed to bring for her weekend stay were clothes and food. Everything else, down to the linens and dishes, was already here.

Dan continued to look around as they made their way past the laundry closet and into the kitchen. He shook his head, baffled. "It's hard to reconcile this with the condition of the rest of the property," he said.

Emily nodded, unable to mask her disappointment about that. "They really let the orchards and barn go."

"You had planned to live here."

Emily nodded. "I'd hoped to close on the property and be living here in my childhood home by Christmas." Sadness swept through her. "But it didn't work out…" She corralled her emotions with effort and moved past Dan, avoiding his assessing gaze. "Would you like some tea? I'm really…cold…for some reason."

"The temperature is dropping outside."

Emily paused in the act of reaching for the kettle. "Maybe I should build a fire first." She'd had one the night before and it had really warmed the house through and through, just as it had when she was a child.

Dan held up a staying hand. "Why don't you let me handle that," he said with a comforting smile that made her very glad he was here. He was, she decided as she set about completing the task, exactly the distraction she needed.

Chapter Eight

"You don't like this idea, either," Dan guessed four hours later.

Emily leaned against the kitchen counter, studying the image Dan had conjured up on his laptop computer screen. The rain was still pounding relentlessly on the roof. "It's not that it isn't a gorgeously imagined building," she said carefully.

Dan pushed back his chair and stood, too. "It's that you don't want to turn your childhood home into a restaurant."

Emily turned her glance to the kitchen window and gloomy landscape outside. "I know it has to be done," she said slowly. This was, after all, why he was here.

"You just can't bring yourself to start the process."

Emily began to pace. "The house is so beautiful just as it is, inside and out." When she had come to see it, before putting in a bid on the place, it had been so easy to see herself living here again, raising her child.

So easy to chase after old dreams.

She swallowed. "It seems a shame to destroy it. And that's what gutting the inside to add on a dining area and a commercial kitchen would do."

So don't, Dan's look said.

"On the other hand—" Emily forced herself to take a deep breath and be practical "—I know the orchards will attract a lot more business during busy season if we have an elegant tearoom and a retail store on-site. With the seed money Tex is willing to put into this venture, if we start now, we could have both up and running by the time the first crop of peaches ripens in mid-May."

Dan's brow furrowed. "Isn't that about the time you're due?"

Good point, Emily thought uneasily. One she hadn't really considered. "A month or so later. I'm due April tenth." She studied his suddenly poker-faced expression. "What?" she demanded impatiently.

He kept his eyes locked with hers. Said, with a great deal of sympathy, "I was just thinking that's a lot for anyone to handle alone."

Emily had heard that a lot since becoming pregnant. She just hadn't expected to hear it from him. She stiffened her spine and glared at Dan. "Thanks for the vote of confidence." She'd thought that Dan understood how very badly she wanted a family of her own, that he approved of her decision to become a single mother.

He spread his hands wide and gave her an understanding look. "I wasn't trying to be insulting."

Emily folded her arms in front of her, her temper spiking. "You succeeded admirably, nevertheless."

Dan smiled at her in the same indulgent way she had seen other men smile at their pregnant wives.

A mixture of wistfulness and pregnancy hormones combined, leaving her feeling all the more out of sorts. "*Now* what?" she asked.

Dan made no effort to hide the affection in his grin. "I was just thinking, we're having our first fight."

Unwanted emotion welled up inside her. "We are not!" she tossed back.

Dan's sexy grin widened. Laugh lines appeared at the corners of his eyes. "I think we are."

Indignant, Emily threw up her arms and sputtered, "To have a fight we'd—" Suddenly she couldn't go on.

"What?" he coaxed, coming close enough to lace his arms around her waist.

The warmth and strength of his body engulfed her, making it difficult to keep track of the argument she was trying to make. Harder still to fight the need for closeness. She drew a deep breath and tried again. "To have a fight we'd have to be…involved."

"Funny." Dan lowered his head and scored his thumb across her lower lip. "That's just what I was thinking."

A thrill soared through her. "Dan…"

He touched his lips lightly to hers in an angel-soft kiss. "Have I told you how much I like it when you catch your breath and look at me like that?" He kissed the side of her neck. "As if you can't help but want me as much as I want you? And I do want you, Emily," he told her in a low, gravelly voice, tangling his hands in her hair, bringing his lips closer still. "So much."

"I—" The rest of her sentence was cut off by a real kiss. Deeply passionate. Sensually evocative. And wonderfully, incredibly tender. A ribbon of desire went through Emily, followed swiftly by a torrent of need. The next thing she knew she was standing on tiptoe, pressing her body to Dan's. His hands drifted lower, sweeping up and down her spine, and still they kept on kissing, while the rain lashed the windows and drummed on the roof.

Emily heard herself moan, and then he was lifting

her in his arms. Carrying her through the hall to the four-poster bed in the master.

He laid her down gently in the shadowy light.

And suddenly there was nothing else to say. Nothing but the need to feel his body stretched out along the length of hers. Quickly they undressed and slid beneath the sheets.

Dan pulled her back into his arms. His touch as hot and sensual as his kiss, he made his way down her body, taking his time. Caressing each curve, stopping to pay tender, reverent homage to the maternal slope of her tummy, before going lower still. Reveling in the intimate contact, Emily closed her eyes and gave herself over to him and the feelings gathering deep inside her.

She had made the baby inside her in the most scientific of ways, thinking that new life growing inside her was all she needed to make her life complete. Dan made her see things differently. He made her feel as if this baby was his, too, in ways that went beyond the facts to something far deeper and more wide-reaching. He made her feel as if a complete family was well within her reach. As if it was possible to give this baby she was carrying a daddy and a mommy. And a brother and sisters, too.

And that was a dangerous idea to have, she knew.

Yet she couldn't stop herself from having the fantasy any more than she could stop herself from responding in the here and now, she thought as their mouths fused in an explosion of heat and hunger. He laid claim to her, his tongue sweeping her mouth, his palms molding her breasts, his thumbs caressing the tender crests. And wise or not, she wanted to lose herself to him. She wanted the bliss and the intimacy only Dan could bring.

EMILY LAY WITH HER HEAD on Dan's chest, her legs tangled with his. She felt content to the point that if she'd had any common sense at all, it would have scared the heck out of her. But she didn't have any common sense. Not when she was alone with Dan. This afternoon had proved that.

The thought that she wanted many more times just like this was more disturbing still. She had become accustomed to being alone, to having no family but the child growing inside her.

Dan made her yearn for so much more.

And she could tell by the look in his eyes, sometimes, that he yearned, too. For a way to fill the empty spaces in his life and heal a family fractured by divorce.

He smoothed a hand through her hair, the movement enough to lull her to sleep. Or it would have been if not for the distinctive ring of her cell phone.

And that quickly, she knew who it was. And what he wanted to know. Once again, she couldn't believe she had let herself end up in such an untenable position.

DAN WAITED FOR EMILY to get off the phone with her future business partner. She walked back into the bedroom, a blanket wrapped around her, her cell phone still in her hand.

He was lying in bed with the sheet drawn to his waist and hands folded behind his head. "What did Tex say?"

Emily's eyes took on a troubled sheen as she related, "He was surprised I couldn't give him a detailed description of my plan for the proposed tearoom. He expected things to come together more quickly."

Tex Ostrander was being completely unreasonable,

Dan thought. And pushy, to boot. "You just got started four hours ago," he said.

Emily stepped into the bathroom. When she came out, she was wrapped in a charcoal-gray terry robe. She dropped the soft cotton blanket on the foot of the bed and sat down beside it. Regretfully she met Dan's eyes. "My dad was always very quick to make things happen when it came to business. And Tex is an impatient man."

"Too impatient, it would seem," Dan said.

"Can't say I mind the interruption, though." Emily compressed her lips together. Regret laced her low tone. "The way I behaved this afternoon…is not at all like me. I don't get physically and emotionally involved with clients."

Dan had thought they were a lot more than personal chef and client. The fact that she never did this just proved it.

But sensing that now was not the time to bring that point up, he let his argument go and concentrated, instead, on bringing her what comfort he could from a business perspective. "Deciding whether to double the width or the depth of the building, or keep the footprint of the house as is and put on a second floor is a big decision."

Emily stood, restless again. "And one that must be made quickly if we are to proceed. The problem is—" she threw up her hands in frustration "—I can't seem to make it!"

It was all Dan could do to ignore his instincts and not take her in his arms again. Aware such a move was not likely to be well received, he stayed where he was. "Maybe you just need to take a break. We could go have dinner in town, relax for a bit, then get back at it."

"No." Emily tightened the belt of her robe. "The last thing we need is to sit across from each other in a candlelit room."

Dan could see how that could easily turn romantic. All they had to do was be near each other and look into each other's eyes to accomplish that. He shrugged. "So we'll go to a bar that's crowded and noisy." Whatever would help, he thought.

Emily pressed her lips together in that stubborn way he was beginning to know so well. "I don't want to end up getting sidetracked with you again." She gathered up her clothing and disappeared into the bathroom once more.

Knowing their lovemaking was over—for now, anyway—Dan rolled off the bed and took the opportunity to get dressed, too.

When Emily emerged from the bathroom, she had her clothes on and her hair brushed. She strode past him to the kitchen. "I'll cook dinner for us while we work."

As Dan watched the sexy play of her hips beneath her jeans, he realized a simple affair was never going to be enough. Not for him and not for Emily. To be happy, they both needed so much more than fleeting intimacy in their lives.

"You don't have to do that," Dan said.

She lifted a hand. "I had planned to cook for both you and Tex this evening anyway, and besides, it helps me think."

Willing to do anything to help her feel better, Dan took a seat in front of his laptop computer and sketch pad once again.

"The thing is," Emily said as she pulled ingredients for a traditional German meal from the fridge, "I could make food for a small tearoom in the kitchen I have right now, if I were offering a limited menu and doing it more or less on my own. Sandwiches and sweets are things that can be prepared in advance."

Dan watched her search the cupboards and pull out a large cast-iron skillet.

"We don't have a commercial cook space the way this kitchen is currently laid out. But we wouldn't need one for tearoom fare." Emily poured a little olive oil into the skillet.

"Seating would still be a problem," Dan thought out loud. "Unless you wanted to limit it to twelve or so customers at a time."

"I'm afraid if we did that, we'd lose more business than we'd gain. Customers coming out here to buy fruit aren't going to want to wait forty-five minutes for a table."

Dan picked up his sketch pad. "Will the retail store be open year-round or just in peach season?"

"Tex wants to ship fruit from his apple and citrus orchards in the Rio Grande Valley for sale here, as well. He'll make more money if he can cut out the middleman. And apples are in the fall, citrus in winter."

"So you'd be year-round," Dan surmised.

Emily nodded and slid German-style Texas smoked sausage into the pan.

"The climate here is temperate. You could always offer outdoor seating under umbrellas, when the weather cooperates." Dan began to sketch what he meant.

Emily stopped chopping red cabbage long enough to look over his shoulder. "I think the tables would look better around the outside of the converted barn."

"Doing it that way would offer a lot more natural

shade," Dan agreed. Inspired, he began to draw a rough approximation of what they were talking about. "You could also configure it to put a small self-serve café in the retail space like they do in a lot of bookstores now. Either at the very center of the space or off to one side in the front. It wouldn't be as formal as a tearoom, but it would probably be more customer-friendly."

Emily went back to the counter and chopped up two Granny Smith apples and slid the pieces into the pan, along with the cabbage and thin slices of red onion. She wiped her hands on a towel and crossed to look over his shoulder again. "Actually," she said, smiling for the first time since they'd entered the kitchen, "I think I like that idea a lot."

Finally, Dan thought, they were on their way to a plan.

The only thing left to do was sell their ideas to Tex.

Dan used a software program on his laptop to create a three-dimensional vision of what he and Emily had talked about. He e-mailed it to Tex. And at eight-thirty that evening, the three of them connected via phone and Internet for a conference call.

"I like the idea of easing into the restaurant aspect of the business," Tex said. "But what about the house?"

"I'd like to live there with my baby," Emily said.

There was a silence on the other end of the connection.

"Are you sure you want to be that close to the retail space?" Tex asked at last. "During peach season, it will open at seven in the morning and close around nine at night. That's a long time to have people traipsing on and off the property, especially when you've got a little baby around. Instead, you both could, as we discussed, live in my parents' old home—rent free— as property manager."

Once again, Dan wondered if Tex was making a play for Emily.

"I'm going to want someone living in the house," Tex continued matter-of-factly. "Someone I can trust."

"You're still going to need somewhere to stay when you return to the property from time to time," Emily countered.

"I can stay in your parents' old place," Tex said. "The commerce won't bother me. And I'd appreciate being close to the construction as it unfolds." He paused. "I'm just thinking about what's best for you and the baby," he said.

Dan had to admit that what Tex was saying made sense.

Emily looked around, her fondness for the house they were sitting in evident. "I don't know, Tex," she murmured. "I'll have to think about it and get back to you."

And that, it seemed, was that.

Tex e-mailed Dan the budget his firm had for the plans to be drawn up, and also a firm schedule, as well as the limit for construction costs. Dan promised to get him something by the middle of the following week. They ended the call.

Looking a lot more relaxed, albeit still somewhat restless, Emily went to the fridge. She opened both compartments then shut them again.

"I can't believe it," she murmured.

Aware he had no valid reason to linger, Dan began packing up his computer. "What?"

Emily swung back to face him. She put a hand to her tummy, clearly distressed. "I'm hungry again!"

Dan strapped his computer between the protective pads in the carrying case. "I can't believe it, either," he said, chuckling affectionately. "We both ate like field hands." He tossed her an appreciative glance, thanking her for the effort. "Dinner was delicious, by the way."

Emily wrinkled her nose. Clearly unsatisfied, she complained, "It would have been better if we could have topped it off with German chocolate cake."

Dan saw no reason Emily couldn't have what she wanted most, now or at any other time. He set his briefcase aside, glad for a reason to delay. "I'm sure there are places in town we could still get a slice."

She studied him skeptically. "You'd really do that?"

And so much more—if you'd let me. But, wary of moving too fast, Dan put aside what he wanted—an entire night in her bed—and shrugged. "We've already done as much as we can or probably should today. Walt and the kids aren't expecting me back until tomorrow afternoon. It's Saturday night. We worked hard. Accomplished a lot, too. And—" he moved past her to peer out the window at the darkness of the November night "—it's stopped raining."

Emily glanced out the window, too. "You're right." She smiled. "It has."

"So what do you say?" Dan swung around to face her and took her hand in his. "Is it a date or not?"

ONCE AGAIN, EMILY THOUGHT, Dan had thrown her completely off her guard by making a move on her when she least expected it.

She swallowed around the sudden parched feeling in her throat. "Dan…"

He tugged her nearer, entwining their fingers as intimately as they had their bodies, earlier in the day.

Emily looked down at their clasped hands.

Dan continued softly, "We've made love twice. Had coffee together once. Yet never so much as shared a piece of cake."

He spoke as if it were a terrible tragedy.

And in a way, Emily thought, it was.

If only they were at the same point in their lives, or even planning to be in the same city after December first. Instead, she was starting a family; he was looking forward to a reprieve from the constant parental duties. She was likely moving home to Fredericksburg; Dan was remaining in Fort Worth, some four hours away. Once she became a lot more pregnant, travel that far would not be advisable.

And that left them nowhere.

Emily forced herself to be practical. With a smile, she offered gently, "Which is perhaps why we shouldn't go down that road."

Dan shrugged, not about to give up. "If we aren't going to be lovers—" he looked into her eyes "—can't we at least be friends?"

Chapter Nine

"Ohhhh," Emily moaned, not sure whether she was still in gastronomic heaven or about to be in overeating hell. Placing a hand to her sternum, she leaned against the outside wall of the German pastry shop on Fredericksburg's main drag. Inside, customers filled the tables, enjoying desserts every bit as decadent and luscious as the one she and Dan had just shared.

Discomfort radiated through the upper part of her chest. Stifling another moan of dismay, she gazed up at Dan, who was studying her with a mixture of amused indulgence and concern.

"I knew this was a mistake," Emily lamented as the first telltale wave of heartburn hit.

And so had Dan when he'd seen the size and richness of the combination German chocolate cheesecake covered in dark chocolate ganache and nuts and slathered with whipped cream. Considering the heavy dinner they'd just consumed, he'd wondered if perhaps the two of them shouldn't opt for something lighter. But Emily, her pregnancy-fueled appetite roaring, had insisted she had room for it all.

Now, of course, she wasn't so sure she had. Who said

it was a good idea to give in to prenatal cravings? she wondered irritably.

Dan shook his head. Hand cupping her elbow, he steered her into the pharmacy next door.

"That may be the case," Dan observed drolly, "but it didn't stop you from eating the last bite of cake."

Okay, so for a few minutes there she'd been as out of control in the bakery café as she'd been in bed with him.

Wondering how she'd become such a hedonist, Emily narrowed her eyes at him. "Are you making fun of me?"

Dan slapped a hand to the center of his broad chest and regarded her with comically exaggerated innocence. "Me? No, ma'am. No way. No how."

More out of control emotionally than ever, Emily stamped her foot in a show of temper designed to distract her from the real issue—her inability to stop wanting more with him. More time, more lovemaking, more everything. "You're laughing!" she accused, indignant.

Dan's rich chuckle was music to her ears. "Can't help it," he confessed with an unrepentant grin. He tapped the tip of her nose. "You're very cute when you're pregnant."

Emily scoffed. "You've never seen me *not* pregnant, Dan."

Crinkles formed around his eyes. "True." His hand slid protectively around her as they moved closer to let another customer pass in the pharmacy aisle. "But I can imagine it."

That was the problem, Emily thought with a wistful sigh. She could imagine being with Dan for a lot longer than the next two weeks, too. Coming into town with him tonight had just made the fantasy all the more real. Warning herself not to get too carried away, she concentrated on the task at hand—getting something to quell her heartburn. "I have to stop eating so much," she said, shaking her head in remonstration.

"You still look very slender for someone who's nearly five months along," Dan soothed as they roamed the store looking for the liquid antacid Emily's doctor had said it was safe to take. His palm slid lower on her back. "Depending on what you wear," he added.

Emily shot him a glance. "I just look fat?"

Exasperation turned the corners of his mouth down. "That was *not* what I was going to say," he returned sternly.

Emily curved her palm over her baby bump and leaned back against the shelf, looking up at him. "Then what were you going to say?"

Dan braced a hand on the shelf, next to her head, and leaned down to whisper in her ear, "That you look cute all the time to me." He smiled.

A thrill shot through her.

Overwhelmed by her deepening emotions, she looked for the clouds in the silver lining. The problem that would keep her from falling head over heels in love with the sexy father of three.

"Not beautiful," Emily assumed, feeling another surge of wholly irrational pregnancy hormones soar through her again. "Just cute."

Looking ready to risk anything to be with her again, Dan curled a finger around a lock of her hair. "Why do I feel this is a trick question?" he asked, his gaze roving over her upturned face.

Not sure where this was going—not sure where she wanted it to go—Emily wet her lips. "Just answer me," she prodded quietly.

Dan let his gaze slowly search her face. "I don't think you want me to do that," he said.

Emily swallowed around the sudden parched feeling in her throat. "Why not?"

"Because—" Dan sighed, looking as conflicted as she felt "—if I start telling you how incredibly beautiful I think you are every hour of every day, it's only going to lead to something we have both sworn off."

Emily released a long, slow breath. "We did that, didn't we?"

Dan held her eyes. "We agreed we would try just being friends for a while."

Another dumb idea, Emily thought. How often did she have romance and passion in her life? Not to mention the completely unforgettable kind Dan was offering? And yet here she was, throwing even a short-term fling away, all in the name of protecting her heart, which was getting broken anyway.

"Now what are you thinking?" Dan asked.

Emily pressed a fist against the increasing pressure in the center of her chest. Pressure she was no longer sure was all due to too much rich food. "That heartburn in a pregnant woman is no laughing matter."

He didn't buy it.

But it didn't matter, because as they proceeded a little farther down the aisle, they located what they were looking for. One transaction at the cash register later, they were outside again. Overhead the moon was clearly visible, and stars shone in the black velvet sky. The rain-scented breeze ruffled their hair.

Shivering a little, Emily uncapped the bottle and swigged the recommended dose of two tablespoons. The chalky liquid coated the inside of her mouth and slid down her throat. She made a face. "I know what the bottle says, but this is definitely not wild berry." She shuddered and made another face.

Dan watched, waited. "But it's helping," he said finally.

Emily leaned against the rough brick facade, liking the warmth of his body. "A lot." She made another face. "Now, if only I could do something about the yucky taste in my mouth." Before it brought on another bout of dreaded "morning sickness."

Dan reached into his pocket and pulled out a small roll of spearmint breath mints. "Maybe this will help."

Their fingers touched as the transfer was made.

Emily put a mint on her tongue. It did help.

"Better?" he asked.

Yes, Emily thought, in that the bad taste was gone. And no, in that her longing for him had just increased a hundredfold.

MONDAY AFTERNOON, DAN met Travis, Jack, Nate and Grady at a local grocery-store warehouse. They were all participating in the local food drive sponsored by the Fort Worth Community Service League. Travis was lending a truck from his construction company. The rest of them were loading up donated goods, which would be delivered to various shelters and food banks in the area.

It was more than a chance for Dan and his friends to get together, it was an opportunity for them to give back to the community that had given so much to them.

And today, Dan thought, it was also an opportunity for him to hit his pals up for a little help in another venue.

While they loaded cases of canned sweet potatoes

and green beans, Dan told his friends about his trip to Fredericksburg and enlisted their help in making Emily's dreams come true.

"I'll ask around, see who's the best in the area for that type of construction," Travis said.

"Same here with the wiring, computer and communication systems," Jack promised.

Nate pushed a dolly loaded with boxes onto the truck bed. "I'll spread the word to all my clients, see if anyone is interested in buying bulk produce from them or underwriting the construction of a restaurant and tearoom," Nate added.

The latter of which, Dan planned to surprise Emily with. "Thanks," he said.

Grady went back into the warehouse for a load of frozen turkeys. When he returned he asked, "How are things going otherwise? Mealtime any better?"

"Lots, actually," Dan said, thinking about what a change Emily had made to his home life.

"Do you worry about the kids getting too attached to her?" Jack pushed the empty dolly down the truck bed. "Thinking of her as a mother figure or anything?"

It wasn't just the kids, Dan thought. He could easily envision Emily as the woman of his house. And that was a dangerous notion. "They know she's planning on leaving us right after the Thanksgiving holiday weekend to move to Fredericksburg."

Nate studied Jack. The most analytical of the group and the only one who didn't have kids, he was always considering every angle of a situation. "You haven't tried to convince her to stay on? Work for your family permanently?"

"No," Dan said.

"Why not, if it's working out so well?" Travis loaded boxes of baby formula and cereal.

Grady grinned like the newlywed he was. "I think I know. Having Emily work for his family complicates things in a way that puts a wrench in other things…."

Leave it to Grady to figure it out, Dan mused.

Not ready to discuss feelings that were still way too raw and unexpected, Dan turned the discussion to another aspect of the situation that was a heck of a lot easier to talk about. "She made it clear to me from the very beginning that she wants to turn things around for the orchard her father started."

The guys considered that. Dan had an idea what they were thinking: there he went again, giving his heart to another woman on a crusade that would end up leaving him in her rearview mirror.

Grady stacked boxes of smoked hams near the door of the truck. Because they had to be refrigerated, they would be last on and first off. "Couldn't she let the guy she's going into business with do that?"

If only they'd just been talking about growing fruit here! It would be a lot easier for Emily to walk away and move on with her life.

Dan vetoed the suggested possibility with a shake of his head. "Tex Ostrander doesn't have the culinary expertise to start a restaurant or develop products to sell in the retail space. Emily does." It was an incredible business opportunity for her, the start of a whole new career that still had the connection to her past she craved. Dan couldn't compete with that, no matter how much he wanted to.

Travis closed the back of the supply truck and secured the latch. "It sounds like a real opportunity for

Emily, but what about you? How do you feel? You want her working closely with that guy?"

Dan hadn't told anyone what was going on with him and Emily. But his friends had seen him when he first laid eyes on her, and knew him well enough to recognize the chemistry brewing between them.

"Yeah, you said he was her ex-fiancé," Grady remarked.

They all waited to see Dan's reaction.

Dan shrugged and tugged off his work gloves. "Why should I care?"

Glances were exchanged all around.

"Not the same as answering the question," Nate teased.

Jack grinned devilishly. "Maybe he's into her."

Travis, the most cynical of the group, said, "Be careful, buddy. We were around to help you pick up the pieces the last time a woman left you to fulfill her dreams." He clamped a hand on Dan's shoulder. "We don't want to have to do it again."

"Do you think Mommy is going to like my pilgrim?" Kayla asked as she put her latest school art project on the bulletin board in the kitchen.

Emily smiled. "I think she's going to love it."

Kayla beamed.

Tommy came in the back door, bag of athletic gear over his shoulder. "Hey, Em? Do you think you can teach me how to make a fruit smoothie? The coach said they're good for hydrating us."

And, Emily thought, they supplied vital nutrients, too. "Sure thing." She went to the well-stocked fridge. "You want one with your dinner?"

"Can I have one, too?" Ava asked, looking up from her thick textbook. "I haven't had enough fruit today, either."

Emily got out the blender and set it on the counter. "Coming right up."

Ten minutes and one culinary lesson later, they were all sipping fruit smoothies. "You're really good at that," Tommy said.

Ava nodded. "You ought to teach kids how to cook."

Kayla smiled through a smoothie mustache. "I'd come!"

Happiness bubbled through Emily. And suddenly she felt it—the kick of a tiny foot or fist against the inside of her abdomen.

As always when it happened, she went very still, not wanting to miss a moment of her baby's attempt to communicate with her.

Ava's glance slid to her tummy and the hand Emily had unconsciously shifted there. "Is the baby kicking?"

Emily nodded as another, harder kick hit her just above the waist.

"Can I feel it?" Kayla asked in excitement.

Emily grinned. "Sure." She held Kayla's hand against her tummy, hoping the baby would cooperate. The baby did.

Kayla's eyes widened. "Wow!" she said. "Feel it, Ava!"

Looking both thrilled and apprehensive, Ava edged nearer.

For a moment Emily feared the baby would not cooperate, but he or she eventually did. Then it was Tommy's turn. And the baby showed off with the biggest wallop to the wall of Emily's abdomen yet.

All three kids grinned. "That was somethin'," Tommy said.

"He's really rowdy!" Kayla agreed.

"It might be a *she,*" Ava countered. "But you're right. The baby is really moving around in there!"

And that was when Emily looked up and saw Dan standing there. She had no idea how long he'd been observing them. Clearly long enough to realize all three of his kids had felt her baby kick.

Kayla rushed over to him and wrapped her arms around his middle. "Daddy, did we kick like that when we were in Mommy's tummy?"

Dan tore his gaze from Emily's and looked down at his daughter. "Absolutely. In fact, you guys were all so rowdy I thought you were practicing to be rodeo cowboys."

Kayla giggled. The older two rolled their eyes at their dad's joke.

Walt came in and went straight to the sink to wash up. "Dinner ready? I'm starving!"

"Just about," Emily said.

Ava moved to the computer on the kitchen desk. "Look!" she said. "It's an e-mail from Mom!"

DAN HADN'T THOUGHT IT WAS possible to be that disappointed. Again.

His kids still reeling, he passed on the opportunity to defend their mom and went straight to his study. Picked up the phone. And punched in the emergency number, routed through the International Children's Medical Service.

As soon as he got her voice mail, he said tersely,

"Brenda, you can't keep doing this to the kids. Either come home when you promise or stay away altogether!"

Furious, he slammed the phone down and looked up, to see Emily standing in the doorway.

She shut the study door behind her.

Disapproval glittered in her eyes. Her voice and demeanor carried a wealth of worry. "Kayla's crying— she ran off to her room. Ava went up to comfort her. Tommy stomped outside. He and Walt are talking by the woodpile."

Dan exhaled.

Figuring there was more, he waited. It wasn't long in coming.

"You should have stayed and comforted them."

"I'm too furious myself to be of any use. Besides, there's nothing to say."

Emily regarded him with a crusader's zeal. "How about 'I'm sorry—I know you are all disappointed and I wish things were different'?"

Dan ignored the knot in his gut—the same one he felt whenever his ex was careless with his kids' feelings. "They know that."

Emily gave him a chiding look. "Do they?"

The room reverberated with an angry silence. Dan stalked to the window. One of his neighbors was decorating for the holidays, placing a giant horn of plenty on their front door. Thanksgiving was almost upon them. And once again, thanks to the carelessness of his ex, his kids were going to feel neglected by their mom. Worse, he knew they would take it personally—not just now, but likely for the rest of their lives. His being hurt was one thing—he'd long gotten past the disappointment of his failed marriage. His kids being hurt was something else entirely.

Dan gritted his teeth. "I am so tired of her doing this to them."

"I'll bet."

"You don't understand."

"I think I do."

And she still thought he was wrong.

Frustration bubbled up inside him. "My kids need a mother."

She perched on the edge of his desk, arms folded in front of her, obviously prepared to listen.

Dan swallowed. Needing her to understand, he forged on, "One of the reasons they've had such a hard time this past year is that there's no steady female presence in their lives."

Emily's expression gave away nothing. "Which is where I come in."

Dan could tell by her tone he had made her feel more a means to an end than a dream come true for all of them. He worked to make amends. "You've seen how they respond to you."

She tensed, seemingly on guard once more. No doubt she was as loath to the idea of being hurt as he was. "They like me as a family friend, Dan."

Is that all she wants to be? Dan looked deep into her eyes. "I think it's more than that."

Another beat of silence fell between them. "We're getting off the subject," Emily said.

Dan lifted a silencing palm. "I don't want to talk about Brenda. Or the situation," he returned gruffly. "It would just be a waste of time."

Emily's eyes filled with compassion. "Dan…" She

reached out to him, in an apparent bid to make him calm down, listen to her…accept her help.

And all he really wanted was to take her up on her offer of comfort, haul her into his arms, forget the hardships of divorce and lose himself in the moment. It would have happened, too, had he not had a houseful of kids and a boatload of parental responsibilities demanding his attention. Upstairs, he heard the clatter of feet and the muffled sounds of both girls sobbing their hearts out.

Barely containing his own emotions, Dan strode past Emily. "I'll get them down to dinner as soon as I can. Given the situation," he growled, "it may take a while."

EMILY WAITED UNTIL DAN LEFT.

Her own feelings in turmoil, she remained there, trying to calm down. Then, knowing what she had to do, she shut the door to the study, closing herself inside, and went over to Dan's desk.

There, front and center, was his address book, open to the page with the phone number for emergency contact.

She picked up the phone and began to dial.

She got patched through to Brenda's voice mail, just as Dan had.

Her message to his ex was a lot different from what his had been.

Finished, she put the phone back down.

This was either going to help or make things a whole heck of a lot worse, she realized shakily. She could only hope it was the former.

Chapter Ten

Early the next morning Emily was just walking out the front door of her building, bag slung over her shoulder and pushcart in hand, when she saw Dan walking toward her. Sunglasses only partially concealing the grim expression on his face, he caught up with her on the sidewalk.

"We need to talk," he said.

She'd been afraid of that. Reminding herself that she had done the right thing—even if it wasn't what Dan wanted or expected—Emily gestured in the direction she intended to go. "I'm on the way to the farmers' market on North Henderson." Which luckily was within a few blocks of her loft. "One of my regular clients needs me to prepare a luncheon for her bridge club."

"I'll come with you."

Emily picked up her pace and Dan matched her stride. "I got a very interesting e-mail this morning," he began.

Emily swore silently. She had been hoping Brenda would do what she suggested when they talked. Obviously Dan's ex had not. "Really?" Finding the temperature a little warmer than she'd expected, Emily used her free hand to unfasten the first two buttons on her wool jacket.

Anger flashed in his eyes. "It had Brenda's flight information on it."

Her heartbeat accelerating, Emily stopped at the corner and waited for the light to change. "That's good, isn't it?" Deliberately she ignored the mixture of disappointment and fatigue on his face.

His expression did not change.

"Walt and the kids got the same e-mail."

A large man tried to squeeze in beside her at the crosswalk. Emily edged closer to Dan, taking in the soap and fresh-air scent clinging to his skin. "So?"

The light changed before Dan could answer her. Emily guided the wheels of her personal-shopping tote over the lip of the curb and onto the street. As she did so, one of the wheels got stuck in a crack in the asphalt.

Before she could even attempt to free it, Dan reached over and plucked the stainless-steel carryall from her grasp and switched it to his other hand. He slid a protective hand beneath her elbow and proceeded to escort her across the street before the light could change again. "So Brenda has apparently changed her mind again," Dan said gruffly. "Now she *is* coming for Thanksgiving."

Emily tried not to look too relieved. She hadn't known how her meddling would work out. She swallowed and turned her gaze to Dan as they proceeded past the crush of morning traffic crowding the city streets. "I'm sure the kids will be happy about that."

"I'm sure they will be—if it happens. If she isn't jerking them around again."

Wishing she could take Dan in her arms and comfort

him physically without it leading to anything, Emily reassured softly, "I don't think she is going to do that."

"Really."

"Really." Her voice was as firm as his was skeptical.

They paused at another crosswalk. Silence fell.

The light changed.

They pushed through the last intersection before the market and into the throng of avid shoppers. One of the first booths contained a display of fresh-baked goods. The aroma of sweet rolls and coffee was incredibly tempting. Catching the look of longing on her face, Dan stopped in front of the display. "What would you like?"

Emily forced herself to be practical. "Maybe on the way out." She needed her hands for shopping.

Dan told the clerk, "I'll have a large coffee—black."

He paid and they continued on with Dan wordlessly simmering at her side.

The pressure became too much. Emily didn't want any tension between them, and she really didn't want any secrets.

"Fine," she said. She swung around to face him, prepared to go toe-to-toe, if need be. "I called Brenda."

That he'd apparently already deduced on his own. His eyes narrowed. "How'd you get the number?"

Emily raised her shoulders in halfhearted defense. "From your desk."

At his glare, Emily propped her hands on her hips. "Well, someone had to do it!"

Storm clouds gathered in his eyes. "Now you sound like Walt."

Emily got back to the business of shopping. "Walt's right, in this instance." She paused in front of the fishmonger. She studied the day's catch, then placed an order for six pounds of fresh salmon.

While it was being wrapped up, she turned back to Dan. "I heard your message to Brenda. It wasn't exactly friendly."

Dan fumed while Emily paid. "I had every right to be angry with Brenda." He pushed the cart to the next venue, a vegetable stand.

Emily gathered bunches of fresh asparagus and field greens, along with lemons and dill. "I am sure you know that sugar works better than vinegar every time."

"Is that what you did? Sweet-talked her?" Dan demanded.

Emily felt herself flush. "Brenda called me back last night and we talked. I told her how much the kids miss her. How much they'd been looking forward to her visit and how devastated they were that she'd gone back to her original plan and wouldn't be back in the States again until Christmas."

"And?" His tone was brusque.

Emily took a deep breath and replied, "Brenda was torn. She wants to be here for both holidays, but she can't be. She doesn't have that much time off. But she wants to spend all the vacation time she does have with her kids."

Dan was silent. The anger went out of him at last.

Emily explained the solution she had offered Brenda. "I suggested that you could put up the tree the day after Thanksgiving and the kids could have their own Christmas celebration a month early with Brenda. I even offered to supply the dinner for them. That way the kids can have two Christmases. One with you, and one with her."

Dan pushed the cart to the next venue. "What did she say?"

Emily looked at Dan, unable to hide the traitorous emotion rising up within her. "Brenda wants Christmas with her kids." Emily paused, unable to help the catch in her voice. "She said it had been too long. That she misses them, too."

IT WAS OFFICIAL, DAN THOUGHT, as he watched Emily. He felt like the world's biggest jerk. "So Brenda really is coming?" he said again for his kids' sake, almost afraid to hope.

Emily walked toward the florist on the next aisle over. Her posture as self-confident as her voice, she looked at Dan and confirmed, "Brenda really is coming for the entire Thanksgiving week. But this time, she wants to grab a cab and go straight to her hotel when she arrives."

Another problem loomed. Dan frowned. "Walt and the kids usually pick her up."

"I know." Emily's voice was sympathetic. "Brenda told me. But she's got a twenty-six-hour journey that crosses multiple time zones. She probably won't have slept and definitely won't have showered. She said, in the past it's been a problem because the kids take her travel-dazed state personally—they think she's not glad to see them and she is. Anyway, the plan is, she'll get cleaned up and nap and then call Walt and the kids. And they can pick her up at the hotel."

Dan hesitated. "Walt will probably be okay with that. He's as independent in his own way as Brenda is in hers, but I'm not sure the kids will understand her wanting to do it this way."

Emily stepped nearer. Her eyes were full of the strength and compassion every parent needed. "It's up to you to make them understand, Dan," she told him, as fierce as any mama bear protecting her cubs. She moved even closer, the scent of her hair and skin inundating his senses. "Ava and Tommy are old enough to get what it is to be so physically exhausted you can barely stay on your feet, never mind make coherent conversation. And while Kayla might not be old enough, she can certainly understand that her mommy doesn't want to feel all 'travel-icky' when they see each other. That her mommy wants a chance to take a bath and put on clean clothes first."

Emily released a beleaguered sigh and stepped back again. "Not that the kids could have gone to the airport to greet her this time. If you took a good look at her flight itinerary, you'll see that Brenda's flying in Monday morning—the kids will all be in school."

Dan exhaled thoughtfully. "Which makes them going a moot point."

"Right." Emily paused long enough to inhale the fragrance of the flowers in her arms. "Anyway, I told her I'd make a dinner in advance and leave it in the fridge so she and Walt and the kids could have their privacy."

Dan caught her arm and held it gently. "Thanks for calling her."

Emily leaned into his touch for a moment, before extricating herself and gracefully stepping away. She dipped her head in a nod, then handed money to the cashier, collected her change and moved on once again. "Consider it my gift to you, too."

She bent to settle the flowers among the other packages in her cart. Then, finished shopping, she turned her cart toward the exit.

Once again Dan fell into step beside her and took over pushing the cart. "I owe you."

Emily shook her head. "No, you don't. This was something I wanted to do. It kind of makes up for—" Abruptly her voice caught and she was unable to go on.

Catching the telltale glint of moisture in her eyes, Dan wrapped his arm about her waist. He knew she was emotional these days, but this seemed deeper than mere pregnancy hormones. "What?" he asked gently as they stepped off to the side.

Emily shook her head as if the action would help ward off the tears. "It kind of makes up for the years I spent estranged from my own mother," she finished in a low, rusty-sounding voice. "Your kids need Brenda in their lives, Dan. Whenever, however, they can get her."

Dan shrugged, his long-held resentment resurfacing. "Which is exactly why Brenda shouldn't have left them in the first place."

Suddenly furious, Emily threw up her arms in exasperation. "Coulda, woulda, shoulda! We all have stuff in our lives we wish was different, Dan. Stuff that should have happened and didn't. And we can spend our lives lamenting those things, or just deal with what is. I choose to do the latter." She shot him a withering gaze. "Your kids are never going to be happy unless they stop resenting the choices your ex-wife made and start embracing them. It sounds like Brenda's doing tremendous things for children all over the world—children who are in trouble, who have medical needs that aren't being met. You should be tremendously proud of that. So should your kids."

Her words were right on target and they stung.

Emily beseeched him with a tender touch. "Look, I know the kids feel deserted by Brenda. I see that." Her lower lip quivered. "I feel their pain. And I can only imagine how hard it is for you, as their father, to stand by helplessly as they've been hurt not just once but over and over again." She let out a long, tremulous breath. "But you can't change any of that, and you're going to have to find a way to make peace with the choices Brenda has made if you want your children to accept them, too."

DAN SPENT THE REST OF THE DAY thinking about what Emily had said to him. She had braved his wrath to do what was in the best interest of his kids, helped him come around to a more objective way of thinking about this situation. Whether she realized it or not, he owed her for that…and so much more. In an effort to demonstrate his gratitude, he left work early, stopped by the florist and headed home, in advance of both Walt and the kids.

To his disappointment, Emily wasn't there when he arrived. When another hour had passed, the girls and Walt were all home and there was still no word from her, he tried to reach her on her cell and then at home. There was no answer at either number.

When another hour passed, and he still hadn't heard from her, he began to get worried. So he drove over to her place and rang the bell. Once. Twice. Finally, on the third try, the lock clicked.

Emily opened the door. She was wearing an autumn-yellow chef's smock and tan cords. Brightly colored wool socks adorned her feet. Her hair was tousled and her eyes sleepy. She yawned and blinked hard, as if trying to make sense of what he was doing there. Never mind with a vase of pink lilies in one hand.

"What's going on?" she asked, smothering another yawn with the back of her hand.

Dan leaned against the doorjamb, thinking how beautiful she was at this very moment and how he would give anything to find a way to keep her in his life. Not just for his children's sake, but for his own. Because she was, undoubtedly, the best thing that had ever happened to him.

He smiled. "I was about to ask you the same question. You didn't show up for work."

Emily glanced at her watch, then at the darkening sky outside the windows. "Omigosh!"

Dan cupped a hand over her shoulder, stopping her before she could rush off in a tizzy. "Relax. Tommy has a wrestling meet this evening—it doesn't start until seven and he's having dinner with the team. Walt is taking the girls out for pizza."

"I can't believe I fell asleep!" Emily ushered Dan in and switched on lights as she went. "I only meant to lie down for a second." She shoved her hands through her hair, still looking a little disoriented. She focused on the vase. "And you brought me flowers?"

Her stunned, slightly bemused expression made him think he should have chosen something a little less romantic than pink lilies. "I wanted to say thank-you for talking to Brenda and getting her to change her mind about coming home for Thanksgiving."

"Oh." Emily's expression went flat. "No problem," she murmured. "I was happy to help." She carried the vase to the breakfast bar and set it down.

Dan followed. "So." He cleared his throat. "How'd your luncheon go?"

"Great. I got several more requests for holiday gigs from some of the guests in attendance. Another couple on my machine. I guess word is beginning to spread that I haven't left Fort Worth yet."

And if he was very lucky, Dan thought, she might decide to stay a good while longer. Long enough for the two of them to make what had started out as an impulsive fling turn into something more serious and longer lasting.

He paused deliberately, then met her eyes. "Are you going to take the gigs?" As expected, his question made her tense.

Emily bit into her lower lip. "I haven't quite decided."

Just as she hadn't quite decided if she was going to go into partnership with Tex Ostrander, Dan thought, comforted to realize that Emily was still contemplating all her options.

He could only hope that when the time came, she would make the decision that would pave the way for them to be together, instead of ensure they would not be.

In the meantime, they had this rare moment without kids, work or distraction of any kind. Dan looked around curiously. Filled moving boxes were stacked everywhere.

Emily strode over to the living-room area of the loft.

Dan watched, taking in her soft curves, and knew if he didn't keep the conversation going, they'd end up doing something completely insensible again.

Emily scooped a stack of brochures off the sofa, where, apparently, she'd been sleeping. "I try and pack a little every chance I get." She piled the velour throw and pillow in the center and sat down on one end. "Have a seat." She gestured to the other.

Dan settled opposite her, aware the linens formed a barrier every bit as effective as an old-fashioned bundling bed.

Acknowledging that wasn't such a bad move on her part—given that he'd like nothing more than to haul her onto his lap and kiss her right now—he looked at the papers spread across the coffee table instead.

Friends. They were trying to be just friends....

"What's all this?" he asked.

Emily tucked her legs beneath her and sat, cross-legged, against the arm of the sofa. She grabbed the pillow and held it to her chest, snug against her breasts. "It's information from the hospital in Fredericksburg. I have to register there for the birth if I plan to have the baby there. And select a doctor." Emily inhaled, looking overwhelmed. "Currently there are seven doctors delivering babies at the women's pavilion there. And my obstetrician here wants me to pick one before I move. We're supposed to talk about it when I go in to have my ultrasound the day after Thanksgiving. I've looked at all their profiles and talked to two so far on the phone."

Dan leaned toward her. "And?"

"They were nice...but I really like Dr. Markham, my doctor here. She saw me through the whole getting-pregnant process."

He watched Emily run her fingers through her hair, absently restoring order to the silky, sleep-mussed strands. "So you don't want to switch?"

Emily shook her head. "It's silly, I know."

"You could have the baby here," Dan suggested.

"Move to Fredericksburg after you delivered, when things are more settled."

For a moment she looked tempted. Dan's hopes rose. Then she sighed and shook her head. "I really need to be at the farm to oversee the construction of the orchard's retail store. Speaking of which..."

Dan knew where this was going. Tex had e-mailed him something earlier in the day, and copied her on it. "I'm looking for local subcontractors now. I should have a written bid ready to present to you and Tex by the end of the week."

Emily smiled. "Great."

Dan slipped back into business mode. "Want to set something up for Friday at my office?"

"Absolutely. Just call and let me know what time."

"Will do."

She unfolded her legs and rose. "I'm going to have a glass of milk. Would you like some?"

Dan threw caution to the wind. "Actually—" he stood, too "—I'd like to take you to dinner."

Her elegant brows rose in surprise.

Aware he might be pushing too hard, too fast, Dan backed off with an excuse he knew she could readily accept. "It'll have to be short. I promised Tommy I'd be at the high-school gym to see his match. But it would give us a chance to discuss some of the finer points of the retail store. It'll make a big difference in the preliminary bid."

Emily relaxed. "I'll be ready to go in ten minutes," she said.

THIS WASN'T A DATE, Emily kept telling herself as she put on a sophisticated black maternity dress and ran a brush through her hair.

But it felt like a date.

Just as practically every moment alone with Dan did.

She really had to get a grip.

Unless Tex insisted they go with another firm—something she would fight—Dan was going to be the architect on this project. She would be in touch with him constantly…for business.

She would no longer be living in Fort Worth or cooking for his family or seeing him nearly every day. The intimacy of their contact would lessen drastically.

It wasn't like she was going to be in shape for anything more for too much longer, anyway, Emily reminded herself sternly. Her tummy was expanding, and although Dan didn't seem to mind making love to her, she knew as her pregnancy progressed, that might not still be the case.

She needed to be grateful for what passion they had shared.

The only problem was, she wanted to make love to him again.

She always wanted to make love to him, she realized wistfully. Wanted to be in love with him and have him love her back. And something in her told her that would never change. No matter where she lived or how much time passed…or how big her waistline got. Or what different timelines they were on, when it came to having a family…

Fortunately for Emily's fragile state of mind, time constraints necessitated that the two of them get down to business as soon as they were seated.

During the appetizers, they discussed the cost of various building materials. They were briefly interrupted when Emily was approached by a former client who wanted her to do a Thanksgiving-week brunch. Emily had enjoyed working for the woman before so she said yes and promised to call her later to discuss it.

During the salad course, Dan asked Emily just how rustic the inside of the retail store should be, and they discussed the various ways they could accomplish that. Between bites of the main course, they talked about where the elevators should be located. They had to put their strategy session on hold again when Emily was spotted by yet another former client, this one wanting her to do a luncheon. Emily knew the job would pay handsomely and would be creatively satisfying so she said yes.

"Sorry about that," Emily said when the business-woman finally left the table.

Dan shrugged as he took a sip of water. A business-man himself, he understood. "It's a busy time of year for everyone in the food business."

Still... "I shouldn't have taken the luncheon gig earlier today, after already figuratively closing the doors on my business."

Dan leveled his gaze on hers. The sincerity in his eyes had her heart hammering in her chest. "But you wanted to do it."

Emily pleated the fabric of the starched linen table-cloth between her thumb and index finger. "What can I say?" She studied him right back. "The money's good." She was unable to suppress a rueful smile. "And there's probably a little ego involved, too."

Dan reached over to take her hand in his, stilling the restless motion of her fingers. "How so?"

She sat back against the sumptuous leather booth and he let go of her hand. "I worked hard to establish myself as one of the best personal chefs in Fort Worth." Knowing the best way to keep her relationship with Dan uncomplicated was to maintain a light tone, she continued with an offhand shrug and a self-effacing quirk of her lips. "I get so many compliments when I cook for someone. I know my food makes people happy." *It's made you and your family happy.* Emily swallowed around the tightness of her throat. "It's difficult to walk away from that." *Almost as difficult as it is to walk away from you.*

"Then why are you?" Dan asked. He held up a palm before she could respond. "I know you want to be part of the effort to revitalize the orchard your parents started. But there's nothing that says you have to move to Fredericksburg before the birth of your baby in April." He looked at her intently. "You could stay here. Continue cooking for my family, take extra gigs, maybe even hire some help to keep Chef for Hire going indefinitely while you oversee the building of the retail store and tearoom at the orchard."

Emily was unsure if he was asking for her convenience—or his. All she knew for certain was that it wasn't the kind of proposal she wanted from Dan. She rubbed her palm over the baby kicking inside her belly, every ounce of maternal protectiveness coming to the fore. "Are you forgetting I'm pregnant?"

His glance roamed her curvy shape.

Apparently not, Emily thought.

She swallowed once again and continued, "I'd have to be superhuman to do all that."

Dan sat back, too, his countenance indomitable. "Okay, then, forget the extra gigs. Just cook for my family while you get the orchard business up and running."

"Tex—"

"Simultaneously oversees several different businesses, in different parts of the state, too."

Okay, so it wasn't Tex she had the problem with right now, Emily acknowledged, working to keep her out-of-control emotions in check. "My deal with him requires I reside on the premises."

Dan tensed. "Have you signed anything yet?"

"No." Emily tried not to feel too relieved. "The partnership agreement is still being drawn up. It won't be official until after Thanksgiving."

"Then there's still time to negotiate." Dan leaned forward and took her hand in his again. "Get what you want out of this arrangement. Don't let Tex steamroll you, Emily. You're tougher and more astute than that."

It wasn't Tex that Emily was having trouble handling. The difficulty was with her growing feelings for Dan.

She looked down at their intertwined hands, amazed at how natural—how right—his protective grip felt. "You're forgetting another aspect of this problem," she forced herself to say. "I have to be out of my loft by the end of the month. I'm going to have to move somewhere."

Dan shrugged. "Fort Worth has plenty of available housing of all kinds."

Emily disengaged their hands. "None that would be rent-free—which is what Tex is offering."

"There's one place," Dan said, more determined than ever. "You could move in with me."

Chapter Eleven

Emily stared at Dan in shock. "Whoa there, fella!"

Okay, so his wasn't his most eloquent proposition ever, Dan admonished himself. But it was probably the most forthright. "It's not like I'm asking you to bunk in with me." *Or sleep with me.* Having the kids around would put an end to those thoughts, tempting as they were. "We have a guest room."

"That not even your ex-wife uses," Emily pointed out.

Dan concentrated on the presumptuous gleam in her eyes. "Only because Brenda prefers to stay in a hotel when she's in town. Otherwise, awkward as it might be, I would be happy to put her up for the kids' sake."

Her posture militant, Emily sat back in her chair and folded her arms. The action pushed up her breasts so their soft roundness spilled out of the sexy V-neck of her dress. A heart-shaped pendant nestled in the hollow of her alabaster skin. "And your offer to me is for the kids' sake, too. Because you want the kids to continue to have home-cooked meals."

"Of course," he said, though that wasn't the entire truth. Yes, she'd brought wonderful changes to his house. And all three of his children were happier than they'd been since their mother had left to take a job overseas. But for the first time in years he had a spring in his step and joy in his heart...

However, his glib offer was, and would remain, a strictly business proposition. Until such time that Emily's talents as a chef were no longer needed in his household, and then he would be free to pursue her the way he had wanted to pursue her from the very first.

Emily relaxed slightly.

Encouraged, Dan continued his sales pitch. "It's not that unorthodox an arrangement. Lots of people have personal chefs who live in."

Emily tensed.

Dan swore silently to himself. Clearly a wrong move where she was concerned. What was the matter with him? Once again, he forced himself to go on with strictly professional enthusiasm. "It could be for a few days or even weeks."

"I appreciate the offer." Emily offered a brisk smile. "But staying under your roof would feel too much like living with you, in the same way that working in your home, cooking dinner for your family almost every night, feels pretty intimate, too. As I told you, I got into trouble that way before—I don't want it to happen again."

Dan saw her swallow, saw the vulnerable light back in her eyes. She looked down and ran her fingertips over the condensation on her water glass, gently rubbing at the moisture until it disappeared. "It's one of the reasons I'm really looking forward to meeting Brenda when she comes in next week." Her throat sounded as if it were clogged with tears. "I need to remind myself that as much as the kids might need and want a mom in their lives, as much as they've turned to me that way in the last two weeks, they still have a mother." She gulped again, trembling this time. "And it's not me."

Emily moved her hand to the swell of her tummy. Rubbing the area lovingly, she said, "Happily, this time, I do have a child of my own. And as such, I have to do what's right for my baby—and that's create a whole new life that will allow me to be with my child every day and every night."

"So you're headed to Fredericksburg on December first?" Dan asked, unable to contain his disappointment.

"If the partnership agreement is signed by then, yes," Emily confirmed.

"THE THING IS," DAN TOLD his friends the next afternoon when they had finished their joint-work session at the McCabe Building in downtown Fort Worth, "I'd really appreciate it if you all would put out the word that Emily may not be closing Chef for Hire after all—at least not right away—and is taking on jobs for the holiday season. Through Thanksgiving, but I think she could be persuaded to do some Christmas and New Year's gigs, too."

Nate, Grady, Travis and Jack exchanged looks as the five of them gathered up the plans and notes spread across the large piece of plywood that had served as their conference table in the unfinished executive floor for Nate's company.

Grimacing at the sound of the nail gun being used in the framing of a set of rooms to their right, Grady asked, "Does she know you're doing this on her behalf?"

"No. And I'd rather she didn't." Dan rolled up the

amended blueprints and slid them into the carrying case.

"Because?" Nate queried.

Dan strode to the tinted windows, overlooking the Trinity River. "She'd probably think I'm interfering."

"Aren't you?" Grady asked.

"Emily has doubts about what she's doing," Dan said, pushing away his guilt. "I think she would have called off her move to Fredericksburg if she didn't feel duty-bound to help restore the orchard her father started."

"Why is that your problem?" Travis asked, shutting down his laptop.

"Because I owe her—for everything she's done for me and my kids the past few weeks."

Another round of looks was exchanged. The recently married Grady slapped a companionable hand on Dan's shoulder. "We all know you swore off marriage when you got divorced."

"Maybe it's time you reconsidered," Jack said kindly.

Dan resented the advice. "I'm just trying to help her out because I don't want to see her make a mistake."

"The only mistake I see here is you not being honest with yourself," Nate interjected bluntly. "Face it, buddy. I'm the devoted bachelor—you're the marrying kind."

Dan swallowed as the unsolicited advice hit a little too close to home.

"Any idea whether she's having a boy or a girl?" Grady asked.

"No," Dan said, wondering where that had come from. He looked at his friends, beginning to get really irked now at all this interference regarding his love life. "What does that matter?"

Nate jumped in with, "Sons need fathers around."

"It'd be a point in your favor," Jack added helpfully.

"Should you ever decide to put aside your fear and go after Emily the way you obviously want to," Grady teased.

Grimacing, Dan realized the guys were right. He was kidding himself, thinking he could let Emily go without first giving their relationship a real shot. The kind of connection they had came along once in a lifetime if you were lucky. He'd be a fool to ignore it.

"Speaking of beautiful women…" Nate murmured.

The service elevator had halted at the other end of the mostly open floor. Looking wonderful in a red chef's coat, jeans and yellow hard hat required by anyone prowling the half-constructed interior of the building, Emily stepped out of the metal cage. She had a bag slung over one shoulder and a folder in her hand. Seeing Dan, she lifted a hand.

"Good luck, buddy," Jack said.

His pals headed toward the elevator. Heart kicking against his ribs, Dan stayed right where he was. As Emily neared him, the sound of a jackhammer from the floor below reverberated.

Wincing at the earsplitting noise, only partially muffled by the solid wall of concrete between them, she cupped a hand around her mouth. "I was going to ask if you had a minute to talk to me!"

Dan knew it must be important if she'd sought him out here. The problem was, the noise level here was intrusive, no matter which of the thirty-nine floors they were on. And although the exterior of the sleek stone-and-glass building was completed, the inside floors were nothing but open shells.

Mindful of his schedule, he glanced at his watch,

then steered her back toward the elevator. When the noise abated to the point he could speak without shouting to be heard, he said, "Sure. If you don't mind riding down to the first floor with me. In half an hour I'm meeting a client there who wants to put in a clothing store."

"It shouldn't take long," she said. "I want your opinion on these contracts."

Which meant, Dan thought, there was something she didn't like. And she wanted confirmation that she was right to feel concerned.

Still, inserting himself in her business carried with it a certain risk. Dan followed her into the cage and pressed the buttons. He stayed in the center of the steel-mesh-enclosed cage. "What does your lawyer say?"

Emily turned her glance from the exposed rails and gears of the lift. Looking as if she felt a little leery in the construction apparatus, she stepped toward the middle, a little closer to him. She braced herself as the elevator went down. "My lawyer said I'm lucky to be offered a partnership where I'm not expected to put up any cash at signing, that will allow me to live on the land rent- and utility-free as caretaker, and share equally in the profits."

The elevator stopped at one. Because Dan had a design consultation with the prospective owners, no building was currently going on. Grateful for the absence of construction noise, Dan stepped out onto the floor. He led the way down the long interior corridor to the back door of the proposed clothing shop. "And yet you have qualms."

Emily nodded. "Taking a job that offers fully paid health insurance and lodging but no guaranteed salary is a risk. I guess I didn't realize how much of one until I saw it all in writing."

Dan shut the door behind them. He watched Emily take off her yellow hard hat and set it down. "So," he said, as he did the same with his, "if you have a good peach crop…"

"And the retail and tearoom business takes off like Tex expects, then I'll be sitting pretty by the end of the year, in terms of my half of the profits. I'll have doubled or tripled what I could have made as a personal chef."

"But if you have a bad crop…" Dan opened the carrying case that held the preliminary plans for the clothing shop.

"Which we both know could happen, given the highly unpredictable weather in the spring." Her expression pensive, Emily watched him spread out the plans on the table that had been set up in the center of the space. "Then I'd have run through all the money I saved for the down payment on the orchard. And the retail business depends on us getting prime fruit to attract customers in the first place."

Dan set up his laptop computer, too. "What was the plan to compensate for a bad crop if you had purchased the orchard on your own?"

Emily pulled out a folding chair and sat. "I figured I'd go back to restaurant work or hire out as a personal chef. Maybe even consult or give some cooking classes. Although there isn't nearly the demand for those services in Fredericksburg as there is here in the Dallas-Fort Worth area."

Dan wanted Emily to be happy—and if returning to her hometown to rear her child was the only way for her to do that, he would support her. "You could still do that."

Emily drummed her fingers on the tabletop. "But I wouldn't own the land. I wouldn't feel as secure." She opened her bag and pulled out the aforementioned contract. "The other thing that bothers me is the no-compete clause." She turned to the paragraphs she'd flagged.

Dan perused them with a critical eye. "Those are pretty standard."

Emily's slender shoulders sagged. "That's what my attorney said."

It was all Dan could do not to take her in his arms. "But?"

Emily squared her shoulders and sat back. "To not be able to work or purchase an orchard of my own anywhere in the state of Texas for two years, should our partnership dissolve, seems a little risky, too. What if I turn out to have my dad's ability to nurture an orchard and grow fruit? What if Tex and I just can't get along?" She exhaled. "What if a smaller place with a lot of potential comes along, and I decide my baby and I would be better off there? I wouldn't be able to act on it."

"You could ask to have the no-compete clause stricken. Or request Tex put in a salary for you to be deducted from your share of the profits."

"I know." Emily clamped her lips together.

Dan pulled out a chair and sat opposite her. "But you don't want to do that."

"I've thought about both things, of course."

He leaned toward her, forearms on the table. "And?"

She paused, looking even more distressed. "I think I'm just getting cold feet."

Dan studied the flush of color in her cheeks. "That

happens to everyone who's trying to get a new venture off the ground," he soothed.

Emily put her elbow on the table and rested her chin on her upturned palm. "But what if it's more than that?" She sighed, looking more miserable than ever. "What if it's gut instinct telling me that going into partnership with an ex-fiancé is a mistake? What if I fail, the same way my mother did?"

Dan's instincts told him she would succeed, the way she'd succeeded in everything else on which she'd set her sights. She just needed reassurance, and the best way to do that was to approach it as methodically as she just had. "First of all," he asked her bluntly, "do you still have feelings for Tex?"

"No."

"Does he appear to have feelings for you?"

Emily shook her head decisively. "No. Whatever we once had is long over."

"Then there shouldn't be any problem going into business together, at least from a romantic standpoint."

Which made Dan very glad.

"Second, from a grower's standpoint, you won't fail. You'll have Tex there to help you run that aspect of the operation."

"True. He's more than proved himself in the orchard business. He's a success three times over."

Dan took Emily's hand in his. The gesture was that of one friend to another, but to him it felt like much more. "The retail and tearoom business might be slower to build, but word of mouth is a powerful thing. So given your talent in the culinary arts, it's hard to imagine that not being a roaring success, too, especially considering the tourist trade in that part of the state every summer. Everyone needs a refreshing glass of iced tea."

Emily broke into a smile. "Or a soothing cup of hot."

He luxuriated in the silky warmth of her skin. "And some freshly churned peach ice cream or a peach sundae."

"Or peach cobbler or pie. And don't forget," Emily said, her eyes sparkling with building enthusiasm, "Tex's family property now features strawberries and blackberries, too. There are dozens of things we can make and sell, just with those three fruits."

"See?" Her happiness jump-started his. "You're already geared for success and you haven't even signed on the dotted line yet."

Finally relaxing, Emily kicked back in her seat. She studied him in consternation, then murmured in a tone laced with wonder, "You don't want me to do this and yet you're urging me on anyway."

Dan had promised himself he wouldn't be chivalrous to a fault again. Wouldn't accept a woman's excuses that anything was more important than the two of them—and the family they were trying to raise.

Yet here was Emily, who had one foot out the door, doing pretty much just that. And here he was, more into her than ever, saying, "I want all your dreams to come true, Emily." He squeezed her hand. *Whether they're my dreams or not.* "It's as simple—" *and complicated* "—as that."

THE NEXT FEW DAYS LOOKED to be incredibly busy and, Dan feared, a glimpse of the days to come. That evening, he missed his dinner because his consultation with the out-of-town clients went well over the allotted time and could not be rescheduled, as they were leaving the next morning. By the time he got home, the dishes were done and Emily was upstairs giving Ava an impromptu fashion consultation and co-reading a chapter of a Beverly Cleary novel with Kayla. Tommy wanted to talk to him about the praise he'd received from his wrestling coach about his victory in the previous night's match. By the time he had, Emily was on her way out the door.

Friday, Dan got home early, but Emily was late getting out of a last-minute gig she'd picked up. When she finally did arrive, the kids commanded every bit of her attention, and Dan was tapped to take Kayla to a birthday-party sleepover at the home of one of her friends. By the time he returned, the older kids had gone off to social engagements, and Emily had gone.

Saturday was a little better on his part. He was there when Emily arrived at four, looking incredibly pretty in an autumn-gold chef's coat, jeans and suede, knee-high boots. She had twisted her hair up in a messy knot on the back of her head. Her cheeks were full of color, her eyes bright and lively.

Once again, the kids preempted her attention the moment she walked in the door, her arms full of groceries for that night's dinner. They kept her occupied until they thanked her for the wonderful spaghetti supper and took off with Walt to go Christmas shopping for their mom's presents.

Happy to finally have a moment alone with Emily, Dan rolled up his sleeves. Her cheeks flushed from the heat of the kitchen, Emily lifted a staying hand. She sent him a look when he joined her at the kitchen sink. "Dishes are my job."

He squirted a dollop of soap into the empty pasta pot and added a stream of warm water. "I can help."

"The point is, Dan," Emily retorted gently, "you shouldn't have to."

But I want to, Dan thought, turning the warm water off. In fact, given his lack of contact with Emily the past few days, he'd take any reason to get close to her.

He studied her, too. He could see the shadows beneath her eyes. "You look tired."

Emily's breath left her body in a ragged sigh. She lounged against the cabinet. "Actually—" she reached up to catch her hair as it started to fall out of its clip "—I am. The past few days have been crazy!"

Dan scrubbed the inside of the pot and rinsed it clean. "What do you mean?"

Emily smiled again, although she was now looking slightly pale. She handed him a dish towel and stepped in front of the sink. "I've had twelve calls in two days for the not-quite-defunct Chef for Hire." She leaned over to put a dish in the dishwasher. "Everyone wants something done right away. It's almost like someone put the word out that I might not be leaving Fort Worth after all."

Here was his chance to tell her what he had done, Dan thought.

Not sure how she would take his less-than-selfless attempt to get her to reconsider leaving the city, Dan ignored the guilt tugging at him and let the chance to confess slide right on by. If Emily stayed, he reasoned silently, he could always tell her later. "What'd you do?"

"Well—" still leaning down, Emily struggled to fit the colander in the washer so it wouldn't bang against the plates "—given that no matter what I do I'm going to need a lot more money than I have right now, I accepted every gig, even the ones scheduled for December first and second."

Looking as if she'd straightened too abruptly, Emily braced one hand against the countertop.

Her cheeks, which had been so pale moments before, now turned a bright pink.

"With some caveats, of course." Her hand trembled slightly as she wiped down the counter where the stack of cleared plates had been. "I told my clients that I had to be out of my loft by then, so I'd have no cooking space of my own and would have to do absolutely all the prep work in their homes, but they were cool with that."

Resting a moment, Emily pressed the flat of her palm against her forehead.

"Anyway, between those twelve gigs and the eight nights I've got left working for you," she stated huskily, "I'll be in a lot better shape financially."

Wishing he could just order her to sit down, Dan again studied Emily closely. "Should you be working that hard?" he asked, keeping his tone mild.

Seemingly irked, she dropped her hand from her forehead and turned her back to him. Shoulders stiff with defiance, she wiped the table. "I'm fine."

Deciding she needed to sit down and have a glass of ice water whether she wanted one or not, Dan set about making them both one. "How are the partnership negotiations going?" he asked casually.

Emily reached behind her for a chair. "Tex agreed to strike the no-compete clause," she reported as she started to pull the chair out with a trembling hand.

A little alarmed by the sudden grayish cast to her

skin, Dan set the glasses down and circled around to assist. "That's good."

Emily took a deep breath and kept talking. "He hasn't agreed to give me an advance on profits via salary. He thinks he's taking enough of a risk and compensating me fairly as is." Her voice was now shaking as badly as her hand.

Dan slid an arm around her waist.

Rather than resist, Emily leaned helplessly into his touch. Another worrisome sign, Dan thought.

"I tried to talk to him about it—get him to see things from my perspective, but...." Emily's voice trailed off. Her lashes fluttered and her hand came up to touch her forehead again.

"Emily?" Dan said in concern.

And then she went limp.

Chapter Twelve

A gray mist swam in front of Emily's eyes. She heard Dan's voice rumble from a great distance away. Gradually it got closer. More distinct. Finally she was able to open her eyes, only to discover she was stretched out on the floor. He was kneeling beside her, cradling her head in his arms, a deeply concerned look on his handsome face. Still struggling to focus on her surroundings, she rasped, "Wh-what happened?"

"You fainted," Dan said.

The tenderness of his touch sent a river of warmth through her. She moaned, not sure whether she was more distressed or embarrassed. Weakly, she lifted her head and felt another tidal wave of wooziness wash over her. "I never faint," she told him with a scowl.

Dan's lips curved upward. "There's a first time for everything," he teased.

Grateful for his steady, reassuring presence—she would have been really frightened had he not been there with her—Emily moaned softly again and tried to sit all the way up. To her dismay, although she was feeling increasingly clearheaded in her thinking, she was still dizzy as all get-out.

Dan continued to hold her. "I'm taking you to the emergency room."

Had she not been pregnant, Emily would have argued. The fact that she was expecting a baby and so wanted to err on the side of safety had her insisting, "Let's call my obstetrician first."

Dr. Markham, it turned out, was already at the hospital checking on another patient. She told Dan she would meet the two of them in the emergency room.

When he hung up, Emily looked into Dan's eyes. Embarrassment heated her cheeks. "We're all going to feel very silly when we find out I simply fainted," she complained grumpily.

She trembled as Dan helped her to her feet. How easy it was to depend on him this way! she thought. "Like you said there's a first time for everything."

A first time for fainting. A first time for falling completely and hopelessly in love. And she was in love with Dan, Emily realized, as another wave of gratitude washed through her. Head over heels in love.

As they checked her in at the hospital, Dan asked, "Do you want me to go back with you or wait in the reception area?"

That, at least, was a remarkably simple decision. Emily had already had to weather far too much of this pregnancy on her own.

"Stay with me." She gripped his hand.

He looked into her eyes as if there was no place on earth he'd rather be. "Whatever you need," he told her quietly.

And Emily knew, in her soul, that he meant it. Just as she would do anything for him.

Her spirits soared as Dan took on the husband role as

if they'd been married for years. He helped her undress and put on a hospital gown. Adjusted her pillows and drew the sheet over her. Then he stood by while Emily's obstetrician talked with Emily, checked her vitals and listened for the baby's heartbeat—which, to everyone's relief, came through strong and clear.

Happily, Dr. Markham agreed with Emily's assessment—she'd simply fainted. "It happens sometimes with pregnant women," Dr. Markham assured them both.

"Any particular reason why?" Dan asked, sounding more like an expectant father than a friend.

Dr. Markham looped her stethoscope around her neck. "When you're pregnant, your cardiovascular system undergoes significant changes. Sometimes that can leave you light-headed or a bit dizzy. These symptoms could be exacerbated if you stand up too quickly, haven't had enough food or drink or get overheated. Or even overdo things physically or feel anxious."

Well, that made sense, Emily thought, thinking she was guilty of not just one but all of the aforementioned causes.

Dr. Markham paused, pen poised over Emily's chart. "What were you doing when this happened?"

Emily swallowed. "I was working in the kitchen, talking with Dan."

Dr. Markham focused on the sudden tension in Emily's demeanor. "About what?" she asked.

Emily knew if her physician was to help her, she had to be completely honest. "Whether I should take on a business partnership with an old friend and move to Fredericksburg next month."

Dr. Markham and Emily had already discussed at

length her situation and the decisions facing her. "Well, you know my feeling about that," the obstetrician said.

Emily nodded and repeated the gist of the aforementioned medical opinion. "Pregnancy and birth are momentous enough without adding the stress of a move or a job change. My being single makes that doubly so. I shouldn't do anything that isn't absolutely necessary until after the baby is born and I've adjusted to being a mom."

Until she'd become involved with Dan, Emily had felt buying the orchard was absolutely crucial to her happiness. Now she wasn't so sure. She still wanted to go *home.* But going back to the place where she'd grown up meant being without Dan and his family, and the challenge and comfort they brought to her life.

"Of course, it's not always possible to avoid such changes. But anytime a person can avoid making life harder than it needs to be…" Dr. Markham said with the practicality that had prompted Emily to choose her in the first place.

"They should." Emily smiled, taking the medical advice with the kindness and care with which it was given.

"But that said, if you decide you want to go ahead and move now, my staff and I will do everything we can to make sure the transition is a smooth one. Meantime—" Dr. Markham looked over Emily's chart "—you're due for an ultrasound soon, aren't you?"

Incredibly excited about that, Emily grinned. "I've got one scheduled for next week."

The doctor made a note. "Why don't we go ahead and do it now, since you're here."

It sounded good to Emily. And Dan would be here

to see it, too. This pleased her more than she cared to admit.

Dr. Markham switched on the machine and smeared Emily's tummy with gel. As she moved the transducer over Emily's midriff, a black-and-white image of a baby appeared on the screen. The head and body were clearly visible. Dr. Markham showed them the baby's strongly pumping heart…the arms and legs…one tiny kicking foot, then another.

"Do you want to know the sex of the baby?" Dr. Markham said.

Too overcome with emotion to speak, Emily nodded.

"Congratulations, Mom. You're having a little girl."

The tears Emily had been holding back spilled over her cheeks and ran down her face. She was touched to see that Dan was just as choked up. Once again, it seemed they were sharing the joy of this pregnancy and the baby to come.

Dr. Markham took some measurements, noted them on the chart. "Everything looks great." She printed out a photo for Emily to take with her and handed it to her.

Emily stared at the filmy image of her baby, cozily curled up in her womb. She could see the side of her little girl's face and her tiny little body. She had a fist pressed nearly to her mouth, as if she was trying to figure out how to suck her thumb.

Dan stood next to Emily, studying the image, appearing equally transfixed. Instinctively he leaned closer, wrapping a protective arm about Emily's shoulders, drawing her even closer to his side.

Emily was suffused with warmth, inside and out. Overcome with feelings of love. This was her baby!

Living, breathing, kicking inside her, evidence of the wonder of life.

Of hope.

Of love.

Of the beauty of the future.

Dr. Markham murmured something about discharge instructions, then ducked out of the exam room.

Emily and Dan exchanged emotional glances. Dan stroked her hair and looked into her eyes. Emily began to cry again. And this time, Dan didn't hesitate. He took her in his arms and held her close. "Congratulations, Mom," he said, sounding every bit as overcome with bliss as she was.

More than anything, Emily wished she could say, "Congratulations, Dad," to Dan. Her baby needed a daddy. Her baby needed *Dan* in her life, as much as Emily did. The question was, could that happen?

And *how* could it happen…if Emily were living a good four hours' drive away?

As if sensing something was wrong, Dan drew back. He cupped her face in his hand and tenderly wiped away her tears. His thumb stroking her cheek, he studied her expression. And in that second, as she felt the love and understanding simmering between them, Emily felt as if they were on the verge of an even bigger change. One that would transform both their lives.

But whatever Dan was about to say was cut off by the nurse who walked into the room and announced cheerfully, "Good news! Your posse has arrived!"

DAN WASN'T SURPRISED to see his entire family in the E.R. waiting room. He knew they cared about Emily. Even Walt had warmed up to her, not just as personal chef, but as an unofficial member of their tribe. Having seen the note Dan had left for them, they clearly wanted to show their support.

What was even more gratifying, though, was knowing how much Emily cared about them, too.

"Are Emily and the baby okay?" Ava jumped up as Emily and Dan walked over to them.

Tommy leaped out of his chair, too. "Why'd you faint?" he demanded protectively, moving around to study her face. "Is that *supposed* to happen?"

"We were worried!" Kayla dropped her coloring book and crayons long enough to declare.

Walt sized up Emily and added with gruff sincerity, "We hope everything is okay."

Emily beamed at the outpouring of love. "Everything's great," Emily told them, hugging each of the kids and finally Walt in turn.

Feeling happier than he had in a very long time, Dan explained, "The doctor did an ultrasound and Emily and the baby are fine."

Ava grinned slyly. "Did you find out what you're having?" she asked.

Tommy elbowed his older sister. "A baby, obviously," he joked, deadpan.

Ava rolled her eyes and elbowed Tommy right back. "I meant is it a boy or girl," she said.

Looking blissfully happy, Emily reached into her purse and pulled out the picture the doctor had printed out for them. Radiating pride, she announced softly to one and all, "It's a girl."

Aware he was as happy as he would be if this were his child they were talking about, Dan studied the black-

and-white ultrasound photo of Emily's baby along with everyone else.

Finally Kayla tore her eyes away from the picture long enough to hug Emily. "What are you going to name her?" she asked, her chin resting on the curve of Emily's belly as she looked up.

Putting her arms around Kayla's shoulders in an instinctively gentle, maternal hug, Emily wrinkled her nose to demonstrate her own confusion. "I don't know yet." She grinned at Kayla, then looked around at the rest of the family to grin at them, too. "Maybe you all can help me come up with some names," she suggested.

The sense of family in the room deepened.

"That'll be fun," Ava declared.

"Awesome," Tommy agreed.

Already moving on to the next topic, Kayla tugged on Dan's jacket. "Daddy, did you ask her yet?"

Guilt flooded Dan. He hadn't had time to bring up the question the kids wanted the answer to.

Emily sent him a wordless, inquiring glance.

"We all agree. We really like having you around," Tommy said.

Ava nodded. "Life at our house is so-o-o much better since you started coming over to cook dinner for us."

"We want you to stay!" Kayla shouted.

"Whoa!" Dan said. "This isn't the time or place to be discussing Emily's plans."

The kids' shoulders slumped dispiritedly. Emily looked, curiously, just as wary of pursuing the matter as he was. Which, Dan guessed with disappointment, told him something he'd rather not know, too.

"The doctor wants Emily to go home and rest," he

continued firmly, putting Emily's and her baby's health first and his own feelings aside.

Walt pulled out his car keys. "I'll get the kiddos home," he promised.

A round of congratulations and goodbyes ensued, complete with hugs and expressions of mutual relief that Emily and her baby were all right. Then Walt gathered up the family and departed while Dan drove Emily to her loft.

En route, he noted she was awfully quiet.

He wasn't sure what to say, either, after the unexpectedly eventful evening they'd had. He only knew he didn't want to do it while he was driving.

It was only when they got out of the car and he saw her in the glow of the streetlamps that he realized why she'd been silent.

"YOU'RE CRYING," DAN OBSERVED in dismay.

Emily turned her head away. Her steps graceful and deliberate, she headed for the front entrance to her building. "I'm just hormonal and overly emotional."

And if I believe that, Dan thought, *you probably have some prime swampland to sell me, too.*

Certain it was a heck of a lot more than hormones upsetting Emily, Dan fell into step behind her.

Pulse picking up, he watched the flash of her long legs and the sway of her slender hips. The funny thing was, he noted silently, Emily had no idea how sexy and appealing she was.

And he couldn't stop thinking about it.

Or how much he wanted her.

Not just as a lover and a friend—or a mother figure to his kids—but as an ongoing, integral part of his life.

The question was, how was he going to make that happen? Especially in the limited time they had left?

Drumming up more business for her hadn't helped. All that had done, he realized guiltily, was prompt more indecision and a fainting spell. Nor could he see himself standing in the way of her goal to return to Fredericksburg to rear her child.

Yet the critical thinker in him was sure there had to be a solution to their mutual problem. A way for Emily to get everything she had ever wanted...and be with him, too.

He just had to put his thinking cap on and come up with it.

Meanwhile he could see that even though Emily had her face turned away from him, she was still silently weeping.

Determined to comfort her, he waited until they stepped into the elevator and the doors shut behind them before wrapping his arms around her and pulling her against him.

"I still want to know why you're crying," he murmured, burying his face in the softness of her hair.

Emily pushed him away. "I'm not! Not how you mean, anyway."

Dan was familiar with tears for no reason. These were not that, he was certain.

The elevator stopped at her floor and the doors slid open. He put a hand across the portal so she could exit safely. Then he stepped out, too, and fell into step beside her. He waited patiently as she unlocked the door to her loft, hit the lights and walked in. He followed.

Stunned, he looked around. The place was practically wall-to-wall moving boxes. Only a few clothes and cookbooks remained unpacked. The kitchen area, however, appeared to be fully functional. Probably because she still had catering gigs scheduled the next week.

Moving almost automatically, Emily shut the door behind them and turned the lock.

It wasn't quite the same as being officially invited in, but it was better than being escorted out, he decided, unable to help but notice how Emily was still surreptitiously wiping moisture from her cheeks.

"And furthermore," she continued, her temper rising, "a *gentleman* wouldn't have noticed!"

Dan teased her. "I thought we had established by now that where you're concerned, I'm no gentleman."

Emily slipped off her coat and pivoted to face him.

"Don't we both wish," she teased him right back. "But you *are* a gentleman. You caught me when I fainted, called my obstetrician, took me to the E.R., stayed with me and drove me home."

What he hadn't done, Dan realized, was throw caution to the wind and make love to her again, despite all the reasons they shouldn't.

"What are those—" Emily threw up her hands "—if not the actions of a gentleman?"

They were, Dan thought, the actions of someone who was very close to giving his heart away. For good this time.

But aware this might not be the moment to say that and have it received the way he wanted it received—with an open heart and mind—Dan said instead, "Those are the actions of someone who cares about you, Emily."

It wasn't what he wanted to say, but it was a start. And a start, he figured, was better than nothing.

Emily considered him for a moment and he was relieved to see that she'd stopped crying.

Her gaze meshed with his, she glided toward him. "You really mean that, don't you?" she asked, looking happier than she had all evening.

Dan couldn't lie about this. He took off his coat and dropped it over a chair. Emboldened by the desire he saw shining in her eyes, he swept her into his arms.

"I want to be part of you and your baby's life, Emily." He stroked a hand through her hair, pressed the other against her spine. "No matter where you ultimately decide to live. I want to know we can still see each other."

And Emily, it seemed, wanted and needed that, too.

"And still," Emily supposed out loud, searching his face and wreathing her arms about his neck, "do this..."

Their lips met. Dan meant to kiss her once, well, maybe two or three times, until she felt better and then call it a night. But the moment he felt her surrender in the way she opened her mouth to his, in the way she gave in to the passion with a soft sigh, all his patient, honorable intentions went by the wayside. Desire thundered through him, fueling a want and need that matched her own. The truth was, he wanted Emily. He'd wanted her every moment since the last time they'd made love. He just hadn't figured she would be up to it this evening. But up to it she was, as she put her all into the hot, searing kiss, intertwining her tongue with his. After stroking her hands up and down his back, she slipped them beneath his shirt to find the sensitive areas along his spine, between his shoulder blades, near his waist.

Blood thundered through him, pooling low. The urgency built, not just to make love to her, but to make her his. Not just for tonight, but for always.

And there was no doubt that she wanted him, too.

He unfastened the buttons on her shirt, slipped it off. Divested her of her jeans and boots, leaving her clad in just a pair of red-satin bikini panties that dipped beneath the sexy swell of her baby bump, and a matching satin bra that barely contained her swollen breasts. His body reacted to the sight of hers. He bent his head again and let the passion take hold.

Still kissing her rapturously, he pushed one strap off her shoulder, slowly, deliberately peeling the fabric down to expose the taut, rose-colored tip. Learning the shape of her, first by touch, then by sight and finally by taste, he luxuriated in the ripeness of her body. In the way she curled against him as her skin heated and trembled.

His own need building as surely as hers, he slipped a hand beneath her knees, lifted her and carried her over to her bed.

Gently he lowered her to the pillows. Turbulent need shimmering in her eyes, she lay on her side, her head propped up on her hand. She watched as he undressed and joined her there.

His need to protect her dictated he do everything with utmost tenderness and care. His desire to pleasure her made him prolong every touch, every caress, every kiss. Until there was no more waiting, only sweet, inevitable feeling as she tensed, shuddered and sighed.

Her body hot and trembling, she reached for him…

Emily had meant to take charge of their lovemaking this evening. To show Dan how wild and wicked and wonderful she could be. Instead, she'd ended up giving in to him, giving over. She had let him dominate, not just her body, but her heart and her soul. And maybe, she thought, her future, too.

But now it was her turn to explore. To learn his body anew, to let the silk of her hair tease the taut muscles of his abdomen and thighs. To stroke and tempt and tease as she took in the musky masculine scent of him. She tasted the salt of his perspiration and the familiar sweetness of his skin. Aware she had never felt more alive, so safe, so loved, so protected, she soared toward the ultimate closeness. Yet still she focused on one seductive plateau after another until he, too, could stand it no more. With a groan that was part contentment, part need, he shifted upward. Sat back against the headboard and pulled her astride his lap.

Emily wound her arms about his neck and shoulders while Dan grasped her by the hips. Their bodies came together as one.

Aware nothing had ever felt so good or so right, Emily melted into his touch. She let him show her the way and set the pace…until there was no holding back the passion roaring through her…no containing the love in her heart. Together they skyrocketed into ecstasy, became suspended in tender fulfillment. And then drifted slowly, inevitably down.

Still shuddering with the aftershocks, Emily molded her body to his and pressed her breasts against the steely muscles of his chest. She clung to him, savoring the moment and the man. She thought about what had happened as he stroked a hand through her hair. Not just tonight, but every time they were alone together—and even when they weren't.

She had tried so hard to deny it, but there was no

getting around it—there was something special here. Something she had never felt before and was certain she would never feel again with anyone else. The urge to go back to the past and bring new life to the orchard her family had built paled in comparison to her desire to build a family with Dan. She could pretend she still wanted to bring up her child alone. That it would be enough.

Or she could be honest with herself—and Dan.

Holding as tightly to the burst of unexpected courage as she was to the feelings of well-being their lovemaking had engendered, Emily drew back far enough to look into Dan's eyes. Her voice soft, she threw caution to the wind and told him what had been in her heart for some time. "I want to be your lover, Dan, as well as your friend. And I want you to be mine."

Dan's brow furrowed.

Clearly, Emily thought, this was not what Dan had been expecting to hear. She hadn't anticipated saying it, either. She held up a hand before he could respond. "I know it's not the usual thing for a woman in my condition to ask. And that you might not want to commit to something like that for even the duration of my pregnancy…" She trailed off.

Dan bent his head and kissed her, and the kiss felt like a commitment, like a bridge to their future. "Consider us exclusive," he murmured, smiling. "Starting now."

And then, just so she would know how serious he was, he kissed her with an intensity that took her breath away and made sweet, tender love to her all over again.

Chapter Thirteen

"I wish I didn't have to go home," Dan admitted an hour later as he climbed out of Emily's bed.

Emily turned on her side to watch him gather his clothes. "But if you don't, they'll likely assume something else is wrong with me or the baby."

When instead, Dan thought with contentment, everything was very right.

"Speaking of which—" he pulled on his boxers and jeans and sat down beside her on the bed "—we never really had a chance to talk about the discharge instructions the nurse gave you."

Emily made a face. "You mean the ones about making sure I'm not working too many hours and am taking care of myself?"

"Those would be the ones."

There was a brief silence as Emily ran her palm over the sheet with the same deliberation she used when she made love to him. She lifted her gaze to his. "You think I've been working too hard, don't you?"

"Honestly? Yes," he said somberly.

Emily sighed and rolled over onto her back. She drew the sheet over the full, womanly curves of her breasts and folded one arm behind her head. The other rested against her brow, shielding her gaze from view. "It's occurred to me, too," she said on a disgruntled sigh.

Dan lifted her hand and kissed the inside of her wrist. "You've looked tired ever since you took on extra gigs."

Emily's lips twisted ruefully. "I've *felt* tired." Her breasts rose and lowered with each long, slow breath. "Between that and all the packing and the stress of trying to negotiate a satisfactory partnership agreement with Tex, it's clear to me I haven't been getting enough rest."

More than ever, Dan found himself wanting to be the one who took care of her and looked out for her. "So what are you going to do about it?" he asked gently, deciding this time he would not stand by idly while it all fell apart. He'd find a way to help Emily and himself gain everything they wanted and needed, even if it meant he had to think outside the box.

Emily shrugged, her worry fading as quickly as his intensified. "I guess I'm going to have to start putting my feet up a little more. Probably stop taking on any more extra work until I do move."

There it was again, the elephant in the room. "And until then?" It was with effort that Dan kept his voice mild.

An emotion he couldn't decipher simmered in her eyes. "I've got one or two jobs a day in addition to making dinner for your family."

Dan wrapped his arms around her and brought her close. "Do you want to stop cooking for us?" He planted a kiss in her hair.

Emily shook her head adamantly, trailing her fingers over his pecs. "I don't want to let the kids down."

"Do you want to give up any of the others?"

She sighed. "Nope."

A frayed silence fell between them.

"I'm a working mom, Dan," she reminded him with a deeply disappointed look.

He made no response. How many times had his ex-wife said the same thing while running herself ragged?

Emily promised in a flat, nonnegotiable tone, "I'll figure it out."

Brenda had said that, too. Only there had never been enough time for family, Dan recalled sadly, never enough time for the two of them. Were he and Emily headed down the same path? And if so, would she end up hurting not just him and his family, but herself and her baby, too?

Or was Emily smarter and better able to compromise?

There was no way to tell as her chin took on that stubborn tilt he knew so well. "I'll work everything out, Dan," she repeated. "I'll find a way to be together with you that won't take away from anyone or anything else important."

Looking into her eyes, seeing the fire of her ambition—and the depth of her determination to be with him and his kids—Dan could almost believe Emily would somehow manage to have it all. Unfortunately he knew how difficult a goal like that was to achieve, especially when the overextended person in question was determined to continue going it alone in the decision-making process.

It wasn't that Emily didn't care what he thought or felt. She'd made it clear in the way she interacted with him and his family that she did. But this was all new territory for her. Maybe if she'd had experience juggling the demands of a relationship, kids and work, she would have understood the hardships of what they were facing.

Unfortunately Dan knew all too well what the odds were of their union succeeding within the parameters Emily was contemplating. Bitter experience with his own family had taught him that good intentions were a dime a dozen. *Wanting* to be with loved ones wasn't enough. For it all to work, sacrifices had to be made.

Speaking of which…

He had a major forfeiture coming up. And like it or not, so did she.

"About my family and the upcoming holiday—" Dan began.

Emily lifted a silencing hand, cutting him off. She sat up in bed, her knees drawn to her chest. "I'm with you."

That was interesting, Dan thought, since *he* barely knew what he was going to say.

Emily clasped her arms around her upraised knees and continued with heartfelt emotion, "I know it's going to be a complicated week, Dan. But I'm ready for it."

The question was, Dan wondered, was *he?*

"Holidays have been tough at my house since the divorce," he said. "Actually," he corrected, "they were tough before then, since there was always a lot of disarray and disconnection in the household."

"I know," Emily said sympathetically, regarding him with kind eyes and a soothing smile. "I guessed as much." She reached over to clasp his hand in hers, the warmth of her fingers as gentle as her voice. "And the truth is, holidays can be a lot to handle for everyone, even when everything in the family is 'normal.'"

"Go on," he said quietly.

Her lips twisted ruefully again. "I've certainly

worked enough of them as a chef, seen how people interact when under stress." She sighed. "And in extreme cases like mine, where I'd lost both my parents—or in the case of your kids, who are still dealing with their mom's habitual absence and the fallout from the divorce—the pressure of those special occasions is even worse."

"I just don't want anyone to be disappointed," he admitted.

She squeezed his hand. "Believe me, I understand, with Thanksgiving now only five days away and Brenda arriving, that you and I are going to have to do what is best for the family and put our own needs on a back burner." She locked gazes with him. "I get that you and I are not going to have any time alone together. And I want you to know it's okay."

Had Dan harbored any doubt about the generosity of her spirit, it would have disappeared in that instant.

It was his own selfish nature, he realized, that bore closer examination. He was tired of hiding his feelings. Tired of having to disavow the best thing that had ever happened to him. Tired of basically lying to everyone around them.

"We don't have to hide in the shadows," he said. "We can let my family know that we're…friends, and we're spending time together."

Emily studied him for a long, silent moment. "You really want to do that?" she asked finally.

He really did.

She, however, clearly did not, if the frown tugging at the corners of her mouth was any indication.

Dan pushed on in an attempt to persuade her. "I don't really see that we have much choice unless we want to wait until we're confronted. Probably at some very in-opportune time." Dan shrugged. "I can tell from some of the looks I'm getting that Walt has already guessed we're—"

"An item?" Emily interrupted wryly.

Dan had been about to call it something a whole lot more romantic. But he was glad he hadn't. He sensed he was pushing her too hard, too fast, as it was. "Correct," he confirmed. "And the kids aren't far behind."

"The point is," she said, "they haven't brought it up, and given the complicated nature of the holiday, I don't think we should, either." She paused. "Our relationship is too new, too special. I don't think anyone should know about us just yet."

"So you want to just get through the week," Dan surmised. Although it was hard to contain his disappointment, he knew it would probably be best to proceed with caution.

Emily nodded. "And see where we go from there."

"I DON'T KNOW HOW TO thank you," Brenda Kingsland said the following Thursday afternoon as she and Emily lingered over coffee in the formal dining room. They were enjoying the peace and quiet while Dan, Walt and the kids dealt with the dishes in the kitchen. Emily had been given a reprieve because she had cooked the meal, and Brenda had been spared because she was a guest. And, as had been proved repeatedly during the past four days, because she was inept when it came to anything domestic.

"This has been the best Thanksgiving ever," Brenda continued with what appeared to be real contentment.

Emily was quick to agree.

She hadn't known what to expect when Dan's ex-wife had arrived in town on Monday for a week-long holiday. Certainly not that she and Brenda would forge an easy friendship. But that was exactly what had happened.

Emily smiled at the tall, lithe physician with the deeply tanned skin and pronounced crow's feet around her eyes. Brenda was dressed in her usual outfit of loose-fitting khaki trousers and shirt and sturdy lace-up hiking boots. Her long, silvery-blond hair was plaited in a single braid. Her nails were short. And her makeup was nonexistent.

The only flaw Emily could see in Dan's strikingly beautiful ex-wife was that she was so tied to her work, she was often oblivious to everything else. She was frequently on the phone or the computer, conferring with colleagues halfway around the world, rendering both medical opinions and managerial advice.

Fortunately, due to the time difference, she did a lot of her work at night and so could spend a lot of time getting caught up with her three children, to their continuing delight.

"Glad I could help," Emily said in response to Brenda's compliment.

Brenda slid the BlackBerry from her pocket and checked for messages. She read quickly, then typed in a response, before pocketing the phone once again. Leaning back in her chair, she sipped her coffee contentedly. "I can't get over the difference in the kids. In the past when I've come home, they've been moody and resentful to the point I'd begun to think it might be better if I just stayed away entirely." She beamed. "But this time they've been really glad to see me, almost relaxed. Dan, too. And that was a surprise. Usually he's tense and irritable. We all are."

She flashed Emily a grateful look. "It's obviously helped, having you around. Making everything run smoothly, reminding us through your own example that we don't need everything society says we do to be happy, that we can get by simply by focusing on what we *most* need." Brenda summed up thoughtfully, "In your case, a baby. In Dan's, a normal family life. And in mine, the knowledge I'm bringing medical care to people in desperate situations."

There was no doubt, Emily thought, that Brenda was not only a very talented physician, but a noble one.

She imagined that chivalrous streak was one of the things that had brought Dan and Brenda together, even as their vastly different goals and dreams had torn them apart. To the point now that not even a hint of sexual chemistry remained between the two of them. They were like distant relations, who while still having the power to get under each other's skin, mostly had no real reaction to each other at all. Hard to imagine they had once lived together and had three children together, whom they both clearly loved.

Knowing it was none of her business, Emily found herself asking curiously, "Do you ever regret the divorce?"

Brenda's reaction was automatic. "No. Dan and I were never all that good together." Brenda grimaced. "Never really on the same page. If it weren't for the intense passion we had in the very beginning and the fact that we had kids we both cared about, we never would have stayed together as long as we did." Brenda made a face. "Dan doesn't do well with long-distance relationships."

Which doesn't bode well for me, Emily thought nervously.

"He tried. We both did. But he's a man who needs a woman around. Not—" Brenda took another long sip of coffee "—a wife who is off on a mission."

Without warning, the kids came back into the living room.

Kayla skidded to a halt next to Brenda. The eight-year-old hugged her mother exuberantly. "Okay, Mom, the dishes are all done! So you can tell us where you're taking us for Christmas now!"

PANDEMONIUM REIGNED for the next two hours. Finally Walt's SUV was packed with suitcases and skis, and Walt, Brenda and the kids headed for the Dallas-Fort Worth airport in plenty of time to make their 7:30 p.m. flight to Colorado.

After four days of constant activity, respective work demands and time with family, Emily and Dan were finally alone.

Emily savored the realization, her spirits lifting even as her body sagged with the fatigue of a long and demanding week.

She turned away from the front windows and saw Dan watching her with the affection he no longer had to hide. Relaxing, she let her feelings for him show, too.

They linked hands and made their way into the living room, where they sank onto the sofa. Dan draped his arm over her shoulders, and Emily nestled into the welcoming curve. She thought about all the surprises the week had brought, then asked, "Did you know that

Brenda planned to surprise Walt and the kids with a ski trip?"

He'd certainly been warmly enthusiastic. But they were *his* kids, too, and it was a holiday weekend, a long one at that. Emily wasn't sure how Dan felt about being left behind.

Dan shifted, then pulled Emily onto his lap. "She didn't share that with me, but I can't really say I'm surprised." He put one arm around Emily's waist, threaded the other through her hair, stroking softly.

He continued matter-of-factly, "We all love to ski. It's a great gift and an easy way for them to celebrate an early Christmas—especially since the resort is providing an already-decorated suite complete with tree. The only downside is that the kids won't get back here until late Sunday evening, which will make getting up for school tough on Monday morning. But I'm sure they'll manage."

Emily flattened her palm against the center of his chest and felt the strong, steady beat of his heart. "What about you?" She noted how delicate her hand looked against his broad, muscular chest. "Are you sorry you're not going?"

"No," Dan said sincerely. He captured her hand in his and rubbed his lips sensually over her knuckles. Then he entwined their fingers and smiled down at her. "Brenda needs time alone with the kids. I want her to have as much as possible."

As usual he was generous to a fault, Emily thought.

"It's just too bad you and I both have to work this weekend," he continued.

Emily's brow furrowed. She shifted around slightly, her bottom rubbing across the hard muscles of his lap.

"I knew *I* had one last gig tomorrow," she murmured. "But I didn't know *you* had to work." Didn't most businesses—like Dan's architectural firm—take the day after Thanksgiving off?

Abruptly Dan's expression closed. "There's a prospective client I have to see."

"I'll be done by around four tomorrow afternoon," Emily said.

"I'm not sure how long my meeting will go," Dan said evasively. Taking her by the hand, he led her toward the stairs.

But until then, he knew exactly what he wanted to do. And Emily did, too…

"ARE YOU SURE THIS IS A GOOD idea?" Grady asked Dan as the group gathered in the unfinished atrium of One Trinity River Place.

"I know you want her to stay," Travis added. "But excluding Emily this way…"

"Emily's had enough stress the last few weeks as it is," Dan said. To the point that the accumulation of fatigue and anxiety had made her faint.

He thought about how exhausted she'd looked the night before, how she'd fallen asleep in his arms immediately after they'd made love.

"Still," Jack cautioned, "if there's one thing I remember well about being married, it's that women like to be *consulted*...."

"And Emily will be," Dan said firmly, "just as soon as I know there is actually something to consult her about."

Nate rubbed his jaw with the flat of his hand, his

expression skeptical. "I hope you know what you're doing," he told Dan finally.

Dan did. He looked at his friends. "Emily doesn't want to leave Fort Worth."

"You mean *you* don't want her to leave," Travis corrected.

"She'd be better off here," Dan insisted stubbornly. "Even her obstetrician thinks so."

"Don't you think that's for her to decide and not you?" Grady argued back.

"The reason she wants to leave is that she doesn't think there is any way she can successfully restore her family's orchard business and still be here in Fort Worth."

"She might have a point there," another voice said dryly.

All five men turned.

The interloper extended a hand and said gruffly, "Let's get started, shall we?"

EMILY COULDN'T BELIEVE it was working out this way. She and Dan *finally* had a chance to enjoy an entire weekend alone together, and they'd barely seen each other. He was gone when she'd woken up Friday morning. She'd called him at noon, but he wasn't answering his cell. By the time he returned her phone call, she was working and couldn't answer him. She thought they'd be together Friday evening. Wrong again. He and the partners of One Trinity River Place were all deep in the middle of some mysterious negotiations that were set to go all through the dinner hour. Emily offered to cook for them—no charge—but Dan had turned her down, saying it was already taken care of.

Trying not to feel hurt he had selected someone other than her to cater the meal, she'd spent the evening finishing up her packing. Saturday morning, she'd been busy supervising the emptying out of her loft and the loading of her belongings onto the moving truck so they could be taken to storage.

She'd thought Dan might come over or at least offer to help with that. He hadn't. Nor had he shown up for lunch. Or been able to meet her for the afternoon movie she'd been dying to see.

Finally, around four-thirty, he called her and asked her to come down to One Trinity River Place to give her opinion on something.

Hardly the romantic date she'd been hoping for.

But he sounded both insistent and oddly formal in his request, so she agreed and drove there to meet him.

He was waiting by the security gate of the twelve-foot-high steel fence that enclosed the construction site, talking with the last person in the world she would have expected to see.

Heart thrumming in her chest, Emily moved forward and extended her hand. "Hello, Tex…Dan." She greeted both with the same careful politeness Dan had used on the phone with her. "What are you doing here?" The question was directed at Tex.

Tex exchanged glances with Dan. "I wanted to talk to you," he said in an all-business tone.

Emily knew her ex-fiancé could be pushy when it came to getting what he wanted, but this crossed over the line. "Our meeting with the attorney isn't until Monday afternoon," she reminded Tex. And although after weeks of indecision, she now knew exactly what she was going to say at that meeting, she didn't want to have that conversation now…and she didn't want to have it with Dan present.

"Actually," Dan interjected smoothly, with a convivial look from Tex, "we'd both like to talk with you."

The weekend took yet another surreal turn.

"Why don't we go inside," Dan suggested.

Feeling at a distinct disadvantage regarding whatever was going on here—and clearly there was something going on—Emily fell into step between the two men. She'd been shut out of some major decision-making when she'd been engaged to Tex. She'd never expected to be similarly shut out by Dan. But to her consternation, that was exactly what seemed to be happening.

The three of them walked in silence across the roughly paved lot and into the beautifully designed stone-and-glass building. Along the way, more than one surreptitious glance was exchanged between the two men.

Finally Emily'd had enough of it. Hands in the pockets of her jacket, she swung around to square off with them. "One of you better tell me what is going on."

"Dan came to me with a business proposal," Tex said. "And it's a good one."

For the next few minutes Emily listened in numb disbelief. At last Tex and Dan finished talking. Still thrown for a loop, she decided to recap, just to make sure she understood the plan that had been developed completely in her absence. "So what you're proposing, Tex, is that you and I go into partnership together, but instead of me being caretaker of the orchard in Fredericksburg, I live here in Fort Worth."

"And oversee the building of the new retail store for all of Tex's orchards," Dan said, "and the adjoining tearoom, which will both be located on the first floor of One Trinity River Place."

"Obviously we'll need to go over the details," Tex said, "and we can do that on Monday afternoon when we meet with the lawyer about our partnership agreement. But I wanted to be here when Dan first broached the subject with you," Tex said. "Just to be sure you knew I was fully on board with this. And have been since Dan and the other guys and I first started meeting yesterday morning."

Still feeling a little like she'd been run over by a Mack truck, Emily signaled her comprehension with a slight nod of her head.

"Anyway, as I told Dan, I've got to get going." Tex paused to shake hands with Dan. "But we'll talk Monday, okay, Emily?"

"We certainly will." Doing her best to control her turmoil, Emily offered a tight smile.

Thinking the matter settled, Tex strode off.

Dan and Emily faced each other in the empty building.

How had it happened? she wondered as the enormity of her mistake hit her full force. She'd done it again, come into a family's home as a personal chef. Only this time, instead of just becoming way too emotionally attached to the kids and even the crusty great-uncle who lived with them, she'd fallen in love with their dad.

Very unwisely, it seemed, since Dan clearly did not understand how much she feared turning into an overly dependent woman like her mother, who leaned on the man in her life for the solution to every problem. And if Dan didn't know that, if he didn't recognize her as the savvy and strong single mom-to-be that she was, then he didn't know her at all! Clearly, she thought ominously, he wanted to mold her into the kind of woman he wished he'd had in his life all along.

"Well?" Dan asked finally, with an arch of his brow. "What do you think?"

Emily glared back. *"How could you?"* she said.

Chapter Fourteen

"What do you mean, how could I?" Dan retorted, not sure why she wasn't happy about what he'd done.

Okay, so maybe his proposal hadn't included her dream of living in the place where she had grown up, but surely she had to see that was no longer possible— if the two of them were to be together. His business was here in Fort Worth. So was Chef for Hire, which she'd yet to let go of. He had kids in school. A home big enough for all of them when they married, as he was sure they eventually would. Hopefully before the baby was born. And it wasn't as if he'd asked her to give up her dream of restoring the orchard business her father had started. He had found a way for her to participate in that—even more lucratively, too! As for being in Fredericksburg, they could always visit and stay in one of the nice hotels or bed-and-breakfasts in the area.

Emily had to know all this, too. Yet she was staring at him like he'd betrayed her in the worst possible way. "You went behind my back!"

Dan clenched his jaw. He wasn't going to apologize for fighting to give their relationship the best possible chance of succeeding, for doing what would make everyone as happy as possible. "Only because I didn't want to present you with you an option and get your hopes up with a plan that turned out not to be viable," he said. "And frankly, before yesterday, I wasn't sure Tex would go for my idea at all."

Emily folded her arms, her expression militant. "But he did."

The sarcasm in her voice rankled. Knowing what was at stake, Dan worked to contain his own temper. "Tex saw the business benefits of putting a retail store for all of his orchards in downtown Fort Worth. Plus, by leasing space on the ground floor, the two of you can have it built to your specifications, instead of going to the trouble of converting a barn. You can open the store in a few months instead of six and stay in Fort Worth. You can have your baby here."

Dan's smile broadened as he thought about how much he'd managed to arrange on her behalf by calling in favors and leaning on his friends. "And even lease one of the residential units on the upper floors for as long as you want, at the business-tenant discount, which will make commuting to work a snap."

Emily shook her head in a parody of being impressed. "You've thought of everything," she murmured.

"I've tried," Dan said. He stepped closer and took her rigid body in his arms.

Emily's eyes darkened. "Except one thing," she said with an icy hauteur that would have sent a lesser man running for the exit.

"What's that?"

Angrily she shoved away from him. "I could never be with a man who disrespected me so thoroughly!" she fumed.

Dan stared at Emily. "Disrespected you," he echoed, stunned. "How the hell have I done that?"

"By not including me in any of this!"

He stared at her in frustration. "I told you my reasons," he reminded her impatiently.

"I know," she scoffed. "You wanted to protect me."

He felt a growing sense of helplessness. "You've been under a lot of stress—as your recent fainting episode and visit to the E.R. proved."

She angled her chin at him. "I'm fine."

"For the moment," he muttered.

"And," Emily countered, her eyes glittering, "I would have continued to be fine had you chosen to talk to *me,* instead of Tex, about your plans!"

Unlike Emily, Dan did not consider his desire to protect his woman from unnecessary stress to be a character flaw. "I'm talking to you now," he said, pushing the words through his teeth.

"After the fact."

He tried to reason with her one last time. "I wouldn't be doing any of this if I didn't respect you," he said quietly.

"Respect me or want to keep sleeping with me?" Her low voice reverberated with hurt and disillusionment. She stared right through him. Her voice was shrill, angry and very sad. "Face it, Dan. You want me here because you don't do well at long-distance relationships."

Her accusation hit him where it hurt. "I'm not going to deny I think they are doomed to fail," he said straightforwardly. "Two people can't build anything lasting if they are never physically together."

"So you came up with a plan to keep us in close proximity."

Feeling more resentful with every second that passed, Dan warned, "I'm not going to apologize for wanting to be close enough to be a part of you and your baby's life, and have you be a part of mine."

Emotion choked her throat. "You seriously don't think you did anything wrong here?" she whispered, aghast.

How could he? When everything he'd done had been because he wanted their relationship to have the best possible chance to succeed. He shrugged and confessed flatly, "I seriously don't."

They stared at each other, neither giving ground.

Emily sighed, looking as if her heart were broken. And Dan knew it was over even before she walked away.

"It's not like we didn't try and tell you it was a mistake," Grady told him that evening as the men all gathered at Dan's home for an impromptu bull session.

Grady opened up five bottles of beer as Travis plated pizza, Jack divvied up the wings and Nate grabbed a roll of paper towels to use as napkins.

Dan switched on the big-screen TV and turned the channel to the Dallas Cowboys football game. With Walt and the kids still in Aspen with his ex-wife and Emily absent, his house was impossibly lonely.

Even if his family had been there, Dan thought on a disgruntled sigh, it still would have been empty without Emily.

How had she become such a big part of his life so quickly?

And why was she being so unreasonable? Didn't she feel as deeply about him as he did about her?

Was it all about needing a man during this momentous time in her life and he just happened to be there? Had she been seduced by the vision of a big, close-knit family as much as by him? Or was it something more along the lines of what his ex had felt, that being with Dan—and the rest of the family—was just not ever going to be enough to make her want to stay and sign on for a lifetime of bliss?

Aware the guys were waiting for some explanation, Dan shrugged. "I'd like to think her unreceptive reaction was the result of pregnancy hormones."

"Face it," Grady said. "You screwed up by not including her in the development of the alternative business plan."

Guilt warred with hurt pride. "I was trying to protect her!" he argued.

"Women don't want to be protected—they want to be included," Travis stated.

So Emily had said, Dan reflected as his friends chowed down. "That's still no reason for her not to forgive me," he grumbled.

"You have to give her time," Nate said.

Dan didn't think time was going to make a bit of difference. He'd seen the disgusted way Emily looked at him before she'd marched off in stormy silence.

Dan continued to defend himself. "It's not as if I set out to hurt her."

"No, just rearrange her life," Grady noted.

Dan looked over at his friend. The McCabe men were known for their way with the opposite sex.

"Maybe it's not what you were offering her so much as what you *weren't*," Travis speculated.

Dan set his untouched plate on the coffee table in front of him. "Speak English," he commanded.

"You're asking her to deep-six her plans to move to Fredericksburg and stay here," Travis concluded as if the problem with that was obvious.

And it seemed to be, Dan thought, to everyone in the room but him.

"And yet from what I can tell," Travis continued sagely, "you haven't offered her anything else that really matters."

The heck he hadn't! Dan thought. "I want to be part of her and her baby's life." In his book that was no small pledge.

"And that makes you different from everyone else in her realm in what way?" Jack asked in his usual linear-thinking way.

"I'm sure lots of people have offered to help her when the baby is born." Grady peered at Dan, considering. "Why did you go so completely over the top to make sure she stayed in Fort Worth?"

Nate jumped in with *his* two cents. "And more important, if you expect her to say yes and do what you want, what are you going to give her that no one else can?"

IT WAS INCREDIBLE, EMILY thought on Sunday afternoon, how cold and empty the loft felt with all her stuff gone, save for one small suitcase and a few cleaning supplies. Incredible to think that life, which had seemed so perfect yesterday, was now one giant mess of lost hopes and dreams.

She filled the bucket with warm water and cleanser.

Set it on the floor. Lowered the mop and then stopped as the buzzer sounded.

Unfortunately it wasn't the visitor she'd hoped to see. But one she needed to talk to nevertheless.

"Hello, Tex," Emily said a moment later, ushering him in.

He shoved his hands in his pockets as she resumed mopping the floor. "Dan told me what happened. I wasn't sure you'd still be speaking to me."

"To either of you," Emily corrected.

Tex stepped to the left of the cleaning. "Look, just because Dan had an idea—which was a great one, by the way—and I concurred with him, doesn't make our idea wrong."

That was the hell of it, Emily thought. Moving the retail business and tearoom to Fort Worth was a great idea. She wished she'd thought of it! "It doesn't make the way you went about it right, either," she pointed out grumpily.

Tex shrugged in concession, moving once again. He watched as she dipped the mop back in the bucket of sudsy water and worked the lever that wrung out the excess moisture. Finished, she slapped the mop back down on the floor.

Tex exhaled and tried again. "Okay, so I had an inkling you'd be ticked off."

And hence had known not to do it, but had gone ahead anyway, just as he had when they'd been engaged in what seemed like light-years ago, Emily thought.

"I also agreed with Dan that there was no point in getting you all excited about something if the business case wouldn't support it." Tex defended himself in the same straight-talking way Dan had. "And since Dan and his friends had one set of information, me another, it made sense for us all to talk before taking things any further." Tex lifted a hand before she could interrupt. "In retrospect, I get that we should have included you from the very beginning of the idea stage, Emily. Frankly, I'm sorry we didn't. But it doesn't *change* the bottom line."

"And that is?"

"Dan had one heck of an innovative idea that could stand to net you and me both a handsome income for years to come. If he went about it the wrong way, so be it. It doesn't mean your friendship with him, if that's all it is—and I'm thinking it's a helluva lot more than that—has to end." Tex paused. "So what's really going on here, Emily?" he asked. "What exactly has you running scared? And why won't you do what you usually do with a problem, which is face it head-on?"

Because, Emily thought, *I'm scared. The stakes are too high.*

But, her more rational self argued, weren't they just as high—if not higher—if she did nothing?

She'd been so very close to getting what she really wanted. What she had always wanted.

"Life takes detours, Emily," Tex said quietly.

Emily knew where this heading. "It's what happens—" she used a popular cliché "—when you're making other plans."

"It doesn't mean that what you want is out of reach. Especially now."

Emily thought about what Tex had said all the way to her hotel. By the time she checked in, she knew what she had to do.

DAN HAD JUST CARRIED the boxes of Christmas lights out of the garage when Emily turned her van into his driveway.

Stunned by how hungry he was for the sight of her, he let his eyes rove over her. She wore a red turtleneck sweater and a black leather jacket. Her glossy dark hair fell over her shoulders in loose disarray. Her lips were a soft cranberry-red, her expression…tense.

He wondered if she had come by to tell him she quit and collect the cooking utensils she'd left at his house. Or if she was going to give him another chance. Her brief glance, as she slid out from behind the wheel and shut the door, gave no clue.

Pulse thundering, he straightened and met her halfway.

In a drift of soft, sexy perfume, she looked up at him. He looked down at her. Without a word, she went up on tiptoe, wrapped her arms around his neck and pressed her lips to his.

Surprise shot through Dan, along with a healthy dose of desire. He kissed her the way he'd been wanting to kiss her for what seemed like forever. She kissed him back in exactly the same way, then ever so slowly disengaged. "I thought we should get that out of the way," she said in a careful, neutral tone that had him wondering if that had been an I-want-to-make-up-with-you kiss or a goodbye kiss. She took his hand in hers, held it firmly. "I also really think we should talk."

Dan nodded. It wasn't like him to let the woman in his life take the lead, especially in a situation like this, where things could easily go the wrong way. But after all that had happened, he figured he should let Emily call the shots, if only to show her how much he respected her feisty, independent nature. "Living room?" he suggested.

"How about the kitchen?" she returned, looking more coolly determined than he had ever seen her.

Hand in hand, they headed for the coziest room in the house—at least since *she* had been there. She moved to the stove and put the kettle on to boil. Her lips twisted in a rueful line. "I've been doing a lot of thinking."

"So have I." *About you. And life. And family. And everything we could still have...*

Emily swallowed and looked him in the eye. "If the offer to continue to cook for your family is still open," she said quietly, "I'd like to take it."

Her proposal wasn't what he'd been anticipating. But it was a step in the right direction of getting her back in his life. "For as long as you want," Dan agreed huskily.

"But only on one condition," she amended, and his heartbeat picked up.

Dan lifted his hands in surrender. "Name it."

She paused. "I don't want to be paid."

Dan let that sink in. "I'm not sure how I feel about that," he said finally. "It's a lot of work."

Emily took both his hands in hers. "It's become a labor of love. And I don't want to be doing it as an employee of your family any longer. I want to be doing it as a, well, friend."

Dan's heart sank.

He'd been hoping for much more than that.

He'd also promised himself he wouldn't leap ahead or steer her anywhere she wasn't ready to go. Not this time. With effort he held himself back.

Her eyes began to sparkle. Tilting her head to one

side, she continued in a low tone laced with mischief, "And I know how you like to think outside the box."

He chuckled ruefully. "My habit of doing that seems to have gotten me in pretty big trouble the last few days."

Emily tugged him close. "Trouble can be good."

Trouble with Emily felt very good. Still, Dan didn't want to jump the shark again. Delighting in the warmth of her body, pressed against his, he rested his hands on her waist. "What are you saying?"

"Quite simply—" her voice suddenly sounded as emotional as he felt "—that I love you." She drew in a jerky breath. "I've been in love with you for a while now—I just was afraid to admit it to myself and to you."

Even though Dan understood, he had to know. "Why?" He eyed her determinedly.

Trembling, Emily splayed her palms across his chest. "Because it scares me," she whispered. "I've never wanted anything or anyone as much as I want a life with you."

Happiness welled up inside him. Aware Emily's eyes weren't the only ones that were getting wet, he admitted gruffly, "I feel the same way." Kissing her sweetly, he murmured, "I love you, Emily, so much."

She held him tight. "Which is why you went to so much trouble to find a way for us to be together."

He stroked a hand tenderly through her hair. And wanting there to be no doubt about the depth of his feelings for her, he said, "So you could achieve your dream of resurrecting the business your father started and owning your own tearoom."

"And staying in Fort Worth to have my baby," Emily said happily. She gazed into his eyes.

Dan flashed a crooked smile. "That's really what you want?"

"Yes. My obstetrician is great. I love the hospital. I love the city. And I especially love being here with you and your family, seeing them—and you—every day." Emily sighed with contentment.

"You sure?" Dan asked as he kissed the sensitive spot behind her ear. "I thought you wanted to go home again."

Emily wound her arms around his neck and kissed him in all the familiar, wonderful ways they had both missed so much. "Home is where the heart is, Dan," she whispered. "And my heart is right here, with you." She drew the words from the deepest recesses of her soul.

Epilogue

Four and a half months later...

Everything was happening at once. "Where's the suitcase?" Walt demanded.

Kayla shrugged and held up the stopwatch. "I don't know. I thought you had it!"

Keys in hand, Tommy raced toward them. Breathless, he pointed to the SUV idling at the curb. "It's in the car!"

Walt looked around, frantic. "Next question. Where is the mother-to-be?"

Kayla eased the door open and peeked into the sanctuary. "She and Dad are still trying to get through their vows. But I think maybe they're done...'cause Dad just kissed Emily and it looks like she's kissing him back—"

"Are they crazy?" Ava cried, wringing her hands. She had thrown down her maid-of-honor bouquet and exited the chapel the moment Emily's first contraction hit. "We've got to get to the hospital!"

"We have time," Dan and Emily said in unison as they strolled leisurely down the aisle of the church.

"Plenty of it!" Emily reassured with maternal ease.

Everyone started to calm down.

Then Emily groaned and tightly gripped Dan's arm. By the time the second contraction in two minutes had passed, she straightened again. Face flushed, she murmured, "Or maybe not."

Dan steadied her. "Are you okay? I could call an ambulance."

"Just call Dr. Markham," Emily said as her body tensed and her face began to flush again.

"I'm on it!" Tommy shouted.

Kayla ran ahead to the SUV and yanked open the front passenger door. "Hurry, everybody! Hurry!"

"I think they might be a little excited," Dan said.

Laughing, Emily demurred. "I think so, too."

Three and a half hours later, the euphoria was even greater as Walt and the kids, still wearing their wedding finery, gathered around Emily's hospital bed to see the newest addition to the Kingsland clan.

"What a beauty!" Walt said, beaming.

"Perfect," Ava said.

"I think she is realllly cute," Kayla agreed as the newborn curled her fist around her little finger.

"A born athlete," Tommy decreed.

His sisters looked at him as if he was crazy. "How can you tell?" Ava asked.

"I just know." Tommy shrugged.

Gratitude flowing through her, Emily took in the familial scene. She'd always hoped to have four children—and a tall, blond, smart and sexy husband to love. And now, miraculously, she did. "I imagine this little one will be like her older siblings, able to do whatever she sets her mind to." Emily grinned at the newly official clan of hers.

"And her mommy and daddy," Dan added.

Together, he and Emily had more than proved that with hard work and determination all their dreams could come true.

Emily's partnership with Tex was proving to be a hit. The retail store at One Trinity River Place had opened on Valentine's Day and was doing a huge business, as was the tearoom. Chef for Hire was still going strong, as well—with personal chefs Emily had hired and now supervised.

Ava had been accepted at Harvard—the college of her choice- -where she intended to study premed. Tommy planned to spend the summer working his first part-time job and attending wrestling camp. Kayla had just celebrated her ninth birthday and was learning to cook.

Walt had officially retired from his private investigative work so he would be free to help out with the new baby, as well as the kids.

And Dan...well, business had never been better.

His home life had never been better, either.

"So what are you going to name her?" Ava asked finally.

Dan and Emily exchanged looks.

"Bet you anything they've been thinking outside the box again," Tommy drawled.

"Please tell me it's not Wheelbarrow or some other completely weird name." Walt peered at them in comical trepidation.

Emily chuckled. "Not quite."

"Is it...Peaches?" Kayla asked, referring to some of the joke-names they'd bantered about the past months.

"Or...Trinity Place?" Tommy teased.

"Cornucopia?" Ava got into the joking spirit. "'Cause you all did meet in November!"

"Maybe it's Thanksgiving!" Kayla giggled.

"Thanksgiving Cornucopia Kingsland?" Tommy guessed.

"Nope. Not a one of those," Dan said.

Emily shifted the baby to one arm and linked hands with Dan. "Shall we tell them?" she asked.

Dan looked down at the baby in Emily's arms. She was without a doubt the most beautiful infant he'd ever seen, and the spitting image of her lovely, dark-haired, blue-eyed mother. And every bit as much a member of their family. "I guess we should," he said, since the moniker they'd picked out was perfect, after all.

Emily looked at the family gathered around. "We've decided to name her Grace, after my mother. And Rei— which means gratitude."

"We'll probably call her Gracie, for short," Dan added.

"Gracie Rei Kingsland." Tommy tried the name out.

"I like it!" Ava said.

"Me, too!" Kayla enthused.

"A fine and fitting Texas name," Walt said with another fond look at the infant. "Speaking of which, I think Miss Gracie looks all tuckered out. So we'll head out and let you three rest."

Kisses and hugs abounded.

Then it was just the three of them. Dan, Emily and the baby. Contentment flooded through him. He wasn't sure how it happened, but he had gotten everything he had ever wanted. And he was pretty sure Emily had, too.

She patted the bed beside her. "I know it's not Thanksgiving, but..."

Dan wrapped his arm around her shoulder, brought her against the curve of his body and settled next to her and Gracie Rei. "But it sure feels that way." He pressed a kiss to the top of Emily's head.

"We have so much to be grateful for," Emily acknowledged in a husky voice.

Dan kissed her again. "So much to cherish."

"There's only one thing we're lacking."

"What's that?"

"A proper honeymoon."

"Actually," Dan drawled, "I think I know just the place."

He left the bed long enough to retrieve his wedding suit jacket and remove a small wrapped box from the inside pocket. "I didn't have a chance to give you this."

Emily sent him a questioning glance as she handed him the baby and he gave her the gift and then warned, "I know I promised you I wouldn't make any more deals with Tex, but in this case, I figured you wouldn't mind."

Emily went very still.

"It's a gift from my heart," Dan said soberly. "And just so you know...everyone—Tex, Walt, the kids, even Brenda—is on board. We all want you to have this and we all felt you should be surprised."

"And to think," Emily murmured, mystified, "all I got you was the promise of a spectacular honeymoon to be taken later."

"Well, now you know where we'll go. Come on. Open it," Dan said.

With trembling fingers, Emily did so. Inside was a

stack of glossy photos. So familiar…and yet not. "This is…!"

"The farm in Fredericksburg, where you grew up. I made a deal with Tex. While leaving the orchards and working parts of the farm intact, I expanded the house enough to make room for our entire family, and bought the ten acres surrounding it, too. So you can go home whenever you want. We can all go. For the occasional weekends and vacations—it'll be our special family retreat. As well as a very romantic place for just the two of us."

The new master suite, Emily noted, rifling through the photos, was especially luxurious. "You really did this?" she croaked, remembering the first time they'd made love there. She envisioned many more days and nights to come. "It's done?"

Dan nodded. Seeing Gracie Rei was once again sound asleep, he tenderly settled her in her hospital crib. "One hundred percent."

Tears of bliss rolled down Emily's face as she looked through photos of room after room. The care and time and attention it had taken to do all this, the fact that Dan truly got what the place meant to her… "Oh, Dan, I don't know what to say…except this is the best gift ever—and I love you."

"I love you, too." Slowly, they came together. Dan kissed her tenderly. "So what do you say?" He held her and gazed into her eyes. "Want to start planning our honeymoon—and our next family retreat? Heck, while we're at it, maybe a swimming pool and a play area in the backyard, too?"

Emily kissed him again, knowing life had never been better. And this was just the beginning! "I certainly do.

But first- -" she snuggled close to her husband, turning her face up to his "—I want to thank you for making all our dreams come true."

* * * * *

We hope you enjoyed the
COWBOYS & BABIES
COLLECTION.

If you liked reading these stories, then you
will love **Harlequin® American Romance®**.

Harlequin® American Romance® stories
are heartwarming contemporary tales of everyday
women finding love, becoming part of a family or
community—or maybe starting a family
of her own.

HARLEQUIN®

American Romance®

Romance the all-American way!

Enjoy for four new stories from
Harlequin American Romance every month!

Available wherever books and ebooks are sold.

HTHMS0414-1

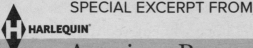
*Looking for more exciting all-American romances like the
one you just read? Read on for an excerpt from
THE COWBOY'S DESTINY by Marin Thomas*

Destiny Saunders marched down the aisle and poked her
head out the door.

Blast you, Daryl.

Even though they'd known each other only six months,
she hadn't expected him to leave her high and dry. She rubbed
her belly. At barely two months pregnant it would be several
weeks before she showed.

She left the chapel, closing the doors behind her. After
stowing her purse and phone, she slid on her mirrored
sunglasses and straddled the seat of her motorcycle, revving
the engine to life. Then she tore out of the parking lot, tires
spewing gravel.

She'd driven only two miles when she spotted a pickup
parked on the shoulder of the road.

A movement caught her attention, and she zeroed in on the
driver's-side window, out of which stuck a pair of cowboy
boots. She approached the vehicle cautiously and peered
through the open window, finding a cowboy sprawled inside,
his hat covering his face.

She slapped her hand against the bottom of one boot
then jumped when the man bolted into an upright position,
knocking his forehead against the rearview mirror.

"Need a lift?"

He glanced at her outfit. "Where's the groom?"

"If I knew that, I wouldn't be talking to you right now."

He shoved his hand out the window. "Buck Cash."

"Destiny Saunders. Where are you headed?"

"Up to Flagstaff for a rodeo this weekend," he replied as he got out of the vehicle.

"What's wrong with your truck?"

"Puncture in one of the hoses."

He peered over her shoulder and she caught a whiff of his cologne. A quiver that had nothing to do with morning sickness spread through her stomach.

"Guess you're going to miss your rodeo," she said.

"There's always another one." He eyed the bike. "This your motorcycle?"

"You think I ditched my fiancé at the altar and then took off on his bike?"

"Kind of looks that way." He kept a straight face but his eyes sparkled.

"Looks can be deceiving. Hop on."

Look for THE COWBOY'S DESTINY
by Marin Thomas in
May 2014 wherever books and ebooks are sold

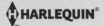
American Romance

The Secrets Of Horseshoe, Texas

Angie Wiznowski has made mistakes—the biggest is the secret she's kept from Hardison Hollister for ten years. The man she loved has the right to know what happened following that hot Texas night long ago. And it could cost Angie the most precious thing in her life.

Hardy has no inkling he's a father…until an accident leaves a young girl injured and the Texas district attorney with an unexpected addition to his family. Blindsided by shock and hurt, Hardy can't forgive Angie for her deception. But as he gets to know his child, old and new feelings for Angie surface. While scandal could derail Hardy's political future—is that future meaningless without Angie and their daughter?

Look for
One Night In Texas
by LINDA WARREN
from Harlequin® American Romance®

**Available May 2014
wherever books and ebooks are sold.**

www.Harlequin.com

HAR75518

American Romance®

BABY STEPS

Handsome surgeon Jack Ryder had a reputation as a
ladies' man until he met the one woman who refused
to be impressed: nurse Anya Meeks. She's carrying his
baby—and she's determined to give it up for adoption.
Jack will do anything to persuade Anya not to put their
baby up for adoption. But with her jaded views on
relationships and family, it won't be easy.
Can he convince her that their love is no accident?

Look for

A Baby for the Doctor

from the *Safe Harbor Medical* series

by JACQUELINE DIAMOND

in May 2014 from Harlequin® American Romance®.
Available wherever books and ebooks are sold

Also available from the *Safe Harbor Medical*
The Surprise Holiday Dad
His Baby Dream
The Baby Jackpot

HAR75220